BUFFALO JONES'
FORTY YEARS OF ADVENTURE

A VOLUME OF FACTS GATHERED FROM EXPERIENCE, BY HON. C. J.
JONES, WHOSE EVENTFUL LIFE HAS BEEN DEVOTED TO THE PRES-
ERVATION OF THE AMERICAN BISON AND OTHER WILD
ANIMALS; WHO SURVIVED THE PERILS OF THE
FROZEN NORTH, THE LAND OF THE MID-
NIGHT SUN, AMONG ESKIMOS, IN-
DIANS, AND THE FEROCIOUS
BEASTS OF NORTH
AMERICA

COMPILED BY

COLONEL HENRY INMAN

CRANE & COMPANY, PUBLISHERS
TOPEKA, KANSAS
1899

Introduction

CHAPTER I

Millions of Buffalo—Their Haunts — So Numerous People Neglected to Study their Habits and Value—Killed for their Hides Only — Ooronado Gave First Historical Account of the Buffalo and the Great West, in 1542—Jones's First Buffalo — Horses Stampeded—"Rained Hail as Large as Oranges"— Buffalo made for Blizzards, Siroccos, and all kinds of Weather — Struggling for Mastership of Herd — Buffalo-Bull Fight... 1

CHAPTER II

BUFFALO JONES

Early Days in Illinois—A Live Deer Tied to Horse's Tail—A Perilous Adventure— Abraham Lincoln Pleads his Father's Cause for $10—School-Days Very Few—Capturing and Selling a Squirrel Fixes his Ruling Passion—A Small Menagerie — Could Conquer any Animal—Asleep in the Field at Midnight— Rescued by Searching Pai-ty—At College — Bound for the Wild West 14

CHAPTER III

"westward no!"

Journey to the Frontier in a Prairie Schooner — Mrs. Jones's Introduction to Camp Life — Plenty of Wolves — Team Escapes on the Journey — Recapturing—Joyous Meeting 30

CHAPTER IV

DESPERADOES

Buffalo Jones as a Farmer—Abandons Farming to Shoot Buffalo— Fails to Shoot Any — Mysterious Mirage — Buffalo Seemingly Running High in the Air—Desperadoes in Camp —"I am Going to Kill You Right Here!"—Rescued by a Plucky Boy 37

CHAPTER Y

THE FIRST nUXT FOR CALVES

Buffalo in Nature's Pasture—Why Not Corral Them There? — Resolved to Try at Last Moment—The Start — Encounter the Old Bulls—Night Search for Water—Companion Extinguishes Beacon-Fire — Feared tlie Indians — Grandeur of Sunrise on the Plains— Discovers a Herd—"Rescuing the Perishing"—Hoi*se Tied to Calf, and Its Mother After the Horse—A Lucky Shot—A Day of Narrow Escapes — Captures Four Calves—Famishing for Water—Penetrates Llano Esta-cado — Letting a Companion Down a Bluff for Water—Rope Slips — Sun "Goes Down on his Wrath" — Last Herd Located— Fourteen Calves Captured — Sheds Garments to Protect Calves from Wolves—White Buffalo 47

CHAPTER YI

INDIANS

Dangers of the Plains — Tenderfoot Stood Little Show Against Indians — Only One Way to Fight Them — Battle with Ar-rapahoes—Gave Them a Surprise — Buffalo-Hunters, and Not Soldiers, Conquei*ed the Indians—Nearly Caught while Skinning a Buffalo—The " Greatest Show on Earth"—Two Hundred Warriors Surround a Herd of Buffalo—Signaling at Long Distance 83

CHAPTER YII

PRAIRIE FIRES

Reminder of World's Destruction — Daylight Turned to Darkness— People Driven Into Cellars, and Breathe Througli Towels and Handkerchiefs—Wild Animals Flee for Their Lives— Like the Roar of a Cyclone — To the Rescue — How to Escape—Many Wild Animals Perish 103

CHAPTER YIII

SECOND HUNT FOR CALVES

Everybody Wanted to Go, but Couldn't, except Two Persistent Strangers, who Drove Into an Irrigation Ditch, where Horse Balked—Wanted Jones to Kill Him — Arriving at "Robbers' Roost"—Wild-Horse Hunter Yery Much Bewildered—" Buffalo, by Jupiter! "—Everything Done in a Min-

ute—Colonel Jones and Mr. Carter Dash After the Herd — Secure Three Calves — Cow Fights to the Death — Searching for Water in the Darkness IH

CHAPTER IX

SECOND CALF HUNT (concluded)

Milking a Buffalo Cow — Excellent Butter—A Long March — Calf Captured by Horse Throwing Rider on its Keck — Strangers After a Bull—Took Both to Kill It, and then Didn't Get Him—" The Herd! The Herd ! "—Colonel Jones Never Lost — Buffalo Right in Camp—"Get Down and Crawl!"— Holes Cut in the Colonel's Tent to Shoot Through — Horses Left to Die — Plenty of Calves, but no AVater—Strangers AVanted Another Trial, then Another 140

CHAPTER X

WILD HORSES — OTHER ANTAfALS

Origin, Habitat, Greatest Number, Size, Color, Style, and Surroundings— Stallion Never Leads, but Drives the Herd — Contest for Mastership—Colonel Jones Always Found Water by Following Them — Speed and Endurance — Prairie-Dogs, Owls,and Rattlesnakes—"Happy Family" Theory not True— Held at Bay by a Monstrous Rattler...167

CHAPTER XI

SUCCESSFUL CALF HUNT "

Extravagant Preparations — Took Domestic Cows to the Range — Competition Quelled — Competitor's Handsome Reward — Sunday in Camp — Herd Discovered—" Hurrah, Boys, Sunday or no Sunday I"—Capture Eleven Calves in Short Time-Pathetic Poem — Shooting AVithout a Sight—AYolves Devour Calves—AVonderful Success — Long Journey for More Cows— Taken for Cattle-Thieves— Colonel Jones Secures Milch Cows at Fabulous Prices — Irishman Sorry He Didn't Ask More — The Typical Cowboy and Ranchman 181

CHAPTER XII

THE ANTELOPE

The Shyest and Fleetest of all Animals — "A Mighty Good Greyhound to Catch a Mighty Poor Antelope"—AVhole City on a Hunt,-Dogs Included — Colonel-Jones Kills More than All 194

CHAPTER XIII

THE LAST HUNT

On the Desert—Sends News by Carrier-Pigeons—Buffalo Discovered— Effort to Corral the Herd — Three Calves Quickly Captured — The Mother's Desperate Charge — Caught in a

Deluge — Hard Ride for a Calf—Roping full-grown Buffalo — Awaiting the Last Opportunity — Forty-two Days and Nights in Pursuit of Last Herd—Colonel Jones's Wonderful Success Recorded in History 201

CHAPTER XIV
BUFFALO ON THE WATER
Colonel Jones Bound for the Old World—Loading Buffalo on an Ocean Steamer—Big Show without an Audience — Seasick Animals— Sensation in Liverpool — Congratulations from Prince of Wales—Accepts from Colonel Jones, Robe made of Buffalo Fur 225

CHAPTER XV
LAST OP THE BUFFALO
Buffalo not of One Family — Organization of a Herd — How Herd was Located — Stampede Equal to a Cyclone — The Cause and Result—Only Method of Escape — Colonel Jones Captures Canada's Last Herd—After Moose — Catalo, the New Race of Cattle — Description and Habits — Need no Artificial Food or Shelter—Robes as Handsome as Beaver.....................230

CHAPTER XVI
DOMESTICATED BUFFALO
Habits as Compared with the Wild Buffalo—Propagation— Takes Nerve to Conquer—Corrals of AVire — Buffalo Kills his Captor — '*John L. Sullivan," which Never Met his "Corbett"—Training Buffalo to AVork, no Boy's Play—Lines Held with a Windlass — Government Responsible for Extermination of Buffalo—Colonel Jones's Proposition to Corral the Last Herd —Warned the Government of Danger—Number Existing at Different Periods — Unwritten Code of Hunters — AVhy Trails are Crooked —How to Kill a Whole Herd 248

CONTENTS VU
CHAPTER XVII
ONE OP THE GREATEST RACES OX RECORD
Opening of the Cherokee Outlet — Oklahoma, "the Beautiful Land"—Horses and Riders Trampled Beneath a Living Avalanche— Genuine "Jehu" and Red-Headed Darling in the Race—The Most Reckless Equestrienne in the World — Facts Never Before Made Known—Colonel Jones Rode Two Horses, and Won the Race 266

CHAPTER XYIII
BUFFALO JOXES'S ARCTIC EXPEDITION
Bound for the Arctic Regions after Musk-Oxen and Other Animals— Route Through Canada — White Girl Held in Captivity by Indians — Leaves Civilization — Alone in a Boat Down the Athabaska River — Indians Oppose his Mission — Boat Capsized and Indians Refuse his Life-Line — Hot Day in the Far North — Crossing Athabaska Lake — On the Peace and Slave Rivers — Big Chiefs Hold a Council to Prevent his Progress 277

CHAPTER XIX
BOUND NORTHWARD
Ordered to Return by Indians—Reaches Great Slave Lake — Tossed at Midnight by an Angry Tempest — Reaches Ruins of Searching Party — Fort Reliance — Treachery of Big Indian Siena 302

CHAPTER XX

IN WINTER QUARTERS

Indian's Wife of Less Value than a Dog—Mercury at Zero October 10—J. R. Rea, a Hero of Heroes—Desperation of Indians — Deaf and Dumb Girl's Sufferings — Children Frightened at White Man—"Hoppy Shompooly" (Sweet Salt), AVhite Sugar — Indians take Provisions by Force—Apply the Torch to Colonel Jones's Cabin — Shoots his First Reindeer — Indians Starving — Conjure Caribou's Return — When they did Come, Colonel Jones Killed More than the Whole Tribe — They Claimed but did not Get Them
....320

CHAPTER XXI

AFTER MUSK-OXEN

Arranging a Musk-Ox Hunt — Mr. Rea Makes a Long Journey with Indians — Caught in a Terrific Blizzard — Greatest Waterfalls of the Far North — Second Niagara — Reindeer Everywhere—Driving Them Into a Corral — Indians Determined to Stay and Eat White Man's Meat—Could Not Drive Them Away '.. 334

CHAPTER XXII

DB8PEHATION IX ARCTIC REGION'S

Indians Left Squaw and Child to Perish—The Scanty Supply Divided with Them—Drove Them Out when Mercury was at Forty-eight Below Zero — Little Ellen Covered with Icicles — Squaw Cvit her Foot as an Excuse to Remain — Colonel Jones's Long Journey in Midwinter — Clothes Frozen Stiff — Failed to Find Indian Village — Frightened Indians to Save Supplies — Reindeer Appear at Last Moment — Indian Frightened Them Away—" Too Mad to Swear"
....347

CHAPTER XXIII

MUSK-OX HUNT

Start for the Far North on Dog-Sleds — Crossing Mountains — On Artillery Lake — Terrific Blizzard — In Blankets Thirty-six Hours, Facing Wind at Forty Degrees Below Zero — On Clinton Golden Lake — Camped in " Land of Little Sticks"— Dog Carried off by Wolves — Colonel Jones's Narrow Escape — Discover New Rivers and Lakes — Musk-Oxen at Last — Kill Six — Description — Indian Superstition — Cross Great Fish River and Arctic Circle — Out of Wood, and Compelled to Return — Guide Badly Lost—Depended on the Colonel's Compass—Arrive at "Little Sticks"—Guide Abandons the Two Nimrods — They Again Penetrate to the Far North 364

CHAPTER XXIV

HEROIC EFFORT BRINGS REWARD

Two White Men on the Barren Lands Without a Guide—Keep Going Until Near the Magnetic Pole—Young Musk-Oxen

Discovered — Old Ones Shot and Calves Lassoed—A "Wild West Show" in the Arctic Zone — Shepherd Dog Devoured by Wolves—Night Made Hideous—Start for Home—Destruction by Wolves Appears Imminent—Fighting Wolves by Night and Traveling by Day — Indians or Eskimos Cut the Throats of the Musk-Ox Calves while Captors Sleep—Ammunition Gone, therefore Compelled to Return — Colonel Jones Fires the Last Cartridge and Hits the Mark — Saved from Starvation—Reaching Cabin in Deplorable Condition.
....380

CHAPTER XXV

AT THE CABIN HOME

Dogs with Hydrophobia — Cuts Steel Chain with Teeth—Mr. iRea's Narrow Escape—In Summer, AV'aiting for Summer— How to Reach the North Pole—A Start for the Sunny South — Fourth of July, but Still Frozen in the Ice — Living on Bread Alone — Mosquitoeg and Gnats in Swarms—Arrival at Fort Resolution — First News of War with Spain—Music in the Far North—"Sweetest Ever Heard"—Colone Jones Fancied he was in the " Spirit Land "—Grand Reception 396

CHAPTER XXVI
METEOROLOGICAL PHENOMENA
"Total Darkness" and "Everlasting Day"—Extreme Temperature of Each Month — Precipitation — Burnt by Cold Steel — Brilliant Display of Aurora Borealis — Mock Suns — Ice Upheavals, etc., etc.......................417

CHAPTER XXVII
INDIANS AND ESKIMOS OF THE FAR NORTH
Differ from Other Indians — Mode of Living in Land of Darkness—Women Slaves — Meat and Fish the Only Diet of the Natives — Marriage Relation — Names of Tribes — Location —Their Habits, Dwellings, Intelligence, Superstitions — Traditional History — Happiest People on Earth, but at Times the Most Miserable — Education Ruins all Indians in that Counti-y who Attempt It 423

CHAPTER XXV
HOMEWARD BOUND
In a Storm on the Lake — Rudder Breaks—Waves Roll Into the Boat—Boat Following is Capsized — One Man Drowned, Others Washed Ashore — Protestant Mission on the Mackenzie River — Catholic Priests Need Attention—A Visit to the Spot where Franklin Spent a Dreary Winter on Great Bear Lake — Picture of his Cabin — Desolation — In the Ramparts — Crossed the Arctic Circle— Fort Good Hope — Sail on the Arctic Ocean—Up Peel's and Rat Rivers— Hundreds of Gold-Seekers Caught in that Desolate Region — Shooting Down the Cascades of the Pacific Slope — Boat Smashed on a Rock — Long Journey Down the Porcupine — Fort Yukon — St. Michael's — Facts About Alaska of Great Interest — On Bering Sea — Reached Seattle — Grand Reception at the Colonel's Old Home — Everybody Sang, "My Country, 'tis of Thee," and "Home, Sweet Home"..................................... 437

INTRODUCTION

It ia the mission of this volume to present, from a carefully kept journal, the thrilling incidents, experiences and observations, together with the results of the efforts of one who has devoted the best years of his life to saving from absolute extinction one of the once most conspicuous, in point of numbers, of all the large mammals on the North-American continent: the bison, or buffalo as commonly designated. He has also exerted his energies in behalf of the preservation of other animals of his native country. The field of his labors embraced all of the great territory extending from the Gulf of Mexico to and including the frozen wilderness, of the Arctic Circle. So remarkable and full of exciting personal adventure have been the efforts of Mr. Jones in the direction indicated, that he has a world-wide reputation, and is familiarly known to the people of both North America and Europe by his well-earned sobriquet of "Buffalo Jones."

His travels in the remote regions of the North-American continent are a chapter of hardships, privations and dangers which rarely fall to any individual in modern times, and show what indomitable courage, self-possession

(XI)

XU INTRODUCTION

and determination can accomplish under the most adverse conditions. At the same time, "Buffalo" Jones has been a close observer of nature,— of all its physical characteristics. In this volume he presents the results of his investigations. The reader will find here many things which will be new to him, and that the book is of thrilling interest, and is instructive as well.
Henry Inman.

FORTY YEARS OF ADVENTURES

CHAPTER I

MILLIONS OF BUFFALO — THEIR HAUNTS — SO NUMEROUS,
PEOPLE NEGLECTED TO STUDY THEIR HABITS AND WORTH
KILLED FOR THEIR HIDES ONLY CORONADO GAVE FIRST
HISTORICAL ACCOUNT OF THEM AND THE GREAT WEST, IN 1542 — JONES's
FIRST BUFFALO — DUTCHMAN'S HORSES
STAMPEDED BY COMING TOO NEAR HERD "RAINED HAIL
AS LARGE AS ORANGES " 1—BUFFALO MADE FOR BLIZZARDS,
SIROCCOS, AND ALL CLIMATIC ELEMENTS STRUGGLE FOR
MASTERSHIP OF THE HERD — GRAPHIC DESCRIPTION OF A BUFFALO-BULL
FIGHT

A FEW years ago,—scarcely a quarter of a century,— millions upon millions of American bison, or buffalo as they are generally though erroneously called, roamed over the vast plains of the intra-continental region of North America. Now, they are so reduced in number that absolutely the last lingering spark of vitality is smouldering on the very verge of extinction. If nothing had been effected toward rescuing them, the buffalo, like the Auk and Dodo, would soon have been found mounted in museums only, as mere specimens ; a silent monument to the wantonness and cupidity of man.

The geographical area over which these immense animals grazed, comprised millions of square miles. When the

(1)

railroads penetrated this heretofore almost inaccessible territory,transportation suddenly became relatively cheap; then there was at once created an unprecedented demand for the beautiful soft robes of the buffalo^ and millions were sent to Europe to be converted into leather. Almost immediately, too, the slaughter of the fated beasts achieved such proportions that annihilation was a question of a short period.

Thousands, even millions, of green hides appeared in the markets of the world, and tourists, attracted by the novelty attending the opening of the continent, which the press announced in graphic word-painting, commenced an indiscriminate onslaught on the now apparently doomed animals.

To a relatively limited number of persons the interior of the country west of the Missouri was well known. To the majority it was a veritable terra incognita. Now, however, there was a phenomenal inrush, whose crowds began to kill merely for the sport it furnished. For miles along the great trunk lines, then wending their way across the so-called "desert," the carcasses of the huge beasts were collected so thickly that one could have walked hundreds of miles, on either side of the track, on their bleached bones.

To properly present the slow, weary, and sometimes discouraging steps which marked Colonel Jones's career in his initiatory attempt to preserve a nucleus of the unfortunate animals (which he hopes and firmly believes will reestablish the bison, with all the superior qualities of this species of the bovine family), it is necessary, in order that the reader may intelligently appreciate his labors, to portray their original haunts, habits, value, characteristics, and the methods he employed in capturing, domesticating, and cross-breeding, as contained in his remarkably interesting journal.

It is an indisputable fact, that notwithstanding the bison had been known to exist on the Great Plains for

four centuries, were at one time almost as numerous as the "sands of the seashore," and that a large number of people had been in constant contact with them, yet the world is really unacquainted with them, even to this day. Had the American bison been a rare species of ruminant, few in number, confined to some remote island or limited geographical area, all that science would have regarded as necessary to know relating to them would have long since been published. Biological societies would have vied with each other to report what they had discovered; the text-books of our educational institutions would have been full of their habits, as they are of the African lion, the camel, or the giraffe. The very fact that they existed in such appalling numbers right at home, as it were, is the reason, perhaps, of their having been regarded of such little consequence, from a utilitarian standpoint at least.

The savage of the prairies knew more of their service-ableness, of their priceless utility, than the solitary trapper, or freighter across the great desert, who merely killed an occasional one for his meat, or to procure a new robe for his own immediate use.

The American bison has been traced backward through the ages by scientists, with a certainty, to a period anterior by a thousand years to the dawn of the Christian era. It has been known relatively well by historians, for at least eighteen centuries..

Mr. W. T. Hornaday, superintendent of the Taxider-mical Department of the Smithsonian Institution, Washington, D. C, in his report to the Fiftieth Congress, sets forth the claim that Cortez, the Spanish conqueror of Mexico, gave the first historical account of the American bison, in the year 1521. He quotes the following extract, written by De Soto, one of Cortez' retainers, after he visited the Zoological Gardens of the Emperor of Mexico, Montezuma:

" In the second square of the same house were the wild beasts which were either presented to Montezuma, or taken

by his hunters, in strong cages of timber, ranged in good order, and under cover: lions, tigers, bears, and all others of the savage kind which New Spain produced; among which the greatest rarity was a Mexican bull,— a wonderful composition of divers animals. It has crooked shoulders, with a bunch on its back like a camel. Its flanks dry, its tail large, and its neck covered with hair like a lion. It is cloven-footed, its head armed like that of a bull, which it resembles in fierceness, with no less strength and agility."

The above quaint description does not by any means give a clear, fair picture of the American bison; particularly, the large tail spoken of does not belong to that animal. The inference is that De Soto did not see a buffalo at all. If he had really seen the American bison, he would have been so enraptured that necessarily he would have been obliged to transmit to posterity a more elaborate report. His description is not accurate. The animal he did see was undoubtedly just what he claimed it to be, a "Mexican bull," with great shaggy shoulders, and exceedingly heavy tail,— which the bison has not.

Mr. Hornaday quotes another Spanish explorer, Alvar Nunez Cabe^a de Baca, as having seen the American bison in southern Texas, nine years after the first-mentioned date (1530). Cabe9a thus describes what he saw:

" Cattle come as far as this. I have seen them three times, and eaten of their meat. I think they are about the size of those in Spain. They have small horns, like those of Morocco, and their hair long and flocky, like that of a merino. Some are light-brown \'7bpardiUos), and others black. To my judgment, the flesh is finer and sweeter than those of this country.

"The Indians make blankets of those that are not fully grown, and of the larger they make shoes and buckles. They come as far as the seacoast of Florida,*

' The whole region watered by the Mississippi and Missouri rivers was called Florida.

and in a direction of more than four hundred leagues. In the whole extent of plains over which they roam the people who live bordering upon it descend and kill them for food; and thus a great many skins are scattered throughout the country."

This last account is not any more satisfactory in its details than that of De Soto's, especially where it refers to the size of buffalo being that of Spanish cattle. As everyone knows, Spanish cattle are mere pigmies compared to buffalo. Cabe§a describes more accurately the Texas cattle than the bison (which are nearer the size and colors of Spanish cattle), so striking in their peculiar appearance to a stranger.

Colonel Jones says: "The fact is, the first herd of buffalo I ever saw, was composed of about twenty old bulls. The gentleman who was with me, Mr. Shultz, first noticed them coming toward us, and we secreted ourselves in a shallow buffalo-wallow, having to lie very close to the ground to prevent their seeing us. Mr. Shultz was an experienced hunter, and both of us were possessed of good guns; but before the animals came within three hundred yards of where we were lying, I said to my partner in a whisper: ' Let us compromise with the monsters; if they will let us alone, we'll let them go by.' Mr. Shultz smiled as I trembled; I could not have hit a whole flock of barns two hundred feet away. The buffalo grazed along, coming so close that at every mouthful of grass they gathered I could distinctly hear a puff from their nostrils, and their teeth grinding together. They appeared to me hideous monsters. They resembled elephants, and as they moved toward us the very earth appeared to shake. I paid no more attention to them; they were too near for comfort, and I shut my eyes, scarcely daring to breathe, when suddenly, like a clap of thunder, came the report of a gun, and I was nearly paralyzed. Mr. Shultz had fired at the leader of

the herd 1 His gun was about as large as a small cannon; the discharge was terrific. When silence was again restored, I discovered that at least one buffalo couldn't scare me 'worth a cent.' "

No one after seeing the majestic creatures would ever describe them as "cattle about the size of those in Spain, with small horns, some brown and some black," etc. Nor does Mr. Hornaday so classify them, in his exhaustive history of the great ruminant, comprising more than one hundred and fifty pages of his report to the second session of the Fiftieth Congress.

The first authentic description of the American bison of the great central plains of the continent, is unquestionably that to be found in the itinerary of Coronado's wonderful march in search of the "Seven Cities of Cibola," during the year 1542. He was also the first white man to tell us anything of that vast region west of the Missouri river, and its resources. He was the primitive pioneer of those early days of exploration; the peer of the "Pathfinder," General Fremont, when time and conditions are considered.

That Coronado saw the genuine American bison, is more than confirmed by the graphic description he gives of them. There can be no mistake after reading the record from the pen of the historian, Castenada:

"The first time we encountered the buffalo, all our horses took flight on seeing them, for they are horrible to the sight. They have a l:>road and short face; eyes two palms from each other, and projecting in such a manner sidewise that they can see a.pursuer. Their beard is like that of goats, and so long that it drags the ground when they lower the head. They have on the anterior portion of the body a frizzled hair like sheep's wool; it is very fine upon the croup, and sleek like a lion's mane. Their horns are very short and thick, and can scarcely be seen through the hair. They always change their hair in May,

and at this season they really resemble lions. They make it drop more quickly, for they change it as adders do their skins; they will roll among the brushwood which they find in the ravines.

"Their tail is very short, and terminates in a great tuft. When they run they carry it in the air like a scorpion. When quite young they are tawny, and resemble our calves."

From the foregoing unique description, any intelligent person would recognize a buffalo, even if its shadow alone were seen.

How it makes an old plainsman laugh to read Castena-da's first line: " The first time we encountered the buffalo all our horses took flight on seeing them, for they are horrible to the sight." The fact is, there is nothing so repulsive to a "green" horse as a sight or scent of a buffalo. Many a man has been left on the open prairie by the too close proximity of a herd of these animals to the horse he was riding or driving; many horses have stampeded, for the same reason, when picketed out to graze. I was once compelled to " hoof it " for twenty miles, from such an experience, and a more delighted individual the reader never heard of, when I discovered it was only that short distance instead of a hundred, and that I did not lose my fine team as well.

I remember at one time meeting a poor German near the Kansas and Colorado line, west of where the flourishing town of Colby is now located, who was in a terrible predicament. It was in the spring of 1872. He was an emigrant to the mountains, and was able to speak only very indifferent English. All his possessions, when I met him, consisted of an old-fashioned muzzle-loading rifle and a pair of nearly worn-out shoes, which he carried in his hand. The antiquated gun was as worthless a piece for those troublesome days on the border as I had ever seen. It might have been one captured by General Blucher

from the French at the battle of Waterloo, and kept as an heirloom in the family of the disconsolate fellow trudging along in the wilderness of prairie around him. He was more than a hundred miles from any settlement, and had in all probability been wandering hopelessly in a circle, for two days or more.

His first salutation was: " Haben sie wasser ? " "Yes, plenty," I answered, at the same time passing him a canteen which had recently been filled from a ten-gallon keg that was always kept strapped to the side of the wagon. The poor fellow was nearly choked. After filling himself, he caught his breath, and told me as best he could that he had lost two horses, asking if I knew where they were — "or do you know nottings?" I grasped the situation at once, and was satisfied he had been too close to a herd of buffalo. This he confirmed by attempting to explain how it happened: He was surprised by a great number of the beasts, and his horses, never having seen such animals before, naturally stampeded, leaving him all alone on the prairie, remote from any assistance. He was a piteous-looking object, indeed. He had given up all hope; had become despondent, and if I had not fortunately met him at this particular juncture, he would in all probability have gone insane, and the wolves battened on his bones before sundown of the following day.

I had passed a hunting-party about fifteen miles back, some of whom I knew; they had incidentally mentioned to me the fact of having picked up a team of " plug" horses, which they supposed some "mover" to Colorado had abandoned to die, they were so miserably thin and weak. From the description given me, and what the German had attempted to convey in his queer jargon, I knew the animals were identical. I really felt sorry for the old fellow, and assured him I would recover his lost team,— at which he was nearly wild. I then said to him and my men, we would go into camp about six miles to the southwest, near the foot of a high butte plainly discernible

from where we then were, and dispatch one of my party on a broncho for his horses—(I always use these ponies on my hunting expeditions), telling him to return by sundown the next day.

Promptly as the sun was sinking in the western horizon the following evening, my messenger returned with the missing animals. They were certainly the most "ornery" creatures one might see in an age; just able to stagger along. What on earth could scare such miserable brutes would have been an indescribable enigma, if it were not known what a herd of buffalo could effect in that direction.

When I met the old man he was in a terrible condition physically: his feet were so galled they were absolutely raw; it was impossible for him to wear his shoes;— yet he was as happy as if he had discovered a gold mine, when the jaded horses were turned over to him. The next morning he started westward again on his lonesome journey, profuse in his thanks for what I had done.

I could relate circumstances of stampedes, until every page of this book would be-filled, showing what a sudden appearance of a herd of buffalo has effected on the plains with the "tenderfoot" in hundreds of instances. I have presented this one, merely to give the reader an idea of one of the vexations which often came to the hunter and the emigrant on their lonely "trails" across the continent, and to prove that Coronado gave us the first intelligent description of the American bison.

To return to the first authentic account of the American bison. It goes without saying, that Coronado's historian gave an unquestionably accurate description, and the intrepid Spaniard saw the real thing. He not only saw the buffalo, but so perfectly does he tell of the *' great plains," that " he who runs may read."

From Hukluyt's voyages. Vol. Ill, (London, 1600,) I

extract a few paragraphs concerning the subject, which are indisputable:

"From Cicuye they went to 'Quivira,' which, after their recent account, is almost three hundred leagues distant, through mighty plains, and sandy heaths, so smooth and wearisome, and bare of wood, that they made heaps of ox-dung, for want of stones and trees, that they might not lose themselves at their return; for three horses were lost on that plain, and one Spaniard who went from his company hunting.

*'A11 that way of plains are as full of crooked-back oxen as the mountain Serrena in Spain is full of sheep, but there is no such people as keep those cattle. They were a great succor for the hungry, and want of bread, which our people stood in need of.

"One day it rained in that plain a great shower of hail, as big as oranges, which caused many tears, weakness, and bowes.

"These oxen are of the bigness and color of our bulls, but their bones are not so great. They have a great bunch on their fore shoulder, and more hair on their fore part than on their hinder part, and it is like wool. They have, as it were, a horse-mane upon their backbone, and much hair, and very long, from their knees downward.

" They have great tufts of hair hanging down their foreheads, and it seemeth they have beards because of the gr6at store of hair hanging down at their chins and throats.

"The males have very large tails, and a great knob or flock at the end, so that in some respects they resemble the lion, and in some others the camel.

" They push with their horns; they run; they overtake and kill an horse when they are in their rage and anger.

"Finally, it is a foul and fierce beast of countenance and form of body.

"The horses fled from them, either because of their deformed shape, or else because they had never before seen them."

Here we find a most accurate description of the buffalo (except the large tail). No one who is familiar with the animal will contest that the beast Castenada writes of is any other than the genuine American bison.

This historian also says, as to the buffalo increasing in age: " They change form and color." The facts are these, from my observations, and handling them for years: the young buffalo, when they reach their fifth month, shed their tawny coat, and assume the natural hue of the adult; that is, seal-brown. The hump, which is one of the most prominent physical characteristics, does not make its appearance until the calves are two to three months old.

The ears of the young buffalo are entirely different from those of the domestic calf: they are small, round, and full of long hairs. The change from a round body to a great hump is very gradual, commencing when the animal has attained about three months, continuing until it is from five to seven years old, according to sex, at which time it arrives at its full growth.

Nature is never more persistent in any of its creations than in that of the buffalo's anatomy, or in its habits so suited to its wild environment. A more perfect animal for the strange surroundings of its habitat could not have been constructed. It is ever prepared for the severest *' blizzard " from the far north, or the hottest " sirocco " of the torrid zone. It is so constructed that it always faces every danger, whether it be the pitiless storm from the Arctic regions or its natural enemy, the gray wolf of the desert. This ghoul of the prairie never is permitted to approach its victim from the rear excepting when overpowered by great numbers; then they are " hamstrung " and rendered helpless. The young bull, also, who contends for the mastery of the herd, always faces his competitors.

A more startling sight cannot be imagined than that of two shaggy monsters contending for the supremacy. With muzzles lowered, pawing the earth with their great hoofs,
raising clouds of impalpable dust from the hard dry sod, over which millions of their compeers have trodden for centuries, they cautiously circle around each other, measuring every possible vantage. Their great heads, matted with "bull-nettles" and "sand-burs" until twice their normal size, are alternately tossed high in the air, then as quickly lowered until their noses come within an inch of the ground. These are the preliminary tactics that gauge the battle, like the knights of old when they threw their gauntlets of steel into the arena. Their short, tufted tails are swollen as a cat's when in the ecstacy of its rage; their backs curved up like the same pugnacious animal, and their hair bristling with the desire for battle. Now, when near enough to each other, comes the supreme moment for which they have been waiting 1 Their eyes appear to send forth livid rays, like that emanating from an electric dynamo, as they charge upon each other with the rush of a tornado at the height of its fury. Their short horns lock with a rattle which sounds like the firing of a battalion, directly over where they stand in their mighty struggle. The spectator is apparently almost paralyzed by the display of energy and exertion of muscle displayed by the

huge beasts, as he breathlessly waits for a lull in the terrible conflict which has completely entranced him.

For a moment one of the combatants has secured an advantage over his adversary: he raises the whole front portion of his heavy antagonist clear from the ground on his horns in a maddened exhibition of strength; but soon, perhaps, he falls beneath his living load;—he has lost his advantage 1 Instantly his opponent profits by the misfortune, and pins him, who was almost the victor a moment before, by the neck to the earth. Then it is that the spectator of the intensely interesting combat, inspired by the sympathy which ever goes out to the weak against the mighty, is seized with an almost uncontrollable desire to separate the ferocious brutes. If he is an old plainsman, however, he knows that his own life would

not be safe for a moment if he attempted it; besides, the monsters will take care of themselves; they are constituted for just such ferocious combats, death rarely coming to either combatant in these conflicts, unless in a close inclosure.

The fight always continues until one of the contestors is conquered. Even then the vanquished animal keejis his face to the victor, moving backward until an opportunity offers itself for him to skulk into seclusion, or out of sight of his now acknowledged master. Should they be closely corralled, death is sure to be the portion of the one conquered, as the bison is relentless, showing no mercy to his enemy in any instance.

The skin of a full-grown buffalo's head and neck is an inch in thickness. It cannot be penetrated by a ball from an ordinary pistol or an old-fashioned rifle, much less by the horn of a competitor; in fact it requires the best modern weapon to make an impression upon such a mass of indurated hide. The muscle of the buffalo has a wonderful adaptation to the requirements of the huge Ijrute; the nostrils are immense, seemingly able to draw in a supply of air to last for a long period; the lungs are comparably large to retain it. Their horns are set at the very best angle to be most effective in the awful battle which invariably falls to their portion at some time in their lives. I very much doubt if the lion is the "king of beasts," or could hold his own in an engagement with &n enraged buffalo bull.

CHAPTER II

BUFFALO JONES

EARLY DAYS IN ILLINOIS HIS PARENTS' PERILOUS ADVENTURE WITH A WOUNDED DEER ABRAHAM LINCOLN

PLEADS HIS father's CAUSE FOR $10 —r- SCHOOL-DAYS

FEW AND FAR BETWEEN THE CAPTURING AND SELLING

A SQUIRREL FIXES HIS RULING PASSION POSSESSOR OF A

SMALL MENAGERIE NO ANIMAL TOO OBSTREPEROUS FOR

HIM TO CONQUER—SLEEPING AT NIGHT IN THE FIELDS

NEIGHBORS AROUSED INTO SEARCHING PARTIES — AN EFFORT AT COLLEGE — BOUND FOR "BLEEDING KANSAS"^ SETTLING DOWN AS A "FAMILY MAN"

CHARLES JESSE JONES, more familiarly known as "Buffalo Jones," (Colonel Jones, as he is by courtesy sometimes called,) was born in Tazewell county, 111., in 1844. His grandfather, Charles, for whom the grandson is named, was one of the pioneers of that State, having emigrated from Scituate, Massachusetts, in 1826, eight years after the admission of Illinois into the Union. "Buffalo Jones's" grandmother was a Nichols, one of the most celebrated families of Boston.

Noah Nichols Jones, the father of the subject of this sketch, was a mere boy when he accompanied his parents to the bleak primitive prairies of Illinois. He married Miss Jane Munden, whose family were of the God-fearing, sterling old-fashioned Virginia Quakers, and from this stock " Buffalo Jones " inherits some unmistakable-traits which occasionally crop out in his nature.

(14)

His father was very early thrown upon the cold world to struggle for himself, dependent entirely upon his own resources for his support. He was a man of great determination ; possessing a strong will; full of energy, which balked at nothing that was possible for a man to accomplish. These characteristics are very prominent in his son, and are the secret of his success in all the novel undertakings he has attempted.

The elder Jones preempted a tract of one hundred and sixty acres of Government land in

McLean county, Illinois, which bordered a small stream called Money creek, where he settled down to the active, hard work of a pioneer farmer, in the then " far West." Here, on this raw wild place, as "Buffalo Jones" himself expresses it, "I went through the ' sweat-box.' I was the second son of a family of twelve children, and from the time I was strong enough to pick up a basket of chips at the woodpile, until I had attained my majority, 'Work, work' was the watchword of our home."

Colonel Jones says that his father was a famous hunter in his younger days, not only because of a love for the exciting sport, but from necessity as well; for in the wild condition of that region, "varmints," as they were pro-vincially called,—deer, beaver, otter, panthers, wolves, and coons,— abounded in the forests, on the prairie, and in the many streams. These were the real source of revenue, rather than the legitimate products of the roughly worked farms. The skins of the animals mentioned, and the flesh of the deer, particularly, were always in demand ; and these were the principal support of the family while, for a few years, the land was being brought into subjection. Of the time passed on the homestead, Colonel Jones tells many incidents, which have,clung to "memory's walls" ever since his babyhood. One of these I'here relate in his own language:

"I was only three years old, a mere baby in tow frocks. We were in the condition of the man digging for the

groundhog, who was to entertain the deacon of his church that day—'out of meat.' My father concluded that he must have some venison, so rose very early that morning,— one of those sharp, crisp, frosty days in January,— jumped on a little pony-built horse that he used to ride on such expeditions, and started for a ' brush-patch ' about a mile from the house, which was a favorite resort of the deer at that season. Arriving at the spot, he took a long circuit around the bushes, and, to his delight, saw an abundance of tracks in the freshly fallen snow. Quietly dismounting and tying his animal to a stout sapling, he walked on through the tall grass which covered the ground outside the brush, when to his surprise he saw, not over a hundred yards from where he had fastened his horse, a large buck with an immense set of antlers, lying in the short herbage,—the great horns, as is frequently the case, betraying his whereabouts.

"In an instant the old-fashioned squirrel rifle—the arm par excellence in those early days — was brought to his shoulder, the flint fell with a crash, the fire flew from it as it struck the pan, but the piece did not go off. Much to his surprise and chagrin, the buck never moved. Whether the animal was asleep or endeavoring to ' play possum,' could not be determined, of course. The gun was hastily inspected to find out what was the matter, as it had seldom before proved false, when it was discovered there was no powder in the pan. In order to make this intelligent to those readers who perhaps have never seen a flint-lock—"a back number" to this generation — let me explain : The ' pan ' was a small reservoir at the base of where the flint was intended to strike, and held about half a teaspoonful of powder; the powder connected with the little tube which entered the gun-barrel, and ignited the charge. My father quickly seized the powder-horn swung over his shoulder by a string of buckskin, poured into the pan some of its contents, raised the weapon again, took an indifferent aim, as the buck's outline was

only very dimly observable, so closely did he hug the ground, and fired. The old flint-lock quickly responded this time, but the deer did not stir. Father walked up to the beast, kicked it, and still it gave no signs of life. He saw at a glance that the ball had struck the animal in the neck, and felt in his pocket for the hunting-knife he usually carried, but, much to his regret, found he had left it at the house. His next dilemma was how to get the deer home. He was not long in deciding that matter. Taking the rope halter from his horse's neck, he tied a knot in the horse's bushy tail, fastened one end of the rope around the buck's horns and the other above the knot made in the pony's tail, mounted, and trotted off briskly, as he had made a bet with his sister-in-law that he would be back with a deer before she could bake the biscuit, which in those days were cooked in one of the old-fashioned ' Dutch ovens'; (such things as stoves were not known in that part of the country.)

" He was in a fair way of winning his wager by hurrying along at the best speed the pony could make with the load he was compelled to drag in such a novel way, but when he had reached about half-way, on looking back he saw to his horror that the deer was attempting to get on his feet, but that, fortunately, as often as he rose to his knees the horse would jerk him down again. The fact is, that the ball had only grazed the cervical vertebrae, or ' creased ' him, as it is called in hunting parlance. This paralyzes all the muscles temporarily, and the animal is unable to exercise any power over them. (This was one of the methods employed in capturing wild horses at one time.) The friction caused by dragging him over the rough and snowy ground had partially restored the circulation, and he was rapidly getting into his normal condition of physical strength.

"Realizing the predicament he was in, my father applied the whip to his now equally scared horse, and the latter fairly flew over the trail with his double burden^ —2

while the deer, continually gaining more and more power, was frantic in his endeavors to escape from his unique position. The great danger was, that the moment the pony should slacken his pace the buck would fight mercilessly, throwing his immense antlers in every direction, probably impaling both horse and rider.

"By this time the family at home were all up, and preparations for breakfast were rapidly progressing. My mother happened to look out of a window, and saw her husband approaching at an unusually fast gait. She rushed to the door, wondering what could be the incentive for pounding his horse in such a manner. Surely, the Indians could not be after him; it was the wrong time of the year for any of the savages to be lurking in the vi-•cinity. Was it a panther?—one of those ferocious and ■dreaded beasts of the settlements which created such havoc among the young stock, and occasionally carried off a stray child. Could it be a pack of hungry wolves ? She was nonplussed for a moment, but soon her husband's voice ■came ringing clearly through the 'opening,' although he was still a quarter of a mile distant:

"' The butcher-knife 1 The butcher-knife! This deer's alive 1'

" This appeal, repeated several times in such loud tones, :showed that he was terribly excited and in danger. As he drew nearer, he gave vent more vociferously to his need of assistance:

" ' The axe ! The axe 1 This deer 's alive 1'

" My mother was young and very active then; she immediately comprehended the situation my father was in, and having been reared on the border, she, like nearly all of her hardy class, knew nothing of that fear which attaches to those women who have lived in a pampered civilization in the thickly settled East.

*'Quickly snatching the butcher-knife from its accustomed place near the mantel-shelf, she ran to the gate, .the pony arriving there with his living load at the same

instant, dashing against the fence in his excitement. Father received the knife from her hand as he rushed by. The pace of the horse was of course now slackened by-coming in contact with the pickets, and in a moment the infuriated deer was on his feet. He made a desperate attempt to break away toward the timber, which nearly threw both horse and rider to the ground. Fortunately, close to the gate stood a heavy farm wagon loaded with wood, around which father whipped the pony, and in so doing jerked the deer's horns into one of the hind wheels, and, his momentum thus suddenly stopped, the animal slipped flat on his side, all sprawled out. In an instant mother (who was somewhat inclined to stoutness, weighing nearly one hundred and sixty pounds, and very strong) was upon the animal, and held him down until father jumped off his pony, came around, and cut the animal's throat.

"Hardly had he accomplished this last act of the tragedy, when a great outburst of childish laughter greeted his ears, and upon looking up, he saw his little three-year-old boy (myself), who had slipped out of the house unnoticed, enjoying one of the most wonderful scenes it has ever been his fortune to witness, even during his own long and eventful career.

"My father was of a firm disposition, and of a small, wiry build. He never hesitated to express his convictions, and was an earn,e8t anti-slavery advocate. Once, when Stephen A. Douglas was a candidate for Congress-man-at-large, father was one of the judges of election, and became politically involved in an altercation with the acknowledged pugilist of the neighborhood. The fracas so terminated that he thought best to go before the magistrate, Edward Burtis, father of A. H. Burtis, now a successful Kansas politician. He paid his fine, and thought no more about it; but the other man felt aggrieved, and demanded a trial by a jury of his peers, in the district court, which was presided over by Judge

David Davis, afterwards U. S. Senator. Father retained two attorneys, Ashley Gridley and Abraham Lincoln, to plead his cause. The fee agreed upon was ten dollars each. It is needless to add that it was well tried, and a verdict of acquittal returned. The amount was cheerfully paid, and ever afterwards Mr. Lincoln and my father were cordial friends. No one mourned the lamented President more than did Noah Nicholas Jones."

Col. Jones attributes a great deal of his inclination for hunting to just such scenes as that above mentioned. His brother John, two years his junior, has many of the same traits, but is a better marksman, especially with the shotgun; though he has never killed so many animals as has the Colonel, not having had the opportunity.

Although of a relatively delicate-looking physique, young Jones was the very incarnation of activity, nerve and muscle during those years passed on the original old homestead in Illinois. He possessed the spirit of emulation to such a degree, that he would never permit anyone of his age and size to outdo him in the labor assigned as his task.

His early education was very much restricted, for, as among all pioneer civilization of the period of his youth, the " district school-house " was the conventional log building, utterly devoid of those appurtenances and educational appliances which characterize our splendid system of to-day. There was no bell, no register, no maps, no blackboard; in fact, nothing that could make the path in pursuit of knowledge an easy one. The benches were constructed of rude slabs, whose legs were rough sticks with the bark on. These were driven into auger-holes, their wedged ends protruding an inch or more,— a fruitful source of torn trousers, as anyone will remember who ever sat upon such instruments of youthful torture.

Young Jones, however, was not a sufferer to any great extent, as his privilege to attend school was limited to

two or three days in the week, and only then when the weather was too cold and stormy to work out of doors on the farm, in winter-time.

His father soon became a very prosperous farmer, working three or four extensive tracts in the neighborhood, acquired by hard work and economy, which, by the time his son Charles had arrived at the age of sixteen, it was his duty to superintend, with their hundreds of cattle, horses, sheep, and mules. This stupendous supervision was thrown almost entirely upon the shoulders of the boy — enough for two or three men. Long before this juncture, young Jones had developed a genius for taming animals. He always possessed a love for animated nature, and the power of subduing fractious beasts to his will. Naturally, he became an expert rider at a very early age, which has served him so admirably on the Great Plains in pursuit of the buffalo so closely connected with his name.

One of the incidents of his boyhood life, he tells as follows:

" When a mere lad about twelve years old, I was sent to the woods with the hired man to saw off logs. Snow was on the ground, and my father was to come with a sled in the afternoon and haul the logs to a mill about a mile away. While busily engaged sawing, I looked up into a tree and saw a fox-squirrel swinging on a limb. I dropped the saw, and followed the beautiful little animal. It was soon high in the branches, and I climbed up the tree and pressed the wise little fellow to the end of a limb, but it gave a spring and caught in the boughs of another tree. Not daring to emulate its method of traveling, I was compelled to descend to the ground, then climb up the other tree. The squirrel repeated its tactics and I mine, until the greater part of the day was gone. At last the little fellow took refuge in a hole, in a large burr-oak. When I reached the place, I thrust my left hand into the hole and grabbed the squirrel. The penalty was, that with his long sharp teeth he nearly cut

off the end of my finger. (Ever since, it has been the unlucky member, and has so often been crippled that it is impossible to bend it.) I held a firm grip until reaching the ground, then thrust it into my coat *pocket, took some honey-locust thorns and pinned the pocket together.

"Presently my father arrived, and finding no logs to load, demanded an explanation. The hired man explained he could not run the saw alone, and Charley had been pursuing a squirrel most of the day. Then a boy about my size received a good thrashing, but he managed to keep his cap over the squirrel to protect it, preferring to receive the blows himself.

"I managed to get the squirrel home; finally had it quite tame, and it proved a comfort to me. One day I was sent to Bloomington, about twelve miles distant, to do some trading. I took Dick (the name I had given the squirrel) along, hoping to sell him for something, as I had made up my mind others could be caught if the sale was made. Dick perched upon my shoulder, and I walked the street for hours, asking all I met if they wanted to buy a pet, but they generally laughed, and said ' No.* Finally a well-dressed man hailed me, and wanted to know if I would sell the squirrel. I told him Dick was a great pet, but if I copld get a fair price for him, would sell, and asked what he would give. He said he had a son about my age, a cripple, and he had never seen anything like a squirrel, and knew he would be delighted with it. Finally he offered me two dollars for Dick. It almost took my breath. I had not hoped to receive to exceed fifty cents, and would have been proud of twenty-five. I had never had but one "bit" (twelve and one-half cents) in all my life, and two dollars appeared like a colossal fortune to me. It was that transaction which fixed upon me the ruling passion that has adhered so closely through life. From that time until this, I have never lost an opportunity in my power to capture every wild animal that rune on legs, as well as some that creep upon their bellies.

HIS FACULTY FOR CONQUERING ANIMALS 23

"Before a year rolled around, after receiving such a princely amount for little Dick, I had caged a good-sized menagerie, consisting of every animal that inhabited central Illinois; had even captured rattlesnakes and extracted their fangs. By this means I had all kinds of curios to sell when the shows came around, and thus realized many a precious dollar.

"The capture of that little animal, Dick, molded the destiny of my whole life. It is the little things which govern the lives of the people of the world. The first money made by a child is never forgotten; he is sure to try the same method again and again. And I am certain if that first two dollars had been made by dishonorable means, such as gambling, stealing, robbing, cheating, begging, or blackmailing, the habit would have fastened itself as firmly upon me as did that of capturing wild animals."

On the farm, if there was an obstreperous animal, either horse, mule, or ox, it was he alone who could conquer it. He relates an incident of this character, which occurred when he was but thirteen years old. His father desired to have a pair of young steers yoked up, so as to break them for service at the plow; but they were so vicious that, after trying for half a day, assisted by two burly hired men, the old gentleman was compelled to abandon the job as impossible,—all badly worsted in their struggle with the ferocious beasts. Then his father and the men left, and went to a neighboring village, Hudson. At once young Charles started for the pasture into which the fractious steers had been turned. He succeeded in driving them into the barnyard and then into the barn, where he threw a rope over the horns of one, and by skillful management drew it up to a beam. He then laid a slip-noose in another rope, so as to get the steer's hind foot into it, when he hitched a steady old mule to the rope, who stretched the steer's leg out to its greatest tension. With another rope he anchored the stiffened leg to a brace ou

the opposite side of the barn from where the animal's head was fastened. All the time that young Jones was thus manipulating, the old mule quietly held the steer in any position desired. The boy then took the yoke and bows; one of the latter he keyed tightly on the animal's neck he had in durance, and then served his mate in the same manner, until they were both so bound together it was impossible for them to unyoke themselves. He then opened the double folding doors and cut the ropes that held them so tightly, when they darted into the barnyard.

When his father returned in the early evening he was dumbfounded to see the steers yoked up, standing in the yard. He became quite vexed when he discovered that Charley had accomplished all alone what he and two men had failed in. The fact was, that after finding that the steers were perfectly unmanageable, he sold them to a butcher while down in the village that afternoon. The next day was occupied in endeavoring to free the oxen from the yoke. They were so wild and vicious that the bows had actually to be sawed from their necks; the consequence of which was, the boy received a good thrashing with the ox-goad for the trouble he had caused.

The great majority of boys of his then age delight in marbles, kites, base-ball, and kindred games; but young Jones was the rare exception to all this. He shunned the crowd of boys who usually congregate in the rural districts, much preferring to be by himself, free to ramble alone through the timber or fields, where he could indulge in his love of nature untrammeled by any uncongenial companions. Birds and animals, whether squirrels, bear, or deer, were his special loves. These he would catch at every opportunity, and tame them in his own peculiar way. Capturing animals was his ruling passion. The more restrictions thrown around him by his parents, the more he became attached to his favorite amusement.

He declares that he was unquestionably the most sleepy-headed boy that ever existed. It made no difference whether he retired as soon as supper was disposed of—it was just as difficult to awaken him in the morning as if he had gone to bed at midnight. At times, in order to awaken him, it was necessary to actually roll him out on the floor and pour cold water into his ears. This exceedingly disagreeable condition lasted until he reached his sixteenth year, at which time he fortunately outgrew it.

At one time, when only nine, he was sent to a distant field all alone to pull weeds out of the corn-rows. When he reached the farthest point from the house, a young quail in an adjoining oat-field suddenly commenced to whistle for its mother. Instantly the boy darted over there, and secreting himself in the tall grain, answered the bird's call several times, but before the fledgling could come in response to the counterfeited mother, Charles was eound asleep.

At home every preparation for supper had been completed; the men were called out of the fields, and when they sat down at the table there was " one vacant chair." *' Why, where 's Charley ? " was the anxious inquiry, " I don't know," all responded, with the exception of one gruff old Yankee, who exclaimed, "Oh, he 's out somewhere watching a gopher-hole, trying to get him for a pet." But this did not allay the anxiety of an affectionate mother, who immediately abandoned her place at the teapot, went to the door, and in an earnest, ringing voice called her missing child. But no response came echoing over the prairie, which was covered with the shadows of night, for the sun had long since set; and the boy's absence began to be a serious matter, particularly to the loving mother, whose countenance unmistakably indicated her solicitude. The hired men then mounted horses; the mother, the female help and all of the children were running in every direction, calling, calling, but calling in vain; only the echoes of their own voices reverberated on the calm night air, or the gradually fading

sounds of the father and the men as they receded in the distance. Every row of corn was carefully scrutinized, for all knew he had been sent there. Every nook and corner where it was believed possible for him to have gone, was thoroughly searched. Then lanterns and torches were hastily procured, the neighbors notified, and the search for the lost boy became a neighborhood affair. This was a common thing in those early days on the border; it was necessary for mutual protection, and in a case of this kind promptness was essential, for the country was still infested with panthers and wolves: so no wonder the mother of young Jones was nearly distracted when midnight arrived, and no word of her boy.

About one o'clock, as one of the hired men was riding rapidly through the oat-field, his horse made a tremendous lunge, evidently frightened at something; upon which the man dismounted, and to his astonishment and delight saw the missing Charley, sound asleep,— dreaming, probably, of the motherless little bird he had set hia heart upon capturing.

Then a shout was set up, and a cheer which all understood, from its tone, to mean that the boy had been found alive and uninjured. A crowd soon gathered around the place where he was found, and the naughty boy, like a successful gladiator of old, was borne triumphantly away to the arms of his mother, who so anxiously awaited his coming.

When Col. Jones had attained his majority, he began to realize he had passed the greater portion of his years in very hard work, like a dutiful son, for the interests of the family. He had been obedient to his father,— so there were no regrets in filial obligations; but he also realized his education had been sadly neglected. Then he determined, now he was released from any further demands on his time, to in a measure rectify the misfortune of the want of early schooling, so far as it was possible at this late day. Having thus determined, under the prompt-

ings of his iron will, (and a little black-eyed girl who no doubt rather liked the awkward chap, yet was ashamed of his ignorance,) he packed up his limited quantity of effects, walked to the railroad station, three miles distant, and took the train for Bloomington. Arriving in that flourishing town, he applied for entrance at the Wesleyan University, located there, for one term at least, in v/hich he was successful.

At this institution of learning Col. Jones studied diligently and earnestly for two years, at the end of which period, in consequence of his close application, he was stricken down with typhoid fever, which affected his eyes very seriously, and he was compelled to abandon his studies and turn to other vocations. Among his classmates at the University was Joseph W. Fifer, since Governor of Illinois, and many other men who have risen to distinction in the domain of politics, law, and literature.

Although obliged to abandon his attempt to acquire an education, he had no idea of sitting supinely at the family hearthstone and grieving over his misfortune, but, prompted again by his indomitable will, he notified his father he intended to start out in the world to seek his own fortune. Of course the father, to whom he had been such a dutiful son, was grieved to learn of his determination to leave the old home, and made several favorable overtures to persuade his boy to remain with him. Among these was the offer of a gift of one of the best farms of which he was possessed, well stocked with cattle, implements of the most approved pattern, and everything ready to commence operations on a large scale. But the young man refused all, determined to seek the "Far West" beyond the Missouri river, to which comparatively unknown region he had been attracted by reading its tales of adventure and hairbreadth escapes, ever since he was old enough to master words of three syllables. He felt sure that in that remote region he could accumulate wild animals to his heart's content, and never lost courage in that direction.

One beautiful morning he packed his little valise, shook hands with his father, kissed his mother and baby sister good-by, and was soon speeding westward over the prairies, full of determination to succeed, and with energy to carry out whatever enterprise he might attempt. He first stopped at St. Joseph, Mo. This was early in 1866, just after the close of the great Civil War. Here he remained a few days, and then started for the wilds of the new State of Kansas. He settled in Troy, Doniphan county, where, having managed to secure a large amount of Osage orange seed, he started a nursery for the growth of hedge plants and every variety of fruit trees. In 1867 the locusts, or grasshoppers as they were erroneously called, visited the State in countless swarms, darkening the air, and in the short space of twenty-four hours every vestige of the nursery had disappeared, except the bare poles of what had been trees; and within a week they stripped them of their bark, completing absolute ruin. This disastrous raid did not discourage the indomitable Jones, however. " Try again " has ever been his motto, and in accordance with its precepts, during the winter he grafted more than 50,000 trees, grapevines, and other varieties of fruit. With the opening spring came the grasshoppers again, and devoured a larger portion of his year's labor; yet by hard work he saved and sold enough to enable him to purchase a small farm of twenty acres, upon which he built a comfortable dwelling, and outhouses to carry on his business. In the year 1869 Col. Jones was married to Martha J. Walton, the daughter of a highly respected farmer, formerly of Laporte, Indiana. Mr. Jones's relations with his estimable wife have ever been of that character which proves that " marriage is not a failure."

The only trouble he experienced was when he would leave home to capture wild animals, to which his wife always objected. Nothing to her appeared so much like a phantom. Her fretting was always of short duration, however, for he was careful to refrain from talking in re-

lation to his starting on an expedition until about ready-to leave, and then only in a vague sort of way. Every time he did go she always protested with increasing earnestness, declaring she had a presentiment that "that would be his last trip." She felt certain that some cow, robbed of her offspring by him, would gore him to death in the most shocking manner, far away from civilization, and his body left to bleach on the desert; or that some hostile band of bloodthirsty savages would capture him and put him to unnameable torture; Indians, Eskimos or wolves would overpower him; a rattlesnake might bite him; he might die of cold, thirst, or hunger. A thousand deaths of horrid character continually pictured themselves to the wife, who was relieved of this mental torture only when her husband returned safely home. His declarations of the wonderful results if successful in his dangerous work — fame, wealth, honor—were but as ashes to her mental lips.

CHAPTER III

" WESTWARD HO I"

bound for the wild west in a peairie schooner mrb.

Jones's first experience camping on the prairie — wolves cut lariat and team escapes — recaptured under difficulties joyous greeting on return to

CAMP

LATE in the fall of 1871 Col. Jones left his home in Troy, Kansas, on horseback, to seek a* place where ^ more game and cheaper land could be obtained. Having business in Marysville, in the same State, he was delayed there until midwinter. The terrific storms which prevailed did not daunt him, however, in his purpose; he is made of " sterner stuff." A prevailing characteristic of his whole life is his determination to carry out to the end any enterprise, no matter how difficult, or what obstacles may present themselves.

On the first of January, 1872, he again saddled hi& horse and pressed forward to the west until he found himself about two hundred miles from home, near the center of what is now Osborne county, on the south fork of the Solomon river. There he discovered a most excellent tract of vacant Government land, on which was an abundance of water and some timber. This he entered, and was soon the proud possessor of one hundred and sixty acres of rich, fertile soil, almost in the center of the buffalo range. All of the preliminaries necessary, required by the United States land laws, having been con-

(30)

eluded, to hold the land, he returned to his old home on the same means of transportation, his tough and faithful horse.

Arriving at Troy, he arranged his financial affairs, and the following April loaded his worldly goods into a large wagon, in which, accompanied by his wife and only child, he left all his old associations, the comforts of civilization and friends, for his claim on the remote plains of western Kansas. This was a severe undertaking, especially for his young wife, who had been reared amidst the luxuries of an Eastern community; but like all our pioneer American women, she cheerfully followed the fortunes of her brave husband, accepting whatever of hardship might befall. None excepting those who have had a-like experience can conceive what such a sacrifice means; what privations must be endured; what disadvantages, must be contended with, and what suffering is the portion of the women who have built up the civilization of the mid-continent.

On the night of the sixth day the precious freight of that lone wagon was to sleep on the ground, having left the last cabin on the "trail" far behind. The darkness and awful silence were oppressive; the latter broken only at long intervals, by the occasional neighing of the horses at the end of their picket-ropes, the flapping of the wagon-cover in,the fitful gusts of wind, or the dismal cry of a hungry wolf in the rocky ravines.

At the first streak of dawn a terrible howling and yelling resounded upon the early morning air, apparently not a hundred yards distant from camp, caused by a pack of persistent coyotes that were patiently waiting for the wagon to move on, that they might feast upon the scraps left from the meals of the "movers "—fighting and snarling meanwhile among themselves, until the time should arrive when they might take possession of the abandoned place, too cowardly to approach nearer while the camp was occupied. Col. Jones of course paid no attention to

such an occurrence: he was familiar with the nature of 1 the animals which were making the disturbance; but to his gentle wife the unusual noise, so foreign to her delicate ears, was a source of torture, and her sleep was continually disturbed.

With the daylight the curious sounds ended, but the long, lank, wistful brutes could be seen sitting on their haunches, watching every movement in camp, licking their chops in eager expectancy of the meager feast that awaited them.

At the moment the red flush in the east betokened the approaching day, Mr. Jones was out of his blankets, and his first thought was of his horses. To his astonishment and discomfiture, the wolves had gnawed in twain the lariat with which they were tied, and the animals were nowhere to be seen. Mr. Jones ran back a mile or more on the "trail," until he reached the crest of the divide which encompassed a view of the country for a long distance to the eastward; but his horses were not in sight, even from that vantage-point. Their tracks, however, were plainly visible in the dust of the desert, turned toward their old home. He thought of the dilemma in which he was placed, and of what Mrs. Jones would say when she learned of the unfortunate occurrence. He was not at all certain whether they would be recovered within a distance of ten, or fifty miles, or whether they were irrecoverably lost, as prowling bands of Indians were in the country, besides many horse-thieves.

He knew that he could not conscientiously keep the facts from his wife, and go in search of them, so he hastened back to the wagon and communicated the direful news.

" What shall we do? " was naturally her first inquiry. " I 'll go and get them," he replied. " I 'll go with you," was Mrs. Jones's quick rejoinder. He knew that was impossible, and persuaded her that it was better to remain with the wagon until he made a thorough search, promising his anxious wife to return before night in any event.

• This was an hour when the courage of any woman would have been severely strained, and Mrs. Jones was sorely tried. She could do nothing but seat herself upon the highest box on the wagon, with her child (a boy only one year old) in her arms, and watch through the weary hours which must necessarily elapse before it was possible for her husband to return. Thus she wearily sat, looking earnestly in the same direction, as Daniel of old, until deliverance came.

Col. Jones was fleet-footed, courageous, and endowed with wonderful powers of endurance; so he started, full of hope, with his rope and hat in hand, coat off, after the renegade team, while his wife watched his form as it flitted like a flying shadow, over hills, across valleys, and through the deep ravines, until the high divide had taken him beyond the range of her vision.

Mile after mile was rapidly left in his rear; the hours rolled on apace, and the sun indicated the time to be nearly noon ; still the tracks of the missing animals could be distinctly seen ever pointing eastwardly. It was becoming a serious matter to their intrepid pursuer; he was far from his camp; could with mental vision see his patient wife straining her eyes in the direction he had gone, in expectancy of his speedy return. He now realized that night would be upon him before he was aware of it, and that he must soon retrace his steps in order to be back at the wagon, horses or no horses. He felt assured, too, that it would be impossible for him to keep up his rate of speed, and that he must slacken his gait. He resolved, however, to continue on for another hour, at which time he would abandon the chase and return to camp, if the horses were not then to be seen.

While he was ambling down a long hill on a run, pondering upon his embarrassing situation, he passed around a short curve in his course, where, to his surprise and delight, he discovered the recreant animals within a stone's-throw. One of them stood perfectly still, with ears erect, —3

listening to the noise their owner had made coming down the hill, and the other was deliberately moving towards him to learn the cause. As soon, however, as they saw it was their master on the run after them, they threw up their heads and tails and were off again, as on the wings of the wind, keeping up their rapid gait as far as the eye «ould see,— for the shelter of the trees soon obscured them.

Many people at such an unfortunate juncture would have given up in despair; not so, however, with a man constituted as is Col. Jones. He was rejoiced at seeing his animals again, notwithstanding they had fled at his approach, and knew that his strategy, learned by a long and varied experience, would enable him to circumvent any apparently hopeless chance on the part of mere brute intelligence. He cogitated for a moment; remembered that the trail made a long curve to the south, and then ■turned northward again. So he started northward, and went down into the valley at the greatest speed he could xjommand, determined to reach the trail before the fright-«ened horses could possibly arrive there. When he came to the creek which flows through the valley, he found it quite deep, and about ten feet wide. Although an excellent swimmer, he did not care to plunge into the cold water, saturated as he was with perspiration. There were •many small trees growing along the margin of the stream, and he was not a moment in making up his mind what to do under the circumstances. Selecting a withy sapling about twenty feet high, hanging towards the opposite shore, he sprang into it, climbed nearly to its top, where his weight bent it over towards the other side of the water, at which instant he sprang from his perch. His calculation had been correct, and he landed with but little room to spare. All this was effected in less time than it requires to read it, and he continued on his way as rapidly as his strength would permit, for it was half a mile before he could reach the trail, on which the

horses were surely approaching, and he must arrive at a certain point before them or his strategy would fail.

He shortly reached a little divide which parallels the creek, and from its crest saw the animals walking briskly almost opposite him. It was too late to carry out the plan he had formulated. If he ran out to head them off, it would only result in frightening them, undoubtedly cause them to stampede again, and all his trouble would have been in vain. He then changed his tactics to meet the emergency which had occurred. Quickly taking in the altered condition of affairs, with that perspicacity which characterizes the old plainsman, he rushed down the divide and up the creek for about half a mile, to a point where a small ravine enters it. He followed the tortuous windings of this ravine for nearly a mile, then crossed the little divide separating him from the other ravine, up which the horses were slowly coming, arriving at the trail in a very favorable spot, with relatively high embankments on either side. Now came the final struggle. Had the animals yet passed out ? Fortunately not. He could discover no marks of their hoofs; all was well so far. His rope was hidden behind him, and the now anxious pursuer was compelled to be very cautious. He wandered slowly back on the trail, loudly singing one of his favorite tunes, fearing that if he came suddenly upon the animals in such a sequestered place without some sort of warning, they would take to flight in another direction. This strategy lasted but a moment, and he was not by any means too soon, for the horses suddenly appeared upon the trail right in front of him. He sauntered along carelessly toward the now interested animals, who pricked up their ears as they stood perfectly passive, seemingly recognizing their master's voice. Instead of attempting to rush off again, they deliberately walked up to him, apparently as much pleased to see him as he to meet them under such favorable circumstances.

The thing was done, and well done, thought the Colonel as he mounted one, fastened the rope around the neck of the other, and started on his return to camp. It was now the middle of the afternoon, and he was at least twenty-five miles from the wagon, so he wasted no time on the return trip. He made the horses atone for the trouble they had given him, by pushing them at the top of their speed, realizing it would not hurt them, as he intended to remain in camp another twelve hours, which would give them ample rest for their journey on the following day. They seemed to acknowledge that they had committed a grievous offense, by willingly doing their utmost to reach camp without any persuasion,— and away they traveled at the rate of twelve miles an hour towards the goal which he was so anxious to gain before the night set in.

It was long before sundown when he reached the high divide from which he could see Mrs. Jones still sitting on the same old box. Of course she could see him also, and signals were quickly exchanged which settled the question of identity, and a great load was lifted from her heart,

The reader, although he may never have experienced an incident exactly similar to that of Mr. and Mrs. Jones, can imagine the mutual joy of such a meeting, under the peculiar circumstances attending it. Col. Jones was no more a hero than his estimable, patient wife was a heroine. In her anxiety, though, she had absolutely forgotten that her worn-out husband had left at the earliest dawn without having eaten a morsel of food; had walked and run a quarter of a hundred miles, and ridden bareback the same distance, and must necessarily be in a famishing condition. He was almost exhausted; asked for a ciip of cold coffee, upon which she realized her forgetfulness. But never was a meal cooked by an unaccustomed camp-fire with such dispatch as that prepared for him on this occasion. He sat down, and realized that his wife was the very best cook in the world.

CHAPTER IV

DESPERADOES

FARMING IN THE FAR WEST — A FRUITLESS BUFFALO-HUNT — LIVING ON BREAD AND NO WATER — MIRAGE INTENSIFIED BY PROSTRATION — BUFFALO RUN HIGH IN THE AIR

DESPERADOES IN CAMP—" IF YOU HAVE ANYTHING TO

SAY, SAY IT D—D QUICK, FOR I AM GOING TO KILL YOU RIGHT here" — RESCUED BY A PLUCKY BOY

IN the summer of 1872 I was an embryo farmer on the new raw prairies of western Kansas, which region just then began to attract immigrants on account of its superiority of soil and climate. I had been a successful buffalo-hunter, had killed thousands simply for their hides, but the idea of my buffalo-rescuing project was but a creature of the brain, not yet perfectly formulated; yet that was the year I determined to * some sweet day ' capture a herd, domesticate and perpetuate the species. I captured about a dozen that year, sold them for seven dollars and a half each, and was delighted to receive even that much. After I had finished my corn-plowing (it was in the early part of August), I determined to go on a hunt, as the week previously I had learned of the main herd of buffalo about sixty miles west of where I had staked out my Government claim.

"Although an experienced hunter, I had not given so much attention to the habits of the buffalo as I have during the past quarter of a century. No doubt it was my lack of buffalo lore, which allowed me to imagine I could any time within the next week go where the herd was re-

(37)

ported to have been seen, and find it tliere still. I took an abundance of time to make my preparation, and employed a young man, a neighbor, to go with me. The day before I left, two strangers came along, who declared they desired to secure work in our section of the country, at anything. I informed them that all the buffalo-hunters were out after hides, which was the principal employment of the few people who lived in the region, and they could undoubtedly get a job of skinning, if they were able to find an outfit going to the range. I was besieged to let them go with me; they promised to help about the camp and skin buffaloes until they were able to find regular work. I finally took pity on the miserable tramps, and consented.

"The next morning we rolled out on our journey in search of the great herd I had heard of. Two days of travel without any incident worth recalling, brought us to where we certainly expected to find game, but not a single buffalo could we see in any direction. I had provided the outfit with three days' rations of meat, plenty of flour for two months, together with other necessary sundries.

"Our meat was soon gone; the fourth and fifth days jmssed, and still not a sign of any game; nor were there hunting parties to be seen anywhere, from which we might have replenished our stock of provisions, or at least our meat rations.

" We had now been living two days on bread and butter alone; the butter was all consumed on the night of the fifth day—the dry bread must serve us until we could kill a buffalo. This condition of things continued until the morning of the sixth day, when we rose very early, ate a piece of bread, drank some water, and then started off on the buffalo trail to the northwest, where the great herd had passed a week previously. Noon came, but nothing in the shape of game appeared, and we had no water. The sun poured its rays down upon our defenseless heads, as only those who have experienced a summer day on the

Plains can imagine. - It was intolerably hot, and the deceptive mirage played its curious pranks with the broiling landscape, by forming the most beautiful lakes, running over with the clearest water imaginable, while their shores were fringed with the shadiest, tallest, and most luxuriant timber; but as we approached the seductive spots, they would vanish like ' castles in the air.'

"At one time, as the wagon was moving slowly along, I was half a mile to the left, and on the border of a prairie-dog village. Here I determined to kill some of the rodents, to make soup, and was preparing to execute my plans, when on looking toward the team I saw a beautiful pool of water, and really believed it to be such, for I reasoned thus: ' It cannot be a mirage; it is certainly water, because I can see the reflection of the team, the wagon and its occupants, in the little lake. I am satisfied it is clear, cold water, and I will hasten and quench my intolerable thirst, for my tongue is actually swollen; I cannot endure the suffering much longer, as I have not had a drop since long before sunrise, and it is now past the middle of the afternoon.' I walked swiftly towards the pond, but on approaching with every nerve at its utmost tension, it vanished, as had the others, and my disappointment was sore, as may be imagined.

" In a short time we arrived at the bank of a dry ravine, or ' arroyo ' as the Mexicans call these breaks in the surface of the prairie, and ordering the men to go down on the south side with the team, I told them I would goto the valley on the north and try to find water. The strangers had been riding all day, and I suggested to them they had better walk awhile to lighten up the load, as the horses were becoming rapidly exhausted and had been traveling rapidly all day without water. One of the men in an insolent manner said: ' We did not agree to make this trip on foot, and don't propose to wear ourselves out,— we can do better. Besides, you are a d—d fool to go down this dry ravine. Why don't you keep on to the northwest ? '

" This was a ' stinger ' to me in my helpless condition, as I had only the lad whom I had brought from home, and immediately realized that they were desperate characters and no doubt had formulated some plan to take my outfit, as their actions for the past day or two convinced me they were nothing more or less than desperadoes. My attention from that time on was given to formulating some scheme to circumvent them. I made no reply to their insolent question, but ordered the boy to drive down the ravine as I had suggested, and to keep in the little valley. Four o'clock arrived, and matters were assuming a serious phase: the hot, dry wind was withering everything,— even my very flesh seemed to be shrinking; my tongue was parched and swollen, while my eyes I could scarcely trust to be right or wrong. I could see lakes and groves; the trees appeared to be approaching, but proved to be only small weeds, while the lakes, too, were merely optical illusions.

"While in this really precarious condition physically, as I staggered along, I heard a rumbling sound, and looking to the north I saw very distinctly six buffalo high up in the air, about ten times larger than usual, and about five hundred feet above the ground, running in space, coming directly towards me. I at once dropped on my left knee, ready to shoot, but could not catch a 'bead' on them, as they danced around in every direction. Nearer and nearer they came, until I could hear the rattling of their hoofs; they must have been within forty yards of me, when I heard them give a great snort, aa they turned quickly eastward and bolted around me. They sailed through the air with their legs making regular motions, as though they were running on the earth, yet to me they appeared circling high above, and soon disappeared from my view. I was really glad when the strange vision was ended; it was certainly a relief, for it appeared to me that I had lost my reasoning faculties, and my doom was at hand.

'* I felt myself perfectly conscious, and realized my situation ; there were my gun, my cartridges, and everything near me in their normal state. I could scarcely believe that a mirage would delude me to the extent described, but that is just what it was. The fact is, the buffalo passed so near I heard them puff and snort, and no doubt could have hit them with a stone had I been able to properly locate their true position. My power of sight being somewhat paralyzed from intense thirst and exhaustion, the mirage was intensified in its deception to my nervous system.

"I managed to struggle on until I reached the wagon, where, under shade of its cover, I rode awhile to recruit my failing strength. By the time I had gained somewhat of my normal faculties and power it was nearly sundown, and the shades of evening helped to brace me up. All of us, including the team, were in a really deplorable condition. I finally saw, while gazing around in search of succor, an object ahead which appeared to be a tree reaching to the sky. But the atmospheric conditions were still playing tricks with me, and consequently I did not dare to decide what it really was that I had seen,— for I had been fooled so often that day I could no longer believe my own eyes. I had lost confidence in myself, and it did not return until the sun had gone down. What had been magnified so greatly, instead of being a gigantic tree was in reality a small box-elder bush about eight feet high. This, however, was encouraging, proving that we were certainly making progress.

" We soon discovered a clump of trees or bushes ahead, which also had an inspiring effect upon our almost worn-out natures, because these objects were indications that moist ground existed there, and that was what we so much needed, for it would indicate that water was near the surface, at any rate. But unfortunately we were still doomed to sore disappointment, for there was none of the precious fluid in the immediate vicinity. We continued

on our weary journey until darkness set in. If I had been alone, I should have felt fairly comfortable, but the two tramps, genuine toughs, had changed into almost raving maniacs, they were so completely overcome by thirst. I did the best I could; assured them that water was certainly near, adjuring them to be a little patient, as I was sure we would strike it by keeping down the ravine, which had now become pretty well dotted with trees. I went out to search for water; took a spade from the side of the wagon, and commenced to dig in the sand which formed the bed of the creek. I found it moist, but could not squeeze out any water; but by putting a few of the damp pebbles in our mouths, it temporarily relieved our feverish and parched throats. Again we wandered down the ravine, which was becoming more densely lined with Cottonwood, ash, and box-elder, and presently came to a ' drift' caused by a relatively large tree which had blown down and was lying across the bed of the ravine (or creek, at certain times of the year). The water had washed out a deep channel under the debris of the logs, but not a drop remained; all had been evaporated under the influence of the intensely hot weather. I again commenced to excavate, this time in the deepest place that had washed out, for I was sure water must be close to the surface. Sure enough! I struck it, but it was so thick with quicksand that it caved in as fast as I could throw it out. Yet I knew that by a little perseverance we would all be supplied and saved from a horrid death. Presently we heard the report of a rifle coming from the direction of down-stream, not more than a half-mile away, and I quickly abandoned operations with the spade.

"We all started for the point from whence came the joyful sound, and a welcome, sight caught our eyes,— a hunter's camp and a well of water in the sand. It was full of the delicious, pure cold beverage, which we relished as mortals never did before or since. They had, besides, an abundance of fine fat buffalo-meat, of which

they invited us to partake freely, as is the custom on the Plains. We soon had an oven of biscuits under way, and by the time coffee was ready we sat down to a most bountiful meal which we so needed to revive our weakened bodies.

"The buffalo-meat was from a young animal — tender, and with an abundance of rich tallow we made a gravy that seemed infinitely superior to the sweetest butter. What a change comes over the hungry hunter when his appetite (which is the best sauce) is appeased I His whole nature is full of unselfishness, and his heart goes out to the lowliest with a full measure of brotherly love; he is then involuntarily a Christian, in the most rigid acceptance of the term.

" I was informed by these generous men that the main herd was about twenty miles north, a few buffalo having been in the vicinity of the camp that afternoon. Although the wants of my physical nature had been abundantly supplied, I was mentally discouraged that night, and slept but little; for, now familiar with the character of the men I had foolishly brought with me, I felt it would be imprudent to allow them to go farther in my company. I endeavored to persuade them to stay with the gentlemen that had so kindly entertained us, who had expressed a wilhngness to employ them in skinning buffalo; and that if a reasonable number were secured, something besides their board would be paid. This did not satisfy the two tramps. They insisted that they were to stay with me until I found them a paying job — which was false. So I determined to abandon the hunt and the next morning start for home, one hundred and fifty miles distant. Breakfast disposed of early, I informed the men that I had all the hunt I cared for, and intended to leave at once for home. This change in the plans they strenuously objected to. I made all sorts of excuses for so doing, and at last told them in a most decided manner that I was certainly going.

"After breakfast, on looking around we saw a large buffalo about a mile farther down the ravine, standing near a high bank. The strangers wanted to go and shoot it. I consented, and they started off with my Henry rifle and an old musket belonging to themselves, while the boy and I hitched up the horses and pulled down the stream about half a mile, to the south of the high bank where the buffalo had been seen ; but we could discover nothing of him or the men. I repeatedly fired mj^ gun and called aloud several times, but received no response. On looking towards the south in the direction we intended to travel, I saw two objects a mile or so away. Supposing them to be the men we were looking for, I turned the team and headed in that direction. The Solomon river was about forty miles to the south, and we expected to make it for our camping-ground that night. We kept watch of the two objects until about noon, when they disappeared. We supposed they had entered the ravine and continued the journey southward, yet thought it very strange, indeed, that these men should be so anxious to travel on foot, as they had been so averse to that method of locomotion the day previous.

" I was very much worried, and thought they could not have been our men or they would have waited until overtaken. Could it be possible they had stolen my rifle, and * skipped ' purposely ? or what was the trouble ? I drove on slowly until nearly night, when we arrived at the river and went into camp, about a hundred yards from an outfit of five men, who had also been on a hunt.

"After sujiper, as the boy and I were talking over the mysterious disappearance of the two strangers, we were very much surprised to see them suddenly emerge from under a bush, not twenty feet from where we sat. The largest one walked straight up to me with my rifle in his hands, and said: 'Old chap, you are my meat now. If you have anything to say, say it d—d quick, as I am going to kill you right here 1' My other gun was in the

wagon, and my revolver lying on a bundle just out of reach. He stood within ten feet of me, with the gun pointing straight at my heart, his finger on the trigger. I knew the least pressure on it by him would settle me for all time, as I always shot with a hair-trigger; besides, it was my favorite weapon for close quarters, and carried thirteen cartridges in the magazine. I had already risen to my feet, and was intending to arrange supper for them as soon as I saw them. So I merely turned my face directly towards them, and very calmly said: ' Shoot, if you think best, but as God is my judge, I have done you no intentional injury.' At the same instant the boy sprang directly between us, and shouted, with his hand up: ' I swear that Colonel is innocent of leaving you; I am more to blame than he, as I urged him to come on, believing you were ahead.'

" By this time the men in the other camp heard the maniacs in their fury, and one of them called out, ' What's the racket over there ? ' I responded, ' Come over and arbitrate this difficulty.' Three of the men came at once, but the crazy fool stood with my gun in his hand, jabbering all kinds of nonsense, refusing to listen to anything; but he had no ' tenderfeet' to deal with. One of the men walked straight up to him and took the gun out of his hands, without any resistance whatever.

"I explained the situation to the man; that we saw the two objects referred to, and believed with all our souls it was the two men preceding us. They claimed that while creeping up on a buffalo bull, I fired the gun to scare him away; that they followed him quite a ways, but could not get a shot. Then they came back and saw us about four miles away, upon which they fifed their guns, and kept on after us, remaining in sight nearly all day. The old hunters could scarcely keep from laughing at their excitement and jabber and ridiculous conduct. They pitied them, and pacified them. Finally they ate their supper, after which they felt much better. I took possession of the guns, extracted all the cartridges, and buckled on my belt of cartridges and revolver, as I did not intend to have any more such foolishness. The strangers soon rolled themselves in their blankets, and were sound asleep, as no doubt it was the biggest ' tramp' they ever took in one day.

" The next morning our friends from the other camp joined us, and all started for the settlements, reaching the first village. Bull City, the second day, where I very promptly told the men that they had been my guests long enough, and drove on, glad that I had disposed of them so quickly. I think that they had really become demented, and not accountable for their actions, yet capable of doing some irreparable damage; either that, or they took the opportunity as a pretext to kill me, and confiscate my team and outfit for their own use. The only thing that protected me was the camp being so'near by. The fact of others being near by was unknown to the desperadoes until the call came from the other camp.

" This was the last hunt I ever made with entire strangers."

CHAPTER V

BUFFALO ADAPTED TO EVERY ENVIRONMENT — WHY NOT DOMESTICATE THEM?—THE LAST OPPORTUNITY RESOLVED

TO TRY — THE FIRST CALF-HUNT — FORDING THE ARKANSAS RIVER FULL OF ICE — A LONG WAY FROM CIVILIZATION — "great HEAVENS 1 AN ELEPHANT, SURE 1 "—KILLS THE LARGEST BUFFALO—A NIGHT SEARCH FOR WATER— AFRAID OF ATTRACTING INDIANS, THE WATCHMAN EXTINGUISHES THE BEACON-FIRE — SAFE IN CAMP AGAIN — COL. JONES ENJOYS SUNRISE ON THE PLAINS, ALSO A " SCENE "—BUFFALO DISCOVERED THROUGH FIELD-GLASSES— FIRST ATTEMPT TO "rescue THE PERISHING"—LASSO TIED TO horse's neck, OTHER END TO CALF — THE MOTHER NEARLY IMPALES THE HORSE AND RIDER — THE COLONEL SHOOTS THE COW, AND PRESSES ON FOR MORE—HORSE FALLS, AND HERD RUSHES TO FINISH HIM—CLINGS TO SADDLE AND ESCAPES — CAPTURES FOUR CALVES — HORSE AND RIDER FAMISHING FOR WATER — MILES FROM CAMP — COMPANION LED ASTRAY BY MIRAGE—DESPERATE RACE FOR CALF PENETRATES THE LLANO E8TACAD0 — COMPANIONS REFUSE TO FOLLOW — DARE NOT RETURN WITHOUT A GUIDE

FOOLED SO OFTEN BY MIRAGE, DO NOT RECOGNIZE WATER

COMPANION LOWERED INTO THE CANADIAN RIVER—ROPE

BLIPS "the sun goes DOWN ON HIS WRATH" LAST

HERD DISCOVERED — CAPTURED FOURTEEN CALVES — THE COLONEL SHEDS HIS GARMENTS TO PROTECT THEM—HERD OP WHITE BUFFALO — LONG JOURNEY HOME

IN March, 1886, after the unprecedented and wide-area " blizzard " of the preceding winter, Colonel Jones, in his itinerary, says : "As I drove over the prairies from Kansas into Texas, I saw thousands upon thousands of the carcasses of domestic cattle which had ' drifted ' before

(*7)

the chilling, freezing 'norther.' Every one of them had died with its tail to the blizzard, never having stopped except at its last breath, then fell dead in its tracks. When I reached the habitat of the buffalo, not one of their carcasses was visible, except those which had been slain by hunters. Every animal I came across was as nimble and i\'iry as a fox. As Watts meditated over the mystery of steam lifting the lid of the teakettle, I commenced to ponder upon the contrast between the qualities of the white man's domestic cattle and those of the red man's cattle (buffalo). Young Watts exclaimed, as he watched the effect of the powerful vapor, ' Why not chain this great giant ? ' I thought to myself, ' Why not domesticate this wonderful beast which can endure such a " blizzard," defying a storm so destructive to our domestic species ? Why not infuse this hardy blood into our native cattle, and have a perfect animal, one that will defy all these elements ? ' I was in the right mood to thus soliloquize and appreciate an animal which could withstand such a terrific ordeal, having personally suffered severe losses in the great storm of the previous winter. I had been caught out in it myself at its beginning, while hunting antelope. The wind blew a perfect hurricane; the snow was twisted and hurled in all directions, until its initial mass, a foot in depth at least, was blown into the air, leaving the ground bare, where it was completely pulverized by the energy of the contending elements into an impalpable powder, filling the lungs of everything animate; drifting through their hair, alternately melting and freezing, until horses, mules and domestic cattle perished by tens of thousands. Woe unto the man who chanced to be caught in its mad career I Many did it overtake who yielded to its fury. By good luck, familiar with the nature of these terrible storms, I made my way to a ' claim-shanty,' leaving five dead antelope on the prairie, not daring to linger a minute to gather them in. I was just in time to save myself and team.

" I remained there as long as the fearful storm lasted, — two nights and a day,— and saw everything had to be protected or yield to its fury. Imagine my astonishment when I discovered that the buffalo alone were exempt; and I then commenced to calculate the worth of this remarkable but almost extinct animal. With my pencil I noted these points : ' The buffalo is king of the blizzard ; he was constructed for the fitful climate of the Great Plains; he was made for the use of a race that had nothing else to depend upon, and must surely be nearly a perfect creation. His flesh is far superior to that of any domestic animal under similar conditions; his robe is a ' solid comfort' when the wintry blasts howl. The hair of the animal's head and forehead is heavy and springy, serving perfectly the office of a mattress and pillow. It» tallow is as rich and palatable as butter; the flesh, when dried, serves for bread; the hide, when tanned, makes good shoes, rope, and leather. Its fur is softer than lamb's wool, and when woven into cloth is the lightest and warmest fabric ever manufactured. The under fur is like swan's down, and makes a perfectly waterproof hat when converted into that article. The rain is shed from it as rapidly as from a duck's back; it is this wise provision of nature so close to their bodies which keeps the animal constantly dry and warm. While domestic cattle are stricken down by the deadly venom of the rattle-^ snake, the buffalo receive its fangs in the long hair and wool covering their head and legs, and then trample the-serpents into the earth with their sharp hoofs. Its fleece may be carded off every spring, after having fulfilled its purpose of a winter's protection to the animal, woven into the finest fabrics, knitted into hosiery, and made into robes and blankets which kings and princes delight to recline under.

" 'The buffalo's endurance is marvelous; as a beast of burden it has no superior. The milk of the buffalo cow is infinitely richer than that of the Jersey. The buffalo-— 4

are decidedly clannish; they do not stray away, neither can they be driven off their range by the severest " blizzard," and, in contradistinction to the domestic steer, always face the storm.

" ' Their sense of smell is so keen, they can tell where a rich bunch of grass is, though buried a foot deep under the snow. They root in snow like a razor-back hog after artichokes. The severest winter has no pangs for these patient brutes. Their sinews serve as thread for heavy sewing; their horns make excellent goblets, receptacles for powder, and beautiful buttons. Their fur spun into yarn affords the best material for hosiery and underwear. Their bones can be converted into handles for ladles and cutlery. When ground, they furnish the best fertilizer for an impoverished soil; when charred, are used by sugar-works in the process of refining.

" 'Where, then, is the animal to be found which can compare with the buffalo, the rejected buffalo? "The etone which the builders rejected has become the chief corner-stone." So it is with the buffalo: when we have fitted it to its proper sphere, it is the chief of all ruminants. I will chain him, and domesticate a race of cattle «qual to, if not superior to all ruminants heretofore known. I, will attire myself entirely in clothing made from the product of the buffalo ^; even the buttons of my clothes shall be made of horns and hoofs of that wonderful animal. I will not rely on the ravens for my "food and raiment," and all may rest assured I will never suffer from the howling blizzards nor for meat go hungry.' "

The 24th of April, 1886, was a bleak, cold day. Early that morning, Colonel Jones, Charley Rude and Mr. Newton Adam^s harnessed up a team of three-year-old mules to a light spring wagon, and a heavier span to an ordinary lumber wagon, determined to experiment with the bounding buffalo.

> See frontispiece to this chApter.

COLONEL JONES DRESSED IN GARMENTS PRODUCED FROM FUR OF BUFFALO AND CATALO.

Their point of departure was the little hamlet of Kendall, on the Arkansas river, in Hamilton county, Kansas, forty miles east of the west line of the State. Here the Arkansas is a very treacherous stream, about half a mile wide, never exceeding five feet in depth, with a quicksand bottom. The several channels continuously change, making its passage fraught with danger, particularly in the spring. There were no bridges in the region then, consequently the only means of crossing was by fording. The slush-ice was thick, the water about three feet deep on an average, although in places the mules were off their feet. It was a hazardous undertaking to venture into the stream—cold, swift, and surging with ice — especially with only one span of animals, drawing a heavy load of corn, flour, bacon, and other provisions for man and beast during a six-weeks expedition.

Kendall is the town built up on the product of its wonderful stone-quarries. Colonel Jones had a force of men with very heavy horses there, getting out the crude rock for his famous " marble block " he was then constructing at his home in Garden City; so he ordered two teams of his immense animals to be hooked ahead of the mules. Then, gathering up the lines himself, and telling the man who brought the horses to "climb on," he cracked his whip over the six animals, plunged into the raging river, and was soon safe on the other shore. Messrs. Rude and Adams followed the indomitable Colonel with the spring wagon, and when they arrived on the opposite bank the extra horses were sent back to the quarries by the man who had brought them from their work.

The course determined upon by the adventurous " buffalo-hunter" was over the apparently interminable sandhills of the region beyond the Arkansas, thence southwest across the plains and deserts of the Indian Territory and the "Panhandle" of Texas: a long, weary march, with the almost absolute certainty of not meeting a soul until their return.

Day after day for a whole week the little party strained their eyes in the vain hope of discovering something which would relieve the tedious monotony of this wearisome journey.

April had almost vanished ; the last evening of the last day was rapidly flitting; Colonel Jones was a half-mile in advance of his companion's team, ascending a "divide." Old hunter as he was, he had always made it a rule when on an expedition after big game on the Plains, never to cross a ridge in a sitting position; always standing up on the seat, which enabled him to see animals or Indians before they could discover his approach. Mr. Rude was lying in the rear of the wagon, leading two saddle-horses, spared from any work, reserved for the chase when the proper time arrived.

"Great Heavens!" suddenly exclaimed the Colonel; "an elephant surel" Then he sat down, gave the off horse a cut with the whip, and whirled the team around to the left so short and quickly that it almost tumbled everything out of the wagon. Away he went at "John Gilpin" speed for about two hundred yards into the ravine; then out he jumped, gave the lines to Mr. Rude, rushed to the crest of the divide with his Winchester, and peeped over. In a few minutes, bangl came the report of the Colonel's gun. He then beckoned for Mr. Rude to come, who immediately drove up the slope for nearly a quarter of a mile, where the Colonel was waiting for him. Three hundred yards beyond was a huge buffalo bull lying on "all fours." He had been instantly killed; never struggled a particle, or rolled over on his side as usual.

This was the first buffalo ever seen by Rude or Adams, and they were so excited- at the extraordinary spectacle, that, as the Colonel expresses it, "He could have scraped off their eyes with a stick."

Mr. Rude, who was nearly six feet tall, was very particular to "size up" the animal by his own standard of
measure. He stood close to the buffalo, and could barely see over the immense animal's shoulders, as it laid in its peculiar position. About a hundred pounds of excellent meat were saved, and the remarkably large head of the animal reserved for mounting.

Dallying with the buffalo until all the daylight of April had disappeared, not a drop of water had been secured; there was none in camp, and, what was worse, none had been met with during their last twenty miles of travel. The horses were jaded, the men terribly thirsty. What was to be done? Colonel Jones kindled a fire of "buffalo-chips" on the highest point of the divide; then, he taking one of the saddle-horses and Mr. Rude the other, leaving Mr. Adams to keep up the signal, that they might not get lost, they started on a search for water. The Colonel was to inspect the high plateau, while Mr. Rude was to follow the course of the ravine, and each with a pail on his arm darted away in the darkness.

Hours rolled on, but no return to camp of either. Mr. Adams became alarmed, fearing the Indians had captured both his companions; so he crawled off in the grass and hid himself, allowing the fire to die out. About eleven o'clock he heard the report of a gun far out on the prairie. He became frantic with fear, for he felt positive that Colonel Jones was killed, as the sound came from the direction in which he had gone Avhen he left camp.

Presently he heard another report, this time due north, immediately followed by two more to the east. This capped the climax of his terrible fright: he now believed that his time had surely come.

Very soon, in his terror, he saw what he supposed to be an Indian riding a pony, passing by the camp. Then he consoled himself with the hope that all of them (of course, his imagination had peopled the entire prairie with bloodthirsty savages) would go by without discovering him. At this moment one of the animals in camp neighed at the sight of the horse going past, on which

Mr. Adams supposed the Indian to be, and in anothei second he heard a voice call out, "Hello, Adams I Where are you ? "

Tt was the Colonel, who had fired his gun and had so disturbed Mr. Adams's nerves,— the former expecting the usual response of a hunter; but Mr. Adams was too thoroughly frightened to remember that he should have returned the report, if indeed he knew anything about camp customs. His long life on the Plains had taught him how to find camp, and the Colonel wandered into his headquarters without the beacon he had started on the hill before he left. The reports from the north were responses made by Mr. Rude to the Colonel's salute, which had only added fuel to the terror kindled in Mr, Adams's breast.

Colonel JOnes immediately renewed the " buffalo-chip " beacon on the top of the hill, by the dull glare of which Mr. Rude was guided to camp. He had been more fortunate than the Colonel in their search for water; for lie had discovered a small pond on the broad plateau, while the Colonel found not a drop anywhere. Fortunately, Mr. Rude had brought enough water back with him to quench the thirst of the men, wet the throats of the four mules, and the horse the Colonel had ridden,— his own having satisfied himself at the pond.

Matters having assumed a more satisfactory shape so far as water was concerned^ they began to prepare themselves for the remainder of the night.

A large piece of the buffalo was deliciously broiled on the coals, superintended by the Colonel, who was perforce as good a cook as he was hunter; coffee was brewed, "slapjacks" fried, and the now comfortable little company kept up a jolly time by telling stories, the interest centering upon the experiences of the Colonel on the Great Plains and in the mountains, until long after midnight, when they rolled themselves up in their blankets.

During the conversation before the cheerful but small

campfire, one of the party remarked that as the morrow would be the first of May, they should inaugurate a " May party." Colonel Jones said that if buffalo were discovered he would place the lasso " wreath " over the head of one, and proclaim it the " Lucky Knight" or the " May Queen," according to sex.

In a few minutes every one of the party was lost in the land of dreams, where came exciting visions of chasing the bounding bison, or of other strange experiences, new to the two gentlemen, who were entitled to that purely Western appellation of " tenderfoot," (Col. Jones had already served his time as a " tenderfoot,") until the gray dawn in the east uncovered its eyes.

While the others were preparing breakfast next morning, Colonel Jones took his field-glass, strolled off in search of water, and in a short time discovered, about half a mile to the southwest, a beautiful pool of the purest and clearest. Such things frequently occur: parties "turn in," having given up the hope of finding water, but in the morning discover a fine spring or pool close by. It seems almost miraculous,— as if some Moses had smitten the rock in the night, as was done in the Desert of old. That this find was relished by man and beast, anyone who has been similarly situated will concede. He returned by way of a very high point, where, adjusting his powerful field-glass, he could not resist stopping to contemplate the magnificent pastoral scene all around him; for the Colonel is a lover of Nature in her quieter moods, as well as in the midst of an exciting chase after her wildest and dangerous creations. The air was so pure that not a vapor streaked the dawn, so that he could see over a vast area. He who has never been alone on the Great Plains and looked across a magnificent stretch of prairie at the moment of sunrise, cannot comprehend the thrill of emotion which fills one's soul as he gazes upon such a scene. There is positively no obstruction to the vision except the convexity of the earth, com-

passing a landscape which is bewildering in its vastness. Colonel Jones stood entranced as he drank in the variety and charming features of the panorama, which only ended in the deep blue of the horizon, while imagination took him beyond and to the " happy hunting-grounds" of the Unknown. Little groups of antelope were either grazing, or, having completed their morning repast, were ruminating in the sunny ravines; bands of wild horses were gamboling on the green hillsides; while here and there a wolf or coyote that had not yet finished its nocturnal prowling, slowly moved toward its den of seclusion as the sun rose in fullness of beauty and splendor. Far in the distance was a herd of perhaps twenty monstrous buffalo, unconscious of the fact that so near was an ijidividual who had enlisted his best efforts in "rescuing the perishing" from annihilation. How slowly they move! — in single file, towards their sequestered nooks, where the grass is thick and tender. Now the Colonel became intensely interested in this group of shaggy monsters, as the light glinted upon their huge bodies. He earnestly gazed through his glass to detect, if possible, if calves were among them, as he did not care for the grown animals. What he desired was the young bison, to raise at his ranch, and thus perpetuate the species. But the group was so far away, the glass was not powerful enough to discern any baby buffaloes. There might be a hundred there, but the fact could not be determined, except by going nearer to them.

Upon this decision the Colonel returned to camp. With the animals all watered, breakfast was hurriedly disposed of, and soon the party was on its way to where the buffalo had been seen, leaving Mr. Adams to keep camp. The Colonel guided, as usual, riding in the light'wagon, leading his Kentucky thoroughbred, already saddled and bridled, with lasso carefully wound around the horn of the saddle, and plenty of small rope to bind the calves, if any were found in the herd.

FIRST ATTEMPT AT CATCHING BUFFALO CALVES 57

Mile after mile was traveled, until about ten o'clock they arrived at the crest of a high divide, where to the northwest, far beyond in a wide valley, a herd of twenty buffaloes were discovered,— the same first seen by the Colonel in the early morning, which by this time, having filled themselves with the nutritious grass, were lying down for their midday rest. Here the team was immediately turned to the left, into a ravine opening into a larger one, situated between the buffalo and their pursuers. Arriving at the larger ravine, a turn into it at the right was made, until another ravine from the west was encountered. Turning into it, the most precautionary measures were adopted. The wind was blowing from the south, and it would not do to permit the scent of the party to be wafted in the direction of the herd, for buffalo will more quickly stampede at the smell of objects approaching them, than by actual sight of the disturbing element: and the odor of a white man is particularly obnoxious to them.

It would not do for the wagons to proceed farther, as the rattle of its wheels would certainly alarm the herd. Colonel Jones then cautiously took his horse by the reins, drew up the cinch, and gave Rude orders to keep up and gather in the calves if any should be caught; to lay on the lash, and be sure not to lose sight of him. Then he led the horse as near as he dared without danger of detection, quickly mounted, laid flat upon the animal, and galloped directly toward the buffalo. Every detail of the Colonel's methods worked like a charm. If he had sat erect upon his horse the herd would have become frightened at once, and been out of sight in a few moments. He did not deviate from a straight line in the slightest. To the buffalo, the object they saw was only a wild horse, looking at it as a very familiar sight; for buffalo and other wild animals are not able to distinguish a moving object from a stationary one, particularly if it is coming directly toward them.

Nearer and nearer the Colonel approached the herd, until he was within two hundred yards of them, when they then commenced to rise and move slowly away. To his infinite delight, as the buffalo stood up, the Colonel saw four tawny calves among them, which had been hidden from his view before, so completely were they masked by their mothers, nestled close to their great shaggy bodies. In an instant confusion ran riot with the herd; away went the animals, all going to the northeast, as if they had been shot out of a cannon.

By this time Mr. Rude had arrived with his mules at the top of the hill, from which commanding position he could grasp the whole exciting scene, and take in every feature of the chase. Being an expert artist, he drew the faithful sketch which will be found on another page.

Colonel Jones was in excellent condition to do good work that morning. Getting so near the herd before it started, and mounted on his best Kentucky runner, it was a combination of strategy and luck. Fearing that when he dismounted to tie a calf his horse might get frightened and leave him, he had fastened one end of the lasso around his animal's neck, so he could be sure of keeping the horse from stampeding while binding the captive.

As soon as the Colonel closed up to the surprised animals, they ran all the faster. Mark how the cows protect their calves, sheltering them almost under their shaggy bodies! But old " Ken tuck " was in his prime, and swept down upon the buffalo like a wolf on a wandering lamb. Now see the lasso, whirling in mid-air, from skillful hand; away it goes, into the midst of the fleeting shadows of the frightened animals; the horse comes to a sudden halt; a tawny calf is rearing and plunging at the end of the rope in its frantic struggles to escape the fatal snare. It is in vain; in an instant the Colonel is on the ground, grasps the little brute, and in some three distinct motions lashes its hind legs close up to its neck, slips the nooses from its head, and with a

single bound that would have done credit to the most nimble circus-rider, is firm in the saddle again, and " Kentuck " dashing after the hurriedly retreating herd. See how the blooded horse sweeps over the prairie I At every jump the sod and dust are whirled thirty feet high in air, to land on the ground a hundred yards in his rear. What a wonderful picture 1 Scenes rivaling the chariot-racing in the Roman Coliseum of old 1 Every hope of success now depended upon the endurance of the thoroughbred ; like a hawk swooping down on its prey did the noble steed again close in on the flying herd. Now the lasso once more is whirled into the air; it shoots out like a cat's paw, and rakes in another calf 1 Its musical voice could be heard distinctly by Mr. Rude. The Colonel was off as quickly as before, but as he was binding this second victim of his prowess, he heard a loud grunt accompanied by a terrible rattling of hoofs, immediately in his rear. Looking up to discover the cause of the strange commotion, he saw the mother of the calf, who, having heard her offspring bleating in its fright, was coming to its rescue, with her eyes green as an angry tiger's, and hair all turned the wrong way. Under the impulse of the maternal instinct, she was swelled with righteous indignation and deliberate determination to rescue her baby or die in the attempt,— apparently feeling as competent to crush the daring robber as if every hair on her body was a keen lance and her horns of Damascus steel. Discretion at this serious juncture was better than valor; with a bound that surprised the Colonel himself, he threw his body into the saddle and sunk both spurs into Kentuck's flanks, upon which the horse darted off like a flash, with the enraged cow in close pursuit.

In an instant the end of the rope was reached; Kentuck whirled into the air like a small boy's top, as the other end was still around the calf's neck. There was no time to unfasten the rope from the horse's neck, as the cow had already passed him, and was fixing herself for another

charge. All that could be done under the peculiar circumstances in which the Colonel found himself, was to run Kentuck in a circle, using the calf for a pivot, or, if possible, shoot the cow. Bang 1 bang 1 bang 1 came three reports successively from the Colonel's forty-five double-action revolver, which he always carried on hunting expeditions ; but still the cow came nearer and nearer. The gallant hunter realized the fact that there remained only two charges in the chambers of his weapon with which to do the work; so he collected his nerve and waited until the furious animal was almost within reach of his horse; then, leaning far back in the saddle, he took deliberate aim, firing for the fourth time. The cow gave a furious snort, and bounded away as if a dynamite cartridge had exploded at her side. She was hit high up in the shoulder, badly hurt, but not mortally wounded. When she had gotten off about a hundred yards, she halted, shook her head, and pawed the earth. Colonel Jones, taking advantage of this lull in hostilities, quickly slipped off Kentuck, tied one of the calf's hind legs close to its neck, then drew the noose from its neck, again mounted, and started after the fleeting herd a mile away, as deliberately as though nothing had happened. The herd by this time had become heated, and their anger was at the highest pitch.

Upon overtaking them, he profited by the lesson he had just learned, and did not attempt to throw the lasso over another calf while the rope was attached to his horse's neck. So, reaching down, he attempted to untie it, but the terrible strain it had been sul^jected to during his little fracas with the cow had so tightened the knot that he found he could not do so. The Colonel was well aware that if he stopped to untie it, it would be impossible to overtake the herd again, as his horse was fast becoming fatigued, and not able to make another race. He concluded that if he pressed the herd hard enough the old buffalo would get away and abandon the calves, which I

they would not do under ordinary circumstances. He then contented himself with an occasional dash between the calf and the remainder of the herd, causing it to bleat and beg for assistance. In every instance the cows and bulls grunted in response, invariably turning completely around, facing their enemy with a solid front of sharp-horned and vicious-looking heads, coming in the very impersonation of brute rage to the rescue of their little one. The Colonel then determined to resort to the expedient of catching one of the calves with his hands, so he could hurriedly let it go if the herd pressed too closely. Reaching over to the right, as they dashed over the prairie, he succeeded in effecting what he had determined upon, by grasping the tail of one of the calves; (buffalo always run with their tails curved over their backs, " like scorpions.") The well-trained Kentuck knew that whenever his rider leaned to the right or to the left it was a signal to turn in that direction. So, when the Colonel leaned to the right to grasp the tail of the calf, the horse promptly turned in that direction, unfortunately striking the calf with his feet,— and in an instant horse, rider and young buffalo were tumbled in a confused mass on the ground I

The calf bellowed lustily, half scared to death, upon which cry for help nineteen of the infuriated bulls and cows started for the intrepid but reckless Colonel with all the intensity of concentrated wrath. He at once realized the terrible predicament he was in, but his inevitable coolness in time of danger did not" forsake him in this instance. Striking the horse a terrific cut with the rope, which brought him to his feet and senses in a second, away he dashed with his master clinging to the saddle, out of the way of the impending clash of the charging buffalo. It was a "close call," to employ a Western expression indicative of escape from almost certain death; but Fortune favored the hunter that day, as she has many times since, and the buffalo were doubly enraged and no

doubt disgusted upon arriving at the spot where the calf stood, to find their enemy vanished like a mirage.

These two thrilling experiences, so closely following each other, did not abate one jot of the Colonel's usual " nerve" : in a moment, like Wellington at the battle of Waterloo, it was "Up, Guards, and at them ! " Again, as soon as he could straighten out matters, he dashed into the herd, running it until one calf, exhausted, was far in the rear. He pressed the old buffalo at such a rate that they were soon so far away they could not hear it bleat. He then deliberately whirled his horse about, galloped back and met the calf, threw the lasso around its neck, dismounted, tied it, and started for the other, the last calf. By careful tactics he succeeded in overtaking the herd, and the last calf and its mother were separated from the herd, when, with the last load in his revolver, he so wounded the cow that she was unable to keep up with her young one, and throwing the lasso over it, he captured the coveted prize.

Three very exciting hours had just passed in the intense desperate struggle to secure what he had determined to do. The sun under the semi-tropical skies of the region was terrific; both the Colonel and his wonderful horse were so worn out, that, after resting for a few moments, they were so stiff that neither could make any rapid movement. What was to be done ? Mr. Rude was nowhere to be seen, although he had received positive orders to run his mules under the lash, and gather the calves as he came to them. The Colonel led his horse, after the animal had recuperated somewhat, to the crest of a high hill, hoping to discover Mr. Rude somewhere in sight; but all was a vast prairie, devoid of everything animate except a large herd of antelope and a small band of wild horses in the far southwest.

A close estimate of the distance from the point at which he had left Mr. Rude, also to camp, was made. He found it to be for the former about fifteen miles and

the latter twenty-five on a bee line, or forty to camp, by the circuitous way in which he had come. It was nearly the middle of the afternoon now; to go straight to camp would take until midnight to reach it on foot, if at all, that day. His tongue was already parched and swollen ; there was an abundance of water in the wagon which Mr. Rude drove, if he could only be found. On the Great Plains, ninety-nine men out of a hundred would become bewildered under the circumstances, lose their course on seeing the spectral lakes of the weird "mirage," and either follow them, or travel miles out of the way to avoid them, until all idea of the right direction were absolutely forgotten. The Colonel plodded along on foot, — all there was left for him to do,— dragging his horse after him, until the faithful animal absolutely refused to go any farther. He then took off the saddle, tied the exhausted horse to it, and started on foot in search of Mr. Rude, and plodded along for two long hours.

Reader, imagine yourself in the Colonel's situation : no doubt left to perish, perhaps, as miserably as Jonah's gourd, " for the want of water" 1 Still the old hunter's courage did not flag for an instant, although the sun was rapidly approaching the western horizon. Just at this juncture he suddenly saw an object far away to the south, moving directly east, which his keen eye made out to be Mr. Rude.

He commenced to run as fast as he was able toward him, but failed to attract his attention until he almost overtook him. He was driving straight for an antelope more than a mile away, which was standing still, looking back at him with that animal's curiosity; and this Mr. Rude said he thought was a man on horseback. He was completely "turned around" and bewildered; had not the remotest idea of where he was; and it would have been doubtful if he could ever find his way back to camp, if the Colonel had not opportunely come up with him. The keg of water was soon tested; " the sweetest and best

beverage ever drank by mortal man," as the Colonel afterwards expressed it, rivaling the sweet springs of Bethsaida.

Mr. Rude had gathered in the first calf, and driven up to the second one, which had caused the Colonel so much trouble; but, having only one leg tied in the terrible struggle, it would hobble around in siich a vexing manner whenever he attempted to approach it, that it scared the mules, and they reared and plunged on nearing it so that he could not secure it at all. He decided to remain there and watch the obstreperous little brute until the Colonel returned, if he stayed a month,—which was in one sense commendable, in another, almost fatal. However, as night began to throw its coming shadows over the landscape, his courage, like that of Bob Acres, "oozed out," and he determined to go in search of the Colonel. Mr. Rude was far from lacking in pluck, but the feeling of utter loneliness, which only those who have been lost on the Great Plains can appreciate, was too trying, and it was no sense of cowardice that drove him to the wi«e conclusion of "getting out of there " and joining the Colonel if possible.

Colonel Jones, after overtaking Mr. Rude, satisfying his inordinate thirst, and lecturing the delinquent in a mild way, took the lines and drove rapidly back to where he had left Kentuck. Arriving there, the noble animal neighed in recognition of his master's approach, who at once gave him a pailful of the delicious water, which soon brought the normal fire again into the wearied horse's eyes.

Both men then busied themselves in gathering up the calves, and by dark were headed for camp, twenty miles away, over an unknown country. The clouds were ominously scudding over the heavens, indicative of a prospectively gloomy journey; but if any man could drive on a "crow line" at night, Colonel Jones was he. His confidence in himself under such circumstances was un-

bounded, for the reason that he could, instinctively or intuitively, at all times, by daj^ or by night, in sunshine or in storm, take the proper bearings of the course he desired to make; could, without any apparent effort, give the exacts points of the compass,— a gift of which very few men are possessed, but invaluable to the hunter.

They traveled until ten o'clock in the exact direction first indicated by the Colonel, when a bright light shone on the distant prairie, which made the hearts of the two weary and hungry souls beat fast with joy, as they had eaten nothing since breakfast, and had no bedding with them. The fire they saw was an effort of Mr. Adams, who had been left in camp early in the morning, when the buft'alo were first sighted. He had been so terribly guyed by his comrades the night previously for letting the signal on the hilltop go out, he was determined not to be found derelict on this occasion ; so he had piled on an extra supply of fuel, the sight of which was so suggestive of supper and a warm bed to the weary and benighted hunters.

Arriving at camp in a short time, the first thought was for the care of the calves which had cost so much time and trouble. They had become very restless during the last hour, constantly bawling for their mothers, in a not very rhythmical strain. Two heavy stakes sixty feet apart were driven into the ground, to which a long rope was stretched tightly, and in which, at a distance of sixteen feet from one another, a light rope was fastened, measuring four feet in length, to the end of which the calves were tied by the neck. This method admitted of a great deal of freedom, relaxing in every direction, and putting all obstacles beyond the reach of the vicious little brutes; for if they had been tied to a post, wagon, or any other substantial object, they would soon have been killed by battering themselves against it.

The next morning the calves were inspected and christened. The one which had been the cause of so much —5

trouble to the Colonel, and whose mother had been in such a rage, rushing upon him so ferociously, was named " Lucky Knight"; the other, which threw Kentuck, and possessed an amount of endurance really phenomenal during the chase after her, " May Queen " ; the first and last one, "Robert Burns" and "Grace Greenwood," respectively. But the dast two named did not survive the tedious journey to the ranch, in Kansas, while the others are among the finest specimens of the buffalo in the Colonel's famous herd.

The next morning the hunters were out bright and early, as the calves kept up such a calling for-their mothers there was but little sleep to be had. As soon as daylight fully came, Colonel Jones was scanning the country for more buffalo, and was astonished at finding ten head not to exceed a mile away, and by the use of his glass could see a fine calf gamboling around the herd. Very fioon he was on his reserved steed, and dashed away for the prize; but the calf was a large, strong one, and made the chase one to be remembered. Once, twice, thrice the lasso was sent out to ensnare the wiry beast, but each time the calf would spurt forward and the noose fell short and only landed on its back. The Colonel determined to make one more effort only, as his horse was nearly exhausted. Spurring his steed to his utmost, he sent the whizzing lasso with all the force he could command ; but the calf made its usual effort just at the critical moment, and the noose fell short, striking on its shoulders, and fell off to the right side. However, as fortune "favors the brave," the Colonel was rewarded after all hope had vanished, for the right hind leg swept into the loop as he sped along, and the skillful captor made & quick jerk that fastened it in the toils. It bellowed lustily, and the herd of ten cows hastened to its rescue. They surrounded it, and the fury that they generated would have made a regiment of soldiers retreat, as they were only about twenty feet from the Colonel. As he was holding

to the rope desperately with his left, he grabbed his broadbrim hat with his right hand, and sailed it into the herd. It lit right under one of the cows, which made her kick worse than seventeen mules. She gave a furious snort and lurch, and made a bee line for the desert, with all the others closely following, except the calf, which was named " The Plumed Knight," in honor of James G. Blaine, and which, like its namesake, maintained the head of the party as long as it lived.

The 3d and 4th of May were passed (excepting a limited reconnoiter, but bootless of success) in taking the calves to a ranch fifty miles to the east for temporary keeping. On the 5th everything was in readiness to move to the southwest. The tent, lumber wagon, and bulk of supplies were left behind, and on the evening of that day the party arrived at the north bank of the South Canadian river.

The channel of this treacherous stream is deep in the earth, its banks very precipitous, sometimes rising almost perpendicularly more than a hundred feet. The animals and men were tired, thirsty, and about worn out. The ravines running into the river were so rough and deep that it was not possible to go any farther up or down the stream that evening, and as night was already upon them, it was a perplexing question what to do in their dilemma. Something had to be accomplished, however, and as usual the Colonel was ready in case of emergency, and, full of fertile ideas, took the initiative,— for the others depended upon him as their Moses. He first ordered all the available ropes to be collected, drove a stout stake of timber in the ground on the edge of the bank, threw a noose around Mr. Adams's shoulders, handed him a pail, took one turn of the rope around the stake, and told him to descend and send up a pailful of water. This was a trying moment for Mr. Adams, but he had all confidence in his comrades at the top of the bank, and obeyed gracefully.

Having reached the surface of the stream, he anchored
himself on a rock and filled the pail, which was drawn up. This was repeated several times, until all the stock was satisfied. He then fastened the rope around his body, and with a pailful of water in his hand, was soon dangling in the air. Drawing him up was not as easily accomplished as letting him down; upon Mr. Rude remarking, "Adams must have drunk as much as a buffalo cow," it caused the Colonel to burst into a laugh, and not another inch could they raise the swinging, faithful Adams. At last, almost in despair. Colonel Jones called out to him to pour the water out of his pail, which was quickly done. There was no water for coffee as yet, and the Colonel, remembering that the want of their accustomed beverage would cause much discomfort, gave orders to lower Mr. Adams again, which was effected more rapidly than was appreciated by the latter, for as he landed in a lump on the small rocks bordering the water's edge, his feet slipped, and he went head foremost into the foaming torrent. The yells to which he gave utterance as the chilling fluid coursed over his warm body were too laughable to describe. But it was no laughing matter—it was getting serious; so the two men above quickly gathered up the slack of the rope and landed him upon a safe footing.

In the struggle Mr. Adams let go of the pail altogether, and it required considerable persuasion to induce him to detach the rope from his body in order that they might send down another. He had lost all confidence in his companions. The darkness was intense. A more dismal situation for a man to be in, probably, could not be found in any country. It required faithful pledges to restore the brave fellow's confidence, which was entirely gone; but the sudden bath to which he had been subjected through the carelessness of his comrades braced him up. Another pail was lowered to him, the last one in camp, which he sent up alone, not daring to risk the loss of the precious fluid as before, by the added weight of himself. Safely on the top of the bank, it was carefully set aside, and the dreaded task of hauling him to the companionship of his comrades above was again commenced. By exercising better judgment and stronger efforts this time, the Colonel and Mr. Rude succeeded; and Mr. Adams was once more in camp, but shivering with cold, wet through, and disgusted. His language was not such as would have graced the drawing-room, so his comrades concluded he had "let the sun go down upon his wrath."

The next day, after driving about five miles north, an almost obliterated trail was discovered, which they followed westwardly until noon, when a crossing over the treacherous Canadian was effected. Camping there for dinner and resting the animals an hour or two. Colonel Jones then mounted his horse, telling his companions to follow him into the '^Llano Estacado'^ (the Staked Plains). Mr. Rude was well educated, and a school teacher; but he shuddered at the Colonel's command, for he like many others erroneously believed that region with its awful name to ears unacquainted with Spanish, to be a veritable terra incognita, a ^^Jornada del Muerto"" (Journey of Death) to anyone who had the temerity to cross it. He uttered no protest, however,— he was too proud and courageous for that, and would have gone to positive annihilation with the Colonel if necessary.

As the little caravan wended its way over the sandhills to the south, upon arriving at the top of one of the loftiest points both of the gentlemen whom Colonel Jones had chosen for companions on this trip actually felt the cold chills run through their nerves as they gazed upon the unwelcome and barren landscape stretching out before them.

As far as the eye could reach, to the very verge of the horizon, there lay an apparently boundless desert of pure sand. The wind howled mournfully over the great waste, blowing the almost impalpable particles of fruitless soil in clouds which simulated myriads of insects, so fine was the hot sand as it was moved by the wind. Sometimes the whole surface, when the fitful gusts were more fierce, resembled a high, rolling sea with the spray flying high, and apparently as unstable as the ocean. To add to the repulsiveness of the picture, dismal-looking black clouds hung like a pall low down on the earth in every direction.

Colonel Jones was more than a mile in advance of the wagons, plowing through the wearisome sand at a fearfully slow rate, when upon looking backward over his trail he saw the caravan had halted, and a signal made by Mr. Rude for him to return. He swept the whole area with his powerful glass, saw there was no danger lurking from any quarter of the compass, so duplicated Mr. Rude's signal by ordering the caravan to come on. These orders were conveyed by well-understood signals. (These signals were made by different movements of the horse, directed by his rider. Riding in a circle indicated move on. To proceed westward, a ride in a circle and then suddenly out to that point of the compass, after which slowly return to where the circle was formed. The same for all courses. To make haste, ride out at right angles to the direction traveled, and back. To come to the commander, two dashes out and return, the speed to be indicated by the one giving the order. Danger, three quick dashes out. Discovery of buffalo in the distance, circle, and two dashes in the direction of the herd.) The caravan did not move, but soon Mr. Rude mounted the other saddle-horse and started for the spot where the Colonel waited, impatient at the loss of time. Mr. Rude's horse wallowed through the sand to within a hundred yards of the Colonel, when the latter shouted, " What's the matter, Rude,— anything wrong?" Mr. Rude made no response, continuing to advance, and as he came nearer the Colonel repeated his interrogation. Mr. Rude looked very pale, and replied that Mr. Adams had refused to go any farther for fear they would all perish on the desert from want of water; that he himself was not particularly anxious to proceed. Colonel Jones's only answer was: "Go where you like; I shall cross this desert. I know you never can find your way home; you would better choose the wiser part."

This was undoubtedly cold comfort for Mr. Rude, as the Colonel whirled his horse, rode straight to the south, in which direction he had been traveling, not deigning to bestow one parting look at his weary and discomfited followers.

As the Colonel crossed a ridge, before he rode down on the other side he cast his eyes back and saw Mr. Rude wending his way toward the caravan; but he kept right on, was soon over another ridge, and out of sight of his companions.

When he arrived at the next ravine he dismounted, w^alked back to the crest of the divide, and with his glass peeped over to watch results at the wagon. He saw Mr. Rude arrive there, hold a consultation with Mr. Adams, which lasted fully fifteen minutes, and then they mounted the wagon and made a direct line for where they had last ∎seen the Colonel. The latter, upon seeing this movement on the part of his comrades, mounted his horse again, ascended in full view, and continued straight ahead as though nothing out of the usual course had occurred.

Mile after mile he worried off; there was no vegetation of any character visible anywhere; the darkness set in very early, so he halted, to wait until the wagon should come up. Here was made a "dry camp," for the drive had been so heavy it was impossible to carry water, excepting that contained in the ten-gallon keg; enough only to serve for drinking purposes for the men. It was a most uncomfortable night—dark, cold, and misty; besides, the relations between the individual members of the party were not of the most cordial nature after what had occurred, which did not ameliorate matters.

The next morning, however, broke clear and bright., having an exhilarating effect upon both men and ani-

inals. Ab soon as the roseate color in the east betokened the coming day, the reconciled gentlemen were well on their way towards the southeast, where a high point stood out very prominently against the sky,— Colonel Jones, as always, in the lead.

By ten o'clock the party had reached the spot, where they joined the Colonel, who had been waiting for his comrades some minutes. When he first arrived there he saw, much to his own surprise, away to the south, about six miles distant, a large lake of water glistening in the sunlight. Was it only a deceptive creation, a receding mirage, which makes the disappointment of the thirsty traveler a thousand times more realistic, or was it real water? He dwelt upon the delightful picture with his field-glass. There were antelopes in the vicinity, and a band of wild horses was approaching the real or fancied lake. He would soon know now. The wild animals approached the spot in a gallop, reached the edge of the apparent shore, halted for an instant, lowered their heads for a few minutes, then turned about and started in the direction whence they came. Water, beyond a doubt 1 Often before had the Colonel observed these maneuvers, only not so early in the day. Often he had been compelled to depend entirely upon the actions of wild horses to discover the wherewith to save himself from dying of thirst.

Of all the animals of the Great Plains, wild horses are safest to rely upon by the thirsty traveler, as they drink every day between ten and three o'clock; while buffalo will go three days or longer at a time without attempting to find a stream or lagoon. Antelope are very changeable in their times and modes of drinking. They frequently get their supply from an old pond or lagoon which has been dry for a long period. Strange as this may seem to the uninitiated, to procure water from where apparently no water is, it nevertheless is a positive fact, as all old plainsmen will testify. The antelope forces his long nose into a crayfish hole, for instance; then, by a process of suction through the mouth, forces the air through the nostrils, this action forming an air-pump, which causes a vacuum, and the pure cold water is forced up to quench his thirst.

The Colonel, now perfectly satisfied he had discovered water, signaled the men to hurry up, which they did; but when the calm, beautiful lake was pointed out to them they declared it was only a mirage, and would not really believe their leader, until they approached so near they saw ducks breasting the rippling waves. Even then they were in doubt whether to believe their own eyes or no. They were only convinced by dipping their fingers into the water so as to have infallible proof,— for they had almost passed the period of believing anything.

The reader will naturally think, perhaps, that these men were the veriest " tenderfeet," or lacking in force: such was not the case. Mr. Rude, as previously stated, was a man of bright intellect, with an abundance of courage and business sagacity; Mr. Adams was a solid farmer, and a man of good all-around ability. The fact is, ninety-nine out of a hundred men, not accustomed to the Great Plains, under such desperate circumstances would have been unable to tell whether they were afoot or horseback.

They arrived at the lake about noon. A camp was made at once, for they had not yet eaten a mouthful that day; so both breakfast and dinner were served together. All now felt much better, and what little animosity remained was dispelled forever.

About two o'clock that afternoon, while the Colonel from a high point was sweeping the horizon with his glass, he saw a buffalo cow far to the west, heading southward. He watched her until she was out of sight, and as she passed beyond the range of his glass, was still going in the same direction as when he first discovered her, traveling at a relatively rapid rate. This was encouragement enough for the Colonel, as he knew by her

gait that she had been frightened and was hurrying to the main herd.

The team was quickly'* hooked up," and all started at a good gait toward the south, not halting until they had covered at least twenty miles.

During all that long distance not an object was visible on the vast expanse, bounded by only the great circle of the heavens. When the sun was lowering in the west, however, nine distinct somethings were seen in the extreme southwest; but they were too far off to be classified, in the rapidly coming gloom. Colonel Jones and Mr. Rude immediately mounted their horses, leaving Mr. Adams to follow with the team. In a short time, after a brisk lope, the Colonel and his companion came in full sight of nine buffalo bulls, of immense size.

By dismounting and leading their horses, or rather, walking by their sides, thus masking themselves, taking care to keep the animals on the side next to the buffalo, they were enabled to approach very near the monstrous beasts. At the proper moment, Colonel Jones handed the bridle-reins of his horse to Mr. Rude, and whispering, " Keep straight on until I shoot," he then dropped on the ground. As soon as the horses had passed from between him and the herd, bang I went his gun, and away went all the buffalo. Mr. Rude was terribly discouraged, and yelled out, "Shoot again 1 Shoot again I "

"Just wait," replied the Colonel; "I only want one for meat."

"But you didn't touch one," indignantly answered Mr. Rude.

"You just hold on, and you'll see whether I did or not," said the Colonel.

Sure enough, at this moment one of the huge beasts began to jump rather stiffly, and in another minute he was lying broadside on the prairie, the deadest buffalo Mr. Rude had ever seen.

The Colonel had adopted his old tactics — pierced the

beast directly through the lungs, which invariably permits him to run a hundred yards or more before he succumbs to the inevitable effects of such a shot.

Mr. Rude was soon busying himself in cutting out the choice of the best parts of the buffalo, for the whole party were hungry for nature's delicious food. He selected that portion which extends from the loins forward to where the neck joins the shoulders, which includes the" hump," * yielding about a hundred pounds of the most tender of all meat, and never found on any other animal. Thus the buffalo is just that quantity in excess of the domestic species of the bovine family to which he is allied.

While Mr. Rude was thus employed, Colonel Jones rode a quarter of a mile toward the south, and coming to the crest of the divide, peeped cautiously beyond, where the buffalo had just passed over, and there saw the last herd of buffalo remaining in the whole world,— numbering, as nearly as he could estimate, about six hundred.

Without attempting to disturb them, he hurriedly returned to where the dead buffalo was, and gathering up a piece of meat the two men were off for the wagon.

It was now rapidly approaching night: where was Mr. Adams ? Nothing could be seen or heard of him. The spurs were vigorously applied, and down the divide they dashed as quickly as was consistent with safety, reached the level valley, and were soon far apart. Finally Mr. Rude overtook the team, halted it, then discharged his gun, at the signal of which the Colonel returned the salute, and was soon with his comrades.

Just as night had closed in, a cold rain and sleet began falling. In the morning there was no abatement of the

' The hump Is a large layer or roll of choice tender meat, extending from the neck of the animal, back to the hips, being much larger and higher Immediately over the shoulders, and tapering gradually back to a small round muscle. This meat lies on the upper portion of the ribs, and tapers to a sharp edge at the crest of the animal's back, supported by false spines or ribs, standing perpendicularly on each joint of the vertebree. They are flat, and range in length from three to eight inches ; the longest being Immediately over the shoulders, gradually becoming shorter toward the hips. This accounts for the crooked backs of the buffalo.

storm, and the party had to content themselves with lying on their blankets under an improvised tent, formed by the wagon-tongue as a ridgepole, held up by the neck-yoke of the wagon, with a piece of canvas thrown over,— all open, of course, at both ends. No fire was kindled, as everything was. soaked with water; so there was nothing cooked. They ate some dry biscuit, which was heartily relished, because the life they were living was very provocative of a good appetite, although they were cold and constantly shivering.

At intervals during the day, when the sky cleared up for a few moments, hundreds of buffalo could be seen facing the wild storm, with a great many tawny calves trembling with cold as they hugged their mother's sheltering sides of soft fur.

Night came on again, but seemed almost interminable to the men, who, cold and hungry, were lying under their imi)rovised tent anxiously waiting for daylight to arrive. At the break of dawn the storm passed away; yet still it was dark, cold and dreary. The Colonel saddled two of his best horses, the mules were hooked to the wagon, and he ordered the men to follow him as rapidly as possible, and to remember the mistakes of the previous chase. The herd of buffalo seen the evening before were in the same position still, just over a ridge about half a mile away.. The Colonel rounded over the little divide, riding one horse, the other running abreast as a reserve. The herd did not stir until he was almost upon it. When the animals discovered their danger they dashed away, cutting into the soft ground with their sharp hoofs, which in a few seconds resembled a plowed field.

The races of this day were similar to those of the da3'S previous, excepting that on this occasion the Colonel did not depend on one horse alone, but changed from, one to the other without checking; nor did he attach the lasso to his horse's neck. He labored under many difficulties, however: the lasso was wet, hard, and stiff,— not at all

flexible; and this was very discouraging, for the calves jumped through the loop, and this was repeated three or four times by one of the little beasts before he was finally secured. The day, too, was dark; the wolves and coyotes very bold and impudent; dozens of them were constantly prowling around after the calves, and to leave one tied any length of time would surely result in its falling into their vicious jaws. Besides, they took good care to keep well up in the chase, watching the Colonel's every movement.

After the second calf was secured, the teams were again lost sight of in the distance, and it would be useless to tie and leave a calf so far away. What to do under the circumstances, was a problem. The third calf was roped and tied. " Shall I leave it, and take chances of the wolves devouring it ?" soliloquized the Colonel. "Yes. Such another opportunity to catch calves will never again occur. I have traveled five hundred miles for this all-important opportunity." So off goes his cowboy hat; he tucks it under the rope around the calf's neck, and on he rushes. A fourth is secured; his coat is left, to protect it from the voraciousness of the gray wolf — the greatest enemy of the buffalo, excepting man. The wolf will not disturb anything that has upon it the fresh scent of man (as he thinks it a trap), unless driven to desperation by hunger; hence the action of the Colonel in thus protecting his game by the methods lie adopted. Here one of his horses became exhausted. The Colonel leaped to the reserve horse without checking their speed, cut him loose, and rolled the steel spurs upon his faithful steed's flanks.

The fifth calf was shortly afterward caught. Colonel Jones took off his vest this time, which he wrapped upon the little creature to save it. A sixth is secured, and one of his boots does service now. The seventh succumbs to his prowess, and the remaining boot serv^es the purpose. But when the eighth was caught, there was a desperate struggle; the horse by this time was all of a tremble, and

covered with foam; and the gallant Colonel, having no-other garment he could well spare, mounted his horse, reached down, and drew the baby buffalo up in his arms. He then started on the backward track. He could see a^ band of wolves encircling the seventh calf, so spurred up " Jubar" to the rescue. He arrived at the spot just in time: the wolves had closed in on it, and were ready to complete their tactics, when they were scattered right and left by the Colonel, who reached down and drew the supposed victim up in triumph. This calf was also carried on toward his goal, with a band of more than fifty wolves and coyotes trotting all around as they accompanied him.

The next calf, fortunately, had been left in a clump of grass, which the wolves had missed entirely. When the Colonel reached it, his courage failed; the danger was too great to attempt taking the third animal up in his arms with the others. He let the calves down on the ground and made a dash at the wolves, shooting at them with his revolver, but they paid little attention to this kind of music.

He was in a dilemma; in a precarious position. Where in the world was the team ? He was worn out completely, and his strength was gradually giving away; he longed to see the wagon; certainly his companions could not be lost. The trail of the herd was visible fully half a mile away.

As often as he would venture off in search of the itien, as often did the wolves return and attempt to get at the helpless calves; so he was compelled to remain and fight the vicious, hungry brutes.

After more than a full hour's worrying with the pack^ he heard the report of a gun, but in an entirely opposite direction from where he expected. Upon this happy turn matters had taken, he made a dash to the top of a high hill near by, where he saw, about a mile distant, the wagon, the driver apparently wandering at random over

> ' ■ '

THE PERISHING" RESCUED.

the prairie. Signals were immediately communicated hj him, and the team headed for where he stood.

By this time all the wolves were aggregating in one large pack around the three calves, and he had to rush down on them in a mighty hurry to save his prizes; yet they hardly noticed him, continuing their movements to jump upon the little buffalo. He stood guard over them^ preventing the wolves from effecting their purpose, only by the greatest efforts, until the team came up,—and to make matters worse, bringing with them another pack of the hungry devils, which had been escorting the wagon for miles. The report of the gun that had attracted the Colonel's attention was caused by Mr. Rude, who had fired at one of the most impudent monsters,—a great gray beast, which fortunately he succeeded in killing.

The men had gathered up three of the calves as they came to them. The three which were guarded by Colonel Jones were quickly loaded, and the wagon going at a& rapid a rate as possible back over the trail of the herd, until the other two calves and the horse that had been cut loose were safely taken also. It was found that the wolves had made no attack upon them; the foresight of the Colonel in putting his clothes around them had prevented it.

When the last little buffalo was placed in the wagon, Colonel Jones sank on the ground, perfectly exhausted. Fortunately, there was a quart bottle of whisky in the light spring rig, it having been brought from home as an antidote to the possible bite of a rattlesnake, the country being full of them. A drink of this was administered to him by Mr. Rude, and it immediately revived him. The team was driven to where chips could be procured. A dinner was elegantly served, consisting of deliciously broiled buffalo-steak, hot biscuits, and excellent coffee,— the first warm meal the tired hunters had partaken of for forty-eight hours. An extraordinary appetite gave a zest to it, such as cannot be appreciated by those who have never experienced a plainsman's capacity under similar circumstances.

Fourteen calves were secured — a whole wagon-box full. The party bade farewell to the " Staked Plains," and drove to the ranch, where they had left the five calves already caught. They then took a bee line for the Colonel's home, and arrived there with ten of the young animals in good health, four having died en route, in consequence of fatigue and indifferent food, for condensed milk was all that could be procured until the Arkansas river was reached. The expedition was a great success, and the first effort at capturing the nucleus of what is now the greatest herd of buffalo in the world.

While on the return from his trip, and when between the two Canadian rivers, in Texas, Colonel Jones says he saw the most wonderful sight in all his long and varied experience upon the Great Plains and in the mountains. It was the day after his last remarkable effort. He was wearily plodding his way on foot, leading his jaded horse, picking out a route homeward for the heavily loaded wagon containing its precious freight. As he approached the top of a little divide he saw what he believed to be a herd of buffalo and domestic cattle mixed together; they were on the right of his course, about a mile distant. He halted, and instructed Mr. Rude to keep straight on, while he would make a detour, and go up the ravine to a point near where the herd was quietly grazing. When the Colonel arrived at the spot he had suggested, he found himself within two or three hundred yards of the mixed animals, and was surprised to discover that instead of all the white beasts being cattle, one only was a white native cow, while the others were white buffalo: a three-year-old, a two-year-old, and a yearling. This was the most remarkable phenomenon he had ever witnessed, and for a moment he did not know whether he was awake or dreaming. He had read of the superstition of the Indian in relation to the white buffalo, and had considered it a sort of phan-

torn,— a phantasm of the red man's brain; now he could scarcely believe his own eyes. There the strange animals stood under the noonday sun, chewing their cud,—white buffalo as sure as the world 1 There were their humps, their small ears, their short tails. They were buffalo; not as white as the " driven snow," but white enough to assure him he had made no mistake in diagnosing the color. What to do he did not know; he was at a total loss to divine. His horse was so completely used up, there was no earthly chance of putting a rope on one of the curious animals, but to capture one would be a fortune, for the great showman Barnum would probably pay ten thousand dollars for it quickly, as a white buffalo was a rare effort of nature. Here were three that could be captured, and the Colonel thought, as did Richard at Bosworth field, "A horse! A horse! My kingdom for a horse!" But other than his own exhausted animal there was none; so he mounted it, determined to do the best he could under the unfortunate circumstances. By lying along the body of his faithful steed, he rode directly toward the herd, but the white cow soon caught sight of him, and rolling her long tail over her back, led the frightened animals at a fearful gait toward the south. The Colonel urged his horse to his utmost speed, but to no purpose; away the white beauties flew, like so many spirits, and in a short time were beyond the vision of their pursuer. As they went over the divide, both Messrs. Rude and Adams got a full view of them, and are competent to verify these assertions made by Colonel Jones, who says he would never have related the facts without being able to substantiate them by the gentlemen who were with him at the time; and " In the mouth of two or three witnesses let every word be established."

Of late years Colonel Jones has figured out the solution of the problem of white buffalo. He declares that all he has ever seen were nothing more or less than exact prototypes of " catalo," ^ the picture of which is given on an-

' A description of this animal will be found In chapter 15. — 6

other page. Those he saw in the herd described were " catalo "; calves of the white cow, sired by a full-blooded buffalo.

A white buffalo was killed on the Smoky Hill river in western Kansas, many years ago. The skin was saved and mounted, and presented to the State Agricultural Museum at Topeka, Kansas, where it may yet be seen. It was also a catalo.

CHAPTER VI INDIANS

INDIANS THE GREATEST DANGER OF THE PLAINS — ALTHOUGH TENACIOUS OF LIFE, THE " TENDERFOOT " HAS LITTLE CHANCE AGAINST THEM — COL. JONES's GREAT SUCCESS IN FIGHTING INDIANS — A BATTLE WITH AR-RAPAHOES — FOOLED THEM COMPLETELY — CASUALTIES

THE COLONEL NOTED FOR KEEPING OUT OF ENCOUNTERS NO LOVE FOR THEM—BUFFALO-HUNTERS, AND NOT SOLDIERS, CONQUERED THE INDIANS — JONES IN CHIEF's CAMP

REFUSES HIM MONEY — BIG BOW " HEAP MAD "— NEARLY

CAUGHT WHILE SKINNING BUFFALO—"VAMOOSE, OR I WILL KILL you" — GREATEST SHOW ON EARTH — TWO HUNDRED WARRIORS SURROUND A HERD OF BUFFALO — SIGNALING FOR AID AT LONG DISTANCE — HOW THEY CIRCUMVENTED THE ANIMALS.

OF course, during Colonel Jones's long and thrilling career on the Great Plains and in the mountains of the West, often absolutely alone for weeks together, he has frequently encountered the wily red man in all his various characteristics. I found, however, in looking over the manuscript of his carefully kept journal, that he everywhere evinces a decided repugnance to giving the facts to the world. To employ his exact language, he says:

" So much has been written about the Indians, I feel it will be an almost useless and thankless task to present the real facts in relation to them, since the domain of fiction has scattered so much broadcast throughout the

(83)

world which is perfectly ridiculous in its perversion of the truth.

"It appears to me that when a novelist has exhausted his fund of 'blood and thunder,' he falls back upon the American savage to recoup himself. I have many hundreds of times been in close contact with these ' unsophisticated children of Nature' as some of our supersensitive Eastern philanthropists are pleased to call them; have dwelt in their lodges, hunted with their great chiefs, battled with them, and am familiar with their cunning, their bravery, their sufferings, and every other phase of their nomadic life. I have been treated with the most i^rofound respect, and conversely, been humiliated, under force of numbers, by the miserable creatures.

" In the days of our buffalo-hunting,—now, unhappily, past forever,—the Indian was more to be feared than all other dangers combined. Intuitively, the red devils knew a ' tenderfoot' even before that specimen of the genus homo had been classified by old plainsmen themselves. The Indian, however, was as afraid of the ' veteran of the border ' as one can imagine, and always evaded an encounter with one of them, unless advised of victory by the ' medicine-man ' of the tribe,— really the spiritual adviser, or priest of the band.

" The Indians of the Plains were more tenacious of life than any race I have ever encountered; a characteristic, I affirm, of all nomadic peoples. The American savage exercises the utmost precaution in regard to his self-preservation. None have been known to boldly measure prowess with the white man when the chances were about equal; nor would a half-dozen of these 'braves' attack a single old plainsman openly, though they were armed with the latest and most approved repeating rifles, and their tactics and strategy equal to the enemy. They blustered and dashed in such a bewildering manner, however, that they received credit for courage and prowess which they did not

possess, and stories are related of them which never had the least basis of truth.

"How often have we read of 'outfits' crossing the Plains in the early days being surprised and surrounded by Indians. How the savages, it was told, encircled the hapless band of travelers. Running around on their ponies in a circle, the Indians gradually closed in upon the excited little group of whites, constantly pouring a shower of arrows into them, while the latter vainly essayed to drive the Indians off. Thick and fast, it was alleged, the bullets were sent into the ranks of the attacking party, without the least effect, ' as the savages threw themselves on the other side of their ponies, thus precluding the possibility of being struck.' (What nonsense ! all modern rifle-balls pass entirely through a pony, or even a buffalo bull.) Also, that the ammunition of the attacked soon became exhausted, and the bewildered and panic-stricken group was captured. How brave and daring this account of the Indian method of warfare sounds! Yet I could take the same number of white men, and all sitting erect in their saddles, encircle the same number of ' tenderfeet' for an hour or more, and not one of us receive a scratch.

" I never realized the philosophy of the Indians' ' strategy ' until I had wasted a barrel of powder and several hundred pounds of lead, endeavoring to shoot antelope while they were on the run at right angles to the line of sight of my Winchester. When I had learned to aim at least two rods ahead of the fleeing animal, when the latter was two hundred yards distant, at once the wonderful knowledge of the Indian (who is never killed by a ' tenderfoot' under such circumstances as related in the story of the fight as told above) and the ignorance of the white man came to me like an inspiration. The explanation of perfect immunity from danger on the part of the Indian while circling around the enemy as described, drawing the fire of a hundred or more rifles, is this: The

'tenderfoot,' aiming directly at the pony or its rider while moving rapidly, misses the object intended, the ball falling in the rear, as no allowance is made for the velocity of the Indian dashing ahead at a tremendous rate; consequently the ball arrives at the spot where the savage has been, when he is at least a rod or two in advance (according to distance from the shooter). The next Indian was always careful to keep fully ten times that distance behind his leader, so that all balls intended to stop the first man, had passed on before the second reached the place where they struck.

" Before I had learned this lesson by experience, I had wasted an immense amount of ammunition, on two separate occasions, in attempting to ' stand off' the repeated dashes of a band of the persistent Cheyennes. Then it was only by good shelter, cool heads and abundant ammunition that we effectually escaped capture, and the tortures unnameable which were sure to follow our falling into the hands of the enemy.

"Years after our first encounter with these ghouls of the prairie, while hunting buffalo near the headwaters of the Saline river in western Kansas, with five companions, and just as we were ready to go into camp, preparatory to loading one of our wagons with hides, we had a brush with the savages under the most exciting circumstances. In the vicinity of where I had determined to make our camp, we had encountered during the morning several small bunches of buffalo, and the indications were favorable for many more within a radius of twenty miles in every direction. We had fortunately discovered quite a large lagoon, or lake, for the prairie region, the very place for a center from which to operate; for, as the reader has already been informed, water is a scarce article on the remote desert, and when discovered a party will linger near it until everything in the shape of game is exhausted in that region.

"At this favorable point we unhitched and unsaddled our horses, fed them in boxes fastened to the rear of tjie wagons and in boxes on the ground, kindled a fire, made coffee, baked some biscuit, broiled our buffalo-steak, and after eating, discussed the situation for a few moments and felt as comfortable as if we were sitting around our own firesides in the far-eastern part of the great State. Presently I picked up my rifle and started off, telling the other men I would walk to the top of the little divide, nearly a mile away, to see if there were any buffalo in sight. I had proceeded about half the distance, when my attention was suddenly attracted by an object rising over the crest of the ridge and as quickly disappearing. I felt almost certain that what I had seen was a skulking savage, but knew that it would not be discreet to retreat, if my conjectures were true, for upon thus admitting I had seen them, they would dash out immediately and cut me off from camp. I did not by any action indicate that I had discovered them; did not even make any change in my gait; neither increased nor slackened it, but swung around slowly to the left for a few hundred yards, walked down a little embankment, and was soon out of their sight. Then I made a bee line for camp, or as nearly so as the topography of the country would permit, and at the same time shield me from view of what I believed to be Indians. When about three hundred feet from the wagons, I emerged into full sight of whatever might be behind me. Then stopping for an instant and looking back, I saw fifteen of the murderous savages dash down to the very spot where I had first passed out of their sight, they evidently supposing (as I had intended they should) that I had continued on my original course. If I had, unquestionably I should have been cut off from my companions a full half-mile from camp. They must have been terribly surprised and angered when they discovered I had completely circumvented them, and was safe in camp.

" I exclaimed to my comrades, who were engrossed with their work around the wagons, ' Look out 1' They at once comprehended the situation of affairs, and were ready with their rifles, shotguns and revolvers. By this time the redskins were all in line, coming directly toward us as fast as their ponies could carry them. I was now within about twenty feet of the wagons, where there was a small buffalo-wallow. Here I stood until the savages were within about four hundred yards of us, then dropped on one knee, leveled my rifle and drew a bead. But at that instant they all scattered in every direction, the majority turning to the left; then, uttering their diabolical, blood-curdling war-whoop, they commenced to circle around us in their usual strategic style. I called out to my companions to lie down and not shoot until I had opened the fire; to keep cool, and aim ahead of the ponies one rod for every hundred yards distance.

"Our horses became terribly alarmed, and it was fortunate we had securely tied them to the wagons, or they would have stampeded, been captured by the savages, and we left without means of transportation, hundreds of miles from our homes.

" The Indians now sent several balls whistling over our heads, and were constantly pressing closer and closer in upon us ; yet we never moved from our position, or made any demonstration whatever. These tactics, doubtless, put them in a quandary: they evidently could not determine whether we were old hunters, saving our ammunition, were veritable ' tenderfeet,' or were so badly scared that we dared not fire. A few moments later their doubts were speedily dissolved, for when they had crowded in until I could plainly see the ears of their horses, having by this time calculated the distance pretty well, I cried out, 'All ready, boys! ' raised myself on one knee, aimed two rods ahead of the front horse, and fired; and by the puff of dust raised by the ball knew it had struck about a foot behind the animal's hind foot, directly in the rear. Then I knew well what to do next time: I aimed a little farther in front, and four feet higher, touched the hair-

trigger at the instant, and watched the result of my shot with as much confidence as though I had the pony so near I could have touched him with my rifle. Spat I went the ball, and instantly the bald-faced animal rolled over and over. Its rider was on his feet before the animal was off his, running away like a wild turkey. Having thus disposed of one of the red devils, I turned my battery on the last of the savages, and sent a ball which crippled his horse very badly; yet the scared Indian applied his whip so vigorously that he soon reached the same little ' cut-bank' that had served me so kindly a short time])efore. My men sent many shots into them, and claimed several horses were badly wounded.

"Immediately after this last essay of ours, every one of the bewildered savages was out of sight. We then walked out to look around the field of battle. On reaching the prominence which shielded the Indians, if any of them remained in the vicinity, we found that as far as our vision extended there was nothing but the tracks of their ponies visible, as they had hurried off. We then returned to the spot where the pony I had shot was tossing in his agony, throwing his head about, and appearing to suffer the greatest misery. I found the ball from my rifle had struck him in the right shoulder and passed out just at the point of his other shoulder, crushing the bone in its passage. In his fall he had skinned his side terribly by coming in contact with the hard, dry ground. A ball from the revolver of one of my companions put the poor brute out of pain. And thus ended what might have been a bloody fight had we not known how to deal with the merciless redskins.

" The band which had attacked us belonged to a party of Arrapahoes that had been harassing the hunters in the region for more than a week previously to our entering the valley, but they did not show up afterward.

" We kept out a strong guard that night, and the next day killed sixteen buffalo. We pulled out for the station

the following morning with a full load of fine skins, for which we received two dollars and thirty-five cents each — an excellent remuneration for our work.

"As an Indian-fighter, I must admit that I never especially desired to get into battle with the savage; nor do I care to boast of scores of scalps, as some self-styled plainsmen do; was always more famous for keeping out of the way of the wily nomads than for seeking their hiding-places and 'itching for a fight.' The 'daredevil' type, or what some would term, brave men, seldom if ever survived those troublesome days, I may have killed an Indian or two; if I did, no one will ever be the wiser, as I do not possess any Indian scalps,—hope none will accuse me of so doing. I must confess, that in those troublesome daj^s I would as soon have killed an Indian as a rattlesnake.

" Some people will doubtless say I was a hard-hearted and strange sort of a frontiersman.

To all such let me say that they never have passed through the scenes, trials and tribulations incident to a life on the Plains, as I have, for if they had they would agree with me in my statements regarding the 'children of the prairie.' If you had been with me from 1869 to 1886, (a i^eriod extending over seventeen years,) harassed, hounded and haunted by these savages; compelled to go hungry, thirsty and sleepless; losing cattle and horses through their devilish machinations; and had seen with your own eyes, as I have, scores of innocent people mutilated, tortured, and even butchered, simply because they were of the hated white race,—it would be indeed a strange thing not to have sworn eternal vengeance against the perpetrators, of such hellish deeds. True, ' time cures all ills,' and it has made me recant many of the vows made in my earlier and callow days on the frontier; still, I remember their detestable deeds as if they were committed but yesterday, and cannot say I have altogether relented, and am certain they have not gained any more love for me than

they originally entertained when I was counted as a ' tenderfoot ' in their estimation. I have ever dealt with them in the sternest and most determined manner, always demanding my legitimate rights under almost every circumstance, yielding to them an equally honest adjustment of theirs, believing that by thus acting I have warded off many a severe encounter and saved myself and party much suffering, to say nothing of possible death.

"The great generals and those in authority in the United States have been credited with subduing the red warriors of the Plains, but such is not the case. The buffalo-hunters conquered the whole Indian race — not by unerring aim at the red devils themselves, while perchance they encircled the camp, or in combat when they often met; but simply by slaying the buffalo, and thereby cutting off their source of supplies. As soon as the red man was compelled to beg or starve, then his proud heart broke, and he plead for mercy at the feet of the paleface; while as long as the buffalo lasted he was richer than a millionaire, defied and baffled the greatest generals and the most formidable armies of the United States and Canada, but at last was compelled to bow to the inevitable buffalo-hunter of no pretensions.

"It will be expected, probably, in this chapter that I relate somewhat of the habits of the Indians; their manner of living, their social customs and tribal affairs. In answer to this expectancy on the part of my readers, I can only say that I really know but little about their social relations; yet I do know some things, more than I care to divulge, as the relation of the facts would only disgust and shock the senses of the refined. Therefore I have let them severely alone in this narrative.

"I always took especial care to avoid the presence of the Indians; never would permit them to loiter around my camp if I could possibly avoid it. True, sometimes they were too numerous, and I have been compelled to put up with some of their impudence; but this rarely

occurred, as I treated them in such a determined way they took the hint (I really believed they feared me) and would incontinently clear out.

"On one occasion, while hunting, one of my horses fell over an embankment and was killed. I could not keep up the hunt without another, so made straight for a camp of Kiowa Indians, about ten miles away. There must have been a thousand of them on a great buffalo-hunt, laying in meat for winter. At my approach there was quite a scramble among the half-naked outfit. An old chief came out to meet me, with bow strung and arrow in place. My salute to him was, ' Good Injun ? ' He replied, ' Good Injun.' I dismounted, and by that time a half-dozen lesser chiefs and braves surrounded me. I said to the chief, 'Sell pony?' He answered, 'Big chief, me. Heap ponies. Got money?' 'Yes,' was my reply. He immediately reached out his hand, saying, 'Me see.' I had not been accustomed to doing business in that way, and shook my head, giving him to understand that when I got the ponies he got the money, and not before. I held four five-dollar bills in my hand,'but was careful that he did not grab them. He made a reach for them, but I quickly drew them back. Upon this he gave a characteristic ' Ugh ! Ugh 1 ' grasped his arrow and pulled the string until his bow was nearly double, and sent the arrow into the soft marshy ground, nearly out of sight, and walked directly toward his tent, never looking back, skulking off like a spoiled child.

"Presently another chief spoke up: 'Heap chief, Big Bow, much mad; sell no ponies. One sleep, come; heap money, good pony.' This was very easily understood, and I made straight for my camp; took pains not to return, but moved about ten miles to where some men were camped on a hunt, and bought a pony for less money than the Indians wanted, and already broke to harness.

" Once, while camping on the headwaters of the South Fork of the Solomon river, in western Kansas, I had wan-

dered about six miles from my wagon, and had killed five buffaloes. It was an hour before sundown, and as may be imagined, I was very busy stripping the hides off the animals. I was leaning over the carcass of the last of the five, just putting the finishing touches to my work, when, happening to glance under my left arm toward the rear, I saw two Indians approaching, tiptoeing along in a crouched position. I did not rise from my position, but walked in my cramped attitude to the opposite side of the beast I was skinning, picked up my rifle, and leveled it on the red devils before they were aware their presence was discovered. They were not more than seventy yards distant, when I exclaimed, 'Halt! ' The Indian in front raised himself to his full height and cried, 'Good Injun, me! ' at the same instant striking himself on the breast with his right hand, while holding his gun in his left. * Vamoose! ' I thundered out, as he continued to approach.

" ' Big Indian, me; good Indian, me,' he said again.

" 'Good Indian goes around,' I replied; but he still advanced. I brought down my rifle on the old chief in such a determined manner that he knew very well what to expect next. He halted, and fairly danced up and down, chattering all the time like a monkey that had been struck in the eye with a quid of tobacco. He yelled out three times, 'Red man's cattle; do, do.' But all I did was to yell back at him, ' Vamoose, or I'll kill you! ' He immediately led off to the right, and the young buck followed.

"I then resumed skinning the buffalo I was engaged on, and appeared terribly brave, while really I was disturbed, and guarantee there were more holes in that hide than there are in the bottom of a sieve, as I kept my eyes on the Indians continually, for I did not know how many of the devils might be in the vicinity, and my scalp might be in serious danger. After the savages had withdrawn, and were about half a mile distant, an antelope com-

menced to circle around them, presently stopping to gaze on the red blankets which both wore. Soon, 'bangl' went one of the guns, and I plainly heard the ball spat, and saw the poor animal attempt to dash away. He reared, walked a few steps backward on his hind feet, and fell dead. The Indians each cut off a quarter of the animal, packed them on their shoulders, and leisurely sauntered off toward the northwest. I watched them until they were out of sight, finished my work, and walked six miles to camp, congratulating myself that I did not meet the fate of the antelope.

" The first thing I did on arriving in camp was to order everything moved about five miles to the east, so as to preclude the probability of an engagement with the savages that night, as they would endeavor to get even with me for the manner in which I had treated them; and how many of them might be prowling about, we had no means of even guessing.

"It must have been nearly midnight when we again pitched our camp, this time in a deep ravine a half-mile from the bank of the river, where we remained unmolested for another week, hunting buffalo. The second day after moving camp I chanced to be in the vicinity of the old camp, and discovered that the Indians had been there, in anticipation, no doubt, of finding us napping. By the number of pony-tracks plainly visible in the soft sand on both sides of the stream, the band must have comprised at least thirty or forty. It is wonderful how quickly one Indian can find another when relief is desired or assistance required. No matter how great the distance, within a reasonable number of miles, help is always forthcoming with a certainty that is astonishing, and seems impossible without the aid of telegraph or telephone wires. Of course nothing of the kind is employed; they communicate only by a series of signs, strange and symbolical in their nature, yet understood perfectly by every member of the tribe, and unfailing in their correctness and effect-.

iveness. Some of these means are brands of fire by night, in daytime by smoke, and by gestures if within sight of each other and on foot, or by the motion they make their horses undergo if mounted; also, by little pieces of sticks stuck in the ground on the trail, or by mounds of dirt or grass, or by a rag, if walking but out of sight of those whom they wish to communicate with and they know are to come that way. By this silent language they can convey to their distant comrades what they wish done as readily as if they could talk to them.

"In the spring of 1872 I was on a hunt for hides^ drifting with the main herd of buffalo to the northwest, having encountered the vanguard at a point on the South Fork of the Solomon, where the mass of shaggy animals crossed that stream. Let me interpolate here, that the buffalo always migrate two or three hundred miles north in the spring, returning late in the fall to their winter feeding-grounds. Aware of this fact, I had learned by years of experience that when they wore thus on their annual move it was much easier to kill those animals at the head of .the,herd than those at the rear, as the latter always stampeded and rushed by if I opened fire upon them, while the leaders if shot at would never turn back any considerable distance, evidently persistently opposed to retracing their steps toward the place from whence they had started, and would also linger a day or two before venturing to pass a creek, river or canon where there appeared any danger ahead. Under such circumstances, where they had been fired at as I have related, we would in those two or three days do the most effective work of our trip. Then, after slaughtering all it was possible to secure, we would stretch and peg the hides on the prairie, flesh side up, and make a rapid drive of thirty or forty miles, and thus get in ahead of the herd again.

"Once, when we had made one of these hurried trips^ and were past the front of the buffaloes sOme three miles, we rolled at a lively gait down to a stream near the Ne-

braska line, which I knew to be the South Fork of the Republican river. We made straight for a clump of timber, where we camped and took a lunch. I then jumped on my pony and hastened back to a high point, where I could overlook the whole country and watch the movement of the slowly approaching herd, in order to be ready to take every advantage of it. Just as I was adjusting my field-glasses to focus on the mass of buffalo two miles off to the south, an Indian rode out from the west side of the hill, and came directly toward me, raising his hand to salute me as he approached. I saw at a glance he was possessed of bow and arrows only, so I returned his greeting with a signal that he might come to me.

"When he rode up I discovered he was a Pawnee, off his reservation. He was a chief — a 'Big Indian, heap ponies,' and his tribe was not considered hostile; so I was really delighted to see even an Indian in that Godforsaken country, as it was at that time. He could talk fairly good

English, and told me he was one of two hundred who were in camp sixteen miles distant from where we stood, out on a buffalo hunt, but they had not as yet seen even a straggling animal; that they were out of meat, nearly starving, and were dancing, and asking the Oreat Spirit to send back the buffalo. I pointed out the approaching herd of the coveted beasts, and he immediately gave vent to his feelings of joy by crying out, ' Heap buffalo 1 Heap buffalo 1 ' His eyes fairly flashed with the prospect of getting food for his hungry people and raising himself a notch higher in his tribe as being a successful chief. After looking scrutinizingly upon the huge beasts in the distance, he exclaimed again, 'Yes! Surel Surel ' I replied, 'Yes, surel ' and handed him my field-glasses, but he shook his head as he looked at the (to him) strange things, and said, 'Two guns; kill Injun.' I shook my head negatively in return, fixed them to my eyes, and said, ' Big heaps buffalo,' and then

placed the glasses to his eyes; and as he saw the apparently close herd, he shouted, ' Ugh 1 Here already I '—at the same moment thumping the sides of his pony with his legs, and, layin'g himself flat along the back of his animal, he dashed ofif until he had ridden about fifty yards in the opposite direction from the buffalo, and had gotten behind the hill, in order to hide from the animals. I never saw a more surprised individual in all my life, than was this Indian on looking through the glasses. Having no conception of the laws of optics, he supposed, as he looked at the buffalo, magnified as they were by the glass, that they were rapidly advancing, and already nearly within range of his weapon.

" Recovering from his bewilderment and now grasping the true condition of affairs, he pulled from his pony an old red blanket, took hold of its opposite corners, one in each hand, remounted, and then, of all the 'fluttering in the breeze' I never before saw anything to equal that of this blanket under the manipulation of the Pawnee. The Indian was signaling to his comrades that there were ' buffalo in abundance,] I could discover nothing in any direction that indicated the presence of other Indians, although I scrutinized every point of the vast expanse, that was cut off only by the great circle of the heavens. He too was evidently keeping a sharp lookout, and presently pointing toward the northeast, called my attention to that portion of the horizon. I could not, however, discern anything until I had adjusted the field-glass to my eyes, when, sure enough, in the dim distance, far beyond the river, on a side-hill, I could make out a band of men on horseback, who appeared to be moving toward us. On the very summit of the elevation I saw another detached figure, apparently an image of the Indian by my side, who was also waving his blanket in response to the signal he recognized at that immense distance. He was repeating the glad tidings to Indians beyond our sight. It is wonderful, as I have previously affirmed, how penetrating is — 7

the vision of the savages of the Plains. Here, where I could observe nothing with my naked eyes (and they were considered as good as any that scanned the Plains), the chief at my side had discovered what required the aid of the glass for me to discern. In this particular the white man blushes for his inferiority.

" In a few seconds the Pawnee again pointed to the east with his whip, and I could now plainly see four men on horseback coming toward us from the direction indicated, one of whom was waving his blanket vigorously, conveying the news to others beyond, as did the first. In less than half an hour there were fully six distinct groups of Indians moving rapidly toward where we stood, and in an hour's time more than a hundred Pawnee warriors were ready for one of the most desperate struggles for food, perhaps, ever undertaken; and others were continually arriving,

" The herd was feeding slowly, and was surely advancing toward the river. We stood passively where we were, watching their seeniingly lazy movements, impatient of the time to commence active operations. In a few moments one of the chiefs rode up to me and said: ' Me go to woods to hide; come too ? ' I bowed my acquiescence, and followed him. The Indians stationed themselves under the bluffs that paralleled the stream, when, leaving them here, I rode down the bank until I arrived at my camp and explained the situation of affairs to my companions, who had by this time become very much alarmed for my safety. In fact, so disturbed Avere they when they saw so many Indians in the distance, that they had hidden themselves in brush-heaps, and only my familiar voice brought them out from their refuge, when I told them to be prepared to witness one of the greatest ' circuses' they could ever hope to see again.

" The herd of buffalo soon made its appearance about a mile away across the valley. The animals were now wandering down a ravine, as they usually do when traveling,

and were heading for a point half a mile west of where we were standing, and directly toward the main group of Indians, who were ' on the anxious seat.' Now we could see the interest the hungry savages took in their prospective dinner. They were very active, hustling backward and forward, and talking in their silent but expressive sign-language (so perfect in its symbolization), so as not to let a sound escape which might stampede the buffalo. The wind was favorable, being strong from the south. On either side of the ravine there was a little ridge, which gave them every opportunity to outwit the wary brutes. On came the shaggy monsters, thicker and thicker, until they appeared like a great cloud or a cluster of bees working around a hive. It was a grand sight, never to be again witnessed by this or generations to come.

"The Indians divided into two parties, one going to the east side of the ridge, the other to the west side, until their line extended fully half a mile from the river toward the bluffs. Arriving at their proper stations, one Indian from each line dismounted, walked to the crest of the low divide, and peeped over. Here each, by signaling, gave information to his companions of the motions of the herd. Finally these scouts ran back to their ponies, mounted, and rode rapidly to the upper end of the line of savages, then rode toward each other, where they met in the low swag of bottom land that lay between the two ridges and in the rear of the herd. Not a word was spoken until they had nearly reached each other, with the long lines of their companions closing up behind them. At this juncture there arose such a yell in concert from the throats Of the watchful savages, never before or since heard by me, that fairly deafened my ordinarily tough ears. A thousand coyotes struggling and fighting in the midnight hour on the remote plains over the carcass of an old buffalo bull driven out of the herd, bears no comparison. Although horrible and blood-curdling, as anyone will attest who has ever heard it, it is as the soft spring breeze

compared to that awful whoop of the Pawnees, which will never pass from my memory though I should live to a patriarchal age.

"While all this commotion was going on in the ranks of the warriors, the guards just over the ridges remained in their places, but kept up the wild j^ells, until the herd reached the crest of the little divides both on the east and west, and those along the river-bank took up the piercing yell afresh, which reverberated through every little valley and mass of rock bordering the stream, until it awakened the echoes of the very prairie in its wildness.

"The herd, which must have contained at least two thousand buffalo, now surrounded by the strategy of the Indians, attempted to stampede, about half running to the east, the others to the west,— none daring to essay the passage of the river, although but few Indians were stationed there.

" When the affrighted herd caught sight of the Indiana and heard their awful yell on either side of them, the two bands of the bewildered brutes circled around and rushed in opposite directions. About a dozen of the now excited Indians, mounted on the fleetest of the ponies, pressed them on, and the noise they made seemed like Pandemonium broke loose. The chasing savages fired at the poor brutes with their revolvers, and the two herds met in a few moments with a shock as terrible as would be that of colliding express trains. Just before the dreadful collision, the Indians whirled their ponies and rejoined the line of guards they had started from. At the instant these scouts retraced their steps, the buffalo in their maddened fright followed them until they reached the ridge, where tjiey were again greeted with a demoniacal yell which caused them to circle again, and back they fairly flew, followed as before by about a dozen fresh Indians. This peculiar strategy was continued for fully an hour, by which time the poor brutes were so exhausted and crippled they could scarcely raise a gallop. Now, taking

advantage of the physical condition of their game, the Indians were in the center of the herd, on the outside, and everywhere,— shooting with their revolvers, or spearing them with lances made of steel, bound with rawhide to the end of long poles.

" Finally, so desperate had the poor creatures become, that they mustered up courage to break through the cordon of savages to the west, and thus escaped further torment from their pursuers.

" During the terrible and exciting encounter I had been seated on my horse viewing the unequal contest with great interest, though moved by that natural pity which wells up in the human breast sometimes, under the most adverse conditions, and I was really glad when the conflict was over.

" I now rode out to the scene of the battle, where there were more than a dozen wounded buffalo still standing on their feet. They were dangerous creatures to approach in that condition, but some of the Indians ventured to rush by them, endeavoring to finish them with their revolvers as they passed, but made very indifferent progress. I carried a ' forty-four' sporting rifle (Sharps'), and asked one of the chiefs if I might shoot the crippled buffalo for him. He replied, ' Yes, if you can.' I then knelt on one knee. *Bang! ' went the great gun, which on the evening breeze resounded sharply on the calm air. One cow tumbled over, and the Indians, attracted by the report, stood as if a clap of thunder had suddenly burst from the cloudless heavens. I fired again, and a second buffalo rolled on the ground. The savages then began to retreat from the vicinity of the remaining wounded animals, and as fast as I could load and fire they tumbled over one by one, until the last was dead. I don't know why, but every shot was better than usual. The old chief was so excited and pleased at my success, he jumped off his pony, caught me by the hand, in his enthusiasm, and exclaimed: " Esta wauo! Heap big white man! " \'7bEsta bueno, is the pure

Spanish for what he intended 'to convey, but, like the ' Greasers ' in New Mexico with their Spanish, and the old mediaeval monks with their Latin, they corrupt the 'b,' giving it the sound of ' w.')

" It was only a few moments until the entire two hundred Indians crowded around me, making the air hideous with their congratulations in corrupted Spanish; after which they all hurried off to secure the delicious humps and hams of the great game. These they bound upon their ponies and started for their camp, nearly every one of them chewing a piece of the raw flesh as he moved away.

"After the Indians had departed, I counted up their day's work. I supposed, of course, from their demonstrations and hurrahs, I would find at least a hundred dead buffaloes, but imagine my disgust when the total numbered only forty-one!

" Knowing the whole band would move to the spot the next day, we drove about five miles to the southwest that evening, where we had fine shooting for nearly a week, as the Indians guarded the river, which the herd was chary of attempting to cross."

PEAIRIE-FIRES

REMINDERS OF THE WORLD's PROMISED DESTRUCTION

STARTED BY HOSTILE INDIANS — DAYLIGHT TURNED TO DARKNESS AND DARKNESS TO LIGHT — PEOPLE DRIVEN INTO THEIR HOUSES AND CELLARS — COMPELLED TO BREATHE THROUGH HANDKERCHIEFS AND TOWELS TO SEPARATE ASHES FROM AIR — WILD ANIMALS FLEEING BEFORE THE WRATHY FLAMES PASSES WITH THE ROAR OF A CYCLONE— EVERYONE TO THE RESCUE — THE ONLY WAY TO ESCAPE ON THE PRAIRIE — WILD ANIMALS BURNED TO A CRISP.

THERE is, or rather, was, no more sublime sight than that of a prairie-fire in the early days of our pioneer civilization on the Great Plains — now a thing of the past, as the region is comparatively well settled, and each recurring year is lessening their probability. Some of the most awful in their results were purposely started by the Indians, who were jealous of the constant encroachment of the whites upon what the savage was pleased to call his own domain, and adopted this method, among their many devilish plans of driving off the intruders, whose cattle and horses suffered fearfully by being deprived of their pasture in this manner. At the present time these fires, while of course limited in area, are still formidable, and rarely occur excepting through the carelessness of the individual upon whose land they originate. Sometimes a spark from a passing locomotive is the cause, and the effect is disas-

(lOS)

trous to whole neighborhoods. Colonel Jones records one of the mighty conflagrations in his journal, which I here give verbatim:

"In the fall of 1872 there occurred in Russell and Osborne counties, Kansas, one of the most destructive prairie-fires that ever swept over any country; not likely to again hapjpen.

" It was in October, that month of incomparable beauty on the Great Plains. There had been an abundance of rain in the early spring and during the summer; consequently all upland vegetation had grown phenomenally rank. Every acre of every ravine and little valley was covered with a luxuriance of vegetable matter unprecedented in the memory of the oldest hunters.

"About the first of August, what is usually a constant feature of our intracontinental climate occurred: the windows of heaven were closed, the rains and dews ceasing to fall. Then commenced those simoons, the hot, scorching winds peculiar to the region, so destructive to crops, and which frequently blow constantly for weeks at a time.

"On the evening of the 19th of October the relatively gentle southwest wind turned into a furious gale, and when night came on we could see far off in the darkness a reflection on the clouds; the first premonition of the awful fate to which the country was doomed. At the incipiency of the affair but little attention was given to it, excepting to admire the beauty and grandeur of the scene, as, like the ' pillar of fire' that Moses and the children of Israel followed of old, the treacherous flames shot upward to the zenith from the far-distant southwestern horizon.

" The next morning the sun rose upon a landscape enveloped in smoke, and all that day the air was so dense that to breathe it was almost stifling. When the darkness, or rather the time for darkness, to make its appearance arrived, the change from daylight to night was awful to contemplate. During the day, what should have been hours of sunlight were thick, smoky, and a diffused gloom like that of a heavy fog spread over the landscape; while the legitimate night was as lurid as the Inferno so graphically described by the immortal Dante. The whole heavens, from the remotest east to the farthest west, appea'red to be melting under a glow that was as red as incandescent hydrogen, and the light so intense you could see to pick up a pin anywhere on the broad prairie. Many of the superstitious really wondered whether the ' last day' had not really come.

" Sleep that night was an entire stranger to all in the settlement, excepting the little ones; and how long it seemed 1 When the sun rose on the morning of the 2l8t, the atmosphere was so saturated with the dense smoke that it appeared as if the order of nature had been reversed,— day turned into night, and vice versa; a mighty pall spread over the earth. Occasionally, when there came a rift in the black smoke-clouds, the sun appeared like a molten ball, intensely red, and swiftly scudding along the heavens,—this apparent motion being only an optical illusion, of course, caused by the swift passage of smoke-clouds as the wind hurled them along in its fury.

" The condition of affairs was now serious, for the sheet of flame was rapidly closing in toward the settlement. The few settlers in our portion of the region in the pathway of the fire demon, turned out and began to break furrows around their homes, rude stables, haystacks, corn-cribs and other property, comprising their all, in order to save them if possible. During the long weary hours that the frightened people had helplessly watched the coming of the fiery storm, the wind had not abated one jot; if anything, rather increased in its fury. No one had dared to put out a 'back-fire,' for fear of destroying his neighbors' property that lay in the fire's pathway. Not a living thing could have withstood the full force of the withering blast. Cattle and horses were hastily driven

into their stables and sheds, while people were obliged to keep indoors, down cellars, or in some sheltered place where the scorching wind could not reach them. The very air was filled with ashes, much of them impalpable, getting into the throat and lungs. Another feature was, great pieces of inflammable debris of ' buffalo-chips' were blown from the sheet of flame (far away as yet) by the force of the terrible wind. It was now impossible to breathe with comfort, unless in some closed room, where the ashes had been filtered from the air as they entered the place.

" The women and children were pale and haggard from excitement and fear, the men exhausted and discouraged; yet everyone fixed his eyes on the awful spectacle of the rapidly approaching flames, as if it were a siren that had charmed him.

" By noon, the roar of the fire as it swept along could be heard above the roaring of the wind, adding new horror to that already paralyzing the silent lookers-on. This appalling feature of the terrible scene sounded like distant thunder, or like the dashing of breakers on a ledge of rocks during a fearful storm. On every side, all over the prairie, could be seen nearly every variety of animal known to the region, fleeing for their lives before the coming waves of fire. Antelope appeared in large numbers ; wolves skulked along, their tails tucked under their bodies,— now stopping for a moment, looking backward, then ahead in their bewilderment, not knowing where to turn next. A few buffaloes drifted by with the other beasts, nearly exhausted with their long race, their tongues hanging far out of their mouths. The jack-rabbit and the cottontail could be seen mingled with the rest of the unfortunate brutes, seeking some i^lace where, they might hide from the impending danger. How I longed for a Noah's ark or a place of refuge for them! But not a bird was to be seen in all the vast expanse of the country. They had long since, from the first intimation of the

fire, forsaken the region, being fortunately supplied with means of locomotion that would swiftly carry them out of the path of the flames.

"Nearer and louder the horrid blasting storm approached; the ashes now sifted through the crevices of the buildings, and then the people were compelled to hide their heads under towels, handkerchiefs, or something of that character, to prevent being smothered by the dense smoke and ashes permeating every place.

" Early in the afternoon, by two o'clock, with a mighty roar the flames reached the crest of the divide only half a mile distant, and we then knew that in a few moments the terrible storm of fire would be ujoon us. Would it destroy all ? In another minute everything suddenly appeared to have turned to flames, but no one dared to uncover to see. Another moment and all was wrapped in intense darkness; relief soon came; the horrid ordeal had ended, and then, ' To the rescue I' was the cry. Now to save our homes and property, which had been in a measure protected by the broad furrows of earth that had been plowed around them. The air was so hot, however, it drove the men back instantly into the houses. Besides, the ashes were still being hurled thickly in the atmosphere by the awful hurricane which the radiation had caused, and it was impossible to live in it without shelter. This condition, after the fire had passed, fortunately did not last long, as the wind soon swept everything clean, and hurled it far beyond. Then the men were soon able to get out and fight the sparks and brands which had lodged in the barnyards and other exposed places, making another conflagration imminent. Many stables and open houses were by this means destroyed on that eventful day.

"When quiet had been restored and the air attained its normal coolness, what a desolate picture the landscape presented I The whole earth looked as if the angel of destruction had visited the region, leaving nothing but wreck and despair in its pathway.

"A few days after this visitation, I went out on a hunting expedition, more for the purpose, however, of surveying the area burned over, than in the expectancy of securing any game. I found everywhere ghastly monuments of the fire's dreadful work; antelopes which had been caught in the cruel flames — some dead, burned to a crisp, others so badly injured they could not even crawl out of my way. One, especially large, had evidently been caught in the midst of the flames; his hair was completely burned off, his feet so perfectly roasted that the hoofs had fallen off, and when I came up to him he attempted to run away on his raw and bleeding stumps. I put an end to his suffering at once, rather than leave him in that helpless condition for the wolves to torture, which they would surely have done.

"This awful fire was in all probability set out by a band of Kiowa Indians who had been hunting in that vicinity, and was no doubt enjoyed by them as much as dreaded by the citizens.

"I have seen a great many such fires on the frontier, and have always been very lucky in not being caught without plenty of matches and something to light them under. The first thing that I would pack in a box when going out on a hunt would be matches, for without them a man's life was in as much danger as from the Indians, in those troublous times on the frontier.

"Many years afterward, near Garden City, Kansas, a friend and neighbor of mine, Clinton Gore, who was driving across a prairie in a light spring wagon, was suddenly surprised to see the flames in close proximity to hira. Realizing his danger, as the wall of fire rolled toward him, he applied the lash mercilessly to his really very fast team, and endeavored to escape before the flames could reach him, which were gaining rapidly; but saw he was too late. He then stopped, attempted to set out a fire, but his matches failed, the wind being too strong, extinguishing them as fast as he lighted one, until his

MR. gore's narrow ESCAPE FROM THE FLAMES 109

entire stock was nearly exhausted. The flames were now almost upon him, and he was in a dilemma which can only be imagined by those who are familiar with the dangers of the Great

Plains. In despair, he snatched a buffalo-robe from the wagon, and, sheltering himself under it, attempted again to light a fire. This time he succeeded; (and this means, i. e., by a cover to break the wind, is the only way a fire can be started when the wind is very high on the Plains.) He paused but a minute, then guided his team in the rear of the blaze, and followed the fire he had started as fast as he could go, but the wind was so terrific that it prevented the flames from spreading sideways very fast. The main fire had nearly reached his rear, and threatened to consume both him and hi& team; so, as he could no longer keep ahead of the flames, he dismounted, laid himself flat on the ground, pulled the robe over him, and held on to the reins until the fire had passed. The horses, although on the burnt ground that his fire had cleared, fully four rods wide, were so-badly burned that within three days the flesh fell from the side next to the flames, and Mr. Gore was compelled to kill them. His face and hands were very badly burned in his attempt to hang on to the team. By holding to-the reins his hands were jerked from under the robe, and for fear the wagon or horses would run over him he threw the robe back from his face so that he could see, which was a mistake. He drove sixteen miles to the-town, where he put up at the hotel and sent for a doctor; he was compelled to keep his bed for six weeks, and came very near losing his life. It is hardly credible that animals could endure so much after being so badly burned, but they crippled along in some way, and finally reached the village, more dead than alive.

" No doubt many of my readers have seen prairie-fires in the middle Western States; but the vegetation there is-very different from the buffalo-grass of western Kansas, which is so full of combustible matter and so short, that

the wind sweeps right over it, causing the flames to be wafted much more rapidly than in those places, and to reach far out in advance. The rapidity with which it travels, and the heat that it produces, seem almost incredible to people who are unaccustomed to prairie-fires. Those who have seen such fires during a hurricane, as above described, will bear witness to the terror it inspires."

CHAPTER VIII SECOND HUNT FOR CALVES

EVERYBODY WANTED TO JOIN COL. JONES'b EXPEDITION

TWO STRANGERS THRUST THEMSELVES UPON HIM — PROVED TO BE "angels unawares" —LANDED IN AN IRRIGATION DITCH ALL THE SAME HORSE BALKED — WANTED

JONES TO KILL HIM—" NO 1 HE IS THE BEST HORSE IN THE expedition" — WILD-HORSE HUNTER LOST — WOULD NOT BELIEVE RIGHT DIRECTION WHEN TOLD—LOST CONFIDENCE BECAUSE GIVEN WATER INSTEAD OF WHAT HE WANTED — "buffalo, BY JUPITER ! " — " EVERYTHING DONE IN A minute" — HORSEMEN DASH AFTER HERD

"tenderfeet" follow, standing in wagon, over hillocks AND dog-houses — MOST GRAPHIC ACCOUNT OF the chase —SECURED THREE CALVES—COW FIGHTS TO THE DEATH—SEARCHING FOR WATER IN THE DARKNESS.

("A Buffalo Hunt Indeed." Written by E. Hough, sketched by J. A. Kicker, eye-witnesses.)

IT was in the month of May, 1887, that the artist, J. A. Ricker, and myself found ourselves in southwestern Kansas, While tarrying at Garden City we learned, through strictly private sources, that a herd of buffalo was within two hundred miles of us at the south, and that within two weeks an efficient effort would be made to find them by an old and successful buffalo-hunter. We had supposed that the last buffalo had been killed during the past season. If there were indeed any left, even the very fewest, it would be news to learn of them, and the event of a lifetime to see them: it ivas the last chance. Added to this interest, which naturally attached to the

(111)

hunt proposed, was the further peculiar purpose of the hunt; which was, not to destroy as many as possible of the little remaining band, but to make a systematic and energetic attempt to preserve the species from final extinction. In short, the hunt was to be a buflfalo-calf hunt, and they were to be preserved for domestication.

When we learned of this hunt, learned its projector, and became satisfied of its success,— if success was a possible thing,— my friend and I were filled with a great conviction that it was an affair in which all sportsmen, as well as all who possess humane proclivities, in this great country, were interested. We were satisfied that we could learn something definite about these representatives of a grand and passing race, and confident that we would find in the hunt something new, as well as something impossible to duplicate. This at least was our conviction. With a determination to go, we set out to get an invitation to join the hunt,— which we had not yet received. We looked up Mr. C. J. Jones, the projector of the enterprise, a gentleman with whom our personal acquaintance was yet only slight. We told him who we were, and what we wanted; assured him that we were "tenderfeet" only in appearance (though neither of us had ever seen a buffalo); and concluded by telling him that Ave felt obliged to join that particular hunt,— peaceably if possible, by force if we must. He had refused fifty less determined beggars, and refused "US also. We begged, and threatened to go on our own hook, ■which he knew would frighten ail the buffalo off the range; so he could not resist our stern purpose. He smiled amusedly, looked us over, made us promise not to grumble if the bread was burned, and finally said, "Gentlemen, if jou will obey orders and not shoot or scare the buffalo in iiny manner without permission from me, I will take you in." All of which we swore would be carried out faithfully.

And now, as delicately as we may, and whether he likes it or not, we must tell about Mr. Jones; for without him

such a hunt, or the pleasure of it, or the story of it, could not have been at all.

The Hon. C. J. Jones is "The gentleman from Finney," when he is in the legislative halls at the capital of Kansas; but when out of his legislator's desk he is just "Buffalo Jones," all over Kansas and the West. There is no man in Kansas so well known, perhaps no private citizen better, in the entire United States. He has built a city, made a fortune, and has gone to the Legislature; but still his old name sticks to him, and will stick so long as time shall last. There is no use of his trying to escape it: he is and will always be "Buffalo Jones."

Time was when Mr. Jones was not so rich. In the "*70s" he was out west in Kansas, away ahead of the "rain-belt," with little to support him but his belief in the future of the country, his ability to " rustle," and no doubt the hope of a blessed immortality if he starved to death. He was mail-carrier, station-agent,— anything he could be. He located the town-site of Garden City, and by his own ability and energy started the town going little by little, until, snowball fashion, it grew bigger and bigger, and finally one morning took a screaming boom, and made him rich. He built the marble blocks which delighted visitors to one of the livest and loveliest towns in western Kansas, and pushed the town yet farther on. It is no wonder the people made him mayor, and conferred further honors on him. But all this time he was only "Buffalo Jones." The big marble hotel which he built had some ceremonies over its corner-stone. It was not known what to name the hotel. "In honor of Mr. Jones," cried one happy speaker, "call it the 'Buffalo Hotel.' " And Buffalo Hotel it was, and has been ever since; and a very good one, too.

In those early days — for ten years ago was early in the history of western Kansas — the buffaloes were as the sands of the sea ; and as

"The blue wave rolls nightly on deep Galilee," — 8

80 daily rolled their countless bands upon the shallow Arkansas. Then, there was hardly a man in Kansas who had not killed his buffalo. Now, there are thousands who will never see one. Where Garden City is, the railway train has many a time been stopped for hours at a stretch by the passing herds; and old trainmen and frontiersmen tell, of these episodes, that there sometimes seemed to be millions of these animals in sight; and far as the eye could reach, from the swarming sandhills on the south to the edge of the northern horizon, the whole landscape was covered with a black sea of surging bodies, and the air was filled with the rumbling bellows of the innumerable hosts. There are few of us now who can actually realize such a scene. There were few then who reflected that the scene could ever be different. It seemed impossible even to think that all those countless herds could ever be destroyed. To-day, where are they ?

In those days Mr. Jones lived in the heart of the buffalo country, and in the midst of the buffaloes. He lived in a town which even now has "buffalo-wallows" within its city limits, and within a gunshot of its marble buildings. He grew fundamentally acquainted with the animals, and learned their every habit, so that gradually he came to be known as the most successful buffalo-hunter on the range. Let it not be misunderstood: he did his full share toward exterminating the buffalo, partly because his necessity was greater than theirs; but even aa^ he destroyed them, he grew to know and regret their fate; and as they faded away from the range, and it became certain that soon they would be gone forever, no heart was fuller of regret than his, and no mind so full of expedients to rescue them. He saw that no game law could jireserve the wild buffalo. Congress had slept on its golden opportunities.

So we were to be in at the last " round-up." To see a buffalo had been our highest wish. Here we were on the last verge of all opportunity. Our hearts ran riot at the

thought, and the question almost tormented us into hysterics. Would we indeed find the herd ?

Slowly, the day of our departure came near. We were like children making their first visit: we could not eat, we could not sleep. We would call around at Jones's office every few hours, and were actually indignant because he did not worry too. He appeared to regret the coming day of our departure, and we shuddered for fear he would back down after all.

In the meantime, at leisure moments, we got together such articles as needed. As we were forced to travel light, we confined ourselves to actual necessities. All our personal baggage, excepting guns and blankets, were packed in a little box, fourteen by eighteen inches in size,— whose principal contents, aside from soap, towels, a spool of thread, and a whetstone or two, were some six or seven hundred rifle cartridges.

We had several canteens, which we knew would be necessary. Three pairs of heavy blankets constituted our bedding. My friend and I each had a rifle, revolver, and knife; and in addition, he took his little pet three-barrel gun, for small game, while I packed uj) my fishing-rod, which always stands at the head of my bed of nights. Mr. Jones's baggage was intended to be as simple as our own, but on the first night out it was discovered that his wife had secreted in his roll of bedding a thin mattress, and also a pillow. We adjudged such luxuries sybaritic, and gave him no peace of them. He also thrust under the buggy-seat, when we started, a dilapidated-looking valise. It contained quinine and a quart of whisky for snakebite, besides various other articles often needed on such expeditions.

It should be premised that our expedition was divided into two forces. The heavy outfit, containing the camp supplies, tents, etc., and accompanied by three men who attended to the camp, left the railroad for the south nearly a week before we started. There were with this wagon a

fine mule team, an extra team, and three of the running-horses— "Jennie," Mr. Jones's favorite Kentucky horse, "Kentuck," and a likely-looking black horse, which, being of Western birth, and therefore nameless, we temporarily christened "Blackie." Aside from camp supplies for a month, the wagon contained over two thousand pounds of grain. The stock was to he kept in as fine condition as possible, for it would be called upon to perform the hardest of work; grass feed would not do at all. With the main wagon went also twelve milch cows. These cows were to be foster-mothers of the young buffalo calves which we were to catch, and were to take the place of the condensed milk which had resulted so disastrously the preceding year. This portion of the cavalcade started thus early because, owing to the cows, it could not be expected to travel more than twenty miles a day, while the lighter outfit was to cover three times that distance. The first team was in charge of Charlie Rude — the man Mr. Jones always "banked" on. He had been on the calf-hunt the year before, and therefore knew the trail, and the i^oints to make for.

On Tuesday night. May 10, Mr. Jones left Garden City by rail for Hartland, which was the point where we were to leave the railroad. My friend and myself started early that day to drive the light rig across, the distance being only about thirty miles. Our vehicle, which was to be the scout wagon of the expedition, was an uncovered two-seated buggy, or light "platform wagon," and our team consisted of a big black horse and a 'little gray. The former was a large "States" horse, and was purchased by Mr. Jones on Tuesday morning, the day of our start, and incontinently hitched up for the trip, without further words; the latter was a weary-looking animal, with a suggestion of "broncho," a bad eye, and a record as a runner. We had no name for the new horse; when we got to Hartland we had unconsciously christened his mate "Gray Devil."

It was ten o'clock Tuesday morning when we pushed our last letters into the postoffice, tossed our traps into the wagon, buckled on our belts, and pulled out from the Buffalo Hotel, followed by the profane regrets of half a hundred men who wanted to go on that particular hunt and couldn't. We drove around the corner of the hotel, and there a transaction was effected at the kitchen window, whereby a certain dark-eyed damsel transferred into our possession a most substantial-looking lunch, and a wish for luck,— in return for which we promised her a buffalo.

Our road lay west along the railroad track, and across the multifold irrigating ditches which environ Garden City. Our first ditch bade fair to stop our trip at its beginning. The water was running along it nearly bank-full, and fairly boiling: for the fall of the country makes even the Arkansas river run six miles an hour at that point. AVe knew the ditch was shallow, and it was not more than fifteen feet wide; and we could see where other teams had crossed ; therefore, in we went. The horses slid down the steep bank to the bottom of the ditch, plunged through it, and struck the other bank with their fore feet just as the weight of the wagon came sliding down upon them from behind. The black pulled true and honest, but the gray "went to pieces," and fell to rearing, pitching, plunging, backing, and lying down in the harness; in short, going through a whole circus-bill of equine performances which we were willing to call " absolutely without parallel." We whipped him vigorously, tried moral suasion, and even, in respect of his ancestry, swore at him in Spanish; but everything was worse than the thing before it, until at last, with a vicious shake of his head, the brute began to throw himself back in the harness, and in a way we never quite understood, pushed us out — on the wrong side of the ditch.

There was a farmer plowing in the field near by. We gave him half a dollar, and he unhitched his team and

came to our help. We meekly took out our own team, and rode them across the ditch. The farmer pulled our wagon across; and we went on our way sorrowful, wondering if there would be plenty of ditches — and plenty of farmers — all the way down to the Panhandle.

There were plenty of ditches that day. At the next one our horse behaved admirably, and pulled straight across without a murmur. At the one following he balked unmistakably, but finally got tired and went on. But about three o'clock in the afternoon we found ourselves stuck fast in the biggest ditch yet, the gray refusing to move under any consideration. We took out the team, and tried to move the wagon ourselves, but our efforts only sunk it and ourselves deeper into the soft, sticky mud. At last one of us started off to a claim-shanty, distant over a mile, to get a team, while the other remained with the wagon, and thought, and thought.

By the time the good-natured Dutchman — for another half-dollar—had agreed to get his yoke of oxen (he had no horses), and had finally rounded them up from the hills where they were grazing, and had come to our assistance, our pride had made us desperate. We would not be pulled out of a ditch by an ignoble yoke of oxen. So we harnessed the black horse to the end of the tongue, and pulled the wagon out in that way. Then we hitched up, drove to the bottom of the hill, stopped again for reasons the most obvious, and engaged in another struggle with perverse horseflesh. We blindfolded the horse, put dirt in his ears, fed him grass, watered him, swore at him, spoke to him in well-dissimulated tones of honeyed sweetness; but all to no purpose. Then our "proud hearts broke." We chartered the Dutchman to pull us up the hill with his oxen, and followed behind, an inglorious procession of buffalo-hunters. We said to each other, "Oh, but won't Jones be a picturesque idiot if he tries to get that horse down to the Panhandle ! "

We managed to reach the way-natation of Lakin without

stopping. Here the gray horse balked on the railroad track, just as the passenger train was coming in, but fortunately he got scared at the cars and ran off, so that we were not left open to the charge of being disguised anarchists. As the team had such a good start, we did not let them stop until we got to Hartland, eight miles distant. Delays are dangerous indeed, with a balky horse; and, as we reasoned very properly, if we never allowed him to stop, he could not possibly give us any trouble about starting,—which, you know, is the chief difficulty with a horse of that kind.

At Hartland we met Mr. Jones. We took him aside, and told him privately to execute the gray beast, or trade him off for a box of cartridges.

" Pshaw! boys," said he; " he is the best horse in the expedition; you don't know how to handle him—that's all. That horse is all right. Did you put a stay-chain on the other horse ? "

True; we had forgotten the stay-chain. We told Mr. Jones we would have thought of that, too, if we had had time.

After some talk with the men who gathered about us, and wanted to go on the hunt and couldn't, we ate supper, had the horses shod, and turned in at the hotel for a good night's sleep; our slumbers being broken only by the apparition of a gray nightmare which balked, and would not be persuaded.

The next morning Mr. Jones mounted the seat with lines in hand; a "stay-chain" had been properly adjusted, and all was then ready to dash into the sandhills south of the river. Ricker and

I knew "Gray Devil" would never pull through ten feet of soft sand, and we did not care to ride on the seat only to freeze in the crisp northern breeze and perhaps be invited to get off' to lighten the load; so we determined to walk.

"Jump on 1 " shouted Colonel Jones. "No, thanks; we will walk a ways; we can make ten miles while you are driving one with that team," I responded.

"Very well," replied the Colonel; "you can walk all the way if you so desire; but let me kindly suggest that I shall not stop, after starting, until noon,"

I looked at Ricker and he at me; we both knew better, but fearing the Colonel might order us to walk all the way, as he threatened, we climbed up into the wagon under protest, smothering our emotions.

No sooner seated, than Colonel Jones tapped the black horse easily with the whip, and he gradually moved off, pulling the wagon by the stay-chain. The little gray brute turned his head clear around to see what we intended to do, and soon learned we were coming on just the same, whether he moved or not, and evidently fearing^ he would be crushed beneath the wheels, dashed straight ahead, nearly jerking us off the seat, and kept up the pace until the first sand-knoll was reached. He then again looked back inquisitively, but a gentle touch to th& black- sent him traveling through, and the gray had to trot right along.

Ricker and I felt terribly disappointed because "Gray Devil" didn't do as we told Colonel Jones he would. I leaned over to Ricker and softly whispered, "I wish to the Lord he 'd balk 1 " Ricker responded, "Just wait until the next sand-knoll is reached, and he will satisfy our longing." But the team kept right along, and such a span of roadsters we never sat behind in all our lives. We made eighty miles that day, a large portion of the distance through sand a foot deep. We passed Richfield and another village, three miles south,—Frisco, emulous also for the county seat of Morton county. Thence we pulled up along the breaks of the Cimarron, heading for a certain bold promontory known as the Point of Rocks, near which the advance team was to have crossed. We now left all houses and signs of settlement, and made down into the valley of the Cimarron and camped for the night. This valley, as far as we could see, was lined with the half-wild range cattle. We felt as if we had indeed

left civilization. The scenery was rough and broken, quite a deviation from the monotony of the Plains. Next morning we ran up between the rocky bluffs on one side and the gray sandhills on the other. Presently we struck a wagon-trail, and after a time found a rope which had been dropped. We thought our team could not be far ahead.

On going up to the Point of Rocks,^ we learned that our party had crossed the stream some distance below. Our informants were some cowboys whom we met. They were out with a wagon from Seattle's ranch, picking up " chips " for fuel. Among the men was Mr. Beattie himself— a bronzed young fellow, dressed in conventional cattleman's garb, and therefore looking exactly like a cowboy. It was rather a surprise to learn that this ordinary-looking young man, engaged in this very ordinary

1 "Point of Rocks" has a historical record of much interest. " Robbers' Roost," a famous resort for outlaws in early days, was located not many miles to the southwest, and being the nearest ranch, the desperadoes that Infested the wilds of No Man's Land could often be found lounging in the vicinity of Point of Rocks. In April, 1882, John H. Carter (father of "Ez.," alluded to hereafter), a ranchman near Lakin, Kansas, stepped into a little shanty at that place, where the telegraph operator was sheltered from the blizzards of winter and the scorching suns of summer, and on the walls was tacked, " Notice ! $1,000 Reward !" It was a reward for the capture and conviction of Thomas Whooton and James McCuUom, two men who had murdered

a section-boss, near Fort Wallace, Kansas, for his money. It was offered by the Governor of Kansas, John P. St. John. Mr. Carter was deputy sheriff eft Ford county, and needed a thousand dollars just as badly as the Governor needed the desperadoes, and on Inquiry among immigrants going to Colorado he learned that two men had crossed the railroad about twenty miles to the east the day previous. Mr. Carter immediately started for the Point of Rocks to intercept them, as he knew they were making for that haven of safety for criminals. When he arrived, he found no one had been there recently. He made his errand known to the proprietor, Mr. Beattie, and the cowboys, and cautioned them under penalty not to manifest any suspicion If the men came that way.

After all had rolled up in their blankets for the night, two men on jaded horses rode up and asked to stay all night, which request was of course granted. Mr. Carter was in a room just next to where they had a lunch, and after a cup of coffee they lay down on the floor, and no doubt consoled themselves that they were safe beyond the strong arm of the law. Little indeed did Mr. Carter sleep that night. He was planning how to make sure of the murderers. As soon as the gray dawn betokened the coming day, he slipped his Sharps' rifle through a window, and walked through the room where the two men and cowboys lay. As soon as possible he was making his way In the direction 'of the jaded horses. When about half-way to them, he found a deep buffalo-wallow. In which he secreted himself. He only had a few minutes to wait, however, when \S'hooton came out of the bouse and made straight for the horses. When within about fifty feet. Carter rose and shouted, " Hands up!" The surprised desperado uttered a terrible oath, pulled out two large revolvers, and immediately sent bullets flying all

process of fuel-gathering, was worth some two hundred thousand dollars.

By diligent inquiry we learned that our men had camped six miles below on the preceding night, and had spent a part of the day before in resting up the stock. They were therefore not quite half a day ahead of us. We crossed the stream on their trail, and followed so hard through the sandhills that at about two o'clock we sighted them through one of the field-glasses. We pushed on rapidly, and overtook them just as they had pulled out of the trail to rest their animals and take a late dinner. Mutual greetings and recountals followed. Then we " hobbled out" the horses, and threw ourselves down in the shade of the wagon, where we ate heartily of the meal which Harry Robinson, who officiated as cook, had ready for us. Part of the bill of fare was antelope-steak, young Carter having killed a buck the day before.

Carter, or " Ez.," as we all called him, was to be quite a figure in the hunt; and a word about him might be well. He is a son of the well-known John Carter, of Hartland: the man who captured the two desperadoes

MTonnd Mr. Carter, who was so enwrapped with dust raised by the balls striking near his feet, and no doubt considerably surprised at the rapidity with which they were coming, that when he returned Whootou's fire he missed his mark entirely. By the time he could reach into his pocket for another cartridge, the other desperado was well on his way to the rescue of his "pard." Mr. Carter saw he must act quickly, and pushed the charge into the rifle and pulled the trigger. Whooton staggered, and finally fell to the ground. McCuUom had by this time arrived where the man lay writhing in pain, and commenced shooting as rapidly as the other had done, and with the same result. Having emptied both revolvers at Mr. Carter, excepting one load, he determined to finish him, so ran with all speed for the daring intruder ; but just as he was within ten steps, Carter was ready, and threw his gun up quickly, took the first shot, and McCuUom dropped dead.

When the smoke cleared away, Mr. Carter found the first man was shot through the shoulder, but not mortally wounded. He had emptied all the chambers of his weapons ; so had the other, except one. He found, also, all the triggers tied back, so as fast as the hammer was raised it would fall, and this accounted tor the rapid shooting. Mr. Carter turned his prisoner over to the sheriff of Ford county, and he finally recovered from £ls wounds. A mob took him from jail to enforce lynch law, but, after snatching a revolver from one of the mob and wounding several of his assailants, be escai>ed altogether. Mr. Carter not having succeeded In securing the conviction of either of the desperadoes, the reward could not be collected, but the Legislature made a thousand dollars appropriation for him, and a brave man was justly rewarded.

The foregoing Is only one of many such encounters in this historic locitlity. I am fortunate In being able to give a good halftone of the noted place. 0. J. Jones.

at the Point of Rocks. His life had been spent on the Plains, and although yet less than eighteen years of age, he had the reputation of being one of the best " ropers " on the range, and in all ways he was a plainsman of ex-

JOMN H. CARTER

perience. Colonel Jones had secured his services for this trip in view of the quick and close work with the lasso among the buffaloes. Charley Rude has already been mentioned as the teamster. We found all the boys jolly, and largely enthusiastic over the hunt.

The stock was all looking well, a& plenty of water had

been found in the buffalo-wallows, left from a recent rain, and it was therefore determined to push as far as we could into a much-dreaded portion of our journey — the drive across the " Flats."

We were now outside of Kansas, and a few miles across the line into that long neck of the Indian Territory-marked on the maps as the "Public Lands," but known all through the Southwest as "No Man's Land." Our road lay along one of the biggest cow-paths in the world —a great northern " through cattle " trail; the trail itself before us, a wide ramification of separating and approaching paths. We knew that there would be water somewhere along the trail, but how far we did not know, and could learn only by steady traveling until found. It seemed not improbable that we would be forced to make a "dry camp" that night, with exception of what water we had in the cask,— which would have been but a drop among so many horses, even if we had not had a herd of cows with us.

As our black horse was beginning to show signs of the extra work which the wily gray imposed upon him by means of that " stay-chain," we replaced him with a horse from the slower outfit, and pushed on rapidly in advance, to search for water.

The grandest sight of the day was a large band of wild horses, driven^ by a magnificent black stallion, which passed within half a mile of us. We watched them a long time through the glasses, and they were in sight for a distance of eight or ten miles. They were tired, and evidently being pursued by a "wild-horse outfit,"—of which sort of hunting parties there were several on the range.

Shortly after seeing these horses, we met a wild-horse hunter, who was badly lost, and most dilapidated-looking in his general appearance. A stampede had carried off all his stock, and instead of his catching the wild horses,

I An explanation ot this will b« found In a chapter farther on.

they had caught his own, with exception of the sorry nag which he .bestrode. The man looked thirsty, and we asked him if he would take a drink, handing him a canteen. His eyes sparkled as he took it, and he drew a long pull at its contents; but a pale, frightened look came over his face when he found that he had inadvertently taken a drink of—water 1 He was expecting something else. He asked the way to the " 0-X " ranch, and we told him; but he rode off in the opposite direction: he had lost confidence in us.

At six o'clock we found a buffalo-wallow which contained an abundance of water, and here we turned out and waited for the boys to come up. When they had done so, we hobbled out the horses, pitched the tent, and ate a supper fit for the gods. We found that the boys had brought a well-stocked mess-chest with them; and in fact, at no time on the trip did we lack for such delicacies as come within the compass of a tin can, or of a hunter's rifle.

Our tent that night was a busy and a jolly one. Colonel Jones and Ez. now began to practice with the lasso, in order to work up their skill and muscle for the coming trial on the buffalo calves; and during their drill hour we were any of us liable to lose a hat, or be tripped up by the heels; while the greyhound, "Don," was roped so often that he would howl whenever he heard the whiz of the lasso. The other members of the party were busy in various camp duties— attending to the cows, arranging the interior of the tent, or gathering supplies of the peculiar prairie fuel, "buffalo chips,"—several years old, no doubt.

The night passed without event, except that a heavy wind rose and blew down our tent. In the morning it was very raw and chilly, and we pulled on overcoats as we started out. Soon after we were on the way, the sky became overcast, and a chilly rain came up. So threatening was the sky that at one time, while in the breaks of

Goiigh creek (another dry stream), we thought we should have to go into camp. It was during this storm that we saw, far off to our left, a small bunch of rapidly moving objects. We had long since formed the habit of scanning with the glasses everything that moved; but up to this time we had found only cattle, wild horses, wolves, and antelopes. As soon as he saw these animals through the glasses, Colonel Jones gave an exclamation of surprise: "Why, they're going against the storm 1 " And a moment later added, "Yes, they 're buffalo, surel "

At once we all caught at the remaining glass. The animals were three or four miles distant, and the rain made everything obscure, so that their shapes could hardly be distinguished, although it could be seen that they were running furiously, and that directly into the wind.

"Boys," said Mr. Jones, "those are buffalo. The buffalo is the only animal that ever runs against a storm. Cattle or horses drift before it, but a buffalo, never."

Presently the course of the animals brought them within a mile and a half of us. Ricker and I kept the glasses on them, and at last we felt that we could really say we had seen our first buffalo. We could see the humps plainly, and could see how low they carried their heads as they went on in their tireless, lumbering gallop. There were only three — a cow, a yearling, and a calf. We were half-frantic to get at them, but Mr. Jones refused to tire the horses by a chase after so small a number, and much to our regret we drove on. Were we then indeed upon the buffalo range ? we asked. Were those indeed Imffalo, and had we indeed — we, who had longed all our lives to see a buffalo — seen these real, wild ones ? Then rose the question. Would we see any more ? When we thought of that, we begged Colonel Jones to turn back, and at one time nearly persuaded him to do so; but he assured us we would see plenty more.

We crossed Tepee creek, finding some water in pools near the trail. Beyond that, the first

water was the

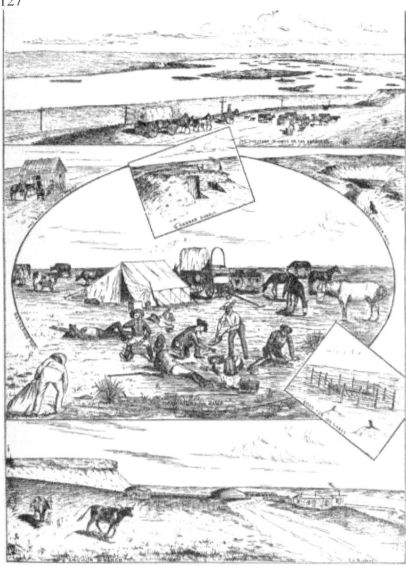

SCENES ON THE JOURNEY

North Fork of the Canadian, here known as the Beaver; and as we were now assured that there was enough along the trail for our cattle, we pushed on across to the latter stream, and took dinner at the "Anchor D " ranch, pretty-near the " jumping-off place " of the world, it being close to the south line of the Neutral Strip and the north line of Texas. On the range, the different cattle outfits are known only by their brands, and a man's ranch goes by the name of his brand, and not by his name. Thus we had heard of the " 0-X " ranch, the "T_V Bar" ranch, etc., etc., but had no idea as to who owned them. We found that the "AnchorD " brand belonged to E. C. Dudley, of Boston, who has about 15,000 head of cattle on this southern ranch, and about as many more on his ranch in Wyoming. Mr. Dudley was not at home; but we ate his bread and bacon just the same.

We were now about one hundred and fifty miles from our starting-point, well down to where we might expect to see or hear of the buffaloes; but, though we made inquiry at the ranch, we could get no news of the herd. They might be at a point known as "Company M," or down on the Agua Frio, or there might be water enough along the San Francisco to hold them, or they might be out on the Flats, at some water-hole known only to themselves : nobody seemed to know. We were not surprised at the seeming ignorance, for we knew that the cattlemen would not tell us of the herd if they were within ten miles of us; and Colonel Jones says he always finds buffalo in the opposite direction from that advised to go. Such jjerquisites as pertain to calf-hunting, the cowboys usually prefer to retain for themselves; besides, seeing in all visitors possible forerunners of the dreaded "grangers," the cattlemen are reticent on that account, and will, if possible, send a man out of the country as ignorant as he came in, and devoid of even the knowledge of the " lay of the land " which a buffalo-hunt would give him. There-

Scene in CB Ranche—Beaver Co, Oklahoma— CE Dodley R.I.P.

fore our leader was not in the least put out by this general "blankness" in regard to the buffalo, and announced to us his intention of making at once for the headwaters of the Beaver,

We were now perhaps thirty miles in advance of the slow-moving heavy wagon, but instructions had been left for the boys to take our trail up the Beaver, and to shape their course for the upper pools of that stream, and there pitch the main camp while we were scouting for the herd with our lighter vehicle. We had with us two extra running-horses,— the gray, and the bay mare "Jennie." The black runner was hitched in with a heavy mate at the buggy. We had also plenty of hobbles for tying the calves if caught, and young Carter was with us in the buggy, ready for work if the herd should be sighted.

We crowded the horses up the trail until it left the breaks of the Beaver, then drove out on the high prairies. We spun across a great expanse, picked our way across the North Fork of the Beaver, and swung off to the left, heading for the upper pools of the main stream, which we knew were dry above a certain point, twenty miles uj^. All the time, the glasses were kept in play, and nothing within ten miles escaped us.

The sun was getting well on in his last quarter, and we were trundling along just at the edge of the breaks of the South Fork, when our eyes were caught by a cloud of dust rising from the other side of a little ridge. We snatched up the glasses. The cloud came nearer. It was approaching. It swung up over the crest. Huge black forms — twenty—thirty — fifty—sixty — rolled and surged along with it, heading almost toward us. No need of glasses now. Our tongues " froze stiff " over the common thought, until, a second later, our leader sprang <5lear of the buggy at a single bound, and shouted in a voice like a bugle —

"Get out the horses 1 They 're buffalo, by Jupiter! •Give me the lasso! "

That they were indeed buffalo, every drop of blood in our veins was attesting. On they came — huge, rolling black hulks enveloped in a circling cloud of dust. A grand "view halloa" burst from us as they passed. They were running strung out in line, buffalo-fashion, and square into the wind. They must have scented us, and obviously had first taken fright when, at a distance of three-quarters of a mile or more, they had "got the wind" of us; but they paid no attention to us as they held on their mad and headlong flight. They passed within three hundred yards, bearing to the left; we could easily have shot into them if desired.

How vanished every ache, pain, and thought of weariness 1 It was not ground we touched, nor hot air we breathed. We were not creatures hampered with flesh and blood, but borne up on the wings of the hunter's exaltation. The very horses snorted and tugged at their ropes. The greyhound flashed out like an arrow from a bow, and, laying a cunning angle for himself, ran into the herd almost at once, where he worried at a yearling, until kicked and beaten out of the dust-cloud; and realizing that the game was too large for him, he ran back to the team and fairly begged us to come on.

The horses were nearly ready. At the first flash of conviction every man was on the ground, and tugging at the load to get out the calf-hobbles,— which of course were at the bottom of the wagon. Then a saddle had to be improvised; a lasso got tangled up, and a bridle was lost just as it was needed. The horses were not saddled, or even bridled, for we were not expecting buffaloes so soon. Everything had to be done in a moment. Colonel Jones, for an old buffalo-hunter, showed himself at least free from all stoicism, and was fairly wild to get into the chase. Never was change in a man's demeanor more sudden. His eyes were riveted on the flying dust-cloud, and he tightened up his saddle-cinch instinctively and without looking at it. But if everything had to be done quickly,

everything was quickly done, and away flashed the two riders, coiling up the long lassos as the horses ran.

The third running-horse could not be spared from the team, as the wagon must follow the chase to pick up the calves. Ricker and myself therefore remained for that duty. We bundled the disordered baggage back into the wagon, sprang on top of it, and whipped off in pursuit, going at the wildest rate I ever tried on wheels, and bound to "get there" if the running-gear held together. The wagon jumped over dog-holes, hummocks and sinks, and the springs clashed together at every bound; but we managed to hold on some way,— can't tell how,—and laid the team flat down in our determination to be in with the crowd.

Short as the time of preparation had been, the herd had passed, and was over a mile away before the riders started. Yet Colonel Jones, after the first burst of racing-speed, held back the pace, and galloped easily on in the rear of the herd, restraining the eagerness of the])ay mare Jennie to close in on the herd. Let it not be supposed that all horses are able to close in at once with these animals. There are few horses which can do so at all. The buft'alo appears clumsy, even when in motion, but its actual speed is surprising, and it holds its gait wonderfully well. In running its action is not stiff-legged, like that of a cow, which places her hind feet directly in the print of the front ones; but to the contrary, the buffalo spreads the hind feet well apart, like a horse, and throws them clear in front of the fore feet, hurling its great body on in a style not unlike that of the racer. The apparent clumsiness of the gait probably arises from the large hump, and from the fact that the buffalo always runs with its nose almost against the ground. The hind feet come up almost on either side of the nose when the animal is at full speed. When running together in large numbers their speed is materially reduced, and it is then that a horseman can most easily approach them. A cow and her calf, alone

FORTY YEARS OF ADVENTURES

■^'/fciT^tX

and at a distance from the herd, would say good-bj'e to almost any horse, with a start of a quarter of a mile. Calves a month old appear to run about as well as the older animals.

But all this time my companion and I were not indulging in abstractions, but were trying to overtake the riders. All at once the herd disappeared over a ridge. Then the cloud of dust appeared over the top, and began swinging off to the right. Like a flash the conduct of the riders changed. With a common impulse they leaned forward in the saddles. The horses sprang forward at four times their original speed, and making an angle of forty-five degrees to their former course, they swept off to the right, across our track, sailed — flew — drifted up along the ridge; topped it; disappeared. Half a mile was saved; and we knew the run was on just beyond the ridge. How we crossed the intervening space I do not know, but in a moment we were over the hill, and making sharp to the right on the other side,— tearing down to where we could see the horsemen leaping into the very edge of the blinding cloud. Colonel Jones and "Jennie" were ahead; the mare seemed to fly. The sight was a grand one. With head well down and nostrils wide, the bay beauty tore in on them, eager as her rider, and was never once called on with the spur. She crowded into the dust, into the herd, pushed out from it a cow and calf, and lay alongside of them in her stride. Then we saw her rider lean forward. Up came his hand, circling the wide coil of the rope. We could almost hear it whistle through the air. The next instant out it flew. In a flash the dust was gone, and there was Colonel Jones kneeling on toj) of a struggling little tawny object, while Jennie stood by looking on complacently. A second later the little object was hobbling around upon the grass alone; Colonel Jones was following young Carter now, and we were making for the calf. The herd at once swept out of sight, and we of course saw no more of it, for we were'

busy with the captive, and had no more fortunate angles offered to save distance.

We drove up to the first victim. He was a comical-looking, round-headed, curly little rascal; we laughed when approaching him. The first thing he did was to utter a hoarse bawl, and charge at us with head down. In doing this, of course the hobble tripped him, and he turned a somersault. Before he could recover, we sat down on top of him—the first buffalo calf we had ever seen. We found that he was secured in precisely the best and most effectual way that could have been devised. The hobble was made of several strands of untwisted rope. At the middle it was tied in a large loop, which was slipped over the calf's head; the two loose ends — which were left of just that length which experience told was right—were slip-noosed. These loops were fastened just above each hind foot, where they sat tight on the i^astern joint, and drew the tighter for each struggle the calf made to free itself. Thus shackled, the captive was unable to make any progress, but at the same time was not choked, or held in any way calculated to injure it. This was the system of calf-hobbling devised after the experience of other hunts. Of course, the adjusting of the hobble took but an instant; and that was necessary, for even after the delay of a minute the herd would gain ground enough to make it hard to overtake.

As we afterwards learned, Carter and the gray horse got into the edge of the herd easily enough, but the horse could not be pushed in close enough for roping-distance, as he was afraid of the buffalo. Carter spurred and "quirted" him in vain; he was just the same old " gray devil," and needed the " stay-chain." Carter was furious at his inability to reach a calf. Colonel Jones again passed him, and went into the herd within two miles of the place where the first calf was caught. He missed his cast at the next calf, but the mare did not stop. As she ran alongside of the now angry animal. Colonel Jones stooped down and caught it by the tail, turning it heels over head, and' before it could rise the Colonel was on top, held it in his arms, and then hobbled it. This was a large bull calf, the largest taken on the entire hunt, and he made a big fight after his fall. It was not difficult to turn him over by the tail,— for the largest Texas steer can be thrown headlong by a horseman in the same manner, while at full speed. But the calf was like a basketful of eels to hold.

The last calf was caught by Carter, who roped it neatly as Colonel Jones cut it out of the herd and turned it toward him. This was a fine heifer calf, and was apparently the idol of her mother's heart, for the latter came very near making a casualty the price of the capture. As soon as the calf was roped, the cow left the herd and charged on Carter viciously as he bent over his victim. Seeing the danger. Colonel Jones rode up just in time, and drove the cow off for a moment; but she returned again and again, and finally began charging at him whenever he came near: so that, much as he regretted it, he was compelled to shoot her with his revolver, killing her almost instantly. This was an unwished result, and was much deplored, for we came, not to slay, but to rescue.

After this last affair was over, both rode on after the herd, which was by this time far toward the darkening horizon. The horses were now well " blown," for they had run in on the herd not only once, twice, but three times, and had gone a distance of eight or ten miles from the start. Colonel Jones soon pulled up, and turned back to find the wagon ; but Carter was angry at his horse, and followed the herd until upon its flanks, though he could not get the gray within roping-distance. The horse came back pretty well "winded," and with Carter swearing at him for a coward. In the meantime my companion and I had, by dint of severe exertion, got the first calf tied up more firmly and secured in the light, wagon, where it required all of our strength to keep it until we devised the plan of piling the heavy tent upon it. We then drove

on along the trail, using the glass all the time to sight the next captive,— which we presently did, at a distance of over a mile from us. We repeated our tactics here, having a great time with this big fellow; then drove on, meeting Colonel Jones before we got to the last calf. Part of the time we had not kept to the trail, but had cut across the curves the herd made, depending on the glass to locate any calf that might be left. As it was possible and quite easy to miss seeing so small an object at such long distances, we were glad to learn that we had found all that had been caught.

It was nearly dark by the time we had the last calf in the wagon, and as soon as Carter came up, ,all started back toward the Beaver. We could not camp, for we had no water, and the horses needed it sadly. As there was none elsewhere within twenty miles, it will be seen how absolutely necessary it was that we find the river. It should be remembered that this river had no water in it, except at certain places; and we did not yet know where those places were. We might have to drive twenty miles after getting to the river-bed, and might have to travel nearly that far in trying to get down through the breaks which fenced in the stream. All this was pretty near to being serious; but it was one of the exigencies of buffalo-hunting,— so we said nothing, but turned in the direction where we knew the stream lay, and ran by the compass and the stars, driving in darkness which grew more dense at every moment. If our leader had been a man inexperienced on the Plains, or unacquainted with the general lay of the country, we would have had a dry camp that night, and would in all probability have lost our calves, to say nothing of any possible discomfiture to ourselves, or injury to our horses.

In an hour or so we came to the edge of the breaks, and began to hunt a way down through them. Ricker and Carter rode off to the right, while Colonel Jones drove a little to the left. We noticed that all the trails appeared to converge at the head of a certain draw, and after driving across them till that fact was established, we knew that they led to water. We therefore followed down this draw, and fired signals for the boys to come in. Presently we heard Carter fire, he having got out on a point at our left. We called to him, and he found his way down into the draw. Ricker had not come in, and did not answer any signal; so, fearing he was lost. Carter went back after him. Colonel Jones and myself, following the draw, presently got into the valley and found water. There was not much, and it was tramped up by cattle and had several dead carcasses in it; but still it was icater, and we were glad to find it.

By the time we had the horses out, and the baggage on the ground, Ricker and Carter got into camp, the former insisting that he was one of the sort that didn't get lost. We all fell to and proceeded to water the horses and get camp up. We found there was no axe or hatchet with us, but were lucky enough to find a hard stone, with which we drove our tent-pins — for it looked like rain, and we concluded to pitch the tent. We had no coffee-mill; but an old buffalo-skull, a bit of canvas and the stone served instead.

Presently the clouds broke, and the southern moon peeped out brightly. It revealed another pool of water below us, and we could see a bunch of ducks upon it. As we had not stopped to butcher our bufi'alo, we had no meat; so Ricker took his three-barrel and shot four ducks, which Ez. fished out with his lasso. When we went down to the water we heard something flopping in it, and discovered that it was fairly alive with bullhead fish. We therefore supposed that the running water could not be very far away. A search soon revealed that a succession of pools began a short distance below our camp. While investigating this matter, a plowed furrow, running down near to the bank of the stream, caught Colonel Jones's attention, and following it up he

found a little patch of breaking, a dugout, and a welL He knew then that we were at Lee Howard's cabin, on the very headwaters of the Beaver, in the Neutral Strip ("No Man's Land"). Howard is a half-hunter, half-freigbter, and half-ranchman, who has squatted on this claim, away out of the world. The water will make him rich some day.

The owner of the dugout was not at home, but we got> some good water at his well, and helped ourselves to a " Dutch oven," a hammer, a piece of kindling-wood, and a few other things which we found lying around, and which we thought would do more good at our camp than where they were. Then, as our little fire of " chips " was going nicely, Ez. soon had some bread baking, the coffeepot simmering, and some bacon and skinned teal sizzling in the frying-pan. Our stove was a buffalo-skull, and our shovel a shoulder-blade. No Man's Land is entirely devoid of timber, and even of small sticks.

While we were getting supper and arranging the tent, Colonel Jones was busy with the calves. Taking a long rope, he stretched it along the ground, fastening the ends to two strong tent-pins, driven to the head in the ground. On this rope he strung his calves, like fish on a trot-line, each calf being tied by the neck, and with its limbs left free. This arrangement gave them plenty of play and kept them from injury, while at the same time it rendered their escape impossible. The little fellows were vigorous and full of fight, and whenever anyone came near they would lower their heads and come at him with a short bawl. We amused ourselves by pushing each other upon them, and found by experience that they could butt hard enough to knock a man entirely off his feet. They spent most of their time standing with head down, back humped up, and tail cocked out, pawing the ground for all the world like an old bull, and from time to time uttering short, hoarse bawls, which sounded much more like the grunt of a hog than the bleat of a calf.

LEE HOWARD.

CHARLES RUDE.

Interested in the actions of our strange and wild little captives, we sat beside them after supper until a late hour. Then we rolled up in our blankets and went to sleep, telling each other that we were the luckiest fellows in all the world.

CHAPTER IX

SECOND CALF-HUNT (Continued)

MILKING A BUFFALO COW EXCELLENT BUTTER CAUSED BY

THE JOSTLE OF THE WAGON—DOMESTIC COWS ARRIVE

LONG MARCH TO THE SOUTHWEST—COLONEL JONES MIRACULOUSLY

CAPTURES A CALF—" TENDERFEET " AFTER BUFFALO BULLS—TOOK TWO TO

KILL ONE, AND THEN didn't kill HIM—CLOUD OF SMOKE PROVED TO BE

DUST— "the HEBdI the HERD ! " COLONEL JONES

NEVER LOST, BY DAY OR NIGHT—"GET DOWN AND

crawl" —BUFFALO IN CAMP THE COLONEL AWAY, BUT

HOLES ARE CUT IN HIS TENT THROUGH WHICH TO SHOOT, JUST THE

SAME—CALF-HUNTERS RETURN TO CAMP IN A DEPLORABLE CONDITION —

HORSES LEFT TO DIE—PLENTY OF CALVES, BUT NO WATER — TENDERFEET NOT

SATISFIED — WANTED ANOTHER TRIAL, THEN ANOTHER

EARLY on the morning of the 14th of May we wer^ astir and preparing for the day's work. We could not expect the main outfit up until the following day, and feared we would lose all our calves before it arrived, for we had not a cow with us, of course, and not even a can of condensed milk. It was decided to lasso a range cow, and milk her by force; but at that early hour no cattle had yet come in to water, and there were none in sight among the breaks. All that could be done, therefore, was to try to induce our panting and suffering little captives to drink of the water which we offered them; but they refused to be comforted, and in-

(140)

BUTTER FROM MILK OF A BUFFALO COW 141

dignantly butted the waterpail endways whenever it was left near them, or charged headlong at a wet rag or a stick.

Colonel Jones concluded to go out on the range and try to find the herd again, then to return, and in the evening either rope a range cow, or drive down in the night to meet our team and get some condensed milk to keej) the calves alive until the domestic cows would arrive. Accordingly, he, Ricker and Carter started out with all the horses, directly after breakfast. It fell to my lot to remain and guard the camp — a duty which, in view of a possible buffalo-chase, I did not relish very much.

At three o'clock our scouting-party returned. They had not found the herd, but had met two buffalo cows, undoubtedly the mothers of the captured calves, whose maternal instinct had led them to return in search of their offspring. One cow was killed for meat; her udder was full of milk, and as there was no water to be had, the Colonel concluded to fill a canteen with the precious fluid, as the day was very hot. After milking the canteen about half-full he corked it up and tossed it into the spring wagon. After about two hours of travel he concluded to take a drink, but the fluid would not come out, and he concluded there must be a dead mouse or some kind of trash in the can. By close observation it was discovered the jostling of the w^agon had churned the milk into butter, which was as solid and yellow as that of the best Jersey right from the creamery, and satisfactory in quantity,— all of which was left in the can until the camp was reached, when it was extracted, salted, and we had one grand feast of hot biscuits and buffalo butter. The wonderful richness of the milk and deliciousness of the butter nerved our leader up in his endeavors to domesticate this valuable animal.

During the day a great scope of country had been covered, but no further signs of buffalo were found, and no water could be discovered anywhere. The flats were entirely dry. It was a problem where the buffalo could be.

Colonel Jones now started down the Beaver to meet the team, giving neither himself nor his horses any rest,— for it was imperative that we get milk, or we would lose our calves. The little fellows began to look gaunt, their tongues black and swollen, hanging from their mouths, while they continually uttered their hoarse, groaning grunts of complaint. The remainder of the party began to move the camp up nearer to the edge of the bluff, where the stench of the decaying carcasses which lay in the water would be less unendurable. The weather in tlie daytime was very warm, though the nights in that country are always cool.

A couple of hours after dark we heard repeated halloos and shots. We replied, and soon heard voices of our own party, and knew that by some unprecedentedly good generalship they had succeeded in getting the cows in,— a full day earlier than they could reasonably be expected. It happened that Colonel Jones went down just in time, for if he had not met them they would have kept on up the flats, and passed our camp, to wander no one knew how far into the waterless country.

Everything was now confusion in camp. We had a great many animals to take care of, and it necessitated work. The cows had all to be lassoed and hobbled — a matter which they always resented; the horses to be watered; supper to cook, and a hundred other things to be done. One of the first of these duties was the feeding of the buffalo calves; and this was one of the most interesting features of the whole hunt. Ez. roped a certain old . red cow, of about as near the right color as any we had, and hobbled her securely fore and aft; then we picked out the youngest calf, and approached — the little fellow butting and fighting viciously. The cow turned her head, and promptly kicked so hard she broke the hobble and sent the calf a somersault to begin with. This did not daunt it, however, and it returned, seeming to take in the situation at a glance. It was strange, but after a few

moments this cow and buffalo calf seemed to "take to " each other. The best of relations were established between them, and within an hour the curly little rascal was lying down by the side of his new mother, chuck full of milk, and "happy as a clam." This calf was never wild after that, but could be approached easily, and was perfectly docile. In the morning we let it loose near the cow, and it followed her about, kicking up its heels and bawling out of very exuberance of spirits. The next day after, the cows were hobbled and the calves' lariats were allowed to drag loose; yet they never made any attempt to escape — even under certain strange circumstances (which will afterward be described). To-day the "little " calf is the tamest on Colonel Jones's ranch, and the "old red stripper" (as she is called, for she has had no calf of her own for three years) is its devoted mother. This cow took a great notion to all the buffalo calves, and would allow two of them to suckle at once, though she would drive off a domestic calf. The buffaloes were emphatic, imperious little scamps, and she seemed to take a fancy to them.

The other calves gave some trouble. They did not take kindly to the white cow which was introduced to them as their stepmother, nor did she to them. One of the calves preferred a beer-bottle, covered with a rag; while the last one, the big bull calf, would drink from nothing but a bucket — though he made a very good supper in that way. And, it may not .be believed, but it is true, he would never afterw-^ard drink out of any but that particular pail, which happened to be painted white outside and in. If any other.was offered him, he would butt it over at once, and prance around, pawing at the dirt, until some one would call out, " Give him the white pail!" The scenes of that night and of the succeeding days, in trying to teach the buffalo calves to assume their new relations, were full of action and spirit, and went to make up a history of interesting experiences that never can be duplicated.

Will excHange work for Old Russian Samavars, Copper ami Brass Dishes, Cand'»-Sticks. Indian Goods and Curios.

FORTY YEARS OF ADVENTURES

It was late when our camp sank to rest that night. The following day was the Sabbath, and we rested, with exception of the "artist fellow," who made some drawings in and about the camp.

The next day we started for "Company M," a certain water-hole situated in a valley, where, years ago, a Company M of U. S. troops were snawed in and spent the winter. In the natural caves where they were mostly quartered there can be seen to-day numerous names cut into the rock, and also loopholes which they made when fighting the Indians. "Company M " is near the west boundary of No Man's Land. There is no house or ranch there, and none nearer than the cabin at our camp; yet hundreds of cattle water at the scanty seepage of the sandy river-bed. Somebody will get rich there, some day.

We drove to Company M with both wagons, taking all the horses but one, and plenty of supplies for a week's trip. We left the bulk of our load at the home camp, covered by the cook-tent. All the cows were also left, and also the buffalo calves. The duty of taking care of the home camp faid all the stock devolved upon Robinson, who was told unceremoniously not to be surprised if we did not get back in a week, or if we did n't get back at all.

We drove between fifty and sixty miles that day, and having a late start, did not all reach Company M until nine o'clock at night. We found but little water, but dug a hole in the sand, and got enough for our use. Out of all the fresh meat we had killed, we had brought none with us, and lived on salt pork until, the day following, we shot a cottontail rabbit or two with rifles, and with the shotgun killed a lot of the big sickle-billed curlews which were so numerous there. We did not kill any antelope at this water, although Ricker and I, who kept camp together, did some brilliant missing at them. They often came in, and if it had not been so hot, and we so lazy, we —

10

could have gotten one on any day. Ricker killed a coyote, but we did not eat it.

For two days the light wagon scoured the country for fifty miles round about, traveling hard and diligently in a most energetic though fruitless effort to find some trace of the herd. On one day three buffaloes were seen, but none with calves; so they were not followed. As in all this time powerful field-glasses were in use, it may be seen that the buffaloes were very, very few in that country. We began to be discouraged — all except our leader, whose resolve to " find the herd " seemed never to flag.

One morning we were wakened by a grand coyote chorus, and before daylight had breakfast over. Just as the sun was rising we saw a little bunch of animals slowly walking toward us, about two miles distant, and on the other side of a wire fence. We turned the glasses on them. They looked like buffaloes. We studied them. They looked wonderfully like buffaloes. We divided in our opinions. Colonel Jones thought they were buffaloes; but we did not wonder at that, because, being "Buffalo Jones," he thought everything he saw was a buffalo. Ez. didn't know; Charley didn't care; Ricker was not certain; I knew all the time they were only cattle. Finally, Colonel Jones fired a shot over toward them from his rifle. At once they strung out into line and tailed off, as hard as they could go. Cattle do not run at the sound of a gun ; buffaloes always do—that is a habit acquired since they have been hunted so much.

In a moment Colonel Jones and Ez. were in saddles and racing ahead, with Ricker and myself a good second in the light wagon, and Charley following with the mule team. We all got across the wire fence, I don't know just how, and followed after the dust-cloud. The wagons were far behind, when, after a half-hour's breathless drive, we saw a horseman appear on the crest of a distant ridge, and he gave us the Plains signal to " Come ahead,"—which is done by riding at right angles to those called if mounted,

■or by repeatedly rising and squatting down if one is on foot. We hurried on, and soon by the glass made out the figure to be Carter, and saw that he had at the end of his lasso a lively red object which we knew to be another buffalo calf. Ez. came riding down on a gallop, the calf running parallel, with the rope stretched tightly. This was the curliest calf caught on the trip, and a fine prize she was.

Ez. had lost his hat, and we learned that Colonel Jones had gone back along the trail to find it and his field-glass, which had been lost in the chase — both of which were found. The calf caught was the only one in the herd, and there were but a dozen buffaloes all told — all cows.

The calf was caught under rather peculiar circumstances. Both horsemen were crowding it; Colonel Jones cast for it, but it dodged the noose, and ran square in front of his horse. The latter ran against it, and both fell, knocking the calf fully fifteen feet away, and throwing Colonel Jones headlong. The latter — according to Jiis version — was satisfied, as he passed through the air, that the fall would kill him; but concluded that it would be as well to go into another world with a calf in his arms as in any other way. He therefore, either by chance or ■by Providence, fell directly on top of the calf, caught it in his arms, and held on until Carter roped it. It was a ludicrous and altogether lucky accident. Neither man, horse nor calf seemed to be much injured.

We bundled the calf into the big wagon, and headed northeast in the direction of our main camp, through terrible sandhills, which made rapid travel impossible. The •day was very warm. We gave the horses all the water left, and started on with many misgivings. We were on the opposite side of the Beaver from that on which we had come up, and the stream made a big bend to the -south, around which we had to travel. Besides, other .streams made into it (all dry, of course), and as the breaks along these are often impassable for some distance up and down, we did not know how far we might have to travel.

We paid little attention to game that day, although we saw a great many antelopes and wolves, but did not stop — except to kill a rattlesnake or two, which we skinned as we rode along.

We did not stop for dinner, but spent our time trying to find out where we were. And, thanks to fortune and hard driving, we at last got up to a little mesa which was familiar, and soon thereafter struck a trail and better country for traveling. We were truly thankful that our leader was not a " tenderfoot " ; for such had best not go hunting in that country, unless he wants to die crazy, and bleach his bones among the sandhills.

At last we saw a bold front of rock, bearing on its brow a little monument or pyramid. (On the other side of the valley was a large gray wolf looking wistfully at our camp.) This we knew was the "Tepee Rock," which stood just above our camp. (These "tepee rocks"—so called from their shape, and are made of stones or large blocks of sod — are signs built up by wild-horse hunters, to mark the vicinity of water, and plainsmen steer for them when thirsty.) In a few moments we came out upon a ridge, and our white tent lay before us, a thin blue shaft of smoke piercing the sultry evening air, and saying somewhat of supper when we should be cool. The water-pool shone in the evening sun, and the cattle were grazing about it or lying near. Our jaded horses pitched their ears forward, and actually broke into a trot. The long and wearisome day was over.

The mule team, with Charley and Ez., came in late. We were thankful that the day had been no worse. During our absence one of the calves had died — the only heifer calf we had, and therefore most valued, of course. This made us feel sad; so on the whole it was rather a demoralized crowd of hunters that gathered around our late supper that night.

After the disastrous march from Company M it became necessary to lie in camp to rest the horses, which were well-nigh broken down under the severe tasks which had been imposed upon them.

One afternoon the camp was out of meat, and Colonel Jones started out to stalk some antelopes he saw coming in. He followed them up into the breaks north of the river, and we heard him shoot. Then presently we saw him coming on a dead run, and with an expression on his face which made us think he had stirred up a bunch of Indians. We sat up and looked at him. He bolted for the nearest saddle, slung it over the black runner, and called out:

" Get out the horses, boys 1 Four bulls just ran out on the other side when I shot ! "

In a moment Ricker was astride of bay Jennie and I of the gray canterer, Colonel Jones's face bearing a look of grim happiness. Calling out to the boys to follow with the light wagon, he turned to us and said:

"Now, boys, you 're going to have that shot at a bull which I have been promising you."

We wanted to go a little faster, then. Colonel Jones rode ahead through the breaks, and found the trail. The bulls had not yet reached the water, and ran when he shot at the antelope. The fact of their running while all the cattle stood still (the valley was full of cattle at that hour) was what had attracted his attention. The shot might therefore be called a lucky one. After a time the trail was found, and our leader cautiously followed it up through the breaks, not knowing how far the game had run. At last he gave us the signal to come on, and we galloped up to the top of the level country. There, four miles ahead, running into the wind, and looming up as large as churches in the streaming mirage which surrounded them, were four huge objects — the buffalo bulls I Down we leaned in the saddles, and with rifles tightly clutched under our knees and reins loose on the horses*

necks, away we flew in pursuit. The horses ran beautifully together, the little gray doing wonders, and seeming to know that it would be unfortunate for him to tarry by^ the wayside at that particular hour.

The bulls were running directly from us, and neither saw nor winded us. After a time they slackened their pace, and then fell into a walk.

"See ! See ! They're going to feed, I do believe ! " cried our leader.

Presently they began to sink low and lower down from our sight. They were going over a ridge. " Quick I Ridel" the Colonel called out; and in a moment we were-racing into a long, low draw which made off to the left. Here we straightened up in the saddles and rode hard to get in before the bulls came in sight.

But they did not come in sight. They were feeding. Closer and closer we bore in, and finally stopped at the-edge of the ridge where they had disappeared. In a providential little hollow we left the horses, throwing the-bridle-reins over their heads; and then we crawled up, parted a little clump of grass, and one at a time took a look at those huge,"black, shaggy, grand-looking animals. It seemed like a dream. People had said the buffalo were gone. I had never hoped to see one thus. Yet those great creatures standing there, lying there, grazing there — those were buffalo; and yet we were — wel The thought was preposterous. It could not be true I

A grim smile was on Colonel Jones's face.

"Five hundred yards," said he; "we'll stalk them." Was the man mad ? They could not be over one hundred yards away. And how could one stalk anything on that flat floor of a country, where you could see a man ten miles in any other direction?—and we could get no closer.

But now the skill of the old buffalo-hunter began to assert itself. We found he knew more in a minute than we did in all the rest of the year. We made a big circle

back and away from our horses, and got the wind to suit us; crawled over a ridge into another draw we had not seen; followed it up half a mile; squirmed over another ridge; worked this way and that, lying flat out much of the time, and growing fearfully warm in the hot sun ; and finally, after three-quarters of an hour of hard work, we found we were some two or three hundred yards nearer the game.

Then, with all possible care, we laid ourselves flat along the earth, and inch by inch crept up to the edge of the shallow little basin in which the bulls were standing. Long before this we had pushed the cartridges into the barrels of the repeaters, dreading the rattle of the levers if we should load close to the game; now, fearing even the tick of the lock, we pushed our guns ahead of us as we crawled. Inch by inch, through five long minutes, we worked for the clump of sagebrush where we must stop. We reached it. " Breathe a little," softly whispered our leader. We breathed a little — mighty little, I did. It was very warm. Not a man of us appeared excited, however, and we coolly arranged the plan of the attack.

" Both of you fire at the big bull on the right," whispered Colonel Jones, "and I '11 kill the one standing on thejeft."

Ricker and I whispered an objection. We did not wish to shoot at the same bull. We wanted to get a head apiece, and each be sure he had killed his own.

" But don't you see," was the reply, "that only two are standing right? I'll give one of you the head I kill. You go ahead; it '11 take both of you to kill your bull — and then you won't get him ! "

We demurred; but what he said was true. One bull was lying down and the fourth Avas standing with his head square away from us. A moment later, the two big bulls advanced directly toward us. They were grand-looking fellows, but how ferocious they looked, with their great heads all covered with shaggy mane 1 Slowly they swung round; they stood right.

" Whist 1 " hissed out our leader. Then, according to the agreement, Ricker felt for his aim, and Mr. Jones began to count. "One." I was dead on the bull's lungs. *' Two." My elbow trembled. We were all lying flat on our stomachs. Oh, horrors 1 I had swung clear off, and it was time for "Three." Bang I went Ricker's shot. The bulls wheeled. I caught hair on my ivory front sight at the instant, and bang! went mine. Bang! came Colonel Jones's, very late. On one knee, now, each of us turned down the lever as fast as he could catch sight, and spit a pile of empty 45 shells in front of him. Our bull was acting groggy. A second bull pulled his left hind leg heavily. The elevations grew, climbed. Some of the shots cut dust, and some did not. The bulls were getting away in spite of us. The shots grew less frequent. Colonel Jones explained how, at his first shot, the lever of his gun had been prevented from driving up the safety-bolt by sand getting into the little groove, and when he pulled the trigger the bolt held it and the hammer did not fall. The bulls were still going. But see! — one is getting sick. He is reeling. They pass a little ridge. They appear beyond. There are only three!

But what is that dust-cloud here at the right, full of running figures strung out in line ? Our leader springs to his feet. "The herd! The herd 1 " he cries.

And now we were in the midst of one of those intensely animated scenes which come but once in a lifetime. There at the left ran the three bulls: four, less one. At the right, fifty cows and calves were in plain sight. Behind us—thank Fortune! Mr. Rude understood his business — there came sweeping up on the full run the horses and wagon, Mr. Rude leading the three running-horses, which they had wisely picked up when they heard us shoot. A moment later, the calf-hunt was on, and Ricker and I were alone on the prairie, watching three fleeting clouds of dust, and wishing we had another horse l>esides the gray. Then we started out to find the fallen bull.

At last, riding over a ridge into a little draw, I came right upon him. He was down on his knees when I first saw him, and when he saw me made a frantic effort to get up. I never saw anything look quite so wicked; his hair was turned forward over his face, and his eyes fairly blazed. The gray horse was scared fairly silly,— and I was in sympathy with the horse. I could not at first get him in very close, so that, what with his dancing and my own eagerness, I missed that whole, entire buffalo four times with my revolver as I circled around him. Then I reloaded in a hurry, and as I passed in front of him managed to put a bullet square in his right eye. At this the great animal sunk down lower and lower, and then rolled over quite dead — I in the meantime putting three other balls into him.

Ricker was back about a quarter of a mile, and I rode to him, and, as he avers, yelling like an Indian. We then together approached the fallen monarch, and for some moments stood regarding the vast proportions of the lifeless body. It was a huge beast, as large, apparently, as two domestic oxen, and lay a black island on the surrounding sea of gray. Ragged and rugged and weather-beaten, with every line of -its frame suggesting burly strength, it was almost pitiful to see the helpless backward cast of the great head, and to mark the rapid glazing of the eye which a moment before rolled in a tameless rage.

We had no idea how the calf-hunters were faring; we didn't worry much about it. We cared less for "the ninety and nine " cows and calves that got away than for the one old bull that went not astray. We got the best supper the mess-box afforded, and sat late into the night, after we had fed the calves and hobbled out our animals, going over the story of our first bull, and telling how Colonel Jones offered us the head of the bull he was '" going to kill."

We did not expect the calf-hunters back until the fol-

lowing day, and therefore did not keep up any fire, but along toward midnight rolled ourselves up and went to sleep. Not long thereafter, one of us awoke, drowsily asking, "Who was that shot?" One of our party responded, "Indians!" We all roused up, and listened. Another shot was heard, faint in the distance. The night was black as Erebus. We fired several shots ourselves, and waited. Presently there came a long-drawn " Halloa 1" We shouted in response. " Some fellows lost out on the flats," we said, By-and-by came the rattle of wheels in the dark, coming down the canon.

"Get up there, you lazy fellows, and get some supper," called out a voice.

Our nightly visitors proved to be our own party, who by dint of hard driving — and, I shall always think, of sheer luck rather than skill — had managed in some manner to find their way back through the hills and ravines that lay along south of the Beaver, and had followed down it to the camp. What a feat this driving in the dark across the trackless plains is, I will leave for the innocent who has tried it to explain. It is a risky business in that country, where to lose the water is almost certain death.

The party proudly showed us three more buffalo calves curled up in the bottom of the wagon; and these it was our first care to properly attend. After that, around the late supper, we listened to the story of the hunt, and heard how the buffaloes had led a long, long chase; how Colonel Jones and Ez. had fairly divided the honors; how another buffalo cow, in a desperate fight to save her offspring, had been sacrificed to save human life; how the close of the chase had found the party miles and miles from the camp, without water, with the horses badly fatigued, and with the choice of a dry, hungry camp on the Plains, or a long and risky drive at night. We heard all these things, told in a conversation much broken by constant interruption of fried antelope and coffee; then took

a last look at onr long string of captives, and retired to snooze away the few remaining hours of darkness in a blissful consciousness of well-earned repose.

Bright and early next morning Colonel Jones "piped all hands on deck," and after a short consultation announced his determination of making a big trip south to the Coldwater (Arfrio), in hopes of finding the main herd, and intending to drive fast and far until that was accomplished. In accordance with this resolve, the light wagon was at once gotten out, a full camp outfit, including our only water-cask, was stowed in it, and Colonel Jones, Ez. and Charley started out on what it was tacitly agreed would be the last hunt. The horses were looking fearfully worn, and we disliked to see them go. If we had known what a terrible experience they were yet to endure, they would not have gone at all. Ricker and I did not join this expedition, partly because there was load enough Avithout us, and partly because we thought our chances for a shot at a bull better if we stayed at the water where we were.

The next day I wandered down the stream, prospecting.. On my return, late in the afternoon, I saw the Tepee Rock,, and soon after, the white tents of our camp. The gray broke into a gallop, and swung up the valley at a great rate, so that in a little while I could distinguish objects about the camp. The first thing I saw was a form in the door of the tent, leveling a glass at me. It was Ricker. He began to wave his hat, and make some motions which I thought meant "hurry up." I did so. Then he was joined by Robinson, and there ensued one of the funniest, and at the same time most ridiculous, incidents of the whole hunt. Those two boys waved their hats, waved the hand-towel, got down on their knees, lay down on their stomachs, crawled out to one side of the tent on their bellies, and made such a series of insane antics that I was entirely bewildered. They were so extravagant, I supposed they were only guying me for having lost my din-

ner. As I came nearer, they said nothing. I became a little nettled, and thought they were a little too foolish even for crazy men. Therefore, I folded my arms and galloped on, whistling composedly, and intending to tell them I thought they were a pair of fools. As I came up they grew perfectly frantic. At last, when within fifty yards of the tent, Ricker gasped out, " Buffalo I "

I whirled my head, and glanced along the opposite side of the river-bed. There, above a little ridge, showed a dozen black humps. I was off the horse in an instant. The herd had come right into our camp 1

" Come into the tent ! " whispered the boys. I cut the straps which held my rifle in place at the saddle, and forgot to tie my horse. I started to crawl across the intervening space, every inch of which brought me more clearly into the view of the buffaloes, which I could now see quite clearly some five or six hundred yards distant. Alas ! before I could reach the tent, they saw me, and away they went.

When I got into the tent, the boys only hesitated about killing me because I was not good enough to die. I tried to explain, but they said that was needless; that I was a large-sized idiot. I remarked that that was n't a starter to what they both were; and on the whole there was a prospect of gore. But just then one of us took a look through a hole in the tent. There was the herd standing on the hillside. They had not run a quarter of a mile.

The boys told me that they had been watching the buffaloes for over an hour, waiting for them to come down close enough to shoot. The old bulls had gone down into the creek-bed, where it was dry, and had wallowed there for some time, one always standing guard while the others wallowed, and taking his turn when another came out to relieve him. None of the herd had yet watered. The glass revealed their number to be thirty cows and calves; there were nine bulls, and tliey kept in a little bunch by themselves. They did not run so far as the cows, and we could see them plainly, lower down the hill.

It was a strange and almost unparalleled circumstance.. There stood those hunted and proverbially wary creatures which we had found so hard to approach, within full view of our flapping tents, looking at them with no apparent suspicion of their real occupancy. I wonder what they wondered ? I wonder if they trembled with any vague-and undefined fear as they stood there, trying in vain to get some knowledge out of the stubborn and contrary-wind?

We watched the herd through the glass for half an hour. Some of the cows began to lie down. They could not be very much frightened. The remainder of the herd began to walk down toward the water. Appetite was prevailing over instinct. They were coming in !

The boys said they would forgive me if we got a shot. I hoped we might. It looked as if we would.

The nine bulls left the hillside, and moved down. A moment later they were out of sight in a little draw. In that moment we made a rush for the other tent, and got there successfully, sixty yards nearer the water.

With nervous hands we ripped slits in the side of the-Colonel's tent, and thrust out our rifle-barrels, changing-from one spot to another, making holes as often as we desired to change, in the attempt to find a place where the swaying tent should still conceal us, as by that time there were more holes than tent; yet it did not disconcert our aim.

The heads of the bulls showed over the ridge — nine big^ black fronts, one after another, all strung out. All nine-came over the crest, sniffed the air, and came down on a gallop. The little buffalo calf, with its long rope tied to-its neck, was playing about its old red mother, a little below the water. The bulls came nearer yet; took fright, and ran back a few yards; wheeled, and came on again,— this time, we could see, straight to a point within gun-range.

" My eyes!" shivered Robinson, " they 're big as meet-

ing-houses !" They did look so. There was one monster, and four were big ones; the others were smaller. They came down to the bank of the stream and turned fair to our aim. We decided they were less than two hundred yards away. We took our places in the door of the tent, shielding ourselves as well as we could with the flaps, and •coolly arranged our plan. We were to shoot from the two-hundred-yard notch of our rifle-sights, each taking a separate bull, and no one to fire until all were ready. Ricker was to count, and all were to fire at the instant he said

"Three."

The nine old bulls stood gazing with wide-open solemn eyes at the white apparition, whose fluttering wings held they knew not what of fate for them. Their great beards swept out sideways in the keen slant of the wind. They were motionless. They were ghostly. It was a singular xind almost oppressive scene. They seemed like phantom animals from the world of a departed race, come back to menace or to warn us. Never in my life shall I forget that moment, for I never saw a more vivid one. When I am old, and close my eyes, I shall see at will those great, ghostly, solemn animals, standing with beards as weep and eyes full of wondering reproach.

A moment of intense and silent inaction passed. We were read3^

"One!" "TwoI" tolled out Ricker's count. Then tit the other pendulum-beat the three repeaters spoke " Three 1"

And what was this? Dust at my own rifle-shot, a foot over the back of my bull 1 And nothing stops for the other boysl The whole nine are off—oh, misery 1

Fairly gnashing our teeth, we all sprang from the tent and opened on the flying herd as they ran. Their course was right up the bed of the stream, and they ran at right angles to us for fifty yards. Bang ! bang 1 bang ! rang the repeaters. Every shot flew high. Those which did not, cut dirt on the*bank beyond, or struck the bulls in the

humps, where they had no visible effect whatever. When they started to rim, I threw up the leaf of my sight, and so did Ricker, we both thinking they would run away from us; but as they kept right along by, I knocked down my eight, and just as they turned around the corner of a little knoll and made off to the left, I got down low enough and sent a bullet with a vicious " phut I " slap into the hip of the smallest bull in the bunch. He strung out behind after that, and was one of the missing later on.

Again we half fancied we could see the dumb protest in the half-savage, half-wondering eyes.

Slowly the night came down. Slowly, out there in the west, those huge figures shrouded up in the veil-fold of the on-sweeping darkness. Slowly, one by one, — sullenly, with breaking hearts, perhaps, for the white men were around them on every side,— they turned toward the setting sun; toward the little, narrow west which remained to them. And that, for us, was the last of the buffalo.

A world of incident was crowded into our short trip; but in attempting even a broken account of it, it must needs be brief.

On the evening of our rencontre with the nine bulls, we had not time to follow and secure the fallen ones before a.n event happened which put an end to hunting that day, and which foreshadowed the close of the entire hunt. We were looking up the valley, when our attention was attracted by a distant pistol-shot and a faint halloa; and presently we discerned a horseman coming slowly down toward camp. We soon made it out to be Carter. He was riding the bay mare Jennie, and his gait was very slow. Presently he dismounted, and came leading her into camp.

We saw at once what was the trouble. Both horse and man were nearly dead from thirst and exhaustion. Carter threw himself on the ground, with a despairing gesture toward the mare. His first words, after he had

drained a canteen of water, were, "I guess she 's sure gonel "

The poor creature looked it, truly. She stood with head down and legs wide apart, wet with sweat, and trembling like a leaf. In her misery at trying to breathe, she blundered and stumbled about the camp, and we soon found she was quite blind, or could see only imperfectly. A moment later she attempted to lie down, but we caught her and held her up, a dead weight between us. Then we poured a straight pint of raw whisky into a pail. Before we could dilute it with water, the mare felt the rim of the pail, and at once drank its contents at a gulp. Whether the Kentucky mare recognized the Kentucky product or not, I do not know; but she drank that whisky "straight." And it was the best thing she could have done. She did not get down at all after that; and in a little while we gave her a quart or so of water, then half a pailful; and after blanketing and rubbing down her legs, she began to prick up her ears and whinny a little. Then we knew she would pull through; and we held a general jubilee, hugging, the game old animal and calling her all sorts of pet names.

"That mare 's sure clear grit," said Carter. "She 's gone over a hundred miles to-day, and has n't had a drop of water. I 've made three big runs on her, and caught five calves without uncinching the saddle."

While Carter was swallowing his supper, we learned from him the story of the calf-hunt. The drive from the main camp south, he said, had been a very long and rapid one, and as near as they could tell, far beyond the Coldwater, when just before sundown they came in sight of the largest herd of buffalo which had yet been found— probably seventy-five or one hundred in number. It wa» too late to make a run that night, so camp was made in the breaks, within a mile and a half of the herd. In the morning, before sunrise, camp Avas broken, and after dividing up what little water there was left — the horsea

PLENTY OF CALVES, BUT NO WATER 161

getting only a very little — the approach on the herd was begun, and the first run was made early in the morning. Two calves were the result of this run, one each for Colonel Jones and Carter. The herd did not make for any stream, but ran out into an undiscovered country of limitless extent. The second run was made late in the morning. The day proved to be terribly hot. Three calves were caught by Carter; but the horses were almost exhausted. Colonel Jones got so far away from the party, or the party from him, that for a time it looked as if he would have to leave his exhausted horse and try the fifty or sixty miles to water on foot. However, he found 'the trail, and, by walking, drove his horse for a time (as he was so near gone he would not lead), and managed to keep it up until he sighted the wagon and signaled for it to come up. The whole outfit was nearly "done up," and it looked a question whether they would all ever get into camp.

It was well for the party that they knew the country into which they came. Colonel Jones recognized a certain table-rock, and knew that camp lay far below them. Had they not been familiar with that part of the country, and had therefore gone up the stream instead of down, they would have lost all their stock, and would probably have perished themselves. It cannot be emphasized too much, that hunting in that country — in the spring of 1887, at least—was a matter which "tenderfeet" and "grangers" would very much better let alone. A party going down on that range would be foolish to start without a thoroughly posted guide. They would get no game, and would stand a large chance of dying of thirst.

When they came to the Canadian (or Beaver), the teams were nearly ready to drop, and it was evident that fresh horses must be had. The black runner could hardly move, and even the tough mule team was "done up." Two of the buffalo calves had died of the intense heat — which is not strange; for in that little spring wagon there were -11

crowded three men, all their camp equipage, a water-cask, and seven kicking young buffaloes.

Carter had therefore come down to get a fresh team, and take back such water as he could. Poor fellow! — he looked weary enough himself; but he did not tarry, and after his hasty supper started back with the spare team, carrying as much water and whisky as he could sling about him in canteens.

We built a beacon-fire near by the Tepee Rock that night, and prepared supper, that it might be ready for the late comers. About midnight we heard their rifleshots, and could presently see the flashes as they fired. We answered, and built up our fire; and presently the party rode silently into camp. They were successful; but the best part of tlieir success was that they got in alive. The black running-horse was left for dead, ten miles back on the trail.

The next morning Colonel Jones suddenly displayed a certain trait in his character which did much on more than one occasion to rob us of pleasures the trip might otherwise have done. He got in a hurry, and abruptly announced his intention of starting for home. Of course it was not for my companion or myself to murmur at his wish in the matter, since it was pure kindness on his part to take us along on the trip; but we did so wish, now that we had fairly gotten the situation of the buffaloes, to stay and rest a few days, and get another bull or two, before we started in. We knew it was our last chance. However, we tried to be resigned, and recorded no protest except that written here. In these columns we wish squarely to reprimand the man who would do so cruel an act as to take us two fellows away from the buffaloes, just when we had fairly found them. We did not even have time to go out and look for the two bulls which we supposed we had killed, although Carter had seen the bunch of bulls with only seven in it, as he came down the night before, thereby corroborating our count.

We left the boys to look up the dead and wounded, to attend to the wearied stock, and bring into the settlements the captive calves, with all the retinue of the great main camp. We quickly prepared the light wagon for the trip, and hitched in the large bay horse and the lucky, plucky little balking gray, who now balked no more, but was grown into high esteem about the camp. Of course, Jennie could not travel. She and all the rest of the horses were to be allowed several days' rest before they were started for the settlements. The nervy mare had "picked up" a great deal by morning, and appeared to be coming out all right. We were glad to see that she was not going to lose her eyesight, but had been only temporarily blind and dizzy. We were glad also for another thing: Colonel Jones went out early in the morning, after a very scanty allowance of sleep, and found the abandoned black horse on his feet and struggling to get down to the water. Whisky and water revived him enough to get him into camp, and his "naturally strong constitution," as the doctors say, brought him through all right eventually.

Colonel Jones, my companion and I started early, taking with us only a very light camping-outfit, some jerked buffalo meat, and coffee. We found our team could do better than expected, and we made a long drive the first day.

By this system of driving day and night,— which I never could see how the horses stood up under,— we held on our way steadily, and almost before we knew it were at the railroad, and at home in Garden City. Once we drove close to 100 miles in 24 hours.

Then followed the queries and congratulations. Our hunt was over. It had been a most fortunate one, all considered. Had it not been so well planned and so well pushed, it might have been called an unlucky one. Certainly, there was good luck in it.

A week and a half after our arrival the boys arrived
with the main outfit, bringing in the bull- and antelope-heads, and the skins of various kinds which we had collected. Of course, we inquired anxiously about the calves. To our sorrow, only seven out of the fourteen captured had been brought in alive. Some had died of stubbornness or sickness ; one had gotten away in the night; and yet another had fallen victim to

a certain brilliant experiment devised by the boys to make a buffalo calf follow a domestic cow. The experiment consisted in tying the calf, to the cow's tail. The calf followed. But unfortunately its neck was broken before they could lasso the cow. At this, the boys did not finish tying up the other calves in like manner, but just herded them along as before. It was harder work, but the net results in live buffalo calves seemed to warrant them in it. Nothing more need be said for Colonel Jones than to remark that he never reprimanded the boys once for the slimness of their returns. He only said, "I wish they had brought in eight or ten, at least."

To-day, in the pasture at the edge of Garden City, Colonel Jones has eleven buffalo calves. Four of these are yearlings, fat as seals, shaggy as sheep, and so tame that you can almost touch them. The other seven are the calves of this year's hunt. They are lively as crickets, and run bawling after their foster-mothers like any other calves. The "old red stripper" supports two, and watches them with the most motherly pride. They run loose with a small herd of blooded domestic cattle. It is the intention, as was previously stated, to raise a herd of buffaloes, and also to experiment with hybridization. It is to be hoped that no accidents will thin this little band, survivors of a doomed race, and procured at so great peril, hardship, and expense. It is of course true that the American people will watch with the greatest solicitude a herd in which they have so great an interest. To-day, too, in the same pasture, "Jennie "and " Blackie " take their ease among the calves they helped to catch;

now and then privately indulging in a run after a calf, just to keep up the memory of their hunt,— which will be their last indeed, in all probability. The gray horse — now posing as a reformed balker—pensively chews buffalo-grass out on the claim of the dark-eyed damsel who gave us our immortal lunch on the day we started out. Colonel Jones, the mules, and all the rest of us, are at work.

Could not the calf-hunt be duplicated by other parties? Hardly; for the reason that men having sufficient knowledge of the haunts and habits of the game, and an in-i clination to secure it, are very few; and of these few, fewer yet are able financially to organize such a hunt. It cost Mr. Jones over one thousand dollars in preparatory and current expenses for the short time which our trip lasted.

Could not hunters pay the expenses, and hire an efficient guide? They could easily hire a guide. Perhaps he would promise everything; probably he would secure nothing. I do not know of any man who would even promise success. The few who know the secrets of that forbidding land are anxious to keep their secrets for their own benefit.

Could a party of hunters not acquainted with the country go into that region with any chance of success ? No. It would be dangerous to try it. Water is too scarce. The path of the hunt might be a Jornada del muerto (journey of death) for a band of "tender-feet."

Is our party entitled to the claim of having seen the last of the buffalo? Not literally, of course. But it is probable that we were the last, or very near the last, civilized hunters to look upon the buffalo wild on its native range. There were features of our hunt which we should not wish to see repeated; but on the whole, we endeavored to act like civilized hunters. Those will be only savages who, for the sake of the few dollars which the hides of the devoted creatures will bring, will plan to finish

their destruction. It was the skin-hunter who has so nearly anuihihited the entire race of these grand animals, changing Nature's plan — tearing Nature's page in this good century. It will not be the privilege of the last members of the race to die victims of any noble, if inconsiderate, ambition. It will be the cool, calculating, pic-ayunish, fiendish skin-hunter who will make the last "stalk." It will be his penny-loving eye which will catch the sight against the last shaggy side. It will be from the worn grooves of his rifle that the last puff of smoke will come, and hang above a grass-covered wallow. It will be his skilled hands which will strip off the last robe. And his comment as he folds it down will be, "I've got the last I"

Poor fool! He will not know — he has not brains enough to conceive — what those words mean, that he has indeed killed the Last of the Buffalo. May those solemn eyes in their last glance blight and wither him I should be the verdict of all true Americans.

CHAPTER X

THE WILD HOKSE —OTHER ANIMALS

ORIGIN OF — HABITAT — GREATEST NUMBER EVER KNOWN

BIZE, COLOR, STYLE, AND FITNESS TO SURROUNDINGS — THE STALLION DRIVES, NEVER LEADS—GRAPHIC DESCRIPTION OF CONTEST FOR MASTERSHIP — DURING THE DRIVE, TO KILL THE RULER RESULTED IN FAILURE — SOME OF THE HEROES WHO MADE FORTUNES CAPTURING THESE ANIMALS— WHEN FAMISHING, NEVER LOST SIGHT OF HORSES UNTIL THEY WENT TO WATER — THE WILD HORSE's GREAT SPEED AND ENDURANCE — PRAIRIE-DOGS AND OWLS: NO SUCH THING AS "HAPPY FAMILY"—RATTLESNAKES AND OWLS INTRUDERS — HELD AT BAY BY A MONSTROUS RATTLER

IN presenting Colonel Jones's adventures in hunting and capturing the buffalo, to neglect relating a few facts concerning the wild horse and some other animals of the Plains would be like the play of Hamlet without the ghost.

The habitat of the wild horse was that of the American bison, where, though never commingling with them in an absolute sense, there were rare exceptions where a single animal might be discovered in close proximity to a herd of buffalo. I remember once having been presented with a two-year-old colt, which had been observed for more than ten months as the comparatively close companion of a band of buffalo, with which he had run for that length of time. All the individuals of the herd seem to have been imbued with that strange affection which sometimes

(167)

manifests itself among our domestic animals, many authentic stories relating to which are current. The probability is the colt was always smart enough not to get tangled up in the herd, or be caught napping; at least I would have advised such vigilance, had I been the instructor.

The wolf, that ever-persistent, hungry species of the genus Lupus, called by the old hunters "loafers," while particularly fond of young colts, also of horseflesh, rarely takes the terribly unequal chances of securing a meal by attempting to capture a wild horse on the open prairie; yet in the woods he is quite the reverse. For some reason he much prefers to depend upon the superannuated buffalo bulls, driven out of the herd by their junior fellows, for his rations; yet when compelled by almost absolute starvation to take the most desperate chances, he risks an attack upon the stately, swift-footed wild horse.

How long the present wild horse has existed on the Plains is difficult to rightly conjecture; for we know that as he is at present physiologically constructed, he is not identical with the wild horse of prehistoric ages. True, as paleontology proves, there was a variety of species of the horse roaming over the Great Plains thousands of years ago, but they, with other orders of immense mammals, became extinct in a remote geologic age. That was, as Huxley and other famous paleontologists have shown, the primitive horse. There was an almost incalculable hiatus between those prehistoric times and the appearance of the present wild horse, whose existence on the Great Plains of Texas, Colorado, Kansas and Nebraska is limited to a very recent day. It is the accepted theory by scientists, that their origin dates back to the wonderful march of the Spanish explorer, Francisco Vasquez de Cor-onado, one of Cortez's lieutenants, who with a small army traversed the vast wilderness of the mid-continent region of North America in 1541. In his itinerary, his historian.

Castenada, relates losing many horses, which escaped during the fearful storms, and from being stampeded by the buffalo. From the relatively few which formed the basis of all that have since occupied the region pointed out, it appears they flourished in a remarkable degree, for as late as 1875 it was estimated by those who were competent judges, that no less than fifty thousand were roaming at will over the prairies of the large States enumerated above.

Colonel Jones devotes some pages of his journal to the habits of the wild horse. He says:

" The habits and methods of the wild horses, their manner of subsisting, and their remarkable intelligence, have ever been attractive subjects to me. Secreted from the view of a large band unconscious of my proximity, I have often abandoned everything else for hours in order to study the curious and graceful picture of a band of horses in their natural state.

"They are of fair size, weighing in the neighborhood of from seven to ten hundred pounds; remarkably well built, their chests large, wide and deep, and their bones of good size, indicating great strength. Their heads are always carried high in the air, the natural position of the species when unrestrained by mechanical appliances, and when moving they are the very incarnation of grace and symmetry. Their eyes protrude more than those of the domesticated animal, for the reason, perhaps, that heredity has stamped this feature upon them by the necessary vigilance of their ancestors imposed by their environment. The mane is very long, reaching to the knees, and the tail usually'sweeps the ground. Taking them all in all, they are the ideal horse. By constant exposure to the fitful variations of climate of the mid-continent region, entirely dependent upon their own efforts for their subsistence, and frequently, to employ a Western but very expressive phrase, compelled to ' rustle' for their living, they have develoj^ed a vitality and strength of

muscle which is wonderful to contemplate. Their extensive travels from place to place in search of fresh pastures, and their sometimes extended races under the inspiration of absolute liberty, have given them an expansion of lungs and nostril assuring an endurance that is phenomenal. These physical attributes, coupled with an indomitable will, render their capture a difficult and tedious process. They are in all their movements as graceful as the antelope, and I know of no more beautiful scene than that of a band of wild horses at play. They are as fleet as the greyhound, and some of the speediest horses of to-day in the East have a straili of their blood coursing through their veins.

"The scientists theoretically claim—those, I mean, who have not really studied them— that they must unquestionably be a weak race, destitute of fine points, because in their common intermingling, without any regard to proper breeding, the best blood would soon run out. This is not the fact, however; nature has provided a compensating law, by which their specially fine characteristics have been preserved. Strength, nerve and endurance are better provided for under that freedom from restraint which a life of absolute liberty assures, than could be attained by breeding the domestic animal handicapped by the conventionalities of the confined state from which no breeder can hope to escape.

"The wild horse in his aggregation is governed by a ruler, who in a band is as absolute as the most arbitrary human monarch; and of course he is the stallion possessing the greatest strength, pugnacity, nerve, and endurance. As with the buffalo, the contest for supremacy in a herd of wild horses is desperate and exciting! The terrible fight for this position between two contending stallions cannot be imagined, and language is hardly adequate to graphically describe it. They approach each other walking on their hind feet, with eyes which simulate balls of molten metal, or the electric light. Their

great mouths are already open, exposing their sharp teeth, with which they inflict most terrible punishment, and in a few seconds the imj)ending shock comes, for which each enraged animal has been preparing himself. Now their keenly cutting hoofs are flying in every direction over their adversary's body, and their powerful jaws grasp neck, shoulders, or any portion they can get hold of. They fight with all the desperation of bulldogs, throwing their whole force against each other; consequently the weaker ' goes to the wall' a terribly mutilated brute. If he is not equal in strength, or lacks in endurance to withstand the awful shocks of his adversary, he is at last hurled to the ground,— kicked, stamped on, and torn by the teeth of his mad antagonist; and if by chance he can rise again, he rushes off, glad to escape with his bare life. Unlike the contests between buffalo bulls, described in a previous chapter, wherein no blood js drawn, those between the wild stallions of the Plains are fraught with sanguinary results. Wherever their cruel teeth are fastened in each other's flesh, their bodies are lacerated in the most horrible manner. When these instruments of warfare slip off the hide where they have taken hold, they snap together, sounding like the report of a firecracker. The conquered animal in his retreat exerts every muscle if he is permitted to rise from the earth where he has been thrown by his adversary, and breaks and dashes off^ •as fast as he is able, pursued for a mile or so by the latter, who cuts and bites him at every jump. He is at last abandoned, and never again molests his adversary, as the poor disabled ' tramp' never forgets his experience as long as he lives,— unlike the Turk, who 'fights and runs away, to renew the fight another day.'

"One of the most interesting sights in connection with wild horses is when the proud high-headed stallion, who* is ruler of the herd, numbering perhaps all the way from twenty to a hundred, first discovers the presence of an intruding stallion in the vicinity. With lofty head, he liter-

ally 'smells the battle from afar'; his tail is thrown out at an angle of forty-five degrees, and he commences to encircle his charge, with his head lowered to his knees, nose turned up like an old gander when angry. This he repeats once or twice, rounding all the animals into a close bunch, where they remain until his return, without the least change of position. He gathers himself u]), as it were, and dashes off like a whirlwind to meet the object of his fury, which is perhaps half a mile distant. Nine times out of ten, however, the enemy has flown long before he arrives at the spot where he originally appeared. Sometimes, the reverse is the case: he meets with a bundle of horseflesh all nerve and muscle, which waits to measure strength with him. Of the many encounters of this character I have witnessed, only one has occurred in which the master of the herd was compelled to yield to the intruding adversary.

"The general idea of those who have heard of wild horses is, that the master stallion leads the herd. This is not the case; he drives them anywhere he desires them to go, for fear the mares will escape, or be cut out of the band by prowling stallions. The monarch of the herd guards them with as much vigilance as a sheriff guards a squad of prisoners, or a shepherd guards his flock when wolves are hungry and desperate. Does anyone suppose the stallion ' leads ' the herd ? No I Such an idea is nonsense, and the person who insists on it only shows he knows not whereof he speaks. Every individual member of the herd is fully aware that any disobedience brings its chastisement, and offenses of this character are rare, for the punishment is severe and sudden. He allows no males in the herd after they have attained the age of one year. When there are signs of danger from any direction, he invariably puts himself between it and the herd, guarding its interest with all the persistency of a Roman sentinel. When danger has been discovered, the mares flee from it, but the stallion stops at intervals, strikes the

METHOD OF CAPTURING WILD HORSES 173

hard dry earth viciously with his fore feet, whistles terrifically through his nostrils, as if to defy all intruders; then whirls and dashes after the fleeing band with great rapidity. When they are overtaken, he whirls around again and repeats the same performance.

" Seldom are there seen to exceed a half-dozen stallions herding together. They usually are found alone. Occasionally one dashes in and cuts out a mate from one of the large herds (one of the requirements to success). He is soon overtaken, punished, and the mare driven by the victor with terrific speed into the herd.

"The wild horse, like that ruminant the buffalo, when man in his wantonness commenced the process of hunting him regardless of the deplorable results which have obtained, was fated to annihilation, and the race is now nearly extinct. During the decade ending with 1885, many of the old buffalo-hunters turned their undivided attention to gathering wild horses, for which there was soon established a demand, constantly increasing. Their method of capturing the beautiful animals was a tedious process, yet very successful, and attended by no injury to the horses. It consisted of continually pursuing the herd,, day after day, sometimes for weeks, allowing it no rest, until at last, footsore, jaded and worn out, the subdued animals could be easily driven into a corral previously prepared for them. In building the corral, the hunter takes advantage of the knowledge he has obtained of the wild horse, which is the wisest of all equine creation, and builds his fence accordingly. He leaves a large opening into the corral, through which the horses are to pass into the inclosure. Then from each end of the walls, at this opening, fences are made in a flaring manner, about a hundred yards in length, and fromi the end of each wing fence a furrow is plowed about a half-mile in length, in the flaring manner of the fence. As all horse-hunters know, the wild horse fears to cross a freshly plowed furrow, thinking it a snare, no doubt. When the

-animals are so fatigued and footsore they can be turned in any direction desired, the hunters guide the band into the large lane between the furrows, then give a yell, and the band rushes pell-mell in the direction of the corral. If they try to avoid it, they come to the furrow and shy away, but have no time to turn about, and are pressed by shouts, shots and yells between the wings of fencing, where there is only one possible way of escape from the fusillade; that is, in the rear. Thus they are rushed through the corral opening, and into captivity. This corral was usually made of logs, stone, or occasionally of only sod walls; and when once securely inside of the structure the lasso was brought into requisition, and the captured animals were soon'hobbled. They were then herded until quite gentle, when they were driven to a railroad station and shipped to some Eastern market, where they were readily disposed of.

"The monarch of the herd was an indispensable adjunct in the drives before the corral was reached, for it was through his efforts and exaction of discipline that the herd were kept together, until they were so weary and footsore the hunter could easily turn them in any direction he desired. Often the stallion would become desperate and charge upon the hunters, who were compelled to flee from his awful wrath, or shoot him, to escape death. If the latter became necessary, it of course ended that drive, —for the band, having lost its controller, would immediately scatter in all directions, and the work, which had perhaps occupied weeks, counted for naught, while the hunter cursed his luck for a month or two.

" Perhaps the most successful wild-horse hunters were those who commenced the vocation as early as 1878. The bravest and most daring of all was E. J. Bell—'Wild-Horse Bell,' as everyone on the Plains called him. He certainly is entitled to the championship, if numbers is the criterion. He captured over one thousand of the wary animals, and almost alone. He never abandoned

but one herd in all his career, and then severe illness was the cause.

"James R. Fulton and John Stevens, both of them among the founders of Garden City, Kansas, were also remarkable wild-horse hunters. To Mr. Fulton belongs the credit of making the greatest single ' catch' ,on record. Aided by Link Fulton (a mere lad of only sixteen, and son of the famous buffalo-hunter Wm. D. Fulton) he drove in and corralled seventy-two head of the most magnificent animals ever caught on the Great Plains. It was accomplished, too, at the time the notorious 'Wild Hog,' chief of the Cheyennes, was raiding the settlements on the border with his band of renegade savages, during the fall of 1878. The cruel and bloodthirsty devils were constantly on the lookout for horse-hunters, as they were short of ponies, but Fulton by his coolness and superb strategy completely outwitted the old savage and all his hosts.

" Mr. Stevens, while hunting wild horses one day, suddenly found himself confronted by seven well-armed savages. They shot his horse from under him, and wounded him twice. Finally, he put a fifty-caliber Sharps' rifle-ball so close to the old chief that the cowardly brutes hastily retreated. Then, under cover of darkness, Mr. Stevens made his way to camp, fifteen miles distant, considering himself very lucky to get out of the scrape as he did.

"To the wild horse I owe my preservation from a horrid death, as, several times when on the sandy deserts without a drop of water, dazed and bewildered from thirst and exposure, and all my efforts to find the precious fluid had failed, I seated myself on a high hill, and with a field-glass watched for a band of horses. On discovering them I was certain of relief, for all I had to do then was to follow, when they made their daily trip to quench their thirst, as they were sure to visit some lonely pool or lake during the day.

"During my expeditions after buffalo calves I have been able to pick up a few wild colts which I raised on cow's milk, until now I am the possessor of quite a band of these hardy animals. I have succeeded in making them perfectly gentle, and they have done me good service, riding after their old neighbors the American bison. The colors of the wild horses are as widely diversified as in the domestic stock. There is one peculiarity in relation to this subject, however, which struck me very forcibly when I first observed it: that is, each band in its primitive state on the Plains is composed of animals nearly all of the same color, or at least of its different variations. Sometimes you find a gray stallion in charge, and then the majority of the animals will be gray; in other instances the controller is black, iron-gray, clay-bank, bay, sorrel, blue (mouse-color), etc., and in these herds the colors corresponding to that of the sire would preponderate. There is a physiological reason for this, which is of course obvious to the intelligent reader, as the offspring resembles the sire in color more than that of the dam, and proves that the stallion once in charge maintains the position for many years.

" Most of the wild horses are excellent trotters, but occasionally I came across a herd of pacers,— remarkably fast, too.

"At one time while hunting on the headwaters of the Smoky Hill river in western Kansas, I saw for several weeks in succession a magnificent gray stallion which was a beautiful pacer. I frequently spurred my pony to the limit of his speed, but failed to press the animal hard enough to break his gait; he stuck to it as persistently as a thoroughbred. I have often since regretted that I did not spend a month or two in endeavoring to capture him; yet I am thankful that I secured as many as I did."

There are other interesting animals on the Great Plains, which, although of no commercial value, are
perhaps worthy a passing notice. Of some of these, Colonel Jones, in his habit of closely observing, has written in his journal, from which I now quote in this relation:

"Nearly every student of the history of our mid-continent region has heard of the so-called 'Happy Family.' According to the legend — for legend it is—the harmonious aggregate consists of prairie-dogs, owls, and the rattlesnake ; and these are falsely supposed to make their home in the same burrow. Of the first mentioned, the term 'prairie-dog,' so far as classification is concerned, is a misnomer. It is not a dog in any sense of the term; no more resembles a dog than a cow resembles a horse. They are not carnivorous at all, depending entirely upon roots and grass-seeds, and even eat the grass itself in summer-time. They belong to the order Rodentia, allied to the squirrel and such gnawers. The prairie-dog is really a species of marmot, akin to that which infests the fields of continental Europe. It is one-third larger than the American gray squirrel, but its tail is not so long and bushy; on the contrary, rather stubby and short. The prairie-dogs burrow deep in the ground; are very gregarious, living in great villages, which are often five to ten miles long and as many broad. These burrows connect beneath the surface, and some of them are from fifty to eighty feet deep, reaching water,— for this quaint animal must drink. It is a sure sign that water is within accessible distance wherever a prairie-dog town is located, and those holes which lead to it are constructed in a sort of winding-stair fashion. In early days of central and western Kansas I located many settlers on homesteads, and always advised them to dig for water in the ' dog-towns'; and I never heard any complaint of dry wells from those who acted on my suggestion.

'^This little rodent is a natural barometer, for from twenty-four to forty-eight hours before a shower he may — 12

be seen busily engaged in banking up around the mouth of his burrow, to prevent the surface-water from flowing into the hole and drowning himself and family. By carefully noting the habits of the prairie-dog I have many a time escaped a drenching, keeping near my tent until the storm was over.

" The wise hunter always avoids camping close to or in a dog-town; not that they are at all dangerous, but because the rattlesnake is certain to be there in goodly numbers, as is the harmless, blinking, diminutive prairie-owl. Now it is true that they are neighbors, but their proximity is not any indication that they are congenial; far from it. The dog-hole is a very convenient resort for the owl in the glare of the day, without any effort having been expended in building a place such as his nature and habits require. He is an ungracious bird of ill omen, repaying the kindness which he avails himself of, by devouring the young dogs. The rattlesnake too, finds it convenient to accept of a dwelling which presents elegant accommodations suitable for his snakeship, by merely taking possession, where he, equally as ungrateful as his feathered co-tenant, delights to fatten on young prairie-dogs. One day, while crawling up behind a clump of weeds to shoot an antelope, I came very near laying my hand on a monstrous rattler. On jumping up to shoot it I saw a pmirie-dog hole near, and thrust the butt end of my gun into the hole and jumped back. The snake was soon at the hole, but could not get in, neither could I get my gun. The antelope became quite inquisitive, and came circling around until it was within gooii gunshot; but it was perfectly safe, as the snake had commanded me to ' stand back' by holding his head high above his body, darting out his forked tongue in rapid succession. I realized my j^osition, and looked in every direction for Indians. Had there been a hundred swooping down upon me, I never have been able to record which death I would have preferred. Finally I ran to the top of a divide, and

signaled my companion to bring the team over. I then took my lariat-rope and threw a noose over the head of the serpent, and endeavored to keep it alive for museum purposes, but drew the rope too tightly around its neck and choked it to death.

" By that time the antelope was gone and we ate ' slapjacks and coffee' for another twenty-four hours, before more antelope came close enough to be shot.

"The rattler was so large that he had swallowed a prairie-dog, evidence of which fact was indisputable as I opened it to discover what had caused such an abnormal increase in his diameter. Of course, only rattlesnakes of the largest size could accomplish a feat of that character. This was one of the first foundations for my disbelief in the old theory of the ' happy family' idea, which I had read of long before, having seen it in an article published in Harper's Magazine somewhere in the '50s,' and at the time accepted it as true, in my boyish credulity. Besides, another confirmatory proof of the falsity of the legend is, that I have often seen dozens of old prairie-dogs chattering around their burrows, as a bird in breeding-time chatters when its nest is in real or apparent danger from some unwelcome visitant, and upon investigating the cause of disturbance, found a rattlesnake in the prairie-dog's burrow, which was a complete bar to its legitimate owner's entering.

" The owls, as stated, are particularly the enemy of the prairie-dog when the latter is busy rearing her young. The prairie-dogs are often obliged to obstruct the entrance to their burrows with dirt to keep the intruders — snakes and owls — out until the little ones are large enough to take care of themselves. To be sure, the mother has to emerge occasionally for food; but she is always mistrustful, taking the precaution to block up the mouth of the burrow with dirt before venturing far away. The snakes are just as obnoxious to the owls as to the dogs. They devour the young birds whenever found. The rat-

tlesnake is among the most deadly enemies of all creatures. If he cannot swallow an animal he will bite it, and death is the penalty in both cases. Who wonders that the Creator doomed his snakeship to ' crawl upon his belly'for all eternity?"

CHAPTER XI SUCCESSFUL CALF-HUNT

EXTRAVAGANT PREPARATIONS — HERD OF MILCH COWS BENT TO THE BUFFALO RANGE — DISCOVERED COMPETITION, CAPTURING CALVES — CALLED A HALT — COMPETITOR SURRENDERS, AND MAKES A SMALL FORTUNE—HORSE BITTEN BY RATTLESNAKE — SUNDAY IN CAMP — DISCOVERED THE

HERD— "hurrah, BOYS, SUNDAY OR NO SUNDAY!"

ELEVEN CAPTIVES AT ONE RUN — WOLVES DEVOUR TWO

COLONEL JONES CAPTURES THREE NEXT MORNING UNDER DIFFICULTIES — PATHETIC POEM — SHOOTING A BUFFALO COW WITHOUT A SIGHT — WONDERFUL SUCCESS IN CATCHING CALVES — MORE CALVES THAN COWS TO FEED THEM — LONG JOURNEY FOR RELIEF — TAKEN FOR CATTLE-THIEVES — SECURES A DOZEN COWS AT FABULOUS PRICES — AVARICIOUS IRISHMAN REGRETS HE DID n't ASK MORE—THIRTY-TWO CALVES ARRIVE AT RANCH — LEE HOWARD, THE TYPICAL COWBOY — JOHN BIGGS, TYPICAL RANCHER

IN the spring of 1888, Colonel Jones again organized au " outfit" for a determined pursuit after the few buffalo calves remaining. He arranged the transportation of the expedition by utilizing a four-horse wagon, loaded with provisions, and a dozen saddle-ponies, thoroughbreds, and bronchoes. He was fortunate in securing the services of Mr. John E. Biggs as a companion and assistant, who was to take charge of aflfairs when Colonel Jones was not present. Mr. Biggs was a typical cowboy, or rather, had been; he was now a ranchman,

(181)

having passed the cowboy period and settled down to the business of stock-raising, with his wife (a beautiful little school teacher, nee Miss Alice Moore, of Ohio) to preside over his household. He was disposing of his herds rapidly, intending to take a rest and recreation, which he declared he much needed. Upon the earnest solicitation of Colonel Jones, who at last persuaded him he could get no better recreation than by a trip on the Plains, he consented (though reluctantly) to accompany the Colonel whenever the expedition was made up.

On the 20th of April the expedition pulled out from Garden City, Kansas, Colonel Jones's home, headed for the southwest; Mr. Biggs in charge, as the Colonel was compelled to linger behind for about a week in order to finish some important business. At the end of that period the Colonel hooked up two of the wildest bronchoes in his herd, to a single-seated buggy, and on the morning of the 26th dashed away, all alone, on the trail of Mr. Biggs. There were several settlers in that portion of southwestern Kansas through which he intended to pass, who had emigrated into the valleys that spring, and on his first night out he was entertained by one of them. The second and third nights, he camped on the prairie alone; the fourth day overtaking Mr. Biggs in the region called " No Man's Land," now a part of Oklahoma. Mr. Biggs was a careful man with stock; had all his life been accustomed to. it; and on this trip, as he had twenty especially selected milch cows (upon which depended the lives of the buffalo calves) to care for, had prudently taken his time for the work assigned him by the Colonel. The latter found everything more than satisfactory, and the " outfit" traveled until camp was made early in the evening. This was on the border of Texas, in the extreme northwestern portion of that State. The cows and ponies were at once turned loose to graze, with a herder to watch them. Twice a day the cows were milked by the herder and "Shorty," the cook; though all the milk excepting

what the party could use — a limited amount—was necessarily thrown away, as the calves had been left at home.

On the morning of the 3d of May, Colonel Jones, Mr. Biggs and one of the teamsters left camp in a light wagon, freighted with five days' provisions, and other paraphernalia for the chase,— four ponies, saddles, etc.,— fully intent on accomplishing something in the line of the business for which they had left civilization. They crossed the Aqua Frio, on the second evening arriving at the Paladura, where, at the head of this stream, about twenty miles from the South Canadian, they established their main camp.

They were now very near the western boundary of Texas, and here were discovered evident signs that buffalo had been in the vicinity not many days previously. The Colonel and Mr. Biggs left on their ponies for a little expedition together, and on the third morning out from the main camp, while the Colonel was carefully scrutinizing every inch of territory visible in the vast region, for the whereabouts of the remaining shaggy wanderers, he saw an object in the distance, which he shortly recognized to be a man on horseback. Supposing it to be an Indian, they rode directly toward it, and discovered it to be Lee Howard, a ranchman from the North Canadian, whom Colonel Jones had frequently met.

"What are you up to now?" exclaimed the Colonel, after the customary salutations had passed between the two.

"Catching buffalo calves," replied Mr. Howard.

" How many have you caught? " anxiously inquired the Colonel.

"Only two," said Mr. Howard.

This was a bitter pill for the Colonel to swallow, as he was aware there could not be more than forty calves in the country — maybe not half that number; and as Mr. Howard was well acquainted throughout the west, and

.184 FORTY YEARS OF ADVENTURES

was a good hunter besides, the Colonel was satisfied his rival would secure his share of them.

Colonel Jones, however, who is never at aloss in a case of emergency, soon arrived at a determination which would quickly settle the matter. He concluded to stop Mr. Howard's career in the line of buffalo-calf hunting, and asked him how much he would charge to work for him during the next two months. Mr. Howard, it seems, was bent on catching buffalo calves for himself, however, and in his reply to the Colonel put his services at such a high figure that he supposed it would certainly l)e rejected at once. He said, laughingly, he would work during the period specified for five hundred dollars. Colonel Jones accepted the proffer l)efore the sentence was fairly completed, not waiting to "dicker," as he felt sure Howard would withdraw the offer if he realized it was being considered. Mr. Howard was too mucji of a Western man to withdraw his word after its having been accepted, as that was a completion of a contract; and out in the region of the Great Plains, the only credit that prevails is a reputation for honor and veracity. So from the moment of Colonel Jones's acceptance of Mr. Howard's proposition, the latter was working for him.

While the two men were discussing the probability of the whereabouts of buffalo, a cow and her calf made their appearance on a little divide not far away. In an instant Mr. Howard was off after the calf, which happened to be one well advanced in age and strength, and the race for its possession continued for several miles, the Colonel following on a canter. The persistent little l^rute was about to get away altogether, when Mr. Howard halted for a moment, stripped off the heavy Mexican saddle from his horse, to relieve it from so much weight, jumped on again l)areback, and the calf was soon in the noose of his rope. While he was tying it, a large rattlesnake struck the horse on the ankle of his fore leg, and it was only by great effort that the animal was saved. The calf was a beautiful

heifer, and when three years old sold for a thousand dollars. So Mr. Howard's salary was doubly paid by the capture of the one calf.

The next day was passed in scanning the country between the Paladura and the South Canadian. Few signs of the presence of buffalo were discovered. The three men were possessed of field-glasses, and separated themselves at a distance of about six miles. Moving to the west, a small band of buffalo were discovered in the afternoon, out of which Colonel Jones caught a calf, the only one in the herd.

It was now Saturday night, and all went into camp near a small lake, such as are frequently to be found during a wet season in the region where the party was. It was decided to rest on the Sabbath — although Sundays are rarely regarded as different from other days, on an expedition of this character. The wind blew very fiercely, almost a hurricane, and it became too monotonous for the wiry, active hunters to remain in camp all day without a tent or even a covered wagon. So the Colonel, impatient of the enforced idleness, proposed that he and Howard should take a ride "just for their health, and nothing else." The former, nothing loath, as anxious to be on the move as the Colonel, acquiesced promptly, and soon they were loping to the southwest. After riding in that direction for a few miles they circled toward the northwest, and were shortly wending their way slowly back to camp. The sun was rapidly sinking in the west, when suddenly Mr. Howard stopped, fixed his glass to his eyes, and said he saw a fine herd of buffalo, about eighty in number, some three miles northeast from where they then were, and the same distance north of camp. The Colonel had left his glasses at camp, but verified the facts through Mr. Howard's, and they quickly rode to the wagon, changed horses, ordered Mr. Biggs to join them, and the teamsters to follow with the team. As he dashed away, the Colonel shouted, " Hurrah, lx)ys, Sunday or no

Sunday 1 " Away the three hunters went, until they approached, by a strategic movement, within five hundred yards of the herd. The sun was just going down, the wind blowing from the northwest harder than ever. The signal was given by Colonel Jones, and though rein and spur were freely given to the horses, the breeze was so strong that little progress was made, as the herd pressed directly toward the hurricane.

"Lie close!" shouted Colonel Jones. Each man obeyed, laying himself close down on his animal's neck, which was a great advantage against the powerful wind. The herd was soon overtaken, and as it required such an effort for them to run against the wind,— as buffalo generally do when pursued,— the herd varied this time, and veered to the south on a line nearly in the direction of camp, in which direction by almost superhuman efforts Colonel Jones had turned them. There were fourteen calves in the herd, and before it had run five miles, eleven of them were captured and tied down. Howard securing five. Biggs four, while the Colonel caught two and then turned his attention to gathering up the calves, as darkness was now on. Night however came so quickly that two were lost in the darkness, and became a prey to the hungry wolves, ever on the alert for such chances.

At dawn the next morning all were out searching for their lost prizes of the night before, and the three that had escaped with the herd. Colonel Jones rode the same "Gray Devil" that caused so much trouble the year previous, and headed to the northeast and up a deep ravine or canon on a gallop, for time was precious. Just as he rounded a little point, there in full view stood eleven cows and the three frisky calves which had escaj^ed capture the night before. They all appeared to be paralyzed with fear, as there was no egress, except to pass down the caiion and meet their pursuers. There was no way to avoid an encounter, as to retreat for assistance would allow them all to escape. The herd dashed by him before

JOHN BIGGS.

he could arrange his lasso; then the greatest chase of the season was fully on. Dashing after them with his usual energy and recklessness, he soon had two of them tied fast on the prairie. The third one, as he expresses it, " was a holy terror to run " ; in fact, all three had been so fleet the night before, that they escaped even the thoroughbred horses,— so no wonder the Colonel hesitated to try them on the gray pony. Only by chasing at angles, and throwing the lasso with great accuracy, were they finally secured.

It was nearly noon before the rest of the party knew where the Colonel had gone, or what he had been doing.

The wagon containing the calves had been dispatched early in the morning to the main camp; the three caught that day were, after some hard work, gotten together, and tied to a rope stretched between two stakes, as before described ; but that evening the largest took a fit of anger, and dropped dead. To-day the two captives and their offspring form a charming group of eleven beautiful and stately buffalo.

The Colonel related the above facts to a group of visitors one day at Omaha, Neb., and shortly afterward was presented with the following contribution from one of his audience:

"RESCUE THE PERISHING."

All day sped on the panting herd,
Nor paused for food or thirst to slake;
An unknown goal before them lay,— They fled alone for life's sweet sake.
^ For life is sweet to all that breathe,
And from the huntsman's cruel aim They sought a refuge safe and sure. And to the lonely cañon came.
Thus sheltered from the glaring sun, And from unpitying murd'rous eyes,
They drank sweet draughts, and herbage browsed As sweet as mj^nna from the skies.
The weary miles were all forgot,
And peace came to that little band;
Night found them housed in nature's fold,. Led hither by " the Shepherd's " hand.
And morning found them still content.
But hark! A sound comes to the ear, A sound which they had learned full well
To hear with naught but trembling fear.
The ringing hoof beats down the gorge.
Urged on by rider yet concealed,— Be told a strife undoubtedly,
To which this little band must yield.
No egress was there farther on;
They needs must wait and meet their foe, While terror and dismay now reigned
Where dwelt content one hour ago.
Ah, not for sport or wild adventure. Came the huntsman that fair morn;
For his daring deeds of valor. Was a purer motive born.
Not to slay — ah, no: to the rescue,
Was his mission pure and high, To lead them out of other dangers
Into which they else might fly;
For the hand that bore the lasso,
Was a friendly hand and true. And led them out of danger's pathway,
Into pastures strange and new.
No more thirst, and no more hunger,
A hunter's target ne'er to be; These the price for being captives,—
What their fate if they were free?
Mrs. Elizabeth Edwards Keith.

At dawn the following morning, a herd of about sixty buffaloes was discovered coming directly toward camp. It was the same herd, no doubt. There were no calves among them, however. Upon Mr. Howard's suggesting it would be well to kill one, as they were entirely out of meat, the Colonel reached for his Winchester, and strode away to meet the approaching animals. Just before getting within rifle-range, the herd discovered the camp, veered to the right, and passed Colonel Jones fully three hundred yards distant. A fine four-year-old cow was in the lead, and this one the Colonel marked for his dinner; but when he endeavored to take aim, he found that the front sight to his rifle was entirely gone. There was no time for fooling; he quickly made a calculation, aimed (or rather, calculated) ten feet ahead of the running beast, — a little high,— then bang! went the gun, spat! sounded the ball, and up went the tail of the leader. Of all the dashing, spurting and " cavorting " that was ever seen, she did her part for about three minutes, and then began to stiffen; her legs stood still an instant, then she dropped. The ball had gone to the exact spot desired, through the lungs! All hands now came up to where the Colonel stood, and when they discovered he had shot the animal BO accurately at such a distance on the run, and without a sight on his rifle, they pronounced it the best shot they had ever seen made.

The cow was a fine fat beast, and afforded meat for the whole party as long as the weather permitted them to keep it.

Five more calves were captured in the afternoon, and the extraordinary success continued from day to day, until twenty-eight were safely secured at the main camp. They were generally frisky; some very stubborn. One in particular was always making trouble. He would run a hundred yards out of his way any time in order to butt over some of the boys in camp, then kick up his heels and return to his foster-mother. I gave him the name of the champion pugilist of the world at that time—"John L. Sullivan"; and he has maintained his title to this day, for he is now and long since has been the master of the herd. He has never met his "Corbett" in man or beast. He it was which thrust his left horn full length into th&

stomach of the celebrated thoroughbred runner "Ken-tuck," and whirled him in the air easily, and with as much rapidity as a terrier tosses up a rat with his nose. The majority of the calves took kindly to their foster-mothers, keeping as close to them as they a short time previously had to their real mothers. Many of the cows appeared as proud of the little orphan at their side as a hen with one chicken; others would fight desperately when the calf approached, yet to no purpose: if the little buffalo was determined to have its supper, it could not be shaken off, as supper it would have.

Success had so abundantly crowned the party's efforts, that a council was called by Colonel Jones, to consider future movements. There were more calves now than <;ow8 to feed them. What to do under such circumstances was a perplexing question. There was no ranch nearer than a hundred miles; besides, ranchmen are very much averse to selling cattle with their brand on them, especially when they know they are to remain on the frontier. The reason is obvious. Suppose anyone desired to steal cattle for a living: all that would be required of him, would be to produce a bill of sale for the animals, with the particular brand of any cattle he had killed, not belonging to himself.

After a serious consideration of the embarrassing problem which faced them. Colonel Jones determined that Mr. Biggs should accompany him to the lower Paladura, where if possible they would buy cows enough to equal not only the number of calves on hand, but the prospective captures as well. Mr. Howard was to remain behind and continue the hunt, securing as many as he could.

Early in the morning the fastest team was turned eastward, with Colonel Jones driving. All that day they drove rapidly, camping just at night in an old dugout made years before entirely underground by hunters or horse-thieves, in the side of the bank. The next afternoon they arrived At a large ranch, but the manager refused to sell a hoof;

would scarcely answer them civilly. They then drove down the valley, turning in for the night at the abandoned stage station of the once little hamlet called "Zulu," in Texas. There was a sod house " held down " by an old bachelor, the only inhabitant of the place, everything else of its former greatness having disappeared with the collapse of the "boom,"—the fate of the majority of the mushroom towns whose ruins may be met with all over the extreme West.

The hermit of the sod house thought they could purchase some cows at a ranch about ten miles down the Paladura. So the next morning, after having partaken of the old man's hospitality for the night, the party as soon as dawn showed itself were rolling over small hills and tumbling through ravines, until they came to the ranch they had been referred to, which was presided over by one Mr. Pat O'Neal. He was snugly " fixed " ; his family was living with him, and all appeared as happy as if they resided in a palace.

It was quite a treat to gaze upon a woman's face once more, but she was as shy as they were familiar, for strangers (excepting horse-thieves) were rarely to be seen in the region, so remote from all civilization, and the presence of the hunting outfit evidently disturbed the lady's equanimity.

Mr. O'Neal soon appeared, and the nature of the Colonel's errand was made known to him. As is the custom upon visits of strangers, he was very inquisitive as to where they were from, and what they wanted with cows. The plain facts, without any equivocation, were related to him, and when Mr. Biggs spoke for himself, he was immediately recognized as the man from whom he (O'Neal) had purchased his start of ponies, some ten years previously, which was one point in favor of the hunters.

Cows at that time in the Western market were worth about fifteen dollars each, but Mr. O'Neal was very loath to part with any, and concluded to make such a price to the Colonel as would bluff him at the outset; but he did not know the persistent Colonel. Mr. O'Neal named forty dollars apiece for the number that was wanted, expecting, of course, it would be instantly refused. The Colonel merely remarked that about half that price would be considered ; upon which Mr. O'Neal gave him emphatically to understand that not a cent less would buy them; in fact, he did not want to sell at all. Colonel Jones at once accepted his proposition, and drew his check for four hundred and eighty dollars, for twelve cows,— all the stubborn Irishman would consent to let him have. Mr. Biggs indorsed the check, which Mr. O'Neal knew made it good.

Mr. Biggs was left to drive the cows over to the camp, assisted by one of Mr. O'Neal's boys, while Colonel Jones hurried ahead to superintend the great work he had laid out before him.

After the Colonel had departed, Mr. O'Neal chuckled, and boasted to Mr. Biggs that "he had played that man for a sucker, and he swallowed the bait readily."

Mr. Biggs asked O'Neal if he knew Colonel Jones.

O'Neal replied, "Yes — know him well by his being so foolish as to pay forty dollars for such cows."

"Yes," answered Mr. Biggs; "but you don't know him. He is known throughout the country as ' Buffalo Jones.' He built Garden City, Kansas; has constructed a marble block which cost him a hundred thousand dollars, and he can command a hundred thousand in cold cash by one stroke of his pen. He is wild on the question of saving the buffalo, and would just as willingly have paid you eighty dollars apiece for the cows as forty."

"Be jabers 1 " responded Pat, after this disclosure, "I wish I had struck him for a hundred dollars apace."

Mr. Biggs frequently tells this story of the discomfiture of the avaricious Irishman, and enjoys it amazingly.

The cows arrived at camp in excellent condition, and the hunt was continued until the last buffalo calf of the season had been secured; in all, thirty-seven.

Mr. Biggs was left in command of the "outfit" and Colonel Jones struck across the country on horseback, with three days' provisions in his saddlebags. He was mounted on his best and fastest animal, and reached his own ranch in safety, having been absent in all just six weeks.

Mr. Biggs joined him at Garden City, July 6th, as soon as the "drive" could be made, with thirty-two of the calves, having been gone from home nearly three months.

Thus ended the most successful expedition after buffalo calves ever inaugurated, without a mishap or a miscalculation on the part of Mr. Biggs the typical ranchman, or Mr. Howard the typical cowboy of the Great West. Mr. Jones alone made the one mistake, as he should have sent forty cows with Mr. Biggs instead of twenty; but "all 'a well that ends well." The exj^ense of the expedition was eighteen hundred and twenty-five dollars. The thirty-two animals and their offspring proved to be worth many times that amount to their owner, besides the consolation of realizing that he had been doing his duty toward preserving the great race of buffalo, and at the same time atoning for his wickedness of former years in slaying so many of the noble animals.

— 13

CHAPTER XII THE ANTELOPE

THE BHYE8T AND FLEETEST OF ALL ANIMALS— "A MIGHTY GOOD GREYHOUND TO CATCH A MIGHTY POOR ANTELOPE "

WHOLE CITY ON A HUNT, DOGS INCLUDED — COLONEL JONES KILLS MORE THAN ALL

THAT old song, "I'll chase the antelope o'er the plain," was a favorite one of Colonel Jones when a barefooted country boy herding cattle on his father's farm. Little did he dream then he would become the champion hunter of this slyest and fleetest animal on the American continent. The greyhound has ever been regarded as the swiftest of all four-footed beasts; but this is not a fact. Where one greyhound may occasionally, under favorable circumstances, outstrip an antelope, there are fifty which cannot keep in sight after running the first mile. There is no better illustration of the relative speed of these flying beauties, than the remark of ex-Governor St. John, of Kansas. He is also a veritable Nimrod. Once, when on a protracted hunt on the western Plains with Colonel Jones (who was an aide-de-camp on his staff, and upon whom he always depended during the Indian troubles on the border), the latter asked the Governor his opinion in relation to hunting antelope with greyhounds. "Well," replied the Governor, "I have arrived at the conclusion that it takes a mighty good greyhound to catch a mighty poor antelope."

(194)

No one realized this quaint declaration better than Colonel Jones. He was possessed of the fastest and best blooded specimens of the breed to be procured in this country and in Europe; had tried them thoroughly, but was compelled to abandon their services, much to his regret. Some of the famous animals would occasionally catch an antelope, but it was such an effort for the dog, that often, for over a fortnight after the chase, it was unable to enter the lists again. Its feet were so badly torn and bruised by running over the dry baked earth of the prairie, covered with cacti, that it was impossible to attempt another run until the greyhound had completely recovered.

Colonel Jones then employed his dogs in another direction,—that of pursuing the deer which made their lairs in the tall grass growing in the sandhills skirting the Arkansas, Cimarron and Beaver rivers, on the south of the first-mentioned stream. These animals are compelled to resort to grass, in consequence of the absence of timber in the region of their habitat.

This was royal sport, as well as a profitable business, the carcass of a large deer readily selling for from fifteen to twenty dollars; and the Colonel lived in a country that compelled him to sell game in order to live,— much to his regret, however. His methods, always novel, evidenced his natural genius in cases of emergency. It was almost an impossibility for a team and wagon to get through those apparently interminable sandhills bordering the rivers of southwestern Kansas. His plan was, to enter the hills on horseback, leading one or two pack animals, by which means he was enabled to go almost anywhere without much difficulty.

The deer always came to the river at night to drink, and next day they could be easily tracked to their lairs in the tall grass by bloodhounds; the mouths of the hounds being muzzled so as to prevent their bellowing on the track. As soon as Colonel Jones had reached one of these hiding-

places by following the trail made from the spot where the deer had dnmk and the frightened animal leaped out, two of the hounds would be unleashed, and before the deer had run a quarter of a mile they would be at his throat with such grip of their strong jaws and great teeth, that he succumbed, after a desperate struggle.

It is a popular belief among the uninitiated, that the deer is fleeter than any other of the ruminant animals; hence the proverb, when it is desired to express swiftness, " He runs like a deer." This is merely a popular adage, however, for the antelope is fully one-fourth faster than the deer. The antelope cannot successfully be captured by dogs as a profitable business. They differ from the deer in their alertness; their almost intuitive knowledge of danger in an instant causing them to flee at its slightest sight or sound. Because of these remarkably developed instincts of the antelope, it became one of the most perplexing questions that ever confronted Colonel Jones, how to secure some of the thousands of those beautiful creatures roaming over the illimitable plains of the Great West, without an expenditure of time that was worth more than the results in a pecuniary view; for mere hunting as an amusement was a thing of the past with the Colonel. He made a careful study of the habits of the animal, after exhausting every device he could think of, and then his efforts were crowned with that success which has always been his reward when he set himself to work out a problem which engaged his earnest attention.

There was a constant and increasing demand for antelope in the market, at values ranging from three to five dollars each, and, as stated, after every plan had failed, the method which Colonel Jones at last adopted, the result of deep study of the nature of the coveted animal, was a phenomenal success. He learned that while wild animals are in motion they do not possess the sense of discerning whether other objects are also moving, or whether they are fixed. This was the key to the problem he had been so

long endeavoring to solve. It was a great discovery, one in keeping with the genius of the man ; and Colonel Jones turned the key very often, indeed,— always to his pecuniary advantage. He would drivc out in the early morning to where the antelope were feeding, and guide his thoroughbred horses toward the herd, as if to pass them. The antelope allowed the wagon to come within perhaps five hundred yards, when they would circle around, then dash away for a half a mile at a terrible speed, stop, and resume their feeding. Colonel Jones would again drive in the direction of the herd, but at an angle which kept them to the right or left, as the case might be, at a distance of about two hundred yards. The herd would stand still, their curiosity excited, until the team was nearly opposite, when off they would da«h, away ahead of their pursuer, who apparently paid no attention to them ; if anything, the gait of the team slackened until the third or fourth round of these maneuvers. By this time the antelope had naturally determined they were not being pursued, and permitted the wagon to come within two or three hundred yards, at which they merely cantered leisurely off on a slow gallop. This was the golden opportunity. No sooner than the last antelope had moved away (and not before), the horses were guided directly toward the herd, and the word given, "Go!" Then, at the height of their speed, the horses, trained to their business, dashed down upon the herd still loping along, unconscious of any change of action upon the part of their follower until the latter was within fifty yards of the contented animals, when a gentle command, " Whoa," was given to his perfectly intelligent team. In an instant they were still as statues, and Colonel Jones was on the prairie with his Winchester rifle pouring lead into the herd at such a rapid rate that a stranger would think the noise coming from a volley of musketry. At every discharge of his gun, from one to three antelopes would roll over like footballs, their velocity being so great that they often turned two or three

somersaults before stopping. Now could be witnessed the strangest feature of the wonderful spectacle: the herd invariably, at this juncture, would circle around the hunter, and all run up in a compact mass as soon as one was hit, the ball almost certainly stopping one or two more, after passing through the first and second antelope. It was no unfrequent occurrence for Mr. Jones to kill from eight to ten as the herd ihade a circuit, at a maximum distance of from two to three hundred yards.

Colonel Jones, having discovered this secret, hunted these animals with great success, and was envied by all old plainsmen, who had never learned the methods he employed, for he carefully excluded from his expeditions anyone who would be likely to understand them. As to the niimber of antelopes he could kill, he was only limited by the time occupied, if the game was plentiful, even if the number only reached into the dozens. He had an open challenge against the world, to the amount of five hundred dollars, that he could kill more antelope in one day than any other man in this or any other country.

On one occasion, just after a hard blizzard, it was reported in the town that there were fully a thousand antelope congregated about ten miles north. Two of the best hunters in the place at once organized a grand hunt for the next day. That evening they called uj)on Colonel Jones, laid their plans before him, and insisted that he must join them on the morrow. The Colonel was not that kind of a hunter, however, for he always planned and executed according to his own ideas, and then carried them out to the very letter. After many apologies he succeeded in convincing them that it was impossible for him to go with them.

At sunrise the next morning, eighteen men armed with Winchesters and shotguns, accompanied by a dozen greyhounds, started out for their anticipated great slaughter, taking wagons enough with them to haul a hundred antelope to market. The day was an ideal one, and the Colo-

nel was out of sorts because he could not be at work with his favorite weapon among the antelope, but was too honorable to go where his neighbors had gone, after he had refused to accompany them. About three o'clock p. M., his neighbor Jessup, an old Quaker, came puffing up to the Colonel's residence, and inquired, " Why don't thee go out to my house and get some antelope for thee and me?" Learning from the kind-hearted old gentleman that there was a small herd of thirteen near his ranch, only three miles distant, the Colonel saddled his thoroughbred " Kentuck" and was soon on the trail to the Quaker's. Arriving at the house, he discovered that the old man's dog had been chasing the animals and they were very timid; so he did not get near them until nearly sundown. When the hunt was over, he had bagged eleven out of the thirteen. The Colonel then hired a son of the old Quaker to haul nine of them to the railroad station, leaving two with the family whose head had so kindly informed him of the presence of the antelope on his ranch. Imagine the humiliation of the eighteen hunters on their return to town in the beautiful moonlight that night, to find themselves the possessors of but seven out of a thousand, and the Colonel having killed eleven out of a herd of only thirteen.

Many such incidents could be related, but one must suffice. It is from his remarkable success with antelope that he enjoys an international reputation as " the champion antelope-hunter of the world."

The American antelope is generally known as the prong-horned antelope, and sheds its horns annually. Unlike the deer, elk, and others of that particular group, it has hollow horns, like the cow, goat, and sheep, and is the only animal of this class which sheds its horns in this way. The bony prong never drops off, but the sheath which covers it slips off, and another is quickly grown to cover it.

The mating season is in October, when the males do

hard fighting, and may be seen pursuing each other with wonderful rapidity, for half a day at a time. Their muscles are then in a great state of development, and it is useless for a greyhound to attempt to catch one at this season of the year.

CHAPTER XIII

THE LAST HUNT !

ON THE DESERT WHERE THE RAIN WAS WITHHELD—LETTERS CONVEYING NEWS SENT OUT BY CARRIER-PIGEONS —

BUFFALO DISCOVERED—EFFORT TO CORRAL THE HERD

THREE CALVES QUICKLY CAPTURED — THE MOTHERS' DESPERATE CHARGE — DELUGE COMES UNEXPECTEDLY—"THE WAY TO CATCH A BUFFALO CALF IS TO CATCH IT"— ROPING FULL-GROWN BUFFALO — DANGEROUS OPERATION

— DESPERADOES CAMPED WITH THE PARTY AWAITING

THE LAST OPPORTUNITY ON " JUBAR "—FORTY-TWO DAYS

AND NIGHTS IN PURSUIT OF THE LAST HERD TAME AS

CATTLE — SO GENTLE THEY WOULD EVEN RUN UNDER THE SADDLE-HORSES, RATHER THAN LEAVE THEIR RANGE — COLONEL JONEs's WONDERFUL SUCCESS RECORDED IN HISTORY, NEVER TO BE OBLITERATED

THE story of the last buffalo-hunt is graphically told in Colonel Jones's journal, under date of May 16th, 1889. There is something very sad in the f ict that at this time the great animals were almost extinct, which less than twenty years previously were so numerous that the United States troops in their expeditions against the hostile tribes of Indians were frequently compelled to fire into the vast herds, to turn them and prevent them from overriding the command.

Colonel Jones's entry recording his last hunt for buffaloes is dated at Arito Blanco, a small stream about

thirty miles south of the Canadian river, in the Panhandle of Texas. Hesajjs:

" I fear this is the most stupendous of all my undertakings. Everything goes to make the task of capturing a herd of wild buffalo more difficult. It appears there has been no rain in this desert for years past. Surely, there must be a Joshua in these remote and God-forsaken wilds, who is withholding the rain. Should we see him, a lasso is just as apt to encircle his neck as a buffalo calf's, until we see the deluge forthcoming.

"Then, too, the buffalo are scattered to the four winds, and hide away in deep canons. They instinctively know their doom is sealed. How different they appear from "those of oldl — the sluggish, drooping, lazy creatures they were. They now keep their sense of sight, smell, sound and feeling wrought up to such a tension that they are often gone long before we have discovered their presence, only their tracks remaining to betray their former haunts. These we discover by the keen scent of our bloodhounds; but it is so dry that they are unable to pursue the trail any great distance.

"Don't be surprised if we do not catch a single animal. The opportunities for such expeditions have passed forever, and can only be read of, by future generations. How sad 1 How shameful! And more, to this and past generations, how disgraceful I

"As I expect to reach the Denver & Fort Worth Railroad in a couple of days, I note here some of the incidents of this exciting expedition, since I sent the last pigeon off to the north three days ago."

It is better, perhaps, that I interpolate here the letter which that pigeon carried, as it will render the story of the final hunt more intelligible to the reader. The pigeon .referred to by Colonel Jones was the first sent away from the locality where he then was, to carry to Garden City the report of the progress of the last buffalo-hunt, where

it was repeated by wire to the Chicago Times, which had furnished the Colonel with carrier-pigeons in order to get the first news of this hunt of all hunts, either ancient or modern. The text of that letter was:

"Arito Blanco, Northwest Texas, May 10, 1889.

" Dick Williams and I left Garden City, Kansas, according to arrangements previously agreed upon, on the 2d day of May, at 2: 10 a. m., with a light buggy, to which were attached a pair of the very best roadsters in the country. In two days we arrived at the headwaters of the North Canadian, a distance of one hundred and fifty-five miles, or an average of seventy-seven and a half miles a day^ which proves the superior endurance of the animals. I found all my men nicely established in camp, eagerly awaiting my arrival and anxious to begin the exciting work for which they had come. They had been prospecting over a great range of country in northwestern Texas, and luckily had located two small herds of buffalo, one of which comprised two bulls and twelve cows.

" Immediately upon this gratifying report I organized an expedition, consisting of Lee Howard, William Terrill, and myself. We prepared a week's rations, a barrel of water, and for our transportation six riding-horses and two mule teams. On the morning of the 6th we drew out, heading for 'Antelope Draw,' some forty miles from our camp, at which point we were certain the fourteen buffalo were hiding in the breaks of the sandhills. This was a sequestered locality, where man rarely penetrated, and where the grass was green, as the snow had drifted on the sides of the divides and moistened the earth, thereby giving vegetation an early start. We arrived in the vicinity of Antelope Draw early that evening, when Howard, who was riding in advance, suddenly signaled for us to halt. In a few moments he rode back to where we were waiting, and reported everything 'all 0. K.,' upon which

we turned off to the left and went into camp for the night, anxious for the contest with the buffalo next morning.

"The day broke dark and drizzling. Nevertheless, we were up betimes, and, breakfast out of the way, we mounted our horses and started for our covey. We routed the shaggy beasts early, and never were animals more surprised. They were terribly alarmed at our unexpected presence, perfectly frantic with fear, and began to stampede in every direction, but they soon joined the main herd. We took everything very easy, made all the 'cutoffs ' possible, thus saving the wind of our horses; while the excited buffalo sometimes made great circles to avoid us, traveling that day at least a hundred miles, while we did not exceed three-fourths that distance.

" The bulls were very poor and shaggy, soon dropping out, leaving the twelve cows, which by the third day of the chase became so gentle we could ride within two hundred yards of them without any difficulty. On that afternoon, as we were passing the mouth of a canon, five immense cows and three baby buffaloes winded us, and dashed out into the prairie, much to our astonishment and delight. Terrill and I were in the light wagon and Howard on horseback. As soon as I grasped ^the situation 1 shouted to Howard: ' Save the calves I Save the calves 1 ' and in another instant he was rushing over the prairie toward them like the shadow of a rapidly moving cloud. Nearer and nearer he approached the frightene<J little brutes, which now, seeing they were pursued, strained every nerve to escape. Howard was swinging his lasso over his head, as is the custom, to give it the proper momentum, and I could almost hear it hiss, its velocity increasing as he gained on the soon-to-be captives. Gracefully it shot far out in a beautiful curve, and coiled around the neck of the calf in the lead, although it was hugging its excited mother's shaggy shoulders. It was a beautiful sight to the true hunter, and was enjoyed by us far beyond any utilitarian result it

might possess for me. Howard was on his favorite horse 'Charlie,' a famous racer among the cowboys of the Canadian. Besides, Howard had been perfectly trained to the work he was now engaged in, as the ranchmen always paid him extra wages to lasso their calves for branding. It was a relatively easy task to accomplish with such a rider on his back, but impossible for a ' tenderfoot,' had one attempted it.

" The calf, as the rope pulled it up short, tumbled in a heap. The horse, supposing it was the cow which was wanted, sped right on until he reached the end of the lasso, when the calf began to dangle like a rubber ball attached to a string. At this juncture, Howard pulled the bridle-reins with a desperate jerk which instantly brought ' Charlie' to a standstill on his hind legs, and in a moment put a noose, he had already prepared, around the calf's neck, took a couple of half-hitches about its hind legs, and then with the graceful swing of a Carmencita,. he swung to his place in the saddle.

" Once more firmly in his seat, his horse was under full speed after the flying herd. A few seconds elapsed, and another calf was floundering at the end of the rope like a trout pulled from the stream by a skillful angler.

" By this time the enraged mother, fairly wild with the development of her maternal instinct, had determined to attempt the rescue of her offspring. She dashed at the enemy with all the ferocity of her outraged nature; her eyes looked like balls of fire; her hair bristled all over with battle, like that of a wildcat at bay; and her tail stuck straight out like the jib-boom of a yacht. She was the very incarnation of fury and fight. I saw at a glance that she meant ' business,'and yelled to Howard: 'GoI Your life 's in danger 1 Go quick 1 ' He obeyed my injunction just in time, for the charging brute barely missed impaling him on her sharp horns, as the plunging horse sprang forward in response to the rolling steel of the spurs. Howard suddenly whirled in the saddle, and dis-

charged his revolver (a big 44 Remington) at the cow just as she reached him. The shot made her stagger, and in a moment both horse and rider were beyond immediate harm, and the cow soon sank to Mother Earth. Our spring wagon was light, and by laying the lashes on we managed to keep v/ell up with the procession. Howard was still in the saddle, and pursuing the calf that had endeavored to overtake the herd.

" ' Five to one he gets the other calf 1' I shouted in my excitement, as the little animal swiftly crossed a small hill,— but of course there were no takers present. Sure enough, as we drove up the hill which had hidden Howard from view for a few moments, I saw he had caught and tied it, and was awaiting the arrival of the wagon to take it with the other captives to camp.

"These calves were captured at the head of the Agua Frio, in Texas. The cows we had been driving stampeded, and we had to abandon the pursuit, as we could not very well continue it and save our calves, which were of more importance just then than the herd just abandoned, for ' a bird in the hand' was worth far more than the buffaloes on the Plains. So we started for camp, and arrived safely, with the calves intact, where they nursed the fine Galloway cows we had brought along for that purpose.

" I shall not at present pursue the cows we abandoned, Tinless we can start as many as twenty-five, and not then until all have dropped their calves. We have seen but twenty-four altogether. Verily, the days of the buffalo ure numbered. There cannot be more than one hundred left in the whole United States, outside of those in the National Park, and they will probably be destroyed by the hunters before winter sets in.

"May 11. Oh, heavens 1 what a night has just gonel Surely Joshua has repented, and asked for rain. Dick Williams and I had camped in a ' draw' or little gulch, a

short distance from the Coldwater, a stream the most properly named in America. Generally, the creeks and rivers on the Plains are misnomers, but this one did not come in the usual category last night. It was cold, oh, how coldl We had nothing with us but the buggy and a tarpaulin, and made our bed with the latter, in the depths of the gulch, out of the wind as much as possible, which was blowing furiously, at the rate of at least fifty miles an hour. No clouds had appeared on the horizon that afternoon or evening, to warn us of coming rain, yet about midnight a veritable waterspout seemed to have emptied its contents upon our defenseless heads. In less time than it takes to record it, we were in the midst of a mighty flood. Underneath us, where a few seconds before the ground was as dry as a powderhorn, it was now filled with water nearly waist deep, and increasing rapidly.

" We quickly gathered all our traps, which were already soaked, threw them into the buggy, and I seized the buggy-pole and shouted in the darkness to Dick, to push; and thus, blundering over the sharp stones, barefooted, we hauled the vehicle to higher ground.

"We were completely drenched; there was not a single dry thread on us, and still the cold rain and sleet continued to pour remorselessly down upon us. Dick, in the excitement, had lost his boots, hat, coat and vest in the 'roaring flood, and I the key to my 'gripsack' as I tossed my vest into the buggy.

"As Swift says, 'The Lord tempers the wind to the shorn lamb.' I had a beautiful match-box which had been given me the year before by a young lady whom I had saved from drowning, while she was roaming through the Rocky Mountains, and in it were the only dry things of all our belongings. On the inside of the safe was a place to strike the matches, and of course it had not become wet. So I struck one of the delicate little pieces of wood, fortunately found my key, opened my ' grip,' where was concealed a pint of whisky (for snake-bites), together

with plenty of quinine. We each swallowed a four-grain capsule of the marvelous drug, and, washing it down with a little of the corn-juice, rolled ourselves in our wet wraps, where we steamed like pigs until the morning sun, much to our relief, appeared on the now clear horizon.

"The half-naked Dick immediately commenced a vigorous search for his lost garments, and fortunately found them lodged in bunches of willows down the stream, half a mile away, and he was as happy as a boy with his first pair of boots. His clothes were saturated with mud, and he had the pleasure of washing them before he could put them on.

"We got off in good time, notwithstanding our mishaps.

" I have delayed sending the pigeon on account of the storm, but it now goes.

" I met one of my boys to-day, and he informs me that they caught another calf yesterday, making four in all. I fear I am too late to capture a herd of any size this season. Will dispatch another pigeon in a few days.

"All well. C. J. Jones."

I now take up the record of the journal where I left it to relate the contents of the pigeon-letter. On that date, evidently in the evening, when in camp, and work had been suspended until the morrow, Colonel Jones wrote as follows:

" We made a drive of thirty miles to the southeast that day, and saw eleven buffalo cows, but did not attempt to disturb them, as I wished to encounter a much larger herd before undertaking to drive any in. As I was turning the team around the head of the gulch, which is about twenty miles above the headwaters of the Beaver river, t^YO large cows with one calf accompanying them suddenly ' winded ' me and went scampering over the prairie in a southwest direction. I had no saddle; neither spurs

nor revolver. Dick Williams, who was to keep near the wagon, riding the fast running-horse 'Cannon Ball,' was fully equipped with all the accoutrements necessary for such an occasion, but he was nowhere in sight. What should I do ? There was a calf worth a thousand dollars, and all that I had to do was to catch it. In an instant I was out of the wagon, off came the harness from one of the horses, and snatching a rope used to picket the team at night, I mounted the animal bareback and was away like a flash.

" By the time I had finished my crude preparations for pursuing the animals, they were at least half a mile in advance. My horse, only a buggy animal, knew nothing whatever of what was expected of him ; he was as green as a tenderfoot on his initial tour of the Plains. I made him understand, however, by the application of the rope, that he was to get over the ground as fast as his legs could carry him. He became convinced of this fact in proportion to the vigor with which I laid on the lashes. In less than a hundred yards away, my hat went flying in the breeze, but right on I flew, regardless of everything but my mission, as I pressed on to the coveted treasure. Only a short distance more to gain, and then I would be between the calf and its mother. The calf seemed to realize this as well as I, and the last hundred yards were the hardest to gain in the whole race. I laid on more of the rope, came closer to the little brute, which now began to grunt like a pig waiting for swill. Suddenly the old cow stiffened her fore legs, threw her hinder parts around in the air, and, using her front legs as a pivot, reversed ends in a second.

"I took in the situation at once, having been accustomed to such tactics before, and by a desperate effort, crowded in ahead of the calf, and bore it away to the northwest. The mother looked first at her calf and myself, then at the other cow, fleeing in the opposite direc-—— 14 tion, when to my surprise and delight, she turned and resumed her flight with her companion.

"At the turn things had taken I breathed a sigh of relief, as I had no revolver with which to protect myself in case of emergencies, and muttered, 'All I have to do now is to catch the calf,' and paraphrasing the celebrated saying of Horace Greeley, ' The way to resume is to resume,' —' the way to catch a buffalo calf is to catch it.'

"Making a noose as I sped along, I gathered up the heavy rope and swung it over my head, preparatory to throwing the precious circle around the hoped-for captive's neck; but my broncho was not used to having anything of the kind flying above his head — the only instrument he was accustomed to was the butt end of a whip in the hands of my hostler, who often had knocked him down with it when he balked in harness.

"You should have seen that broncho dodge and buck. He was worse scared than the game we were pursuing, and his antics gave the calf an advantage.

"The calf soon broadened the distance between us of more than the length of a dozen ropes. Still, 'all I had to do was to catch the calf.' It was ' a ground-hog case,' but I was satisfied that without saddle, spurs, or proper lasso, I was not going to succeed, and concluded the best thing was to turn the fleet-footed little rascal down towards the east, where I had last seen Dick.

"I swung my rope again, but for a different purpose this time, laying it on behind me in such a vigorous manner that the broncho quickly appreciated what it meant, and accordingly got down to his work without any further misunderstanding between us, and I soon had the calf turned and headed in the right direction.

"We had already traveled fully six miles, and as we went lumbering down the grade I began to realize that I had no saddle under me. Yet this was the last chance, probably, to catch a wild buffalo calf, so I must not grumble at any of the contingent inconveniences of the occasion; consequently I immediately rose superior to my discomforts.

"While thus cogitating, I presently came in sight of * Starvation Peak,' an elevated plateau extending into the valley of the Beaver, and separated from the high plains contiguous to the river by a channel or gulch about fifty feet wide and a hundred feet deep; its sides rocky, precipitous, and its top, which juts out like a headland, inaccessible except from the valley on the north of it. What the legend is from which it derives its name, I do not know. When I neared this strange formation in the otherwise relatively smooth elevated country, I saw Dick coming to my relief. He had seen my predicament (chasing the calf) with his field-glass, from the farther side of the valley, but in ascending to intersect me he rode up to the peak, supposing it was the great plateau which I was on. He was not aware of its abrupt termination, but pulled up in time to save himself from precipitation down the precipice. For a few moments he stood upon its awful edge, reminding me, as I gazed at him, of one of the bronze equestrian statues which grace the parks of the nation's capital. He seemed to me fixed there for a quarter of an hour—perhaps it was not a single minute— when he wheeled his horse, rode back to the point where he had ascended, and then disappeared from my sight, in the valley.

"All this time I was dashing on, nearing opposite the spot where I had seen him pass out of my vision, when suddenly I saw him coming up the ravine as rapidly as his horse could carry him to intercept me. I halted on the instant, waiting for him to reach me, when we changed animals, I grasping his lasso as quickly as possible, and away ' Cannon Ball' shot off with me after the much-fatigued calf. My lasso twirled in the air, as with one desperate throw I placed it around the neck of the beautiful heifer I had been chasing under such difficulties all the greater portion of the afternoon. We soon had it in the buggy and rolled off for camp, which was reached safely at 2 o'clock that night.

"We now have five calves running with our milch cows, all doing finely. Our special artist has taken some photographs of them and the varied features of our camp-life, as well as places of interest; but these I am sorry I cannot forward to you at this time.

" On the morning of the 12th one of our cowboys, Granville Thompson, left us on a tour to the north>yest. He was to meet us at camp the second night, but failed to put in an appearance. We retired without him, knowing he was no ' tenderfoot,' but perfectly able to care for himself, unless disabled by some accident. The next morning, however, fearing that some misfortune might have overtaken him, all the men occupied themselves in searching for their lost comrade. He was'met at noon the next day, having been without food or shelter for fifty-two hours, during which time it had hailed, rained and sleeted. He was very pale, and nearly dead; but a little whisky, hot coffee and some substantial food, prepared and administered by our noble and trustworthy chief commissary, J. W. Kennedy, soon revived him. He stated that he waa subject to heart disease, and before he had gone twenty-five miles from camp the morning he left us he was seized with a severe attack of dizziness, fell from his horse, and knew nothing until late in the afternoon of the next day, when he recovered, finding his animal quietly grazing near him. He was so bewildered that he could not tell where he was, or how he came to be in such a position, and only by the sheerest accident struck our trail. I do not intend to let him take any more such chances, but keep him close in, while some of our ' tenderfeet' will venture out.

"The pigeon now goes. Each of us will throw one of' our old shoes after it for luck. C. J. J."

"May 16, 1889.

"After sending off my letters yesterday, I heard there were a few buffalo lingering in the vicinity of Mustang creek, so immediately broke camp to go there.

"I continue my journal in our new camp on the Mustang, where we arrived early this evening, and are ready to commence operations in the morning, as I have concluded not to any longer ignore small herds, but take what comes to my fortune.

"When I left home on this expedition, I hoped to find a herd of at least twenty-five or thirty buffalo, and * round ' them up into camp in a single drove. But, instead of the animals being in herds, we found they were scattered in small groups of two or three; consequently we are forced to change our tactics, and I have decided to depend upon the lasso and capture each buffalo separately. To-morrow will decide permanently as to what we can accomplish."

" The morning of the 18th broke bright and warm. We mounted three of our strongest and fleetest horses, and started out for the hunt. On arriving where the buffalo were, we found that the herd consisted of only three cows, and as it would not pay for the trouble of driving them, we decided to rope one by way of experiment.

" Lee Howard was appointed to do the lassoing, but it was to be on the fore leg only, as we all well knew that to attempt to catch a buffalo cow around the horns or neck would be as fruitless of results as to lasso a locomotive going at the rate of thirty miles an hour. De Cardova, the moment Howard had succeeded in roping the fore leg, was to 'heel' her (catch a noose around the cow's hind leg), and then stretch her out so quickly she would not have time to gather herself in her surprise. ,

" Everything now ready for the attack, I took the hobbles, consisting of two log-chains, two feet long, with exceedingly heavy straps at the ends, having strong buckles.

We cautiously maneuvered until within a hundred and fifty yards of the cows, when, at a given signal, we dug our spurs into the sides of the horses, and dashed frantically over a small hill which had hidden the buffalo from our view.

"Never have I seen buffalo so completely surprised: they were absolutely paralyzed, standing as motionless as if glued to the earth, tremblingly gazing at the cyclone of horses and dust which was forced upon them, until we were within seventy-five yards, when they fled with that wonderful energy characteristic of their species, each one leaving an arc of dirt in its tracks, one end beginning at their heels, the other ending in our mouths and eyes.

"We still gained on them, however, handicapped as we were, though we could scarcely see; our eyes were full of water, dirt and dust, and we could have furnished enough material to make mud-pies for a whole kindergarten. The wind, too, was blowing almost a gale from the northwest, which was another cause of hindrance to us, our bodies catching its full force, and thus acting as a brake on the speed of the horses. The buffalo had a decided advantage of our animals under such circumstances, as buffalo always — unlike deer, elk, and some other of the ruminants— run against the wind.

"Fortunately, the contour of the country suddenly changed, and our game was compelled to alter its course, swerving more and more to the left, thus giving us the advantage. We constantly gained on the runaways, soon coming within twenty yards of them.

"Howard was on his horse 'Charlie,' De Cardova, an expert roper, on ' Cannon Ball,' while I ' held the fort' on 'Kentuck.'

"Our opportunity had now arrived; we all realized it without a word or sign from anyone. Howard's lasso began to swing around his head; ' Charlie' appeared to, and I really believe did, intelligently know what was demanded of him, for the moment he heard the whiz of the rope above

him he made a gallant spurt up to the cows, which were fairly plowing up the earth in their efforts to escape.

" Howard unfortunately allowed ' Charlie ' to crowd too close, and not being able to watch the eyes and quick motions of the three cows at one time, found himself in a critical condition. One of the frightened beasts, the second cow from him, on his right, made up her mind that ' leg bail' would not any longer serve her at this particular juncture, and acting upon her decision, dashed furiously at the horse, but in the moment lost in changing her huge quarters half-way round, was balked in her desire to disembowel the active animal. She got in just behind 'Charlie,' and in front of De Cardova, when, seeing she would miss her original mark, she threw her head around and struck ' Charlie ' a well-directed blow with the side of her horn, causing him to stagger for a few steps; yet he still dashed bravely on, the rope whirling in the air all the time.

"I had about made up my mind that Howard was really afraid to throw the lasso under the close circumstances in which he was placed, but was deceived ; he was only waiting to make a sure thing of it, for in a few seconds away went the rope like a flash of lightning, while my heart alternately fluttered between hope and fear, and I almost held my breath, waiting for the result.

" No sooner did the lasso leave the skilled hands of Howard, than ' Charley' was so suddenly stopped that he fell back on his haunches as if he were shot. The rope had struck its mark. How the great shaggy monster rolled over and over, like a grizzly turning somersaults! But De Cordova, knowing his part in the tragedy full well, by a simple twist of his right arm placed his rope over her hind leg as he swiftly dashed by, before she could gain her equilibrium.

"Now for the crowning struggle 1 Each horse understood his duty, just what was expected of him, and pulled back, with his head to the enemy, like a bulldog holding

on to the ear of an antagonist in the pit. Howard had caught the right fore leg around the fetlock, the exact place intended, and all the efforts of the cow to get on her feet were in vain ; she was tighter than any vise could have held her.

"It was now my turn to finish the last act of the drama, and I was determined not to be behind in my part. I slid off of ' Kentuck,' but took care to hold fast to the rope, one end of which was tied around his neck; and as I approached the cow, the vicious beast grew more desperate than ever in her rage, acting as if she were a carnivorous animal and wanted to devour me. She struck at me with her horns until her ribs rattled, as her head pounded her sides in her fruitless efforts to reach me; then she used her loose foot, kicking and striking until she was actually exhausted. I finally buckled the hobble on her loose front leg, but could not manage to get it on the hind one; so I took my lasso, threw it around the hind leg, ran the rope through the ring of the chain next to the fore leg, drew the two near together, and fastened them in that position. I then had no difficulty in adjusting the hobbles firmly. Now everything was ready to turn her loose.

"As soon as the horses commenced to slacken the ropes, she would begin to struggle. I gave the order for both of the men to detach the ropes from their saddles at the same instant, but was very careful myself to be mounted on ' Kentuck' before giving the signal to put my order into execution.

" The ropes slackened, she was-on her feet in a moment, with back bowed, tail curled over her back, nose almost touching the ground, hair all bristling in her rage, eyes green as goggles,—in short, the very incarnation of fight to the death! She made all sorts of attempts to charge upon us, but would only tumble for her pains; and when she tried to run, the only effect was to shake the ropes off her feet,— which was just what we desired, only the boys

had to ride forward and pick them off the ground without dismounting.

"We watched her a few moments, then bade her farewell for a few days and returned to our camp, where we discussed the advisability of hobbling, instead of driving the remainder of the buffaloes into captivity.

"I concluded to try this plan at all events, and sent out my assistants in different directions to reconnoiter for the whereabouts of the last herd, which did not exceed twenty-five in number. I gave them orders to return next day, knowing that some of the party would Burely find the buffalo by that time, as there were but four places where they could water, and they v/ould leave their tracks where they had been to drink recently.

"My brother Henry was left to guard the home camp, and take care of the calves already caught. He was a man of varied experience, both on the Plains and in civilized life; having been marshal of several large cities in Illinois, a conductor on one of the great trunk railroads, and had also served with success as a private detective. I had therefore no hesitation in leaving him in charge, although we knew that many horse-thieves and cutthroats were lurking in the vicinity, and it required a man of nerve to assume the grave responsibility. I had loaned one of my teams to the sheriff of Haskell county, Kansas, who said he was pursuing a horse-thief. He returned in a few days with the stolen animals, but the tliief was missing, and it was generally understood and believed that the officer had killed him and left his bones to bleach somewhere on the Staked Plains. I also learned that the alleged thief was merely trying to get out of the country, to prevent a money-loaner from taking his only team by virtue of a chattel mortgage he held on them; also, that he was in possession of several hundred dollars when he left home, which should have liquidated the debt. If we had been informed of the real facts, my own team would have had

more flesh on its bones, and the unfortunate man still be alive.

"After we had gone on our search for the herd of buffalo, at sundown of that day, three of the most desperate characters that ever infested the region rode up to camp, alighted from three most magnificent animals, and told my brother they desired to put up with him that night. He was well posted, and spotted the fellows at once; the leader being easily recognized by the absence of one finger, which had been shot off some years before, and he was known by the name of 'Three-finger Jack.' My brother could do nothing but treat them as gentlemen, and permit them to have their own way. He prepared an excellent supper, from the best articles in camp: buffalo-steak, antelope, potatoes, bread, butter, and a variety of canned goods.

"There were two apartments to the dugout, and my brother invited them to sleep in the inner room, to which they strenuously objected, however, declaring they wanted to be near the door in case anything happened to their horses. All three carried a Winchester each, and two large revolvers, and slept with them at their sides.

"Henry was compelled to occupy the inner room, but was careful to bar the door. He had recently returned from the East, and had brought with him a very fine pair of trousers, which hung upon a nail in the apartment occupied by the desperadoes. In the morning the trousers were missing; but he went right ahead to get a nice breakfast, saying nothing until the men had finished. Then he said:

" 'Boys, I have tried to treat you as nicely as I know how; now won't you please leave my trousers, as I certainly shall need them before I can reach any place where I can procure another pair.'

" In a moment everything was as quiet as the grave. At last one of the men spoke up, and said:

AWAITING THE LAST OPPORTUNITY FOR A CALF, ON JUBAR.

" 'We haven't got your pants. What's the matter with you ?'

"'Yes,' answered my brother; 'this gentleman has them on under his overalls, as is plainly seen.'

" Then spoke the accused :

" ' Well, what are you going to do about it ? '

" 'I can do nothing, of course,' answered my brother; 'but I consider you no gentleman, after being cared for as you have been, to deliberately steal my pants.

" 'Then come and take them,' replied the other, as he placed his hand on his revolver.

"My brother didn't want them just then, nor has he at any time since !

" While out making calculations for the grand drive of the last herd, I saw a cow and calf coming from beyond a low ridge; I quickly dropped down on my horse, 'Jubar,' whirled him about, ran back a few rods, and awaited the last opportunity for a buffalo calf.

"The cow came moping over the divide, and failed to notice me, as my horse understood his part of the program, and never moved. When within a hundred yards,, the calf gave a grunt, which I recognized as an indication that it had discovered my presence. The cow whirled around, and started off at a terrific speed, and as the calf was a large one it held its place close to her shaggy side. All I had to do was to give 'Jubar' the rein, and he-did the rest. Within half a mile he overtook the fleeing objects, and as I whirled the lasso in the air, the cow made an extra effort, leaving the calf a few feet behind. It was just what was needed, and I laid the golden wreath around the neck of the last buffalo calf ever captured.

"And here (though I dimly realized it at the time) the curtain fell, the lights were out. The drama had been played for the last time, and the curtain will never again be rung up.

"After establishing camp on the headwaters of the Paladura, we all went out to reconnoiter the whereabouts of the last herd. In the evening, De Cordova reported having discovered twenty cows and one bull about eight miles from camp. The next morning, after an understanding or code of signals and orders of operation had been written out by me, the signal was given to move. Mr. Howard had command, and was to follow the herd, ' to the ends of the earth,' if necessary. The company was never to lose sight of them, day or night, if it could be prevented. Should the herd escape during the night, bloodhounds were to be put on its trail until the buffalo w^ere overtaken; but resort to this method must not be had if by other means it could be avoided.

" Those in camp were always to keep watch from a high butte by day and by night, and like the devoted Aztecs, ■who keep the fire glowing for the return of Montezuma, so the watchman was to always keep a beacon-fire on the summit and watch for signals.

" When the drivers of the herd were sighted, the reserve at camp was to go immediately with fresh men and horses to relieve those who had been on the drive. Never ■was there more systematic organization.

"Everything ready, Howard with one other man started twenty-two full-grown buffaloes,—twenty-one cows and heifers, and one bull. The bull had been wounded, and on the second day became so lame that he dropped out of the herd.

"A light rain fell the night before starting them, and the weather was favorable, the recent rains making it easy to track the animals, which was necessary in the mornings, after the shades of night had vanished.

" The buffalo at first endeavored to shake off their pursuers, especially at night, but by ten o'clock the next day they were sure to be overtaken. They invariably held a straight general course; therefore the tracks could be easily followed, while the pursuers' horses could take a swinging trot. When first sighted the herd would go ' all to pieces,' but by proper strategy and even movements on our part, would soon come together.

"It was the fourth day before the camp was sighted.-Men, team, and saddle-horses were in a deplorable condition. Only one water-hole had been found, and had it not been for the water carried in a barrel, the pursuit must have been abandoned. During the first three days' drive the herd avoided water altogether, which shows their endurance on the desert to be equal to that of the camel, and their capacity for ranging a great distance from water to be unprecedented.

" When camp was reached, Howard, like a true veteran Boldier, refused a furlough, and joined the relief for another trial. To be sure, it was a great relief to him to secure a fresh man and team, as he could sleep in the spring wagon as it wended its way over the Plains. It was agreed that Mr. Howard should remain with the herd until I should call a halt."

Now, as the animals had become somewhat tractable and could be turned in almost any direction. Colonel Jones, having urgent business at home, took a saddle-horse and began his wearisome journey to Garden City.

It is claimed that Napoleon, after laying out his plans of battle and giving his generals minute orders of operation, would invariably lie down and take a nap, until the victory was won. Not so with the Colonel. He concluded his business the day after reaching home, and then organized another expedition, separated twenty-five of the domesticated buffalo from the cattle on his ranch, and drove them over 200 miles to the main camp in Texas. The next morning after arriving there, he dispatched a messenger on a fresh horse, with orders to Mr. Howard to drive in the twenty-one buffalo, which he had now well under control. The order was promptly complied with, and the third day the two herds were introduced to each other

near the camp in a ceremonious and fitting way. They all appeared to enjoy the occasion as much as if they had been exiles and had reunited on their native soil. The herd was then started for the Colonel's ranch at Garden City, but as soon as the wild buffalo reached the limit of their sequestered range they sniffed the air, turned " tail to," and made a straight line for their familiar haunts. All the cowboys on earth could not have turned or checked iiheiT pace; neither would they be circled off their course, as they would have run under the horses had they not moved aside and let them pass. Had there been any material in that region with which to build corrals and fence pastures, there would have been no trouble in saving this, the last little band of American bison on the great southern plains of North America.

When Mr. Howard made his report, among other things he said:

"We started the buffaloes, and followed them continually day and night for forty-two days, changing horses about twenty times. The buffalo became very thin and footsore, and seemed so lame they could scarcely walk, yet would not allow us to approach nearer than two hundred feet, when they would start off and run with as much alacrity as though nothing was the matter with them. Often we could trail them for miles by the blood left in .their tracks."

Colonel Jones further says:

"I determined to single out, lasso and hobble them, as we had done with the cow previously (although it had died of a 'broken heart'). We finally succeeded in accomplishing this, employing the same tactics as before. Mr. Howard was always depended upon to make the first •catch; he seldom miscalculated, and nearly always caught with the first attempt. We captured all except four, but one-half died within twenty-four hours after being hobbled. They usually took fits, stiffened themselves, then

dropped dead, apparently preferring death to captivity. It appeared to me they had the power to abstain from breathing.

"We worried along with the remainder, but they eventually died before arriving at my ranch in Kansas, We were fortunate enough to bring seven calves safely in, all of which lived, and helped to materially swell the herd."

The great historian, T. C. Hornaday, Superintendent of the Taxidermical 'Department of the Smithsonian Institution, in the year 1887 was commissioned by the U. S. Government to capture, alive, a lot of buffalo calves for the purpose of perpetuating the species in the National Park at Washington, D. C. He made a trip to Montana, but failed to save a single specimen; and thus came to realize how difficult an undertaking was the capture of the buffalo. In his report to the second .flMeiOTi of the Fiftieth Congress, among other things he satd:v^

"Mr. Jones's original herd of fifty-seven buffaloes constitutes a living testimonial of his individual enterprise, courage, endurance and skill in the chase. The majority of the individuals comprising the herd, he himself ran down, lassoed and tied with his own hands. It was the greatest feat ever accomplished.

" For five consecutive years. Colonel Jones made an annual trip to the uninhabited and desolate ' Panhandle ' of Texas, to secure buffalo calves out of the small herd of one or two hundred head, which represented the last remnant of the vast number of buffalo that formerly roamed in the extensive region south of the Canadian. Each of these expeditions involved an expenditure of money, and an elaborate 'outfit' of men, means of transportation, camp equipage, and other paraphernalia necessary to the successful result of the perilous undertaking.

"Perhaps the most expensive and critical adjunct to the Appointments was the herd of from a dozen to forty

fresh milk cows, which had to be taken along for the support of the captured calves. Without such natural nourishment they would have died of starvation.

"The country so often visited by Colonel Jones was sterile, barren, desolate, and almost devoid of water. It may well be imagined, therefore, that to enter its desertlike area was a task that the majority of men would naturally shrink from, attended as it was with a constant struggle against the hardships incident to such a wilderness. The few buffalo remaining were exceedingly wary, and difficult was the labor of finding them. The ground of the region, however, was admirably adapted for running them, consisting chiefly of level prairie, giving the horses employed by the hunter an advantage, and he experienced no trouble in overtaking a herd whenever it was sighted, or in being able to ' cut out' and lasso the little animals he had come so far to capture.

"The skill and daring displayed in the several expeditions by Colonel Jones and his confreres excites the wonder and admiration of the reader, and far exceeds anything that has ever before been experienced in hunting wild game for the purpose of capturing it alive. Some of the results of Colonel Jones's expeditions seem incredible. During the month of May, 1889, he with his party not only captured seven calves, but also eleven full-grown cows, of which latter, many were lassoed while rushing in their maddened speed over the prairie, then thrown and hobbled, and all in a shorter space of time than it requires to tell it. Others were actually 'rounded up,' herded, and held in control until a bunch of tame buffalo was driven out to meet them, thus making it possible to get them all to the ranch. This was a remarkably brilliant feat, and can be properly appreciated only by those who have themselves endeavored to capture the buffalo, and know by experience how difficult the task, to say nothing of the extreme danger in an undertaking of this character. T. C. Hornaday."

CHAPTER XIV

BUFFALO ON THE WATER

BOUND FOR THE OLD WORLD — LOADING BUFFALO OJf A VESSEL— BIG SHOW WITHOUT AN AUDIENCE — ANIMALS SEASICK IN A STORM — CAUSE A SENSATION IN LIVERPOOL

INVITATION TO VISIT HIS ROYAL HIGHNESS THE PRINCE OF WALES — HE ACCEPTS A ROBE, MADE OF BUFFALO FUR, FROM COLONEL JONES.

[EXTBACTS FBOM COLONBL JONES'S JODBMAL, 1891.]

AT McCook, Nebraska, September 28th, 1891, as the sun poured down its fiercest rays, I was busily ^ engaged in pitching a load of hay into the mow of a barn. I paused to wipe the perspiration from my face. Just then a small boy looked up at me and said, "Is your name Jones?"

"Unfortunately, it is," was my reply. I lowered my fork and he stuck an envelope on the tines, which I raised uj) and opened. It was a cablegram, and read as follows :

" Liverpool, England, September 28,1891.— C. J. Jones, McCook, Nebraska: Proposition accepted. Ship at once. Letter, N. Y., care Cunard line. Webster."

The proposition referred to was one I had made two weeks previously to A. M. Webster, manager for C. J. Leland, a wealthy English nobleman, offering to deliver at Liverpool ten full-grown buffaloes, for a certain consideration. The news was joyful, as the price was a fabulous one.

— 15 (225)

Mr. Wayne Boor was in the mow lugging the hay back, and was nearly smothered. I called him to the window and asked him how he would like a trip to England. He looked dumbfounded, and stared at me fully a minute without speaking, and then not until I had explained more fully. I told him as he had been with me five long years, had been so faithful, and needed a rest, I would give him a tour of the Old World free. " It is more than I ever dreamed of," was his response. He could not pitch any more hay, but acted like a small boy who had never been anywhere, just before going to his first circus. The next day we took a coil of rope to the corral. I saddled "/Jubar," my faithful horse, which had never failed me in time of need. Mr. Boor was mounted on a good steed, and with a cowboy, Frank Smith, we commenced the lassoing and corraling of the ten buffaloes. They were fat and rollicky, but by desperate riding and expert lassoing we soon had ropes on the ten desired, and in the corral. I then had them and a portion of the herd photographed ; the illustration will be found on another page. The animals with ropes around their necks are the ones which went abroad.

On the 19th of October, 1891, I loaded five pairs of my finest full-blooded bisons on board a palace stock-car, at McCook, Nebraska,— the animals destined for Liverpool. Accompanied by Mr. F. W. Boor, I left home to take them over the mighty deep. Everything worked admirably, and at the end of a week the car was safely run onto the White Star Steamshij) Company's docks in New York city. Then the question was, how to get the shaggy beasts on board that great monarch of the seas, the " Runic." Gangways without sideboards at least six feet high, were of no use. Finally, such a gangway was l)rocured, and the buffalo taken from the car, one by one. To avoid the crowd that would naturally gather upon such an occasion, the labor of transferring the buffalo to the steamship was commenced about 4 o'clock in the morn-

ing, while all was quiet and no loungers about. The glare of the electric lights on the dock set the bewildered beasts fairly wild with excitement, and one of the best " shows " of the season, without much of an audience, was played around and among the thousands of boxes, cotton-bales and packages of every description, lying on the dock awaiting shipment. One monstrous bull had apparently concluded he required more music; so he mounted a piano-box, and thrust one foot down through it. The keys he struck gave notice to all that he had gotten up to "G." Tlie next animal climbed nine points higher in the scale; while the last off the car broke his rope and ran frantically over everything that chanced to be in his course, for fully an hour. By that time I had procured a lasso, thrown it over the obstreperous brute's neck, and he was quickly hauled up the gangway to his proper place.

All were-on board, and everything ready for the novel voyage at high noon, the 27th, at which moment the vessel steamed out into the river, and away for Sandy Hook, twenty-five miles distant. Arriving at this point, the pilot was lowered to a little skiff awaiting him, and the Kunic again started for her proper element, the deep sea. The Runic was then one of the largest and fastest freight steamers crossing the Atlantic.

The Runic's cargo on this trip comprised one hundred thousand bushels of wheat, hundreds of bales of cotton, two hundred and seventy-eight head of fine bullocks for the English market, besides a great variety of other valuable articles. All went smoothly the first afternoon and night out, but the next morning, the 28th of October, the wind blew a stiff gale from the north, which made most of the " tenderfeet" (or in this sense those unused to the sea) dreadfully sick, affecting even the buffalo in the same manner; besides, the waves had rolled over their sheds, •causing them to shiver with cold. And as I climbed along the])ens that morning, to examine into the condition of my valuable pets, a mighty wave dashed over the vessel, nearly strangling me. I finally managed to reach the animals and locate them; found them all alive, but more than half their number as sick as some of the passengers in the cabin. The great beasts would lie stupid, grate their teeth, and rest their noses on the deck. Their eyes were sunken and dim, showing the extent of their suffering; a really pitiable sight. The captain was very attentive and kind to the poor animals; he ordered the sailors to cover their sheds with tarpaulins, to protect them from the spray which was continually flying over them with its freezing coldness. This continued for four days, when the storm culminated in a furious gale, tossing the goodly ship about like a cork on a mill-pond. At times the buffalo were mid-sides in the sea, as the water occasionally rolled upon the deck. Yet they endured this better than their experience of the second day, as they had now recovered from their dreadful sickness, and were taking their food with a relish.

On landing at Liverpool there were a half-dozen artists waiting to sketch the animals, and the next morning all the leading journals of London were decorated with pen-pictures of what they termed " The Buffalo King and some of his subjects."

After delivering the buffaloes, Mr. Boor and I spent a week in London, ten days in Paris, three days in Glasgow, and then returned to London, where I received many invitations to be entertained and dined with the royalty and other dignitaries, among whom was Sir Walter Gilbey, President of the Agricultural and Fat Stock Association of the British Isles, Through him I received an invitation from the Prince of Wales to visit his Royal Highness on the following Thursday. Sir Walter was to accompany me, but as I had already purchased my steamer-ticket for New York, and as urgent business was awaiting me there, I folded up two beautiful rugs, woven from the fur of the buffalo, and sent one each to Sir Wal-

HIS ROYAL HIGHNESS THE PRINCE OF WALES.

ter and the Prince; also some pictures of my herd of buffalo at home, together with letters of regret and the reasons why I could not comply with their requests. I saw Sir Walter Gilbey afterward, and he assured me it was useless to send the robe to the Prince of Wales, as it would be against all precedent for him to accept a present from anyone outside the royal family. A few weeks after reaching home, however, I received the following

letters : [Letter from Sir Walter Gilbey.]

Elsenham Hall, Essex, 1st January, 1892. C. J. Jones, Esq. — My Dear Sir: I have heard from Sir Dighton Probyn that the Prince of Wales accepts, with pleasure, the beautiful buffalo robe which you left in my charge, to offer to his Royal Highness. You will, I have no doubt, in due course receive a proper acknowledgment of the same.

The elegant robe which you so kindly presented to me has proved most useful. After three severe attacks of influenza, cold "weather affects me, and the warmth of your kind present, during the past month, has added greatly to my comfort.

Accept my sincere wish that you may have health and happiness this New Year. Yours very truly,

(Signed) Walter Gilbey.

[Letter from his Royal Highness the Prince of Wales.]

SANDRINOnAM,

Norfolk, 30th Dec. '91. My Dear Sir: I am directed by the Prince of Wales to thank you for your letter of the 8th instant, forwarded through Sir Walter Gilbey, and for the handsome rug which you sent for his Royal Highness's acceptance, and which the Prince accepts with much pleasure.

The Prince has always taken the greatest interest in the American buffalo, and agrees with you in regretting the wantonness of the slayers of such a noble race.

His Royal Highness wishes you every success in the efforts you are making to reproduce this almost extinct race of animals.

I am also desired to thank you for the photogi'aph which you have sent to his Royal Highness.

I remain, my dear sir,

Truly yours,

(Signed) D. M. Probyx, General Comptroller and Treasurer,

CHAPTER XV

LAST OF THE BUFFALO

LIKE PEOPLE, THEY BELONG TO MANY DISTINCT FAMILIES

THEY ORGANIZE LIKE AN ARMY — HOW THE HERD WAS

LOCATED BUFFALO STAMPEDE EQUALED A CYCLONE — THE

CAUSE AND RESULTS — A MOST GRAPHIC DESCRIPTION, BY ONE WHO

KNOWS ONLY METHOD OF ESCAPE CANADA'S LAST HERD CAPTURED BY

COLONEL JONES — ATTENTION TURNED TO CAPTURING MOOSE — SUCCESSFUL HUNT IN

MANITOBA. CATALO — PROGRESS IN CROSS-BREEDING

DESCRIPTION AND HABITS OF THE NEW RACE OF CATTLE

THRIVE WITHOUT ARTIFICIAL FOOD OR SHELTER — HARDY AND FERTILE — ROBES AS HANDSOME AS BEAVER-SKINS.

A GREAT herd of buffalo on the Plains in the early-days, when one could approach near enough without disturbing it, to quietly watch its organization and the discipline which its leaders appeared to exact, was one of the most interesting objects ever witnessed. One of the striking features of the spectacle was the apparently uniform manner in which the immense mass of shaggy animals moved. There was a constancy of action indicating a degree of intelligence to be found only in the most brainy of the brute creation.

In the event of a "stampede," every animal of the separate yet consolidated herds rushed away together, as if they had turned mad at once; for the buffalo, like the Texas steer or wild horse, stampeded on the slightest provocation—frequently without any assignable cause.

(280)

Like an army, a herd of buffalo always put out its vedettes to give warning in case anything beyond the ordinary happened. The sentinels were always to be seen in groups of four, five, or ten, sometimes even twenty miles distant from the main body. They were invariably old bulls that had been whipped out. When they were apprised that something was approaching that the herd should get away from, they ran directly to the center of the great mass of their peacefully grazing congeners. (A good hunter always knew where the main herd was by the direction in which the guards ran.) Meanwhile, the young bulls, also on duty as sentinels on the edge of the main herd, watching the vedettes, the moment the latter moved on a lope for the center, raised their heads, and in the j)eculiar manner of their species gazed all around and sniffed the air as if they could smell the source of impending danger. Should there be something which their instinct told them to guard against, the leader took his position in the rear to guard danger's point, the cows surged in the opposite direction and the calves crowded to the center, while the rest of the males gathered on the flanks, indicating a gallantry to the fair sex which might be emulated at times by the genus.homo.

The reader will find the following extracts from Colonel Jones's journal of intense interest. Here is his graphic description of a " stampede ":

"During the third of a lifetime spent on the Great Plains of the interior of the continent, I have witnessed many stampedes of buffalo, wild horses, and Texas cattle. Twenty-five years ago a stampede of buffalo (which then roamed in vast herds, numbering millions) was an everyday affair; now, such an occurrence is impossible. What caused the huge, shaggy monsters, accustomed to the tornado, the vivid lightning, the terrible hail that frequently accompanies the sudden, short storms of the prairies, the wolves, and the thousand-and-one strange phenomena of nature, to stampede at apparently nothing, is one of those

problems that will admit of no solution. Sometimes it was a flash of lightning from a dark cloud; again, a cry of a starved wolf; the appearance on the horizon of a single figure; a meteor; or perhaps something as insignificant as the barking of a prairie-dog, sitting on the edge of its burrow. If a single animal snorted and started to run, if only a rod, all others near it would start in an opposite direction from it, and thus others were frightened until all were a surging mass. A herd once started, I have seen the whole jirairie for miles absolutely black with the fleeing beasts. There was nothing so indescribably grand, yet so awful in its results; the earth, shaken by the heavy tramp of their hoofs upon the hard ground, fairly reverberated as they passed a given point. Woe to him, her, them or it that stood in the way of the mighty throng of infuriated, maddened animals ! Nothing but annihilation, absolute and complete, their portion.

"A buffalo stampede, indeed 1 How few there are today who have ever passed through this thrilling experience ; this moment when the heart fluttered at the roots of the tongue; when the pursuer, revolver or gun in hand, the spurs rolling on the sides of his frightened steed, endeavored to force him nearer to the most horrid of all beasts to the eye of a horse. Still on and on, like a cyclone in its fury went the great mass, the living cataract, plunging up as well as down the hills and over the plains, tearing and cutting every vestige of vegetation; and woe unto any and all living creatures that chanced to be in its pathway 1

"Often have I heard the heavy rumble as if a terrific peal of thunder were reverberating in the distance. I could see a great cloud without water. I could feel my blood run cold and my hair stand on end, as I knew that the sound was not thunder, but the roar of the beating hoofs of a living avalanche. I knew the cloud which was approaching nearer and nearer was not rain, but dust and dirt thrown high in the air by the nimble feet of the

countless host of buffalo. To flee from their wrath would have been the height of folly. All that could be done was, if possible, to find a high bank which they could not ascend, and station myself on the highest cliff and rest content until the herd had passed by. If no such retreat was near, then I must rely on my trusty rifle, which was always with me, both day and night. To be sure, I did not depend on shooting them to lessen their number, but to divide the herd and turn their course. This was done by elevating the weapon over the herd just enough to miss their great humps that rolled on toward me like millions of iron hoops, bounding in the air at every little obstacle encountered. Then, when they were within fifty yards, the trigger was touched and the ball whistled furiously over their heads. The buffalo, with one great impulse of dodging the missile, swerved to the right or to the left, owing to which side of them the bullet had passed. Then a great rent or split would open out, and the moving mass would pass by on either side. With wonderful instinct, those coming up in the rear would follow the footprints of their leaders, and the great rent in the herd would remain open for hours at a time, for a quarter of a mile both in front and behind, when they would gradually come together in the rear of where I stood, and thunder along in their mad career. It is true that one animal alone could not have made any impression on the great phalanx; but there is unity in strength, and both were absolutely required in such time of peril.

"Such sights and sensations cannot be satisfactorily pictured to the millions of people now living and those unborn. I regret exceedingly that the kodak was not a more ancient contrivance, so that a true representation could have been taken from life and handed down to those who will now only be permitted to read pen-pictures of the days which will never more return."

As soon as the stampede ended, the single herd was broken up into many smaller ones that traveled relatively close together, but led by an independent guide. Perhaps only a few rods marked the dividing-line between them, but it was always unmistakably plain, and each moved synchronously in the direction in which all were going.

This distinction of groups unquestionably represented different families of the buffalo race. Colonel Jones positively asserts that there is no doubt of this fact. He says:

"Each small group is of the same strain of blood. There is no animal in the world more clannish than the buffalo. The male calf follows the mother until two years old, when he is driven out of the herd, and the parental tie is then entirely broken. The female calf fares better, as she is permitted to stay with her mother's family for life, unless by some accident she becomes separated from the group.

" The resemblance of each individual of a family is very striking, while the difference between families is as apparent to the practiced eye as is the Caucasian from the Mongolian race of people.

" These groups are as quickly separated from the great herd after a stampede, as is a company of soldiers from its regiment at the close of 'dress parade.' The several animals know each other by scent and sound; they grunt similarly to a hog, but in a much stronger tone, and are quickly recognized by every member of the family. When separated by a stampede or other cause, they never rest until they are all together again.

"A pathetic sight was sometimes witnessed when the mother of one of these families was killed at the first shot. They were so devoted to her they would linger, and wait until the last one could be easily slain. Often have I so crippled a calf that it was impossible for it to follow

REPRESENTING THE AGES OF BUFFALO.

METHOD OF SKINNING BUFFALO.

the herd, and its pitiful bleating would hold the family until I could kill all desired. Should the calf be wounded in the fore or hind parts, the old cows would actually support the parts so crippled, and it would walk away on the normal parts by such aid. Sometimes when I now lasso a calf of those in domestication, and attempt to lead it away, the mother will quickly place herself in front of her baby and thrust a horn under and often through the loop of the rope, and hold the horse and rider perfectly solid; while if the rope is slackened, she in some instances will free the calf entirely. Such intelligence appears almost human. Often while hunting these animals as a business, I fully realized the cruelty of slaying the poor creatures. Many times did I 'swear off,' and fully determine I would break my gun over a wagon-wheel when I arrived at camp; yet always hesitated to do so after several hours had elapsed. The next morning I would hear the guns of other hunters booming in all directions, and would make up my mind that even if I did not kill any more, the buffalo would soon all be slain just the same. Again I would shoulder my rifle, to repeat the previous day's experience. I am positive it was the wickedness committed in killing so many, that impelled me to take measures for perpetuating the race which I had helped to almost destroy.

" Th* mastership of a herd was attained only by hafd, fearful struggles for the place. Once reached, however, the victor was immediately recognized, and kept his authority until some new aspirant overcame him, or he became superannuated and was driven out of the herd to meet his inevitable fate — a prey to those ghouls of the desert, the gray wolves.

"The natural life»of the buffalo is much longer than is that of domestic cattle. I frequently saw animals so old their horns had decayed and dropped off, which indicated that they live to a patriarchal age. I saw a buffalo cow

in the zoological garden in Paris which was thirty-one years old, and am sure I have seen wild ones from ten to fifteen years older."

From the Chicago Times, dated at the time when Colonel Jones purchased the famous " Stony Mountain" herd of bison, which made such a stir, I extract some facts connected with the shipment of the animals and their stampede, which is germane to this chapter:

" La Tauche Norbert, of Regina, the government seat for the northwest territories of Canada, is in the city, en route to the eastern provinces. Last evening he entertained the loungers in a corridor of the Palmer House rotunda with stories of that northern region; but what held his listeners best was his account of a shipment of buffalo from Stony Mountain, Manitoba, to Garden City, Kansas. He said: A few months ago, C. J. Jones, a prominent ranchman of Kansas, paid a visit to Major Sam Bedson, warden of the penitentiary, to whom he made an offer of cash for the magnificent herd of buffalo belonging to him. The price offered, twenty thousand dollars, was not fancy enough for the gentleman who worked the corner on the last remnant of an almost extinct animal. More money was demanded, and for a few weeks negotiations for a transfer stood still. Meantime, Major Bedson notified the Dominion Government that such an offer had been made, and asked what inducement would be made to prevent the herd's removal to the United States.

*' It is understood that the Dominion Government made a bid, but the recent transfer shows Colonel Jones on top, at a cost of about twenty-five thousand dollars. A week ago Saturday the first consignment from the famous herd was loaded at Winnipeg, on the cars of the St. Paul, Minneapolis & Manitoba Railroad, and they are now en route to the Kansas ranch.

"Among those who witnessed the loading of the animals were several ' old-timers' in the Northwest, who ten years ago thought nothing of a sight of great herds of buffalo in a stampede across the country, and there was a feeling of sadness at parting with the shaggy monsters; and well there might be, for specimens on the far Northwestern plains are now as scarce as hen's molars.

" The distance from Stony Mountain to Winnipeg is about twelve miles, and when thirty-three of the ninety-five had been separated for shipment, they were driven across the open prairie to the Winnipeg stock-yards. Three or four naughty old bulls, when half-way on their journey, sniffed the air, saw trouble, and with a sudden ' right about' threw down their heads, and with their tails high in the air took the crow-line for their old quarters. Horsemen armed with heavy cowboy whips and steel prongs charged after the truants, but the animals, their ancient vigor having returned to them, soon reached home. Wlien the others arrived at the Winnipeg yards, they too turned tail, but were headed off, and soon driven across the railroad. Jones ordered, as soon as the herd was across, that a train of freight cars a mile long be pulled up to the end of the railroad fence, and thereby prevent a stampede back across the railroad. Everything worked exactly as the great general had planned. The stockyards were on the north side of the road, and how to "get the buffalo into such a trap was apparently beyond human skill; but Jones is the most wonderful schemer ever seen in the Queen's domain, beyond question. He had a hasty fence built from the north side of the gate on the west side of the yards, in a circular fashion, and made it fast to the east end of a car, then ordered the coupling-pin pulled and the east end of the train moved to the east one car-length. As soon as the buffalo saw daylight between the cars, they made a furious dash for their old home to the north. Jones was well mounted, and pushed those in the rear up into the herd. Every buffalo leaped

clear over the track, and the circling fence guided them through the great gate into the stockyards. Jones then jumped from his mount upon the gate and gave himself a mighty push from the fence, and swung in front of the whole herd, which had reached the limits of the pen, realized the trap, and were retreating,— but too late. The mighty gate had closed, and Jones was standing triumphant upon it, as calm and composed as if nothing unusual had occurred, while crowds of people enjoyed this greatest victory our people ever witnessed.

" Then the buffalo began a stampede inside, and trouble commenced in dead earnest, which was as exciting to the spectators as a duel in the dark with knives, between a couple of Southern editors. When the buffalo realized they had been caged, they began a fight among themselves, and some fierce encounters were waged between the old fellows. They tossed the younger ones skyward on their horns, and gored them as they came down. A dog that had been used to the now maddened brutes got in among them, and in less time than it takes to tell it the unfortunate canine was reduced to a grease-spot and flying particles of hair. The fight lasted for nearly an hour; so the idea of getting the buffalo to march on the gangway was about abandoned, and would have been but for the action at this juncture of an infuriated bull who took it into his head to inaugurate a stampede. The old fellow had been making trouble all day, and ' waded in '" to eclipse all his previous efforts. Gathering all his strength, he got behind the rest of the herd; then Jones prodded him furiously. It was then he commenced to make it unpleasant for his companions, bellowing at them, and driving his monstrous horns into their flanks. In this way, from pure devilment, buffalo have from time immemorial worked up a grand stampede. In this instance the herd were compelled to forge ahead, and, having no other plank to travel, had to march into the car, the ' limbo ' prepared for them. But when the old brute

who had caused all the rumpus arrived at the car-door and saw where his skill at stampeding had landed him, he tossed up his head in his characteristic way, and with a look of disgust wheeled around, cleared several fences from seven to ten feet high, and was soon observed as a small speck only, far down the prairie, while all attempts to turn him back were like endeavoring to make the Mississippi river run up-hill.

"When the buffalo had made good his escape, Mr. Jones closed the iron car-doors with a clang, and the world's first car-load of buffalo was soon speeding on its journey to their far-away home in sunny Kansas, and Canada lost one of her greatest opportunities, which will be regretted by all true subjects of her Majesty's domain."

On one of his trips in Canada, Colonel Jones heard of some moose whose habitat was about forty miles out of Emerson, in the Dominion. True to his innate love of hunting and preserving large game, he at once determined to secure some of these animals, none of which he had ever seen alive. His first and the principal idea which controlled him was, if possible, to get one or two young ones, and add them to the stock of wild ruminants on his ranch at Garden City.

He started on the chase (or rather, hunt) in his usual methodical way; for, as previously observed, he is a very practical man, and never does a thing without giving the subject his serious thought. Then if he determines a thing can be accomplished, he never lags until it is consummated. The story of his success in this instance cannot better be told than in his own description of the expedition:

" My original intention was to penetrate the northern regions, as far as Alaska if necessary, in search of young moose, elk, and such other herbivorous wild animals as could be found. While waiting at Emerson for a train,

I entered into conversation with a half-breed Indian about wild animals, and much to my delight and sur-i:>ri8e, was informed that he knew where there were two old moose of prodigious size, and several young ones. I at once investigated the responsibility of the savage, as, from a long experience with them on the Western Plains and in the Rocky Mountains, I was familiar with their love of boasting and occasional carelessness of the truth. I was rejoiced when my landlord assured me that the Indian was responsible and perfectly reliable. Upon this, I immediately sought a team to convey us to the coveted spot where the moose were said to frequent. I found a liveryman who informed me he had a team that could 'get there.' By the way, I learned very soon that this stable-keeper was the once celebrated hurdle-rider of Cole's circus, and I was not long in making terms with him for the team.

"My landlord (himself an old hunter) was to accompany me on the proposed trip, and in less than an hour after hearing of the moose we were all three in a comfortable spring-wagon, bowling over the prairie at the rate of a mile in eight minutes, headed for the tamarack swamp where the moose were known to be. Our guide first took us to where some Indians were camped, digging snakeroot. We were to get one or more of the bucks to go with us. They were only too glad of the opportunity; but I had to hire the whole ' outfit.' Their astonishment was great when they learned a party was going for moose without guns, and when the guide explained my method of getting big game, a lonely old buck stretched himself back and exclaimed with a sneer, ' Squaws I' This to me was a decided insult, and if I could have spoken his horrid language, would have let him know that I had killed more big game in my life than his whole tribe. Perhaps it was as well that we could not converse together, or we might have had a regular cowboy ' round-up' before I had accomplished my mission.

"We were now ready to turn in for the night. The Bun had long since disappeared. I took out my watch, and to my surprise discovered it was ten minutes after ten, although the twilight still lingered in the little valley. The red-margined clouds in the northwestern sky looked as if the sun had only just passed below the horizon. At first I supposed my watch had been gaining time. Then I remembered I was nearer the northern regions, where often is seen the ' midnight sun.' We spread our blankets and rolled in for the night. I never suffered so much from cold, even in January.

" The sky soon became quite clear, and in the morning (June 26th) the ground was covered with frost. I routed the Indians out at break of day, which came about half-past two o'clock, and we partook of a lunch, with a cup of strong coffee to wash it down.

" Our early meal disposed of, we started for a grove of poplars about a mile distant from camp, where it was reported the moose had last been seen. Arriving at the grove, two of us remained outside the clump of timber to watch if any thing ran out, while six Indians and the guide went into it to search for the moose. They had been gone, it seemed to me, long enough to have traveled over the whole area, with an hour to spare, when suddenly I heard a tremendous rattling and snapping of sticks and brush. At the same instant I saw, above a quaking-ash, a huge head, which I immediately made up my mind was nothing less than a grizzly bear. There I was, without even a revolver, and the worst of all wild animals coming directly toward me. What could I do but stand and ' face the music ' ? By the time I grasped the dreadful situation, if my conjectures were true, I saw very plainly that what confronted me was not a bear, but an immense female moose 1 Her long legs looked to me like fence-posts. She passed only a few yards away, making a ' bee line ' for a tamarack grove, half a mile distant.

"Now for the fun I A sharp watch was kept up, hoping — 16
to see a calf following; but no calf appeared. In a few moments I saw the head of our guide emerge from the brush, and to my unbounded delight he held in his arms something that looked like a young colt. Great heavens 1 What is it ? A moose, indeed ? Who ever dreamed of such a looking creature ? Legs like handspikes four feet long; head almost like a bear, with a neck only six inches in length; body like a young calf, except it had' a well-defined hump on its shoulder. When standing it was as large as a young Norman colt; really stood higher, though its body was not quite as heavy. It was the greatest curiosity I had ever seen, and I felt very proud of its acquisition to my collection of wild beasts,— particularly so because the moose is, like the buffalo, nearly extinct. It is now a magnificent animal, as large as an average carriage-horse.

" The guide had routed two calves: one escaped in the underbrush, while the one he captured endeavored to ascend a steep bank and fell back into the arms of the guide. We spent the day looking for the missing animal, but to no purpose.

"When I shipped the buffalo from Canada, I took the moose to my ranch at Garden City, and as my time was occupied looking after the buffalo, I finally sold it to the owners of a park at Hutchinson, Kansas, where it appeared to thrive in that sunny clime. When the Manitoba herd was added to the buffalo I had before captured, they numbered one hundred and thirty-five, a portion of which I took to Salt Lake City, where I disposed of them. Those at Garden City I experimented with for several years.

" I turned my attention to carrying out my original idea of producing a race of animals, by engrafting the buffalo upon our domestic cattle.

"As to the new variety of animals so produced, I should not close without saying something in particular as to thia discovery.

CATALO COW, THREE-QUARTERS BUFFALO

DESCRIPTION AND HABITS OF CATALO

243

" I have been very diligent during the past five years in endeavoring to produce a race of cattle equal in hardiness to the buffalo, with robes much finer, and possessing all the advantages of the best bred cattle. To say that I have succeeded, without furnishing the proof, would merely cause derision ; so I have photographed a number of these wonderful animals, which will give a slight idea of what has been accomplished. The reader may have further and ocular demonstration by seeing for himself.

"To these cross-breeds I have given the name, ' Cat-alo,' from the first syllable of cattle and the last three letters of buffalo (cat-alo); thus forming a suggestive nomenclature for the new animals.

CATALO COW. Seven years old. Weight, 1620 pounds.

" Catalo are produced by crossing the male buffalo with the domestic cow. Yet the best and surest method is the reverse of this. Only the first cross is difficult to secure; after that, they are unlike the mule, for they are as fer-

tile as either the cattle or buffalo. They breed readily with either strain of the parent race — the females especially. It is very difficult to secure a male catalo. I have never been able to raise but one half-breed bull, and he was accidentally killed before becoming serviceable.

"The half-breeds are much larger than their progenitors of either side; the cows weighing from twelve to fifteen hundred pounds. Major Bedson, of Manitoba, succeeded in raising a male half-breed, but unfortunately made a steer of him when young. At five years old he was butchered, and dressed twelve hundred and eighty pounds — equivalent to a live weight of twenty-four hundred and eighty pounds.

" The quarter and three-quarter buffalo are not so large as the half-blood; they are about the same size as ordinary good cattle. The seven-eighths and fifteen-sixteenths buffalo are of the size of buffalo, and resemble them in shape and color. The fur of the three-quarter and seven-eighths buffalo makes the finest robes. This fur is perfectly compact, and when bred from the black strain of cattle, is as handsome as that of the black beaver. Some of the half-bloods are excellent milkers, yielding a fair quantity of milk, \Vhich is as rich as that of the Jersey. The nearer they approach the full-blood buffalo, the less quantity is produced; but the milk is correspondingly richer, as the milk of the full-blooded buffalo cow is richer than the Jersey's.

"The catalo are quiet animals, so long as you keep hands off. They are good feeders, have excellent appetites, and are invariably in excellent flesh, though fed on any kind of provender. I have successfully wintered them on the 'range,' without any artificial food or shelter, as far north as Lake Winnipeg. They withstood the cold when the mercury reached fifty degrees below zero, without artificial food or shelter.

"I have succeeded in crossing with almost all the different breeds of cattle, but the Galloway is unqiiestion-

ably the safest, most satisfactory, and produces the finest and best robes.

"Thecatalo inherit more of the traits of the buffalo than of the domestic cattle. They face the blizzards, and when the first of the unwelcome storms appears in early winter, the domestic cow and her calf bid adieu to each other,— the cow drifting with the storm, while the calf faces the blizzard and remains with the buffalo herd.

"There is one peculiar thing about the catalo: they all have 'solid' colors; i. e., they are either black, seal brown, brindle, or white. I never saw or heard of a spotted catalo.

" They are somewhat inclined to be cross, and when the cows have young calves at their sides are exceptionally so.

"After all my experiments in cross-breeding, I feel confident it can be made successful, if the right class of cows la secured and they receive the proper treatment, without which none can hope for success. I did not only make a failure, but two or three of them; yet by persistent efforts, succeeded in a remarkable degree in producing the very kind of animal my imagination dwelt upon while in western Texas in 1886."

CHAPTER XVI

DOMESTICATED BUFFALO

HABITS OF DOMESTICATED BUFFALO, COMPARED WITH WILD
— PROPAGATION TAKES NERVE TO CONQUER THEM —<-
CORRALS OF WIRE ; FENCE-RAILS NOT EFFECTIVE — BUFFALO KILLS HIS CAPTOR " JOHN L. SULLIVAN," WHICH
NEVER MET A " CORBETT "—BREAKING BUFFALO TO HARNESS— NO boy's play —COMPELLED TO HOLD THE LINES WITH A WINDLASS — CONGRESS HELD RESPONSIBLE FOB EXTINCTION OF BUFFALO—COLONEL JONES's OFFER TO CORRAL A HERD — GOVERNMENT PROPERLY WARNED OF THE DANGER, BUT IGNORED IT—THE NUMBER THAT EXISTED AT DIFFERENT PERIODS — UNWRITTEN CODES OF HUNTERS—WHY THE TRAILS ARE CROOKED—HOW COLONEL JONES KILLED A WHOLE HERD.

UNDER domestication the buffalo loses but few of its normal characteristics. The greatest change appears to be in a diminution of its power of scent, which serves it so admirably in its wild state, and in an increase of the power of vision. In their natural condition the eye is rarely depended upon to locate the whereabouts of an enemy, while their sense of smell is so wonderfully developed that neither animal nor man can pass them on the windward side within two miles without being immediately discovered;- indeed, often a herd has been stampeded by the scent from a single hunter even four miles away.

Under domestication much of this keen instinct ap-

(246)

pears to be eliminated from their nature; this in consequence of a change in their environment, which, as scientists have proved, completely metamorphoses the character of man, after even only one or two generations; and this applies equally to the brute creation, so far as observation extends. Now, by the radical change in their surroundings, the buffalo absolutely fail to recognize anything by scent, depending entirely on sight or sound — a complete reversion in this particular from their normal state of freedom. Colonel Jones affirms that "under certain conditions they sometimes, in their domesticated environment, scent water, especially when ravenously thirsty and when but a short distance away, while in their wild state I have known them to scent it when it was miles distant."

He says further: "While wild, it is an impossibility to turn a herd from its general course; under domesticationy however, the buffalo yields as readily to the cowboy's will in this particular as do our native cattle. Yet they will never allow themselves to be driven into a close corral, barn, or any other inclosure without a domestic cow in the lead, or they are ' tolled ' in by some seductive food or salt. A corral made of wire only has no terrors for them, as in such an enclosure they are able to see in all directions. They are strong feeders, taking kindly to corn and all other grain, as well as to root crops; their appetites never failing until their capacity has reached its limit.

"They propagate as readily as do the domestic cattle, when they have large inclosures and are not disturbed too much. In close confinement they are not at all prolific. When they do breed under such circumstances, the offspring is almost invariably a male; consequently the race would shortly become extinct, unless great care were exercised, as nature revolts at such an innovation.

"When I first seriously talked of domesticating the buffalo, I was severely ridiculed by people who had had

some acquaintance with the few which had been tamed. They were loud in their protestatioiM; declared it was an impossibility; success could never follow the experiment, as no fence except a high stone wall would hold them; there had been boards innumerable smashed, and the old-fashioned rail fence scattered in all directions by the vicious animals, which delight in balancing the rails on their horns, and then tossing them high in the air, running from under and kicking up their heels at every jump. That after their escape from confinement they would raid the neighboring farms, doing immense damage, until finally some enraged individual would shoot them to rid himself of the trouble they caused,

" I tried many styles of fence when first engaging in the undertaking, and of course experienced many of the •difficulties pointed out; but when I stretched five or six barbed wires to fair-sized posts a rod apart, with a stay between, I had no further difficulty in restraining them. I kept from fifty to a hundred buffaloes on a section of land (six hundred and forty acres) for more than a year at a time without a single one going through the wires. Even one acre fenced as above will prevent a hundred buffaloes from escaping, as effectually as could be desired.

" The cows are very cautious when an attempt is made to corral them, particularly if they have calves by their «ide, as they seem to fear their little ones will be trapped. The cows always mingle with the males until the calves are about five months old — from May 1st to October; after that time they separate, the calves, yearlings and two-year-olds remaining with the cows, while the males over two years old isolate themselves. The reason for this is easily explained; there is a motive in it. The males are very important factors in defending the calves from the wolves, which were the greatest enemy the buffalo in their wild state had to contend with. The separation does not occur until the calves are strong enough to take care of themselves. The bulls are very rough with

their horns, and the cows keep beyond their reach, especially while carrying their young. The calves are all dropped in April or May.

" The buffalo very naturally dislike a horse, and during the summer months it is a difficult task to drive the bulls with that animal, as they seem to take a special delight in showing how they can run him over the prairie at their own sweet will, often when the rider is doing all he can to prevent it. He may use his whip vigorously, and even give the cowboy yell, but it has little effect, unless he has the nerve to dismount and walk out to meet the enraged animal,— not at all times advisable; though I had one man in my employ who would persist in so doing, and he always came out victorious. I discharged him for his courage, and he no doubt lived much longer in consequence of my action.

"I am firmly of the opinion that there are very few buffalo, excepting the master of the herd, that cannot be subdued by man, if he only possess the nerve to face them, never yielding or turning his back toward them. As long as you confront them and continue to advance, they invariably surrender just before the apparently supreme moment arrives. If yoii turn your back, even for an instant, they will rush at you with all their natural vigor and rage, and unless there is a fence or other good place of refuge near, you are gone. A man should never turn under any circumstance, but back off, whether he be on horseback or on foot, until he is out of danger of the ferocious beast's horns. The bull, fortunately, always gives warning that he is going to charge, by lying down and rolling in the dust, or by tearing up the earth with his formidable horns, pawing up the turf with his feet, and roaring, or puffing,— something in its sound like a locomotive ascending a steep grade with a heavy load. Another premonitory sign is that the enraged bull always holds his tail high in the air before the impending charge.

" I know of only one instance where a man was hurt by

a domesticated buffalo. This was in the case of Mr. A. H. Cole, of Oxford, Nebraska. An old buffalo wanted to go out in the road to fight a domestic animal which had just sounded the challenge, roaring furiously and pawing up the earth in his rage. The buffalo bull in front of which Mr. Cole stood was six years of age. His keeper attempted to turn the buffalo back, but the pugnacious animal objected; upon which Mr. Coje, becoming disgusted, wheeled suddenly around and started for a pitchfork which stood a few rods from him, when the bull, imagining he had bluffed Mr. Cole, made a furious dash at him and drove one of his sharp horns into the unfortunate man's back, from the effect of which he died in about ten days. Had the man retreated backward, keeping his face toward the animal, there would not have been the slightest danger; the bull would never have made an attempt to charge him. What is true of the buffalo in this respect, is also true of all animals. A person should not lose presence of mind if ever caught in such a predicament, and never forget to face the beast, unless certain he can make good his escape.

"I have had but one buffalo in my herd that was inclined to be dangerously pugnacious— 'John L. Sullivan.' He is master of all others. He is a perfect dictator, ruling his congeners as absolutely as was ever a subject by imperious monarch. Should any one of the growing bulls, however, some day muster up courage to attack and conquer him, all the males in the herd will join in chasing him for many days, until he will not dare show him-.self again. Were he in a wild state, the wolves alone would cordially welcome him, only to hamstring and devour him as a reward for his ' cussedness ' while in power. ^Sic temper tyrannis.^

"Ever since the hour man was given 'dominion over the beasts of the field,' it has been one of the chief objects of his ambition to subject the various animals to his will, for the purpose of compelling them to share

JOHN L. SULLIVAN.'

the burden of labor imposed upon him by the fiat of nature. From the diminutive shepherd dog, which has been trained to take care of the flocks, and thus relieve his master from much of the incessant worry incident to their keeping, to the ponderous elephant capable of carrying tons of weight, man's prowess in subordinating these creatures to his demands is proof of his superiority ___ over the brute creation. The horse, beyond all others, has been of the greatest service; nor must the patient ox be forgotten; nor the'ship of the desert,' the camel, which is entitled to its meed of praise. But of all beasts of burden, in considering the requirements of strength, vitality, endurance, and capacity, the buffalo is incomparably greater than all others mentioned. To be sure, reared in absolute idleness, without being required to labor in the slightest for his support during ages of a *■ long ancestry, it is natural he should be inclined to an obstinacy more persistent than is found in almost any other beast, with a manifest unmanageableness growing out of his freedom from all restraint in his natural state; yet when forced to act, he, like all other animals, reluctantly yields to the ruling power of man. The party who undertakes to control a full-grown bull must be confident of the fact that he was given dominion over all the brute creation, and is able to exercise that power, or he will never successfully perform what he sets about to do.

"I have devoted a great deal of time, patience, and money, to say nothing of the danger experienced, in order to demonstrate that the buffalo is not only a practicable but tractable animal, when he has been carefully trained. I have taken the little buffalo calves and yoked them together; but the determination of their spirit of liberty immediately developed itself. At first they fought as furiously as gladiators. They would lie down, roll over, and put themselves into all sorts of strange positions, not infrequently reversing ends, each one headed in a different direction; they reared, plunged, kicked and 'cavorted'

around like a circus-horse. Their kick was the very incarnation of ' cussedness,' and if you attempted to hold one by the ear, he would double up like a wasp, and knock your hand away by a stroke of his hind foot. . If you stood immediately in front of them, they would jump with all four feet on your body. For weeks they would continue in this obstinate condition, although kept yoked together all the time. By patience, however, and continual efforts in handling them, they finally succumb, acknowledging the superiority of their master.

"Now, as young buffalo possess such characteristics when an attempt is made to subdue them to the yoke, you may well imagine what would be the case in an attempt to conquer a stubborn old bull, who possesses all the traits of the calves I have endeavored to describe in part,— only augmented ten fold, besides the faculty of buffalo in always keeping their faces to the foe, which is their nature, as I have shown.

" The buffalo bull has no more formidable enemy than another male of his own species, and when two are yoked together both are equally terrified. They cannot escape, and the first thing each attempts is to conquer his unwilling mate. Both whirl in an instant in their endeavor to face each other, but the yoke holds them in such a position that it is impossible for them to effect it. The only result is, their heads are thrown around against their sides, like a horse when suffering from colic. They continue in this awkward position for several days, when they begin to realize that neither can harm the other; but before they are made to stand up straight, and refrain from constantly trying to meet each other in combat, weeks elapse. At last, after months of careful handling, and extreme patience on the part of their trainer, they become accustomed to their restraint, and are properly ' broken,'exceeding in courage and strength any other animal subjected by man to assist in his burden of labor. The buffalo when thus subordinated to the will of their

master are excellent travelers, as they walk rapidly, yet never trot, but change from a walk to a gallop, which gait they are able to keep up for miles without apparent fatigue,— a feat impossible with oxen. The buffalo has great endurance, and cannot be run down by a horse. His mighty shoulders and double-strength loins, by virtue of the hump (which is composed of muscles of great strength), and his capacity to endure fitful climates so long without water and food, and his many other points that excel any and all other animals, all go to make up the greatest beast of burden known to mankind; and it is strange that the animal was never before effectually brought under absolute control. Since the windlass has been successfully used, no doubt some day the buffalo will be considered a valuable animal with which to lighten the loads of mankind."

The picture on a separate page represents a team of seven-year-old bulls, one of which is the famous "Lucky Knight," captured by Colonel Jones on the first day of May, 1886, causing him so much trouble, the story of which is related in a previous chapter. The other, with large knobs on his horns, is the animal which killed Mr. A. H. Cole, his owner; was afterward purchased by Colonel Jones, and broken to work by that "buffalo king" when the animal had attained the age of six years — a most remarkable victory of the power of the human will over that of the brute creation.

Colonel Jones, in writing in his journal of this particular pair, says:

" They are gentle, and work well together, but their keeper is ever warned never to give the one that has murder charged to his account, an opportunity to repeat the crime. This team is employed in drawing feed to the other animals on the ranch in winter, and in summer is used in plowing, with excellent results."

They are driven with hemp rope lines, made of the best material, attached to heavy, forged iron bits in their mouths, at one end, at the other to a windlass so arranged on the vehicle that the driver can control each line by winding it up, by simply turning a crank. There are two of these cranks. The driver holds one in each hand, and the brakes are adjusted by his feet, so that the teamster can draw harder with one hand and foot than four men could without the windlass.

It was a happy contrivance, as every other method failed completely to control the strong beasts; and now it has been used so long that the animals are easily driven by the Colonel with his hands alone, with as much pleasure as if they were a span of carriage horses, except that when they desire to drink, when passing a brook or other watering-place, the windlass must control them. They go fast or slow, as he desires. But without the windlass and brakes, they would never have been conquered.

Only a few years ago the American bison was considered as worthless (except for its hide) by everybody save the American Indians, who alone appreciated it to a somewhat limited extent. They subsisted almost exclusively on its flesh. In the fall, during the dry weather on the arid plains of the interior of the continent, where even the "gentle dews of heaven " refused to " fall upon the earth beneath," where a carcass would dry up like an Egyptian mummy, these children of Nature assembled and slaughtered great numbers of the bison. At this season the animal was fat, and in the golden prime of condition; and later, in November and De'cember, the robes were black and perfect.

The tallow of the buffalo is as yellow and rich as "Jersey butter." The flesh is tender, juicy, and through the process of drying, served for bread; the tallow as butter. This "bread and butter" was stored in the animal's own skin for winter use; while the savages, as long as the

fine weather lasted, during their prolonged hunt, reveled like pigs in clover on the delicious portions of the buffalo, in former years regarded by the white man as repulsive and worthless.

It is true of nearly all j)eoples, that the more abundant an article becomes, the less it is appreciated. Never was apothegm more applicable than is this to the buffalo. If anyone had taken the trouble to give but a passing thought to the subject, at the proper time, a great economic problem would have been solved — the benefits to be derived from domesticating and propagating the buffalo, an animal for which Nature had provided the Great Plains, and fitted the wandering ruminant to withstand the vicissitudes of fitful climatic extremes.

The accompanying table was compiled by Colonel Jones, and presents a very fair statement of the number of animals roaming over the Great Plains, and the number slaughtered, outside the National Park, during the years specified:

Tear.
No. of Buffalo.
No. Killed Past Year.
No. Killed for Hide*.
January 1,1865 January 1,1870 January 1,1871 January 1,1872 January 1,1873 January 1,1874 January 1,1875 January 1,1876 January 1,1877 January 1,1878 January 1,1879 January

1,1880 January 1,1881 January 1,1882 January 1,1883 January 1,1884 January 1,1885 Jan-uary 1,1886 January 1, 1887 January 1,1888 January 1,1889.

15,000,000
14,000,000
12,400,000
7,500,000
2,500,000
1,500,000
1,000,000
700,000
600,000
525,000
455,000
395,000
325,000
245,000
160,000
70,000
20,000
5.000
1,000
500
150
1,000,000
1,600,000
4,500,000
4,000,000
1,000,000
500,000
300,000
100,000
75,000
70,000
60,000
70,000
80,000
85,000
90,000
50,000
15,000
4,000
500
350
150
40,000
800,000

3,500,000

3,200,000

700,000

350,000

240.000

75,000

60,000

50,000

52,000

60.000

70,000

77,000

80,000

46,000

13.000

3,500

450

300

In this unparalleled slaughter, thousands of individuals sought the vocation for a profit. Many of them had had no experience whatever, and in thousands of cases mortally wounded their game, which escaped only to die far from the place where they were shot. In the foregoing table Colonel Jones has figured closely from his own observations, and no doubt is approximately correct. Some readers may think that the number reported for 1865 somewhat exaggerated, but the Colonel says they were like the angels recorded by John in Revelation — innumerable. To a person not well posted on the subject, it seems impossible there could have been as many as related. In his calculations. Colonel Jones has balanced the increase against death by wantonness and natural causes. It will be observed that in 1871-2 was the greatest slaughter. Farmers on the frontier left their excellent tracts and went out to kill buffalo f9r their hides, which suddenly grew in demand. It was a rich harvest for them, as it was no uncommon thing for two men with a team to clear from thirty to fifty dollars a day, and many "outfits" killed as high as two hundred of the animals in the same time. Each "outfit"was easily traced over the prairies by the peculiar method adopted of skinning its game. Some would take off the hide in excellent shape, leaving the head on the carcass, and then turn it over by main strength, while others cut off the head, and rolled the carcass on its back, using the decapitated mass to block up the carcass, thus facilitating the process of skinning. Some would drive a sharp steel rod through the neck of the animal and into the hard ground about eighteen inches, cut around the head back of the horns, split the skin on the belly, skin around the legs, then hitch a rope to the hide at the neck, and attach the rope to the doubletrees or to the rear of the wagon. To this the horses were fastened, and with a crack of the whip the team peeled off the hide as easily as taking off that of an onion. Others, who were fortunate

enough to possess two teams, would hitch one of them to the horns of the buffalo, and the other to the skin, thus holding the latter solid, and the team at the skin would at the word, jerk it off. Occasionally a man would go out alone on horseback. If he was,anything of a "cowboy," his operations in skinning were about as follows: After the upper side was skinned, he fastened his lariat around the under fore leg of the buffalo, as it lay dead on the ground; then backed his horse up to the back of the carcass, very close to it, and, tying his rope around the horn or pommel of his saddle, easily turned the huge mass over. Some, who did not own a horse, hunted alone, hiring a team to convey them to the buffalo region, established a camp near one of a neighbor-party, and then killed the buffalo, piling up hides all over the prairie for a week or two, then would hire a team to haul them in to the station. These isolated hunters would alway pray for a herd of cows, as the bulls were so immense and heavy to handle that it was almost useless to undertake it; yet when cows and young animals were not to be found, they attacked the bulls.

Their method of saving the hides was to sever the head, skin the upper side of the carcass, then take off the upper ham and shoulder, extract the paunch, and if the lone hunter was a Sampson he could roll the balance of the huge carcass over so as to complete his skinning. Hunting the bulls alone was the hardest work. Colonel Jones says, he ever attempted. Yet he has killed as many as ten in one day, sold the hides for two dollars and fifty cents each, the hams at three cents a pound; each animal netting him eight dollars, or eighty dollars for his day's work. He could more easily dress three cows than one bull, and the cows would net about five dollars when near the railroad, and the weather sufficiently cool to permit the shipment of the meat to the markets of the large cities. Nearly every hunting "outfit" possessed some kind of a mark, or brand, which they cut on the hides as soon as — 17

skinned, and woe to the individual who had the temerity to appropriate this property: no need of lawyers or lawbooks in those days.

Colonel Jones gives the following interesting information regarding some of the rules by which all hunters on the Plains were governed in the olden days:

" There were certain unwritten codes which governed all hunters, and he fared ill who transgressed any of them. For instance, when a buffalo was killed, with his knife the hunter would cut some place on the animal indicating its ownership.

Again, the hunter who first fired a shot at a herd was as much in control of them, against all other parties, as though he had raised them from calves. No matter how

badly other parties needed meat, they must keep their distance.

" The man who would deliberately pass on the windward side of a herd while another was " stalking," or creeping up on them, was liable to have a ball whistle close to his ear. While a ' tenderfoot' I tried the experiment, and can still hear the whiz of that rifle-ball, which passed uncomfortably near.

" Should a crippled animal escape from a hunter, and be killed by another, the one who first drew blood was the owner. Two shots in quick succession were always given, and repeated, until relief came, when needed.

'* The latch-string of the hunter's cabin or tent was always supposed to be on the outside and convenient to all visitors excepting the 'red man '; in other words, a hungry or thirsty hunter was welcome to quench his thirst with tea or coffee and appease his apj^etite with the best food in camp, and share the blankets, whether the owner was at home or not."

The American bison has been described by many writers, but in detached articles. To do justice to this remarkable animal would require a whole volume. They

are purely American in their form and peculiar habits; bovine in their anatomical structure, but differing in many ways from the ox, which is the type of the genus Bos. They are strangely fitted to the distinctive features of their special habitat, an extent of country which is now the garden spot of the continent, made exceptionally fertile by the manure, bones and flesh of the millions which have lived and died there during centuries past.

An average-sized bull is five feet ten inches in height, at the withers; girth around the heart, nine feet three inches; from end of muzzle to tip of tail, ten feet two inches. The hair and fur on the shoulders are about four inches long, and on the hind part, in winter, about an inch and a half. The average weight of the bulls, when in fair condition, is about nineteen hundred and fifty pounds. They have a broad, short face, with eyes set in the side of the head, thirteen inches apart, instead of in front, as is the case with most animals. They have beards like a goat, though much heavier, and often twelve inches long. The tail is the indicator of the animal's temper, as he invariably erects it when making any wrathful demonstration. Captivity does not change his form in any particular, unless when he is confined in small, close pens; nor is he changed in his many curious traits and the acuteness of the senses, except in that of smell; but he is more inactive than in a wild state.

The wood or mountain buffalo was once quite numerous in the Rocky Mountains, but is now extinct. They were of the same species as the buffalo of the Plains, but much smaller, shorted, with a round, "mullet" head, and much darker. The differences in the characteristics of two breeds were no doubt caused by their environments and by interbreeding.

Buffalo seldom roll in the mud, contrary to the general supposition, but excavate their " wallows " by pawing up the earth. The dust then blows away, and their shaggy coats are filled with dirt, which is shaken off at pleasure.

They shed their coats in May, and regain their fur as soon as the frosty nights appear in the fall, the "guard-hairs "alone remaining on through the heated summer. Their robes are prime in November and December, the fur being dark, soft and elegant; while later on it becomes faded, harsh, and unattractive.

Their mating season commences about July, and usually lasts two months. They seldom mire in swamps, as they have a happy faculty of wallowing through the mud after the manner of a hog. In their flight, they seldom gallop uphill, unless closely pursued, but invariably gallop down when scared or followed. When wounded they leave the herd and seek the most secluded spot possible, in the deepest canon, where they remain until fully recovered or die. They generally start to run against the wind, but do not persist in this trait, contrary to the deer, which never fail to run with it when pursued or scared. When frightened or pursued, the buffalo move much more rapidly when traveling toward the wind; and their sense of smell is so acute they know the instant there is danger ahead.

When you read of buffaloes " trotting off," you may rest assured that the author of the statement knows nothing of the habits of the animal. They invariably walk or gallop. They are naturally very stubborn, and yield to an enemy only after heroic efforts on their part. They never retrace their steps after once starting in a direction, and Colonel Jones often profited in his hunting adventures by knowing this trait.

They never pursue a straight course in traveling. Their eyes are so placed in the head that it is impossible for them to see directly in front; and especially is this true on account of the heavy locks on their forehead. Neither can they look backward, on account of their immense shaggy shoulders, hence they are compelled to keep one side or the other turned in the general direction in whicli they are going. Not being good travelers sideways, they

look ahead with one eye and to the rear with the other, deflecting to the right and then to the left for a distance of two or three hundred yards. Thus they always have one eye covering the ground they are advancing over, and the other looking behind, watching for an enemy or the horns of their companions,—some of which are ever ready to test their strength by thrusting their sharp weapons into the flanks of those that precede them on the trail.

Colonel Jones gives his own method of "stalking" the buffalo, as follows:

"The successful hunter managed to place himself in the pathway of the coming herd ; laid down in a ravine or behind a knoll or divide, until they were as close as possible. Then everything depended on the accuracy of the first shot, in order to get a stand on the herd, and it was always aimed for the heart or backbone of the leader, when within one hundred yards of the animal; at the lungs if farther away. If the heart or vertebrae were hit, the animal fell in its tracks; if in the lungs, it ran from one to two hundred yards before dropping, which took the herd much farther ofl^. After firing the first shot, I would wait until the animals stopped, which would be about a hundred yards from the place where the wounded one had fallen. I would remain perfectly quiet and motionless until one of their number had assumed leadership and led off in the original general direction of the herd, they taking care to avoid the dangerous place where their leader had fallen. No sooner were they started than a bullet would be sent into the leader's vitals. The herd would run back a few rods, gather into a comj)act mass, and appear to hold a council, grunting and moving about in as small a range as possible. Then another would lead off to the other side of the danger-point, but keeping as near the old direction as he considered safe, when a well-directed shot would bring it down. If these three shots were fatal, the herd was mine; if either one failed to kill, they went on their way

rejoicing, excepting what few could \)e brought down by the shots sent after them as they ran. If the three were killed, the herd became completely demoralized, and none would venture to lead, knowing danger to be in front of them, and that death was certain to any which attempted to go to either side. Their stubborn natures would not allow a retreat. They would naturally bunch together, and stand still until the last one was killed, provided the hunter did not get excited and fire too rapidly, or did not rise up so high as to betray his whereabouts."

The curious deviating from a straight course, as has been explained, is the cause of the crookedness of the buffalo trails yet to be seen on the prairies of the remote west. Colonel Jones positively affirms that a trail cannot be found anywhere that is longer than four hundred yards without a change in direction, yet the general course of the herd would be comparatively straight for a distance of thirty or forty miles.

"Buffalo" Jones, in his efforts to perpetuate the American bison, has accomplished more than all others who have attempted it on a smaller scale, trying to follow his example; and had his earnest pleadings to those in authority for help in carrying out his project on a larger scale, been listened to, to-day the Government would have been in possession of the large herds then in existence in "No Man's Land" and southeastern Colorado, numbering two or three thousand, and the increase of their progeny for the past dozen years.

As early as 1887 Colonel Jones went to the National Capital, where he plead with the United States Senators and Representatives of Kansas in Congress to enact a law which would protect the small herd of buffalo referred to in the preceding paragraph. Year after year he has warned our law-makers, and those higher in authority, that unless some measures were taken to prevent it the bison would soon become exterminated. All appeared

interested in having something done, but no one appeared to take the initiative. True, Representative Lacey, of Iowa, offered a resolution giving Colonel Jones a pension for life in recognition of his success in rescuing the last of the buffalo, but the Colonel refused to allow it to be considered by Congress.

In the spring of 1896 he personally called at the White House, and laid this subject in all its details before President Cleveland's private secretary, Mr. Thurber. He also visited the Secretary of the Interior, Hon. Hoke Smith, and filed a proposition with his department, of which the following is a copy:

To the Honorable Secretary of the Interior, Washington, D. C:

Having been notified that no appropriation was allowed by Congress for the preservation of the remaining buffaloes in the Yellowstone National Park, and that only $1,000 is available that could be used for that purpose, I hereby make the following proposition, with a view of preserving them from a speedy extermination, viz.:

If appointed with authority to preserve the buffalo in the Yellowstone National Park for the Government of the United States, I will furnish the means myself, proceed at once to the Park, and use my utmost endeavors in that direction. If possible, I will corral them. If I should fail, I will make a report to the Department of the true status of affairs and what is needed to preserve them.

Upon I'eceipt of said report, the Department is to pay me $500. Should I succeed in corralling the herd, or a portion of them, I will accept $200 per month and actual expenses while engaged in capturing and preserving the herd, the Government to have all the benefits of my service; provided, the amount be paid over to me, or my order, within one year from my sworn report and itemized vouchers. Should the Government fail to pay said vouchers as above stipulated within one year from receipt of my report and vouchers, then I will deliver to the Interior Department of the United States one-half of the buffalo captured, and am to retain the remainder of the buffalo and have the privilege of keeping them corralled in the Park, or removing them at any time to any part of the world as my own property, or the property of those who assist me in my undertaking.

Very respectfully, 0. J. Jones.

Pekry, O. T., June 9th, 1896.

The Assistant Secretary, Mr. Sims, appeared to be in earnest as to the action necessary to be taken. He wrote his acceptance of the proposition and signed it, then sent it to Secretary Smith for ratification, but the latter refused to santion it, and the bison were left to the mercy of the public. When the Superintendent of the Park made his next annual report he admitted, "The hand of man is against the bison," acknowledging, in a lengthy report on that subject, that there was no hope of preserving them.

Again, in April, 1897, after President McKinley had taken his seat, and the new administration was fairly settled down to business. Colonel Jones visited the City of Washington, and found there was five thousand dollars available for the protection of the bison in the Yellowstone National Park. He was confident that not to exceed twenty or thirty of these animals were yet remaining there, but believing some measures should be taken for their preservation, and to enlighten the American people on that subject, he submitted a proposition to the Interior Department, of which the following is a copy:

New York Gity, April 26, 1897.

Hon. Thomas Ryan, First Asst. Secretary Interior — Dear Sir: I desire to call your attention to the fact that the American bison is on the verge of extermination. A great number of the magnificent herd that roamed in the Yellowstone National Park have been slain without mercy in the past two years. As near as can be estimated, 250 out of the 300 have been wantonly murdered for their valuable heads and hides. Unless heroic measures are adopted at once, the remaining few will meet the fate of their kind before another year passes.

Having had many years of active experience in capturing and rearing over one hundred head of these noble animals, I am confident the only thing to do is to corral the remaining band, and thereby reproduce a herd that every true American will be proud of.

I have captured and reared with my own hands buffalo of all ages, and know every trait and habit of the animal. I could refer you to thousands who would testify to my success in rescuing and

preserving the bison, as well as all other valuable American animals that inhabit my latitude.

If the Government desires the American bison rescued and perpetuated, and will give me reasonable pay, I will be pleased to undertake it. Confident that it can and should be speedily accomplished, I am

Yours very truly,

(Signed) C. J. Jones,

("Buffalo Jones.")

Unfortunately, no action was ever taken by the Department upon these propositions, and the United States lost forever its greatest race of native animals.

At the close of the year 1898, by close calculation, there were over five hundred domesticated buffalo scattered throughout the world, the lineage of which is traced back to the efforts of Colonel Jones.

CHAPTER XVII ONE OF THE GREATEST RACES ON RECORD

OPENING OF THE CHEROKEE OUTLET OKLAHOMA, "THE BEAUTIFUL LAND" — HORSES AND RIDERS TRAMPLED BENEATH A LIVING AVALANCHE—GENUINE " JEHU " AND RED-HEADED GIRL IN THE RACE — THE MOST RECKLESS EQUESTRIENNE IN THE WORLD — FACTS NEVER BEFORE MADE KNOWN REGARDING THE OPENING OF OKLAHOMA

WHEN the proclamation of President Cleveland was promulgated, Colonel Jones was living in Omaha, Nebraska. He realized there was to be a great race, and knowing so well the art of making long and successful rides, he determined to once more enjoy the sensation so often realized during his life of adventure, and lost no time in getting in line. He relates the advent of the opening in a clear and dispassion-&te manner, as follows:

"Many, many years ago, I read in a newspaper: ' There is a tract of country about as large as the State of Massachusetts, lying south of Kansas in the Indian Territory, called in the Indian language, 'Oklahoma,' which by interpretation means 'The Beautiful Land.' Little did I at the time think that I should be the first paleface to enter that picturesque spot for a home. A third of a century rolled on; then the newspapers announced that a portion of ' the beautiful land ' (known as the Cherokee Outlet, in Oklahoma) would be thrown open to settlement on September 16th, 1893; that it was

(266)

unlawful for any person to enter upon that land or even pass over it prior to that date. The penalty for violation was a forfeiture of any and all rights to ' prove up' on a tract of land or a town lot. It will be remembered the ' Outlet' was a tract of land seventy miles wide adjoining Kansas on the south, and extending from the Arkansas river on the east 800 miles to the westward. It was known as the ' Cherokee Outlet,' from the fact that it was many years ago set apart by Congress as an outlet for the Cherokee Indians to the Great Plains, where roamed millions of buffalo upon which the red men depended for food. The Government finally bought this tract of land from the rightful owners, the Cherokee Indians, and organized a ' free-for-all' race to citizens of the United States, to determine who should win the prizes to be given away.

"At this particular contest—for that is just what it was — the Government offered a quarter-section of land and a town lot to the one first establishing himself thereon. All were to start simultaneously from the line bordering the strip. Thus it required horsemanship of the highest order, as there were about six contestants for each tract of land. Paul Revere, Putnam, Jennie McNeal and General Sheridan all have left the never-dying story of their dashing and daring rides. They were inspired by purely patriotic motives, yet so far as the physical aspect of their memorable deeds is concerned, the history of this opening presents acts of individual nerve, dash, and endurance, equally, if not more wonderful. Although the promptings were entirely of self-interest, these rides were comparable to anything which has been attempted in feats of horsemanship. Many of those who rode in that fearful struggle, some of whom went down to their death, will no doubt be regarded by generations to come as heroes and heroines; for after all, it is frequently the act of the person and not always the motive inspiring him which causes him to be regarded as such.

"It being contrary to law to enter the coveted land before high noon, of that date, comjielled thousands to congregate at the nearest point, nine miles south of Perry, where was located the United States land office, and all knew it would be the largest city in the Territory. United States soldiers were stationed along the line to guard against intruders and give the signal at the appointed time, when all were at liberty to enter legally. A great many had stolen through the line the night before, and were classed as ' sooners.'

"I was waiting on the extreme left of the assembled throng, with two horses,— my old buflfalo-horse 'Jubar' and the strongest and best race-horse to be had in the State of Nebraska; each one rigged with the lightest saddle possible, weighing only eight pounds each, while a strong rope about three feet long, attached to the ring of the cinch of each saddle, held the horses together. I had learned while running wild horses on the Plains that the poorest old wild horse I ever found could outwind the best blooded grain-fed thoroughbred attainable. I had reasoned out the cause to be that the wild horse carried no load, while the thoroughbred was compelled to carry about one hundred and seventy pounds, including saddle, which ' cut his wind ' very quickly. I often experimented at riding two horses in the chase after buffalo calves.' The method adopted was: As soon as the horse ridden commenced to wheeze, I would quickly change to the other, without checking them in the least; the horse would immediately catch his wind, and by the time the other became winded, the first would be fairly rested, when I would change back to him. By thus changing back and forth I could make unprecedentedly long races and quick time. The change was made by throwing the leg over the horse's neck toward the one I desired to mount, in the style a lady rides, then, placing it on the rope which held the horses together, I threw the other leg over the horse's

back, and was firm in the saddle, without checking, no difference at what rate of speed we were going.

" With this knowledge and experience I took my place in the great cavalcade with as much confidence and determination to win the race as if all others had been mounted on Mexican burros. Many of the would-be winners asked what I intended to do with the extra horse. I made no explanation, excepting that I intended to ride him. No one had the least idea of my intentions until about a mile after starting, when those nearest witnessed the first change from one horse to the other while going with such terrific speed. Instead of being angry, as I had supposed would be the case, a great shout went up from fully a hundred or more, while those nearest expressed themselves in such language as, 'That's the fellow that will get there I He 's a winner,' etc., no doubt realizing they were racing under disadvantages.

" There were fully eight thousand horsemen who awaited the signal at the starting-point. As the noon hour approached they became more and more anxious; even the horses realized that a great race was in prospect, as they pawed the earth, reared and snorted in their eagerness to go. The horsemen were lined up twenty deep, one behind the other, standing side by side for a mile along the line.

" The soldiers rode back and forth in front of the vast array, to see that no one entered before the proper time. When ' high noon ' arrived, one of the soldiers discharged his gun, which all understood to be the signal to start, and the great race was on. It was one of the most exciting and desperate struggles ever recorded.

" Being on the extreme left, I started straight north for Perry, Fortunately, the divide swung to the northwest, and soon I was on its crest. Having been in so many exciting races on the Plains, and in lassoing and driving buffalo bulls in chariot-races, I was not disturbed in the least, consequently noticed many things which no doubt

others failed to recognize. The first thing that attracted my attention after starting was the mighty buzz and roar of the horses striking the weeds and grass with their feet, and the rattle of their hoofs on the hard, dry earth. It brought back most vividly the olden days, as it was a duplicate of the sensation when in close proximity to a buffalo stampede.

" When about a mile out, and just after changing from my race-horse to Jubar, I heard someone in the rear shout in thundering tones, ' Get out of the road! Get out of the road 1' I was just slacking up a little in order to cross an old trail which had been partly grown over with grass, and fearing a deep gutter was hidden beneath, having been whipped out by the wind, as is often the case, I knew it would be dangerous to go at full speed across it. When safely over, I looked back and saw a magnificent team of horses hitched to a buckboard, and a man standing thereon, his coat off, while he was laying on the lash unmercifully. On the seat sat a young woman, with hair as red as red could be. Just then the horses leaped the old trail, the wheels went deep into the gutter, then flew high in the air, which sent the man and woman fully four feet upward. As they came down, both grabbed the seat, holding on for their lives. The horses circled to the left, and it was the last I saw of the ' Jehu' and his red-headed darling. The ridiculousness of this incident afforded me so much amusement that I indulged in a good hearty laugh, which I could not help, though I knew they must have been badly hurt and their lives in peril.

"Just as I was making my second change of horses, about two miles out, a horse ahead of me fell dead. The animal I was mounting gave a tremendous leap to clear the feet of the fallen beast, which precipitated my right foot to the ground between my two horses. Having a good grip on the horn of each saddle, and my left foot across the rope which held them together, I gave a spring from the ground while the horse was high in the air, and

with a mighty pull with my arms as he came down, I went up safely into the saddle. On looking back I shouted to the unfortunate man, ' Stick your stake and claim the land 1' It was a beautiful tract, but I afterward learned that the man's leg was broken in the fall, and that he was sent to his Eastern home. I learned also that the soldier who gave the signal had his horse knocked down, and both horse and rider were trampled to death by the resistless avalanche.

" When within three miles of Perry, two men and a lady, ' sooners,' came dashing up out of a ravine just to my right. Having fresh horses they had advantage of all others. The lady rode a jet-black charger, and was one of the most reckless horsewomen I e"^r saw, and would have done credit to the 'Rough Riders.' I whipped my horses severely, but could not pass her. It was humiliating to be compelled to go into Perry with a lady leading. I jumped to my old favorite buffalo-horse Jubar, cut the rope that held the horses together, and dashed past the mysterious equestrienne. On looking ahead, I saw the two houses which composed the city of Perry. The trail made a detour to the left in order to descend a steep bluff, which dropped off*into a deep valley, lined with trees and brush. Seeing nearly a mile could be saved by making straight for the houses, I left the trail and went thundering down the bluff for fear the lady would again pass me. The grass was high on the side-hills and hid innumerable flat rocks, some ten feet square, and Jubar was right among them before I knew of their presence. Knowing he was surefooted, I quickly decided it would be better to let him have his own way than to check him, for by so doing I would throw him off his well-directed course. Having a slack rein he never checked his gait, but passed safely over precipitous rocks with almost incredible speed. About half-way down I saw that he was going to land on a large flat stone which was tilted up at an angle of about forty degrees. I felt certain his feet would go from under

him and he would land on his left side. I quickly jerked my left leg up high, that I might not be caught as many are who fail to keep their legs in an advantageous position when on a falling horse; but, contrary to my expectation, he appeared merely to touch the stone, just enough to send him to a good footing, and I breathed much easier when we reached the trees and brush.

In the descent I passed eight or ten horsemen, and continued the wild ride until reaching the ravine, which was about eight feet across, with a high bank close beyond. I reined the horse a little diagonally, and he made one of his famous leaps and passed along without checking, I then crossed the main stream and ascended an almost perpendicular bank about forty feet high, which was accomplished by the horse running up obliquely while I ran at his side until reaching the level, when I was again on his back. In ascending I passed the last two competitors, and it appears to me the fastest race I ever made was the last mile to the claim adjoining Perry on the south, where I stuck my flag and claimed the land as a homestead. I then proceeded to the'city,' arriving there before all others, except 'sooners.'

"My race-horse I never saw afterward, but learned that the lady and her escorts while following me came to the ravine which Jubar had so gallantly cleared, and here her horse while attempting to leap the ravine went with such force across it that he struck the bank and broke his neck. The gentlemen caught my race-horse, which was endeavoring to follow me. The lady mounted it, and arrived at Perry in time to secure a valuable lot just east of, and facing the public square. This lot she sold within a week for five hundred dollars. Being a 'sooner,' she could not have proved up on it, and merely sold her quitclaim. The lady was from the Indian Territory, near the Creek Nation. She was known to all that portion of the country as one of the best deer- and turkey-hunters of the region, and took great delight in riding her race-

horses with deer-dogs in pursuit of the wild animals of that country. I am only sorry I do not remember the name of this, one of the greatest equestriennes of the age. " Jubar that day made his last race, as I promised that if we won he should forever be on the retired list; and he now roams the green pastures of ' The Beautiful Land.' "

During Colonel Jones's long and eventful career on the extreme frontier he has met with all kinds of desperadoes, and some who, though always having possessed good reputations, would be much scandalized should their true character be made public. In private the Colonel has related to me some of the most daring and reckless personal adventures that occurred in the palmy days of such characters as the James and Younger brothers, and later with ^' Billy the Kid," whom the Colonel helped to capture in 1882, in New Mexico. He was often accosted by stage-and bank-robbers, footpads, cattle- and horse-thieves. But he refrains from allowing anything recorded in this book of such experience; giving as a reason that there are 80 many false narratives floating through the country relative to such characters, the reader might confound the truth with fiction.

—18
SECOND PART.
BUFFALO JONES'S ARCTIC EXPEDITION.
CHAPTER XVIII
BUFFALO JONES
BOUND FOR THE ARCTIC REGIONS AFTER MUSK-OXEN AND OTHER ANIMALS — ROUTE THROUGH CANADA — WHITE GIRL HELD AS CAPTIVE BY INDIANS — IN A BOAT, ALL ALONE,
LEAVES CIVILIZATION NATIVES OPPOSE HIS MISSION —
BOAT CAPSIZES AND INDIANS REFUSE HIS " LIFE-LINE'.'
SUNSTROKE IN A FRIGID ZONE—CROSSING LAKE ATHA-BASKA — ON THE PEACE AND SLAVE RIVERS—BIG CHIEFS HOLD A COUNCIL TO PREVENT HIS PROGRESS
AFTER Colonel Jones had spent several years on the coast of the Gulf of Mexico, whose

climate did not suit his active nature, and under its influence he was becoming sluggish, he returned to Oklahoma, where he served as sergeant-at-arms in the House of Representatives.

After the session closed, he became restless and the spirit of adventure swelled within him. He had often read of the mighty musk-ox, the most remote animal of the world, and realized there never had been any in captivity. Although it was almost like crossing the "river Jordan," and into another world, he never rested until on his way to the lonely shores of the Arctic Ocean.

(277)

He narrates that most wonderful of expeditions that he (and I might say, or any other man) ever attempted and survived. When the reader remembers that Sir John Franklin, a half-century ago, with one hundred and thirty-seven heroes, backed by the British Government and with the cooperation of the United States and Canada, as well as the friendship of the northern Indians, all perished in that far-away northern zone, he will concede, at least, that Colonel Jones's stupendous undertaking (part of the journey all alone, and never to exceed one companion) surpasses anything in the way of northern explorations ever accomplished. It also proves that the Colonel is not only a hunter of exceptional skill, but a "killer" as well, or he would have perished from starvation.

He relates the facts of his daring undertaking in thi& and the following chapters:

"At daybreak on the 12th of June, 1897, I boarded the lightning express train of the A. T. & S. F. Ry., at Perry, Oklahoma, for the Arctic regions, and ere I returned the sun had risen and set four hundred and ninety-five times.

"My route was by way of St. Joseph, Omaha and St. Paul to Winnipeg, in Canada. From there I went about a thousand miles northwest to Calgary, on the Canadian Pacific R. R.

" When near it, the largest city of that far-away northern country, we found all the creeks and ravines swollen into rivers. There had been a great flood — no one knew to what extent, as no news had been received from either the west or north. The telegraph wires were all down, and no doubt there were innumerable washouts, as no trains had been met or heard of, from those directions, for twenty-four hours.

"At last we came in sight of Calgary, on the south fork of the Saskatchewan river, which must be crossed to get to the city. The train was halted, and all the crew walked ahead to inspect the bridge. The water was up to the stringers, and an angry-looking torrent it was.

"The majority of the inspectors decided it was passable, but one of the passengers, who took it upon himself to speak on all occasions for the traveling public, objected most strenuously, declaring he was an expert railroad man, and that the train would surely go down, as the bridge was already more or less twisted and wrenched from its proper place. Presently the bell rang and the train moved slowly ahead, while the ' guardian of the public ' stood on the ground near the end of the bridge waiting for the train to be submerged and then he could say, 'I told you so.'

"The cars barely moved, which made it evident that the engineer realized the danger which unquestionably threatened him. The bridge vibrated to and fro, but that was all, and the great 'mogul' engine was soon safe on the embankment. Before the last car entered the bridge, when the rear end of the train was passing our excited 'protector,' he caught the railing and swung upon the platform of the rear coach, and we were soon in the once beautiful city.

" Everything appeared to be wild with excitement; even the animals showed it. The horses running loose carried their heads high and trotted over the vacant blocks, tails up, and occasionally snorted as if danger were imminent. The dogs barked and howled alternately.

"As soon as I arrived at the Queen's Hotel, I could see people lining up along the banks of

Bow river, that skirted the city on the north. Some had ropes, others axes and all kinds of sticks and poles. It did not take long to determine what caused the excitement. I could see houses in the river, upset in almost every conceivable shape; some were on their sides, others bottom upward, some floating down the jiver, and others sliding gradually into it. I found the great iron bridge had been undermined and warped in all kinds of shapes. Wagons and horses

could not cross, neither would the police permit pedestrians to pass.

"On the opposite side of the river were hundreds of white teepees, which I learned were occupied by Indians from far and near, who had assembled to do honor to the Queen's Jubilee, which was to occur the next day. For months they had been looking forward to that eventful time, and the longed-for day was near, when they contemplated a great feast, and thus to show to the agents of the Great Mother that they were loyal, and no longer the hostile bands that had been the terror of that God-forsaken country for a length of time that the memory of man could not compute. They realized that in order to secure plenty of provisions, they must come with all their tribes to the Mecca of the Western World and show their devotion to the Great Mother. They made as big a show as possible, and all put on their best,— which was generally a pair of overalls and a plaid shirt for the men, and calico dresses for the women. They brought their ponies, dogs, squaws, papooses,— in fact everything, even the halt and the blind members of their tribes. No one able to hobble could be induced to stay behind; therefore all came.

"I soon learned that a mysterious white girl had for the first time in many years been brought within the pale of civilization. I had once heard there was such a person held in captivity by a tribe or lodge of Blackfeet Indians, and was very anxious to learn all I could concerning her whereabouts, ancestors, and how she was being treated. But the question then was how to cross the river to where the red men had pitched their tents.

" The police were guarding the wrecked bridge, as there was no certainty what minute it would be submerged. By assuring them I was intending to assist a man, already on the dangerous structure, to fasten a rope to a house lodged against the upper side, near the shore where we stood, they allowed me to pass. I made a noose in the rope, threw it over the corner of the house, and handed the man the line.

He commenced to work his way to shore, and I concluded then (and to be sure not before) ta get to the opposite shore. This was accomplished by descending a swag in the bridge to the water's edge; then I went hand over hand, clinging to a railing, to where the bridge stood at ita proper height. I found the police guarding the north as well as the south end of the bridge. There was no trouble to get off the bridge, but getting on was a different proposition. There was a great throng of Indians at the north end, all anxious to enter the city. I grasped the rope that was stretched across the entrance to keep the surging crowds from forcing the police backward, and slipped under.

"Here I found myself among an excited band of Indians. One big ugly-looking redskin made a surge toward me, and shouted in broken English, ' How, Buffalo Jones I ' I was dumbfounded. Could it be possible that some of the enemies I had battled with many years ago had wandered to this far-away country ? All the encounters I had ever had with various Indians during my long career on the Plains, flashed through my mind. I had seen the fellow before, and as soon as the first flash of the startled sensation had passed, I responded, " Hello, Number Nine 1 ' It was cruel in me to betray the poor fellow, but it was, not intended on my part. He was sharp, and could speak fair English. ' My name is Jack,' was his quick response. I caught my senses and said, ' Yes, Jack, I know you well; you were number nine of our hunting party, six years ago, after moose in Manitoba.' 'Oh, yes,' he said; 'didn't we have a h—1 of a time with that old bull moose? ' I said, ' Don't mention it,' and beckoned him to follow me, which he did (with pleasure, no doubt).

" The facts were the Indian was an ex-convict from the penitentiary at Stony Mountain, Manitoba, Canada. He was a very active cowboy, and an expert with the lasso. I had purchased sixty-five buffaloes from the warden of the penitentiary, Samuel Bedson; and when I desired to lasso.

and hobble them in order to get the unruly brutes to the cars, they brought out 'No. Nine,' to assist me. At the penitentiary the only way a convict is designated is by his number; by name, never. Therefore I addressed him as 'Number Nine.' Luckily I turned it off so that the English-speaking Indians, and the white people, standing near, did not mistrust his identity, as he was not known in that locality as a jail-bird. Now I was delighted to meet even an ex-convict so far from my native land; besides, there were hopes of finding the white captive that I so much desired to meet. Although a Cree, Jack could speak the Blackfeet language. He knew the girl quite well, and assured me he knew where she was. He told me the Indians had kept her as far from the city as possible, and would never permit her to be alone, for fear the white people would steal her. From Jack I learned the girl was fully seventeen years old, and lived with ' Winnipeg Jack' and his squaw; that they had raised her from a babe. They had once lived in Montana, U. S. A., and while at Fort Benton, seventeen years before, there was a great storm that covered all the earth with a white blanket of snow. The morning after the storm had abated, a beautiful paleface woman appeared at their wigwam with a bundle in her arms. They asked her in, and built a big fire. Presently she removed a heavy shawl from the bundle, and there was a beautiful little babe, about two weeks old. Jack's squaw had also a young papoose girl; but what a contrast I The strange woman was well dressed, iind apparently quite young. She told Winnipeg Jack, as his squaw could not speak English then, that she wanted them to take her babe and raise it; that she had no husband, and was going to leave it. Jack told her they had one papoose, but she rose and left the babe lying on a deerskin mat,—and that was the last and all they knew of the mysterious paleface, except what an old pilot on a steamboat at the wharf had told them. He said that the mother of the babe was from St. Louis; had come up the

Missouri river on his boat; had been deceived by a man that he knew well, and to hide her misfortune had taken the opportunity of giving the child a chance for its life. The big brave and his squaw soon became attached to the little stranger, and when they realized they were to keep it, were at a loss for a suitable name for the fair little white waif. They remembered the storm when it came to their wigwam, and as it was as white as the blanket of snow that had spread itself over the face of the earth, they gave her the name of ^ White Blanket." And thus the little paleface was christened, and her name became known throughout the Northwest Territory, by all the red men of the Plains.

" Many other things of great interest did Jack, 'Number Nine,' tell me.

"While he was explaining things to me as we walked along, we saw two squaws coming toward us. Jack looked up and said, ' White Blanket!' and as we neared them, I saw one was a very large squaw with black hair, and skin nearly as dark. She was fully fifty years old. By her side, sure enough, walked the white maiden. The girl was about seventeen years of age, of medium height, slender, fair complexioned, with a few freckles on her cheeks. Her hair was what might be called dark auburn; it was in two braids, and hung far below her waist. She wore a calico dress, rather reddish in color; it was short for her age, and might have been taken for a bicycle dress, as worn in the cities. She wore red stockings and moccasins handsomely worked with beads, with a cross made of glass attached thereto. Around her was a checked shawl that hung loosely about her shoulders.

"As we approached. Jack said, 'White Blanket, big white man, Buffalo Jones.' I shook hands with her, and then with the big squaw. Neither of them grasped my hand as I had wished. They were very shy, and did not want to stop. I asked White Blanket, 'Can you speak English ?' She answered softly, ' Me English little speak,'

•but kept her face from me; she pulled her shawl over her head, and I noticed they endeavored to get away from us. Being determined to get a photograph of the stranger, I had carefully loaded my kodak with films, and had it under my left arm, ready for a snap-shot if possible. Jack had told me it would be difficult, as Indians were afraid to have their pictures taken. Seeing I was getting the cold shoulder, I thought maybe they knew of Jack's hard character, and wanted to elude him. I whispered to him, telling him to stay where he was and I would talk to the girl. He smiled, but it did not discourage me. I walked after the women, and soon .overtook them. Having foreseen the difficulty of ' standing in' with Indian girls on short acquaintance, I had invested a half-dollar in candy and nuts, of which I knew Indians were always particularly fond. Walking up close by the side of the fair girl, I asked in as persuasive tones as I knew how, 'White Blanket like candy?' She pulled her shawl closely over her face and turned it from me. I then stepped in front of her; she and the squaw stopped, but turned their heads away. I repeated the words, and she answered, 'Got some?' My answer was, 'Yes, heaps candy and nuts; look here.' She did not look, but reached her hand back for the candy; but I insisted, ' Look here, I want to see your face.' Then she burst out at me: ' No good white man. Me know what you want; white man no get it. Indian die soon white man get picture.' The old squaw spoke to the girl, and they started back for the teepee. I was not to be shaken so easily, but walked right along with the young miss, giving her candy every few steps. She appeared nervous, and walked pretty fast,— which suited me, as I could get along easily, while the old squaw soon fell behind, and I could talk more freely. By this time she would peep at me through the shawl.

"Finally she said, 'Where you live?' I pointed to the south, and told her 'Far, far away. No white blan-

kets where I live,— no snow, no ice, no cold; sun high over the head.' Pointing to some flowers near by, I told her ' Flowers there all the year; apples, oranges and fruit plenty.' She had been peeping through her shawl till I could plainly see two steel-gray eyes, but nothing more. Finally she asked in a soft tone, ' Heaven ? ' I had been endeavoring to describe the place where I had been the past year,—the Gulf coast and Mexico. But when she asked if it was 'Heaven' where I was from, it was too ridiculous to think about. It quickly brought back to my mind that place of torment, where the mosquitoes and gnats reign supreme; where the alligators and moccasin snakes make life hideous; where the centipedes and tarantulas never cease from troubling and the wicked have no rest. I ' haw-hawed ' aloud, and the poor girl no doubt thought I was shouting because she realized there was a place of rest for poor Indians in the Great Hereafter. We were far ahead of the old squaw, and I insisted on getting the girl's picture, but she told me: 'Injun mad, white man get picture; Injun 'fraid white man see picture and take White Blanket far, far.' Finally, when we arrived at the wigwam, she said, ' Come when see sun,— one sleep. Maybe big Injun give white man picture.' All this time her head was wrapped in her shawl. The old squaw soon arrived, and I said good-night, as there was no hope for a picture before the morning sun, at least.

" I was disappointed, but still had hopes. Presently I came to where Jack was, and we hurried to the bridge, as the sun had already gone behind the northwestern hills.

"The police were still on duty, and I feared my lot was to lie that night in a wigwam, or on the grass, without even a blanket. I walked up, boldly lifted the rope, and started down the bridge as if nothing was wrong. One of the police shouted, 'Hold on, there! ' I looked around and pointed to the other end of the bridge, and said, ' I have permission from the other side.' The other officer spoke up and said, 'All right, sir; I remember

you.' I passed over as before, but when I reached the end of the bridge, found the river had risen fully eighteen inches, and I was obliged to pull off my shoes and wade across the bottom to higher ground. The next morning I was out before sunrise, and started for the bridge. There was no one near it; the river had fallen about two feet, and I passed over without difficulty. My friend Jack awaited me at the bridge, and we soon stood at the side of ' Winnipeg Jack's' wigwam. I called in a mild voice, ' White Blanket! White Blanket 1 ' but no ' blanket' responded. I repeated in louder tones, ' White Blanket, come; Buffalo Jones, candy plenty'; but all the sound that could be heard was the barking of a little dog that stood uncomfortably near my heels. I was as determined to see the Indian girl as was brave Hiawatha to see his Minnehaha. Long and loud did I call and beat against the wigwam with a long stick. Jack lifted the wigwam, and said, 'I get her! ' I took a snap-shot at him in the ridiculous position while lifting the tent. Finally, when the side of the teepee was raised, the old squaw crawled out, and in very broken English said, 'White Blanket sleep.' I insisted upon having her wakened, but the stupid old squaw merely yawned and said, 'White Blanket sleep.' And in her solemn attitude I took another snap-shot. The train was to leave for Edmonton, 200 miles north, at 8 o'clock, and I realized it was time to be on my return to the city; so I went my way sorrowfully to the hotel for breakfast. It was evident that Jack had told the truth when he said it would be hard to get her picture, and that white men had even gone to their reservation and offered as high as $25 for one, but had never succeeded in getting it. She knew what a kodak was, as I could never induce her to uncover her face after seeing that treacherous little instrument.

"The washouts on the railroad had been repaired, and our train pulled out on time. That night I found myself four hundred miles north of the northern boundary of

WHITE BLANKET, CANDY PLENTY."

WHITE BLANKET'S FOSTER-MOTHER.

the United States, at Edmonton, Province of Alberta, on the north fork of the Saskatchewan river. This point is the most northern limit of civilization. There are not to exceed a thousand inhabitants in the thriving little village. The main industry is the fur trade from the far-northern countries. The next day or two was devoted to arranging to go, as did Abraham of old, into a country I knew not of. I had often heard sermons preached about that wonderful journey, the loneliness and dangers that surrounded it, and how terrible an undertaking it would be to attempt to penetrate the wilds where human feet had never trodden. Who could tell what the next step would reveal while wandering in such a far-away country ? Yes, I had lain awake nights and endeavored to imagine myself in such a deplorable (?) situation, and to draw conclusions as to what to do when in every conceivable perilous position. If shipwrecked, I would swim ashore. Acting upon this suggestion, I bought a life-preserver, made of rubber, to buckle around my body. If violent storms came, I would wrap in blankets made of buffalo's wool. I provided two pairs. If rain and sleet, would cover with rubber. I provided myself with gossamers and rubber blankets. If I encountered mountains and ice, would wear shoes with steel calks. And thus I kept adding to my storehouse. My mission was to bring out from the Arctic regions musk-oxen alive, if possible; also silver-gray fox, marten, and other valuable fur-bearing animals, to propagate on an island in the Pacific ocean. I provided traps of every description, chains suitable for animals of all sizes, ropes and swivels, bridle-bits, leather for headstalls, bull-rings for the noses of the musk-ox, chain hobbles with heavy leather straps, and every conceivable article that I thought serviceable. But the most valuable thing of all others, as I figured, was not neglected,— shepherd dogs, of which I procured seven. To be sure, they were too small to work to sledges, but I

could procure large dogs of the Indians and Eskimos for that purpose in the far North.

"In the line of provisions, I laid in 1,500 pounds of flour, 400 pounds of bacon, besides beans, rice, oat-meal, coffee, tea, sugar, and such minor articles as one needs on trips of this nature. When I came to load a lumber-wagon, I found it would carry but little more than half my outfit. Another team was secured, and I climbed upon one of the wagons with a dog-whistle in my mouth, as it took continual calling to keep the little dogs together. The fourth day, through mud, rain, mosquitoes, and large horseflies (known in that country as ' bulldogs ' on account of their propensity for blood), we reached Athabaska landing, on the Athabaska^ river, one hundred miles to the north. There, on the south bank of that swift mountain river, I built my boat. I gave it a finishing touch on the evening of the 13th of July. It was 25 feet long, 9 in the beam, and had a capacity of 5,000 pounds. That night I was kept busy until eleven o'clock, transferring my supplies into it. At sunrise the following morning I weighed anchor and started off. The day was an ideal one, and I flattered myself I should find easy sailing, but before going five miles discovered that my craft was entirely too large to be successfully managed by one man, and that it was drifting dangerously near the shore; while immediately ahead was a treacherous shoal. The Athabaska river is noted for the number of these shoals and rapids, and to steer clear of them requires constant vigilance and good seamanship. I managed, with the aid of a large oar, working it first on one side and then on the 'other, to pass safely over.

"About three o'clock in the afternoon a terrific rainstorm overtook me, and I was thoroughly drenched. I protected my supplies by covering them with a tarpaulin, but did not dare to crawl under it myself, as the wind

1 Athabatka, aa Indian word meaatng " without a spirit"; or, as we would liberally translate it, "Ood-forsaken."

was constantly drifting the boat out of its course. As soon as one of these peculiar tempests cleared away, another would follow in quick succession, and they continued until sundown, when I pulled to the shore for the purpose of camping. Just as I was going to land I cast my eyes toward the bank, and saw a group of forty squaws and children intently gazing at me. I immediately turned into the current again, upon which the Indians set up a lamentation. They had expected I would certainly land, and it would be a grand opportunity for them to beg supplies.

"After passing a bend of the stream, and now being out of sight of the beggarly savages, I turned to the shore and tied up for the night. The first act after fastening my boat securely was to loose seven shepherd dogs and one bloodhound, that I had kept chained for over a week to prevent the Indians from stealing them; consequently they were very savage. One of them I had purchased from a half-breed boy, who informed me that the animal was a mixture of collie and spaniel; that he was ' a scrapper from 'way back.' The moment I turned him loose he stationed himself on the bank of the river, and as fast as the other dogs landed he ' went for' them individually, and gave them such a shaking that their howling soon informed the Indians in the whole region where I had camped.

"Another storm was brewing, and I hastily set fire to a pine log, made a cup of tea, spread my robes under a clump of trees, and after partaking of the frugal meal was soon wrapped in my blanket, listening to the pattering of the rain that had commenced to fall on my rubber tarpaulin.

"The Indians, very shortly after I had retired, found
their way to my camp, but ' Scrapper,' as I called him,
led the whole pack of dogs in a break for the intruders,
which I encouraged by 'sicking' them on, and in a few
— 19
minutes the redskins incontinently dashed away through the brush, and left me to sleep peacefully.

"I was off the next morning by four o'clock. The wind blowing from the right point, I improvised a sail, and made excellent time through the mazes of my tortuous course. At eight o'clock that evening I arrived at the upper end of Pelican rapids, where I was to meet a man who was to accompany me to the 'Barren Lands,'—Aleck Kennedy, a half-breed. I found three men stationed at this place, who were boring for petroleum under the auspices of the Canadian Government. They informed me that Kennedy had gone away, and left word he could not make the promised trip. I had contracted with three men in the United States to go with me; another at Edmonton, three at Athabaska Landing, and this Kennedy, who had been vouched for as absolutely reliable by the Hudson Bay Company; but all of them had backed out I What should I do? The dangerous rapids were just ahead. I had been warned of them by every boatman I met on my journey. I knew also that there were dozens of similarly treacherous places below, but had started for the north, and go I would, pilot or no pilot.

"At half-past four the next morning I whistled to my dogs, and was soon pulling through the splashing water. The roar of the falls ahead resembled the sound of distant thunder. I shot down the turbulent current, applying the oars vigorously, so as to give the boat a greater momentum than that of the stream, which would enable me to steer among the rocks without dashing upon them. As soon as safely by one treacherous-looking ledge, I again worked at the oars, and when near the immense boulders, rushed to the helm, and with a long sweep guided my trembling craft through the rapids, sometimes receiving a few scratches and Inimps. I encountered other rapids at short intervals for fifty miles. At last the boat drifted into still water, which reminded me of the old-fashioned mill-ponds of my boyhood days. I then realized that the

GRAND RAPIDS OF THE ATHABASKA.

HUDSON BAY CO.'S BOAT 'SHOOTING" A CASCADE IN THE NINETY-MILE RAPIDS.

great rapids were near. I had been warned not to attempt to go over them, at my peril.

"As I was rapidly approaching them, and could plainly hear the seething of the foaming current as it gathered momentum every instant, four boats, all occupied by Indians except one in which were two white men, came flying by, each manned by five men—four at the oars and one holding the sweep. Three passed between me and the shore, and swung in to land. I was following in good order, when a gust of wind careened my boat and forced it against a boulder whose sharp point barely rose to the level of the angry water. I realized the danger, but was powerless to avoid it. The boat nearly upset, then suddenly whirled about and sped on, stern first. This threw me still farther out into the current, and as I was endeavoring to right the boat, the last one of the other party put in between me and the shore. As they were manipulating their long sweep, it struck my craft and shoved me still farther away than ever. It appeared as if the fates were against me, but I rushed to the bow and threw my ' lifeline ' to the crew of the boat. One of the oarsmen caught it, but the steersman yelled out for him to drop it, which he did, and the next instant I was carried rapidly toward the great cascade. I was cool, and said to myself, ' Now for one more trial 1 ' and, grabbing the oars, pulled for the shore as I never before pulled. At this juncture, one of the mounted police (who are at that far-away place to guard against casualties and prevent ardent spirits from being smuggled to the Indians), saw my danger, and waded far out into the water and shouted for me to throw him my line. It was all coiled up, and gathering it as if about to lasso a buffalo calf, I let it fly so as to light in the water above the soldier. As I intended, it drifted against his legs and he caught it, and I was luckily towed to the shore just in time to escape the dreadful cataract.

"I asked the steersman who had ordered his oarsman to let go my line, why he did so. He exonerated himself

by saying, ' It was better for one man to be killed than six.' That was poor consolation for me, and I read him the cowboy 'riot act,' telling him I hoped to catch him in as tight a place before we reached the Great Slave lake; then I would teach him a lesson in Christianity. I asked, ' Do you know what I will do? ' ' No,' he replied. I said, * I will rescue you and all others, or die in the attempt.' He was humiliated at the reproval.

"All goods shipped up or down the river must be transported by land over an island at least half a mile long, having a channel on each side. (See cut of west channel.) It is an interesting sight to watch thirty or forty Indians at one time carrying furs and merchandise on their backs, making this portage. They are so trained as beasts of burden that they carry on an average from two to three hundred pounds each. They do not seem to be as lazy as our southern Indians; when they work, they go at it with a zeal that is commendable.

"The Hudson Bay Fur Company has a tramway over the island, but free traders are not allowed to use it. It requires all kinds of scheming to get a cargo of furs up the river. In ascending with a loaded boat, when the foot of the falls is reached, several men are sent around to the upper end with a heavy rope about five hundred feet long. A canoe is procured at the police station, and by going far above and floating down the center of the river, the upper end of the island is reached. Then they go over to its lower extremity, tie a log to one end of their rope, fasten the other to the immense rocks, and throw the log into the seething waters. The crew on board the boat below dart out through the eddy, catch the line, and haul their craft up through the great frothing swells, that look almost insurmountable. Many boats lie at the foot of the falls, completely disabled from blows received in thumping against the great boulders. Many a man has been hurled to death by attempting to descend the falls, and none ever survived the ordeal.

"I remained here three days, and made a contract with four Indians to take me and my cargo to Fort Smith for twenty dollars (forty skins).^ On the 18th of July they loaded their own freight, while I was engaged in loading mine, consisting mostly of flour, bacon and other provisions. A third of my goods were already either in the boat or on the rock to be put in, when the interpreter said : ' Let us understand ourselves : we are to have eighty skins (worth $40) to take you to Fort Smith?' 'No, indeed 1 ' I responded; ' our contract is that you are to have forty skins' ($20). He said nothing in reply, but motioned me to take my goods back to the island, which I did. The Indians thought there was no other way to get through, and determined they would extort all they could get from me, but I was as determined to stand by the terms of our agreement or have nothing to do with them. This outlook was discouraging, as I very well knew it was impossible for any human being to run the ninety miles of rapids by himself and come out alive. What was I to do ? The soldiers would not permit me to go alone; they said it would be an act of suicide. So I went back to the island and set up my tent. Although discouraged, I was determined to make every effort possible to carry out my plans. The Hudson Bay Company had discharged several men, who were all bound southward for their homes. They had already been in the northern country for from six months to a year, and were anxiously counting the days when they would once more be with their families on the reservations.

" I made another attempt, and by paying twenty dollars in advance induced a large, fine-looking Indian to accompany me to Fort McMurray, ninety miles away. He had been very anxious to become a pilot, and had frequently tried to get his employers to send him out as one.

' A "skin" i8 an imaginary valuation, at one time based on a beaver-skin as the unit of value, worth about fifty cents of our money ; but a beaver is now worth twelve "skins."

He reflected that here was an opportunity to show his skill, which might be of value to him in the future, as the pilot who can run all the rapids without knocking a hole or two in a flatboat commands a high salary.

"All the men employed by the Hudson Bay Company told Joseph Deserley, the Indian I had hired, that he was a fool to try to guide a boat with only one oarsman, while all other boats had four; that no one man could pull a boat fast enough in the rapids to give it the momentum requisite to steer it accurately, as the pilot would necessarily be occupied all the time at the helm.

"No attention was paid to this sermonizing. We managed to get the boat around ready for loading, and by extraordinary exertion the work was soon accomplished, and we dropped safely down one of the most difficult rapids, I plying the oars with all the skill and energy possible. The eyes of all the Company's men, and those of the crews going down the river, were upon us, to witness what they supposed an impossibility. As luck, or pluck, would have it, we shot through without touching a single rock, and as we rounded the curve, saluted the gang of officers and Indians on the island by waving our hats, and darted out of sight. We shot over the big and little cascades at a certain point where a current of water from both the right and left appeared to meet, forming such a roll that we scarcely noticed the fall, the boat merely shipping about two bucketfuls during the 'shoot.' It is the only place where a boat can descend with safety; and even there, if not exactly on the crest of the swell, a boat will swamp.

" The Boiler rapids are the dread-of all navigators, as no boat can go through without making a circuitous winding among many boulders; and the least variation from one particular route invariably proves fatal. The way these falls received their name was from the fact that the Hudson Bay Company were taking a large boiler down the river on a large scow, the boiler to be used in a steam-

'■-■ -'■"^'-
EDMONTON.

BOILER RAPIDS.

boat they were building at Chippewayan. The pilot became 'rattled,' and lost his course. The scow struck a boulder, and was divided in halves; the boiler dropped to the bottom, and has never been discovered. Ever since, this portion of the river has been knoAvn as ' Boiler rapids.' In fact, this stretch of ninety miles is a continuation of cascades and rapids, making the journey one of continual dread and exciting adventure.

"When we arrived at Fort McMurray we had made the ninety miles without a scratch, while three of the other four boats in venturing the dangerous passage had from three to four holes apiece knocked in them, one nearly sinking. The very Indians who had refused me passage smashed their boat, and were badly scared.

" The extraordinary efforts exercised by myself in this perilous undertaking were so great that I was nearly exhausted ; and my hands were covered with blisters.

" Here I paid off my pilot w4th an extra fee in the shape of a pocket-knife and other trinkets so pleasing to the savage, which he prized more than the original sum of money which I had given him. I also gave him such a first-class certificate that it would have entitled him to a similar position on a fast-line American steamer crossing the Atlantic ocean. I shall never forget the expression on my rough pilot's face when we got into any difficulty dashing, among the rocks; the poor fellow could not speak one. word of English, nor I of Cree. When in the most dangerous places he would yell most hideously, ' Scow ! scow I pemi-scow ! ' which I soon learned meant, ' Row 1 row I row hard I'

" Sunday, July 25th, was an uneventful day. I was. again captain, mate, pilot, and deck-hand, navigating down the Athabaska quite peacefully, excepting now and then when compelled to row briskly to keep from being thrown against a boulder, or drifting upon a bar of quicksand. On Monday morning I passed the mouth of Red river, which I afterward learned was the home of Siena,.

the liberator of the Slave tribe of Indians. At noon the sun shone very bright and hot; yes, hot! and in the frigid zone. The thermometer undoubtedly would have registered one hundred degrees, if I had had one to hang in the shady part of my craft. Three of the boats were far in advance, as they had floated all night. The wind was blowing stiff and strong from the southwest;

it struck me fair, and was fast propelling me on to a sandbar. I pulled for my life 1 It was impossible at first to perceive any re-spouse to my desperate efforts. Finally, however, the boat yielded to my exertions, and in another hour was floating down the river northward again. At this juncture I lost all consciousness, and when reason returned I found my boat lodged near the north end of a long island. I had over-exerted myself, and the result was a slight sunstroke. Realizing in some way what had happened, I managed to get hold of a towel, and with it applied water to my head. I recovered sufficiently to enable me to think, although my brain was in a measure paralyzed. I found my valise, and tried toget at my medicines, among which was camphor. My mind was not lucid enough to distinguish it from anything else, so I must have substituted Jamaica ginger for what I really wanted, for when fully recovered I found my camphor-bottle tied up just as it came from the drug-store: the ginger had evidently been opened and a tablespoonful used.

" I soon became aware of the fact that if the other boat passed me on the opposite side of the island I would be in a dilemma, so I pushed off and managed to land again at the end of the island, where I tied up and awaited results. Had the other boat passed, or not? was a problem that worried me very much. I laid down under some bushes, and patiently watched for an hour at least. Finally, a,round the bend on the opposite side from where I had lodged first, I saw the boat coming; I cut loose and drifted into the stream, and as the craft came near I asked permission to tie to it, which privilege was most

graciously granted. Soon I was almost insensible, but toward night regained strength and reasoning faculties. We camped for the night.

" On Tuesday I was able to paddle my own boat. The wind shifted more to the westward, and blew a gale. My course was almost northeastwardly until reaching Lake Athabaska. I converted one of my tarpaulins into a sail, which sent me flying at the rate of ten miles an hour. At eleven o'clock in the morning I found myself high on a sandbar. The only way to avoid it was to jump into the water and ' boost' the boat off, which was not a very pleasant job, as the day was cold. At one o'clock the lake appeared, and almost before I knew it I was forging^ through its great waves, which rolled like those of the-Atlantic ocean. Had it not been for the warning of the crew just ahead, in another moment I would have rushed beyond the limit of safety; but by pulling desperately swung my boat into an inlet to the left, when, by wading in mud and water to my shoulders, I at last anchored to the shore of a small island, on which I builta fire among the driftwood. I now changed clothing, and felt more comfortable. It seemed the coldest day I had ever experienced, as a cold, sleety rain was falling.

" Let me interpolate right here, that I left my home in Perry, Oklahoma, in a rain-storm, and since then not a day had passed, up to this time, without a downpour.

" It is impossible to row on Lake Athabaska, excepting in a calm. I floated along the shore through the reeds and rushes, made one more camp directly opposite the post of Chippewayan, and the next day again entered the lake; but on account of the prevailing high winds was-unable to use my oars, and my bark was so tossed on its waves that I was obliged to again tie up.

" The region is a perfect paradise for waterfowl; ducks, were constantly in sight, accompanied by their young, feeding on the abundance of snails and bulbs found in profusion. Many Indians live in the Athabaska lake re-gion; they depend for subsistence chiefly on fishing and hunting.

" In the evening I rowed up a bayou to the forks of the river, and down another stream, in order to get as near the fort as possible. At eleven o'clock that night I went into camp seven miles south of Fort Chippewayan, the wind blowing furiously. At three in the morning I a,woke, discovered that the wind had ceased, and was soon off for the fort. I had not proceeded more than a mile before a breeze began to rise, and by the time I had gone three miles it struck squarely against the bow of my boat. It was too late to retreat; the only thing to do was to continue across. I threw myself with all force on the oars, and pulled till ten o'clock, when I arrived at an island about one mile distant from the fort. I was so exhausted from my efforts that I could go no farther, but after a cup of coffee and plenty of whitefish, pulled over to the fort, where all the Indian boys and girls of the village had congregated to see ' Buffalo Jones,' the man who had rowed a flatboat across the lake alone.

"At the village of Chippewayan the Catholic Church has established a mission, as has also the Church of England. Both have schools for the children, and fine gardens in which are grown every variety of vegetables common to that far-away northern country. Potatoes do exceedingly well, and wheat sometimes ripens as far north as this; the best bushel exhibited at Philadelphia in 1876 was grown at this place.

"Athabaska lake is seven miles wide at the mouth of Athabaska river, which flows into the lake on its south side. The lake is 240 miles long and about sixty miles wide. There are no dwellings on its south shore, as it is one vast rnarsh, once evidently part of the lake, but is gradually filled in by the immense amount of sediment washed down from the mountains and the great fertile plains through which the stream flows. Some day the lake will be no more. It is said that the wind never

ceases blowing on this vast sheet of water, and the stories of many disasters are current among the inhabitants. They say, also, that many boats have been driven out to sea by the heavy west and northwest winds, never to return.

" Here I overtook the four Indians who broke their contract to carry me to Fort Smith. They had preceded me about two hours. One of them, John Tindell, thoroughly repented of the mistreatment I had received, and told me that if I would allow him to take his goods into my boat the other fellows might go on alone (as he was only their interpreter), and he would help me through to Fort Smith. I did not hesitate very long, and we soon loaded six hundred pounds of flour and other supplies that he had journeyed eight hundred miles to procure for winter use, and started for the river that rises four miles west of the village. The wind was blowing furiously against us, and we drifted to the southwest. I took out my map and asked Tindell why we should not take the channel that puts out at the southwest corner of the lake and runs both ways, to Peace river and from Peace river to the lake, according to the height of the stream.^ 'All right,' he replied, and we shot through the great rolling waves of the lake, missed the channel that leads to the river, and were blown high on to a sandbar. We managed to retreat and get into the channel, but found the water flowing to the lake very slowly. As the wind was partly in our favor, we put up our sail and went up to where the stream crosses another,— a curious phenomenon, two rivers crossing each other; perhaps it is the only plac6 in the world where

' This may appear somewhat contradictory. The explanation Is this: The direction of the water varies according to the volume of water in Peace river, and the direction of the wind on the lake ; i. e., when the Peace river Is swollen from freshets, its water is forced through a small river about forty miles long into the lake; but should there be a strong east wind, the water of the lake would be forced up in the west end and the water would run into the Peace river. Again, when the river is low the water of the lake always flows into the river, except when there is a strong west wind that forces the water of the lake to the east end; then the water of the river empties into the lake. So about half of the time the water in the short river runs In one direction, and haU in the other.

such a thing occurs. When we reached the other stream we found it was flowing slowly toward Peace river; so we went westward again thirty miles, and at sunset on the Ist of August entered the waters of the Peace.

"I was very much surprised at its width—so much greater than I expected; it was fully a mile across, and, as far as I could see to the west, of the same breadth. We swung to the north and floated toward the Slave river, which is thirty miles below, and where the Peace intersects the main river out of Lake Athabaska. The wind had been against us all day, and I was very much fatigued. I told Tindell to keep watch and I would sleep, part of the night; so I threw myself on some sacks of flour and was soon dreaming I was at my old occupation of holding down the Legislature of Oklahoma, as sergeant-at-arms. When I awoke, the boat was in an eddy just above a sharp fall over boulders, and Tindell was rolled in his blanket fast asleep. I quickly grabbed the oars and shouted to him to guide the boat, and we were soon safely past this dangerous place.

"The 2d of August was the first whole day without rain since I had left Oklahoma, nearly two months previously. The wind was in our favor most of the time, and by hoisting sail we made rapid progress.

"We soon reached the great falls of the Slave river, where we hauled the boat and cargo on the shore to avoid sixteen miles of dangerous rapids, which cannot be successfully passed. The Hudson Bay Company has oxen at this place to portage its goods around these, the last falls to be encountered. I had only about fifteen hundred miles farther to go, and I felt encouraged in the reflection that my journey would soon be at an end.

"It was August 3 that I landed here (Smith's Landing), a Hudson Bay post, half-way between Forts Chippe-wayan and Resolution, where I was invited to a council of ' great chiefs.' An interpreter told me with great solemnity that these men had come a long way to meet me. They

had heard of my advent into the country, and warned me not to take any animals out alive; they were nearly starved to death already, and if I took musk-oxen away all other animals would follow and the people surely perish. I listened attentively until they had finished; then I told them that I had come three thousand miles, not to destroy, but to preserve the very animals they had been killing for their subsistence. That they must learn to foster and propagate them or they certainly would perish of hunger. That they must do away with their foolish superstitions; make fences, cut hay, capture the moose, reindeer, musk-ox, buffalo, and other animals; keep them where they could always have them for meat when the winter winds whistled around and snow covered the earth. All of this was repeated to them by their interpreter, to whom they attentively listened, and agreed to take it under advisement.

" I intended to keep right on to the habitat of the musk-ox. I did not expect to violate any statutes of the Northwest Territory, and as long as I had the law on my side, felt that I should succeed. Of course I expected to encounter many difficulties in bringing the animals out alive, but had no idea of abandoning the project. The Indians I met belonged to three tribes: the Chippe-wayans, Crees, and Slaves. I expected to have some red-hot times even in that cold country, and hoped to return to the United States by the first of December of that year, unless prevented by the red devils that were already showing such a defiant spirit."

CHAPTER XIX

BOUND NORTHWARD

INDIANS ORDER HIM TO RETURN — REACHES GREAT SLAVE LAKE — TOSSED AT MIDNIGHT BY AN ANGRY TEMPEST FINDS RUINS OF SEARCHING PARTY, FORT RELIANCE INDIANS CONGREGATE FROM EVERY QUARTER—TREACHERY OF "big Indian" biena

I REMAINED a week at Fort Smith, waiting upon the humor of the Indians to assist me in going around the rapids, which are sixteen miles long. The Indians alone are depended upon to make the terribly exciting and dangerous passage of the river. It is as much as a white man can endure to traverse swamps and climb the apparently interminable hills and battle with the swarms of persistently voracious mosquitos, saying nothing of attempting to " shoot" the rapids.

The ways of the red men of the North are as dark and mysterious as are those of their brethren farther south. The Indians I had employed to assist in making the portage with my boat and goods were six days on their way across the portage, and on the first day only did they even show a disposition to accomplish what they had promised. Then I was coolly informed that they would not carry any more goods across, because they had learned my mission was to take live animals out of their country. In fact, they impudently told me to pack up my traps and row south again. I firmly informed them that I would take my goods and myself where I pleased, and would go north

(802)

BIG INDIANS" THAT WARNED COLONEL JONES NOT TO CAPTURE WILD ANIMALS.

HUDSON BAY CO.'S BOAT GRAHAM, ON THE MACKENZIE RIVER AND GREAT SLAVE LAKE.

in spite of their protests. At last they appeared to understand that I was not to be intimidated by any of their threats, and they let me alone.

On the 10th of August I associated with me Mr. William Armstrong and J. R. Rea, two of the most determined and successful pioneers in the whole northern region. I also sent for Mr. David Van Nest, of Oklahoma, who had promised to join me if his services were required. I had made up my mind that if four white men were not able to control matters connected with our little expedition, I did not intend to call in requisition the aid of any of the Indians to help us out.

It was my purpose to remain there for a few days, then proceed to Fort Resolution, on the Great Slave lake, thence three hundred miles northeast, where our camp was to be established. I expected to reach the latter point by the 10th of September, and on the first of the following month hoped to start homeward. Should the musk-oxen be found too far away for us to return by the 20th of October, the lake would doubtless be frozen over and preclude our passage on the return trip by open water. I intended to send news to Fort Resolution by a shepherd dog, to be forwarded to Edmonton by a dog train, which leaves there in midwinter for the latter place, more than a thousand miles distant. I had not heard a word from the United States since the 24tli of June, and did not expect to until my return from the " Barren Lands" to Fort Resolution.

Probably the people of the United States entertain the same idea which I did concerning this remote region, viz., that the farther north one travels, the colder the temperature becomes, both in summer and winter. This is not the case. Frost does not make its appearance at Fort Smith after the first of June, or until about the middle of September; while at Winnipeg, on the North Pacific Railroad, I have seen heavy frosts as late as June 26th and as early as September 10th. Many will doubtless be

surprised at this, but the cause is very simple: here, there is no night worthy of the name, from May 15th to September 15th. The sun does not disappear excepting for a very few hours each day, so that during its absence the atmosphere has hardly time to cool off by radiation before "Old Sol" reappears above the horizon to reheat the earth and repel the frost that would certainly come were it not for this provision. A thousand or more miles south of here the case is different: there, the long nights permit an almost complete radiation of the heat many hours before the sun makes its appearance again, and frost is the consequence. Besides, the relatively short days do not permit the earth to become thoroughly heated before night is on again.

I found some of the finest gardens in those high latitudes that I have ever seen; vegetable life appeared to be present everywhere in midsummer. Potatoes, beets, turnips, peas, and cabbages, and many other kinds of edible roots and succulent plants, reach perfection. Many varieties of berries common to the United States, together with red and black currants and the dry-land cranberry, reach a stage of lusciousness unexcelled elsewhere. I found a red-currant bush on an island in the Great Slave lake loaded with fruit, every berry of which was as large as a cherry. I procured a dozen cuttings, and hoped to propagate some of the "Barren Lands"* productions at home. The reason for this seemingly paradoxical condition of vegetation is easily accounted for. There the sun shines almost continuously for many days, and although the seasons are very short, the prolonged light and frequency of showers induce as perfect results as it is possible for nature to effect. During the winter months the weather reaches the extreme of cold, which is intense, with but little variation of temperature.

The absence of bugs and most other insects, which further south, in their season attack everything in the way of vegetation, is one of the notable features of that region.

Reptiles are unheard of; but the gnat and mosquito are monarchs, though their reign is of short duration.

The inhabitants of the Slave river country are all Indians, with the exception of a few traders who venture out there to collect furs from the natives. Their principal food is game and fish; very few ever accumulate an amount of furs sufficient to permit them to indulge in the luxury of a sack of flour, worth from fifteen to twenty-five cents a pound. The men are the most consummate and artful beggars in existence; and when they fail to accomplish their ends they send their squaws to try their luck. If they are unsuccessful, the little children are forced into the service. Often small girls only ten to fourteen years old would come into our camp, and remain for hours, even far into the night, unless they received a morsel to eat, or were driven away. They did not speak a word, but watched every movement, and if very, very hungry would crowd nearer the fire where the cooking was in process, and if given a scrap to eat would leave only to return the next morning, continuing their visits as long as we remained in that locality. I am told that the problem of food is getting more desperate each returning season. The Government makes no provision for their support, as no treaty has ever been made. Surely, the future of the northern red man is deplorable to contemplate.

At sunset on the 13th of August I took leave of Fort Smith, which is situated at the north end of the great falls, about sixteen miles north of Smith's Landing. It must be remembered that in referring to places I visited as 'forts,' they are not in any sense apposite to the term; no troops have ever been sent into that desolate region, hence, the so-called forts have never been garrisoned. They are merely trading-posts of the fur companies. My embarkation was a gloomy one; the clouds hung black and dismal over the limited area of vision, for high embankments lay in every direction. Scarcely had I pulled 20 —

to the center of the great river when the rain commenced to fall in torrents, and a terrible darkness overshadowed everything, and I was compelled to row to the shore, wet through and chilled to the bone.

Oh, how dreary and desolate the traveler's camp in a cold storm, isolated from all sounds excepting that of his own voice and the continuous dropping of the rain I By spreading a tent to protect my goods and crawling under a part of it, I managed to sleep until daybreak. What a blessing it is that one can sleep under such circumstances, forgetting all his troubles; perchance to dream of happy days, vanished forever I On awakening, his cares are multiplied, the dream having increased them by the disappointment of its reality.

On the 17th of August I caught a first glimpse of the Great Slave lake. There I met an old half-breed, from whom I learned that many years ago the Cree Indians of the south had come to this far-away country, captured the natives, and carried them back to their own villages, W'here they were doomed to a hopeless bondage of slavery. The raids of the southern tribes were of such frequent occurrence and so successful in results, that th^ name " Slaves " became the appellation of the northern tribes, and from them the lake and the river were given their names by the first white men who entered the region.

I was compelled to leave my boat at Smith's Landing, as I could not induce any of the Indians to assist me in making the portage. I borrowed a boat below the rapids, of a trader at Fort Resolution, and came through with it. I might have been obliged to remain there all winter, had I not met some kind white man who showed me the mercy which the Indians denied, as they had a grievance against me. I found on arriving at Fort Resolution that the Indians had sent a letter on ahead of me by their runners, commanding their people not to assist me in any way.

I was compelled to build a boat suitable for traversing the dangerous and turbulent waters of the lake, and had

only the assistance of my friend Mr. Rea, and of a half-breed Indian who bade defiance to the traditions of his tribe and the dictation of the headmen. There was no large timber in the vicinity, and the only resource was the driftwood. We were obliged to follow the shore for many miles before any logs were found suitable for our purpose. Then we had to raft them to our camp and saw them up by hand, to get lumber to construct the boat. All this took valuable time, and before the boat was ready for launching the weather was growing colder and more disagreeable.

There are no people north of Edmonton that one can employ, excepting the Indians. I had engaged numbers of them to assist on my journey and in building boats, but invariably every one broke his promise, and refused to continue even for double the wages ordinarily paid. For that reason I made up my mind that Indians would not work. When I arrived here, the mystery was solved. It appeared there had been mysterious messengers sent ahead, and after me, from Edmonton, who carried orders warning all Indians of the purpose of my mission; and ordering them to refuse me any assistance whatever, and to place all the obstacles in my way possible, even to killing the animals I might capture, rather than permit them to leave the country.

What surprised me more than anything else was that some of the Hudson Bay Company's officials prompted the savages to take the action which they did, particularly Dr. McKey, of Chippewayan. He came out boldly, and advised the Indians in my presence not to give me assistance in any form; and when he saw they could not turn me back, he took it upon himself to read me, from a volume of statutes, the law in relation to killing game in the Northwest Territory, notifying me that if I violated it he would "prosecute me to the bitter end." He said he had called his people together to take the subject of my intentions under consideration, and that they were very

indignant, etc. To be sure, I did not kill any game, and the Doctor was not smart enough to follow me to find out whether I did. I learned he had an Indian woman for a wife or mistress; had a houseful of half-breed children to look after, and I presume these facts, as well as his being a hireling of the Hudson Bay Company, prevented him from keeping an eye on me.

A letter had also been sent ahead of me to the high priests and big chiefs, bearing the commands I have referred to. I tried hard to get a photograph of the letter, but the Hudson Bay Company's interpreter at Fort Resolution, who had it in his charge, declared he had lost it, which I knew to be a subterfuge to prevent me from photographing it. The document was one mass of hieroglyphics and characters, readable only by the natives.

I had only one hope of success, and that was the aid of Messrs. Armstrong, Rea, and Van Nest. They agreed to stay with me until we were successful, if it required ten years. I was told all along the route by Hudson Bay Company traders that I would never take a musk-ox out of the northern country, and that I was only wasting my time to attempt it, for the Indians would never help me in the least. More than that, if I did get any, the Indians would kill them rather than permit them to go out of the country alive. I now believe and realize the fact that some of these traders knew of the conspiracy and the letters that had been sent in advance of my coming.

A.S a rule, I found most of the white men of the northern country were very hospitable and kindly disposed; particularly so was Mr. James McKinley, of Fort Smith* He has charge of the Hudson Bay Company's headquarters there, and superintends the transportation of their goods across the portage. Their freight is hauled on two-wheeled ox-carts. The oxen are wintered in sheds, with an abundance of choice hay for forage, cut near that place. I desire to mention among the employes of the Company those who were very courteous to me and as-

sisted me in many little ways, Mr. Gaudet and Mr. Cam-sell. Ed. Nagle, of Fort Resolution, is a free trader on his own responsibility. He is a gentleman in the strictest meaning of the term. His wife is the only white lady in that region.

When September arrived the nights were chilly, and when the rain was not pouring down it was generally frosty and cold. Money is no inducement to people in this region; they do not know what a dollar or a shilling is. I have often heard political speakers assert from the stump that they wanted "a dollar good the world over." I am certain they were never out of the United States, especially never in the land of the aurora borealis. All the gold or silver dollars in the world would not have purchased nails enough to build my boat, for the nails were not to be had there. Even if there were plenty, the Indians would not trade them for coin, as their unit of value is a " skin."

A skin was originally a beaver-skin, and all values were based on it. A beaver-skin at present is worth "twelve skins," a marten is worth "five skins," etc. They do not even have greenbacks, gold, silver or copper to represent their unit of value. It is worse than any fiat money ever advocated, as its basis is only imaginary; still, it serves all demands.

Fortunately, I had brought with me about fifteen pounds of assorted nails, and they were of more value in boat-building than all the gold or silver I could have carried.

On the 6th of September my boat was completed. The little yacht was a ' daisy'; twenty-two feet long and six feet beam. The wind and rain were strong from the east. Northeast was our course, yet we were obliged to go five miles westward to round a point that incloses a bay. What an experience we had after leaving Fort Resolution on the 6th 1 I had often been told of the perils and hazards of the "Great Spirit lake"; that it was the most

treacherous of all waters; that the storms rose when least 'expected; the waves so short and choppy that no boat could be constructed that would withstand the tempests, and many were the bones of human skeletons that strewed the bottom, where bottom was to be found; that in numerous places no bottom had ever been discovered,— which is no doubt true, as we had no line sufficiently long to fathom it.

On the 8th of September came a howling blizzard from the north, but we were in a good harbor, and suffered but little from the raging storm. On the morning of the next Hay the wind shifted to the west, exactly in our favor, and we sailed eastward to the "Point of Rocks,'* where it again veered to the southeast. Here we were compelled to sail northeast to an island fifteen miles away. The wind was blowing a perfect gale, but the Indians who accompanied us agreed to make the venture, and at four o'clock we set sail. After going about five miles the wind shifted due east, which was almost a headwind to where we were going. Then the heavens began to roll and tumble; the waves commenced to emulate them, while the gale increased in fierceness, piling the billows up in great black masses. Then came a tempest of wind with increased velocity, heaping them higher and higher, until they seemed to reach the low black clouds above them. What a night it was! In the stern sat " Old Siena" (the Indian had passed the allotted threescore and ten), guiding our frail bark, as the mighty waves tossed us about like a straw. The old fellow would occasionally emit a groan, which seemed as if it might be his last; at £imes I could not see his form, crouched down under the inky blackness surrounding us. All the others could do was to bail water as rapidly as possible, and by herculean exertions we managed to keep our craft afloat on the angry surf.

Hour after hour slowly—oh, how slowly 1—passed away; where we were, no one could tell. None of the

Indians could speak a word of English, much less could I speak a word of theirs,— the language of the "Yellow Knife" tribe.

Mr. Rea and an Indian in another boat, of the same dimensions as mine, started at the same time we did, with an agreement that we were to keep as near each other as possible, thus making the risk of life much less than if we were far separated. They had been driven from us, or we from them, but which, no one could tell; there were, however, never two more helpless crafts tossed hither and thither on the dark deep sea. It was long after the midnight hour as we still struggled with nature's most dangerous elements, wind and water, when suddenly appeared, a little to the right, a black object. I shouted to the old savage in the stern, and pointed toward it. He spoke to the young Indian, in the bow, and he responded, "An-noe I " I had no idea what " annoe " meant, but from the joyous tones of the young savage's voice, I felt certain that it must be land. Unfortunately, the wind was blowing directly from it, which made it impossible for us to land. I made signs to turn and tack, so as to make it if possible, but the old fellow shook his head and yelled to his companion, and immediate!\'7d' a most exciting colloquy occurred between them, which made me feel uncomfortable indeed, for I really thought we had missed the island and were drifting to sea. Finally the old savage bore heavily down on the long sweep he used as a rudder, and we changed our course more to the left, and sped on more swiftly through the foaming surf, with the wind bearing harder on our broad sail than before, and in a moment we were in the trough of the terrible sea, the huge waves striking the boat sideways. Then of all the rolling and pitching I had ever experienced (and I have twice crossed the Atlantic, sailed on the Gulf of Mexico, and all the great lakes), it was that hour in our harassing position that night, or rather, morning.

Again our young Indian yelled out, "Annoe 1 annoe 1 '*

(island). Just ahead I saw a dim, dark object. Imagine the sensation that came over me; the chills traversed up and down my spinal column ; I trembled between hope and despair. It was only for a moment, happily, as my pilot swung the boat still more to the left, so as to make the leeward side of the island. I could clearly see the trees waving before the maddened tempest, and hope predominated; fear was left behind, for in a few moments we were brought into one of the prettiest little harbors I ever saw, with mountains of moss-covered rocks on all sides.

Where was Mr. Rea ? We fired guns and carried torches to the highest peaks, but there was no responsive signal. A bright beacon-fire was kept burning at the apex of the loftiest mountain we could ascend. Then we rolled ourselves in our blankets, wet, cold, and disturbed in mind, — at least I was, for the safety of my companion. I was soon asleep, and enjoyed that rest we all so much needed after our adventurous and dangerous voyage.

At the first streak of dawn the beacon-fire was again kindled, to make smoke, and our guns discharged, but there was no response excepting the reverberating echoes. About eight o'clock, however, the young Indian*pointed to an island several miles distant to the northeast, and exclaimed, "Con! " (fire). I could plainly see a streak of blue smoke ascending from among the little peaks, and by the aid of my field-glasses could easily discern the mainmast of a boat. This was indeed joy for me; breakfast was hurriedly prepared and disposed of, and as the wind had completely subsided, we soon were plying the oars, and after a long pull, joined our comrades, who were without bread or meat, as the provisions had all been loaded into my boat. When we reached them, mutual congratulations were had on our fortunate escape from watery deaths, and we all indulged in a social cup of tea, exchanging experiences regarding one of the most terrible nights that had ever fallen to our lot.

The old chief and two young Indians had been employed by Mr. Rea to pilot him to Fort Reliance, before it was known that I was to accompany him. There they were to take him on a musk-ox hunt in October, and had the contract made in writing, and witnessed at Fort Resolution. True, the old chief did not sign it, for the simple reason that he could not write; yet its terms were acquiesced in verbally. But when he discovered I was to be one of the party, and that I was to get musk-oxen alive, he was horrified; and when we arrived at Fort Reliance and demanded to be piloted to the place where the herd of coveted oxen were to be found, he absolutely refused to move a step further under any consideration. We explained to the other Indians, as best we could, the stipulations of the contract, and in his presence denounced him in the bitterest terms to be found in their language.

On the 22d of September we arrived at Fort Reliance, having made three hundred miles since leaving Fort Resolution. The prevailing wind during our voyage had been from the northeast, and on the 9th of September and up to the 21st we had it directly ahead, or no wind at all. Oars were our only propelling power, and we consequently made slow progress, especially against the furious wind and a heavy sea.

About three o'clock in the morning of the 21st, a brisk breeze came from the west, and we rolled out of our blankets, hoisted our sails, and went flying through the foaming water. We were then within forty miles of our destination (Fort Reliance), but as the sun rose higher in the heavens the wind abated, and again we were left to our only resource, "paddling our own canoe," and obliged to cross a large bay fifteen miles in width. At sundown we reached the opposite shore, all tired out.

After we had partaken of our evening meal we fully expected to lie down and indulge in a good rest. The Indians had been firing their guns all the afternoon; it is a common custom among them, when approaching a village

S14 FORTY YEARS OF ADVENTURES

after they have been absent for a time, to fire a salute as aoon as within hearing distance. The longer they have been gone, the more salutes are given. Also, if they have been successful on their hunt the number of salutes is increased accordingly. The Indians told us they would row us to Fort Reliance, fifteen miles ahead, if we would permit it, and that we might sleep in the boats. We decided to allow them their own way for once.

Being very tired, we were soon fast asleep, but were suddenly aroused by the report of a gun a little distance ahead. On looking up, "Old Siena" and young Pierre were tumbling over each other after something, for a moment I could not tell what. In another moment Pierre had my Winchester and was sending shot after shot straight into the air, while the old chief had my double-barreled shotgun and was going through the same performance. It was my favorite breech-loader, and he was running the shells into it as fast as possible, while the younger one was emptying the magazine of my Winchester, and was in the act of reaching over for a bag of cartridges to dispose of them in the same manner. I grabbed hold of it first, and that put an end to their fun for that, night. All this time there was a continual blaze of flashes from the guns on the shore, and also from those in the flotilla of birch-bark canoes just ahead of us. It was a wild-looking scene. It did not take them long to get to our boats, and then we must shake hands with " the whole lot. Old Siena said, "La teal la teal "and all of us understood what that meant. He was going ashore and give his hungry friends a great feast of tea and "molar metsou" (white man's dinner), but Mr. Rea and I concluded that as we had just finished a hearty supper it would last us until midnight, at least. Mr. Rea shouted to Old Siena as he was swinging my boat to shore, "Elal" (no). By signals and what few words of the Slave language we could command, we notified the chief that we must either go on until midnight, or no " la tea."

This was cold comfort for the Indians, who had been without tea for months, and perhaps years without tasting bread. We were well satisfied that the whole tribe expected to feast off our supplies as long as they held out. The Indians all laid down their oars, and our barks drifted before a stiff easterly gale in the direction whence they had come. Finally, Mr. Rea made the old chief understand that when we should reach a point five miles away, that we had noticed before dark, we would have "la tea." Upon this gratifying intelligence the oars were quickly put in motion again; one large canoe shot off ahead, and before our boats were half-way to the objective point, a brilliant fire was burning there. It was nearly midnight when we arrived. A quantity of tea, flour, some bacon and tobacco were handed out to the Indians. We then rolled up in our blankets and slept in our boats until daylight. When we awoke, the whole group of Indians were seated around the fire, drinking tea and smoking their pipes. They had not slept a moment during the whole night; it was the greatest "hurrah" they ever had.

On the 22d we pulled about four miles farther to the northeast, and landed at Fort Reliance at 9 o'clock a. m. On our arrival, there came swarms of Indians from every point of the compass, for several days, but we shut off on all their begging, excepting to give them some tea, enough for one meal only. They appeared very much disappointed. Doubtless they had expected to spend several weeks with us, helping to enjoy our winter supply of provisions.

Fort Reliance is not and never was a fort in the commonly accepted definition of the term. It is where Capt. Geo. Back, of the Royal Navy, passed the winter of 1833-4, sixty-five years ago. Capt. Back was Sir John Franklin's most trusted friend, and on his first expedition to the Arctic regions, through most heroic efforts, relief reached Franklin and the few survivors of his party, at Fort En-

terprise, during the winter of 1820. Fort Reliance was built many years after the last-mentioned date, while Capt. Back was in search of Capt. John Ross, who had almost been given up as lost in the eternal ice of the Arctic Circle. A little history of the relief expedition will not be out of place here:

** Owing to the long absence of Capt. Ross, of the Victoria, in the northern seas, a relief and exploring expedition was organized under command of Capt. Back, intending to reach the north coast of America by descending the Great Fish river. This was supposed to flow in a northeast direction, and reach the sea at no great distance from the longitude in which Perry's ship ' Fury' had been abandoned in 1824. It was known that Ross would endeavor to reach this spot and take some of the store of provisions piled up on the beach. Capt. Back, therefore, in 1833 reached the Great Slave lake, and advanced by Aylmer lake to Clinton Golden lake, and made an examination of the headwaters of the Fish river. Then he returned to the wooded country by way of Artillery lake to winter. At the eastern end of the Great Slave lake he built his winter quarters, and called the place Fort Reliance.

" Early in the spring a start was made, and during the summer he successfully descended the river to the sea, and by fall had returned to his former winter quarters, where he passed the winter of 1834, and then returned to England."

The old quarters were of great interest from a historical point of view. Capt. Back chose this spot on account of the abundance of wood in the vicinity for the construction of his cabins and for fuel. It will be remembered that Capt. Back passed through Hudson bay, up the Saskatchewan river, and down the Athabaska and Slave rivers to Fort Resolution and Clinton Golden lake and

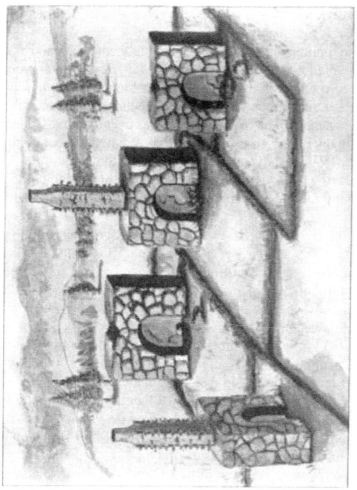

back to Fort Reliance, during the summer of 1833. He returned from Clinton Golden lake by way of Artillery lake, the same route which we followed when in pursuit of musk-oxen. In his report to the Admiralty he said:

"At Cat, or Artillery lake, we abandoned our canoe and performed the rest of our journey on foot, over precipitous rocks, through frightful gorges and ravines, heaped with masses of granite, and narrow ledges where a false step would have been fatal."

The buildings the gallant captain constructed were of logs, but they were long since destroyed by fire, and the only relics of the once substantial cabins are the stone chimneys, by the fire of which those early explorers kept themselves from freezing, and experienced those hard8hij)8 which are now a part of the history of the search for the Northwest passage. There are four of these remains of chimneys, and the only marks by which one can distinguish the outlines of the cabins are the moss-covered ridges that mark their place. The chimneys were of gigantic dimensions, measuring five by eight feet at their base; two still standing, whose tops are fourteen feet from the ground, show their height. The mortar employed in their construction was clay, without any admixture of lime, but its place substituted by sand. The clay had to be conveyed in boats from a point four miles up the river. The Indians knew where it came from, and showed us the si)ot; it appears to be the only clay in all that barren region. Grass had been worked into the mortar, after the Mexican method of making their sunburnt bricks or adobes, or such as the children of Israel used excepting when Pharaoh denied them the straw. The mortar seems to be as good to-day as when first used. The cabins, judging from the charred remains of portions of a bottom log, had been destroyed by fire, and they were so well preserved that I extracted a stick about a foot long from one, which was reasonably sound.

We found several articles in digging among the ruins, among them a file, and a portion of the head of a keg. They were discovered near the chimney, covered by ashes which probably saved them from that disintegration which marks everything else belonging to the hardy explorers-The piece of keg referred to evidently once held some alcoholic stimulants; for in the early days of Arctic exploration, existence in that frozen region was deemed impossible without it. Now, happily, that theory, like many others, has been exploded. We neither took with us, nor touched a drop of spirits during our long and adventurous journey into the far North; never deeming it at all requisite,— despite the intensity of the cold, darkness, and continual disagreeable weather. No doubt many former explorers would have been better off, had they done as we did.

These ruins are situated at the extreme northeast end of- Great Slave lake, at the mouth of a stream which drains Artillery lake. Pines and birches have sprung up all around the historic spot, which gives the place the semblance of a beautiful but abandoned park. I succeeded in photographing the ruins before disturbing them in any particular, and regard these pictures as among my most valuable* souvenirs, as we undoubtedly are the only white persons who have visited this historic spot since it was abandoned.

The distance of the ruins from Fort Resolution is about three hundred miles. The route to them is through groups of islands, many of which are nothing but huge masses of rock, while others are richly clothed with pines and deciduous shrubs, the ground beneath carpeted with bright moss. Their elevation above the water varies as greatly as their physical formation; frequently rising more than a thousand feet, with walls that are sheer perpendicular from six to eight hundred feet, and their horizontal length often extending for miles. The formation of the rock of which they are composed appears to be a species of flinty

granite varying strongly in color, with the lines of stratification distinctly marked.

The water of the lake north of the chain of islands is almost transparent,— so clear, in fact, that an object fifty feet below the surface can be distinctly seen; while on the south side, next to Peace, or Slave river, the water is muddy and full of silt. This chain of islands reaches from the east shore through the center of the lake nearly to the most western extremity.

The lake abounds in fish of several varieties, all of which are of excellent quality. Whitefish predominate, which are very oily,— a statement which probably no one would believe without having had ocular demonstration as we had. The number of trout is also marvelous, especially in the clear water described in the preceding paragraph. There is another fish Which it is believed is found only in this lake and its tributaries. It is fairly eatable, and is caught only with a spoon-hook, baited hook, or net. It is colloquially called "cony," which seems to be a corruption of some word whose derivation I could not clearly make out, but probably the French " inconnu, " These fish are used principally as feed for the dogs.

Trout are generally caught by spoon-hooks and lines from a boat, by the method known as trawling. I once regarded it as great sport to catch trout in the manner indicated, but hauled out so many in the Great Slave lake it was no longer a pleasure, but hard labor. White-fish are captured only by nets.

Fish in the lakes and game in the forests bordering the Barren Lands are in great abundance, and are the only support of a vast multitude of human beings,—the many tribes who live on the shores of the lakes and the streams tributary to them.

CHAPTER XX

AN Indian's wife of less value than a dog — mercury
AT ZERO OCTOBER 10 J. R. REA, A HERO OF HEROES —
DESPERATION OF INDIANS — CRUELTY TO A DEAF AND
DUMB GIRL — CHILDREN FRIGHTENED AT WHITE MEN ON
TASTING SUGAR, THEY SHOUTED, " HOPPY 8H0MP00LY1 "
(sweet salt) —INDIANS TAKE PROVISIONS BY FORCE
THEY ALSO APPLY THE TORCH TO COLONEL JONES's CABIN
HE SHOOTS HIS FIRST REINDEER — INDIANS STARVING
CONJURE THE RETURN OF THE REINDEER—WHEN THEY DID COME,
COLONEL JONES KILLED THEM—INDIANS ENRAGED— CLAIMED BUT DID NOT
GET THEM

AN Indian regards his wife, or mate (as that is the term that represents it in the far north), with less ^ consideration than he does his dog. They are, it is true, of greater value from a purely utilitarian standpoint, because they are able to work both winter and summer, while the dog works only during the former season. While the wife was employed in erecting the teepee, perhaps sick from constant exposure, hardly able to gather sticks to keep up the necessary fires, with the thermometer ranging from fifty to seventy degrees below zero, the husbands would be idling in our cabin from early morning till late at night, leaving their comfortable places at the last moment before we closed the door to retire. Frequently, to rid ourselves of their vermin-infested presence, we would make a bowl of gruel and a pot of tea for an ailing squaw, which we sent to her by the hands of the children. In a few moments the "buck'*

(320)

Indian \Vould start for his lodge, hoping, no doubt, to rob the poor woman of the only comfort she could enjoy.

The greatest annoyance we experienced was from the Indians, who crowded into our room; and no matter how many were already there, they always seemed to think there was room for one more. We refrained from ordering them away, for it would have been an insult to the whole tribe; and we needed their assistance as guides in the musk-ox hunt.

As soon as we learned there was no prospect of obtaining any musk-oxen, and that we would not be ready to return before the winter set in, we determined to pass the weary days, weeks and months in the land of the aurora borealis. We were only partially prepared for the siege, as before leaving home I had taken no thought of spending a whole year in that remote northern portion of the continent. I did not even provide myself with an overcoat. I had plenty of blankets made from the fur of the buffalo, which served me on all occasions, and they doubtless were often the means of preserving my life.

We each possessed an axe, felled the dry timber, about eighteen inches at the butt, and built a cabin sixteen by twenty feet, which was sufficiently large to admit sixty or seventy Indians at one time. We were compelled to raft the logs for its construction from four to five miles, and carry them on our shoulders fully one hundred yards, a good load for four men. Timber was only found in sheltered ravines. In fact, these ravines are the only fertile spots in all that region, the formation of the whole country being nothing but great mountains of stone. We lost no time in preparing ourselves, and on the 2d of October moved into our hurriedly constructed cabin. That night it blew a hurricane, accompanied by a terrific fall of snow. It may be imagined how grateful we were to be so well housed from the raging blizzard. I had been on the road for nearly four months ; had not slept under a roof or in a bed during the whole time. The rain had poured —21 upon me nearly every day during that period, and most of the time I was literally soaked; but now what joy and comfort we could take !

The snow that had commenced to fall when we luckily got into our cabin, continued without interruption for several days, and on the 10th of October the mercury sank to zero; on the next day, four degrees below. We had no lumber for a door or glass for a window, but utilized blankets for the openings, which made our quarters rather dark and dismal, even very cold, as the clay we used for daubing and the earth floor had been covered with water from the continuous rains, and was still thoroughly saturated. After the 11th, however, the weather moderated, and we took advantage of it to hew some timber into thick boards, and made a door. We also used a white shirt to cover the opening intended for a window, which admitted some light,— besides an abundance of healthful ventilation !

My companion, John R. Rea, was born in 1857, near Kingston, Ontario, Canada. His parents were in but moderate circumstances, and John was obliged to work to help maintain the family. His schooling was like that of boys in similar pecuniary condition. He served an apprenticeship at blacksmithing, and he apparently had a taste for that art. He is about 5 feet 8 inches in height, and weighs 190 pounds; is well-muscled and courageous. He is apparently a natural-born mechanic; of a. quiet disposition; says but very little, but what he does-say is always full of meaning. His broad chin and high cheek-bones do not betray his character, as a more resolute and determined man to carry out any and every undertaking is seldom met with. He could sing but one song, "The ship that never returned"; and I must confess, the doleful music had no charms for me. He was-just the kind of metal needed throughout our journey, and was a very useful man. Mr. Rea had already passed one winter on the Mackenzie river. With some canvaa

JOHN R. REA.

we had been using as a tent, he made harness for our four big dogs; also built a sled, and we soon piled up plenty of good dry wood, that we had to haul nearly a mile over some pretty rough roads, or rather, no roads at all.

October was a blustery month. Snow-storms were frequent. The ice was thick on the bays and margin of the large lake, and the fish had departed for parts unknown. The reindeer were expected daily, but as time rolled on they failed to put in an appearance, bringing only disappointment and hunger to the Indians, as well as to ourselves. Eatables were getting very scarce, and the Indians continued to come from all directions, hoping to beg meat and a cup of tea from the mysterious palefaces who had invaded their domain. I had often read of the few expeditions to the far North ; how the savages had begged and robbed the members of their subsistence, and how they had suffered from hunger. I had made up my mind not to be caught in the same dreadful situation, and believed myself smart enough to circumvent the Indians; but the white man who can outwit one of these northern tribes ought to pack up and start for their country at once. He would be of great service to the few traders there who attempt to carry on a legitimate business 1

These miserable creatures would make all kinds of excuses and promises; tell what great people the whites were; bring tongues of the caribou; follow us around, and declare that their children were starving; that their fathers or brothers had gone to Fort Resolution for provisions ; that as soon as they returned we should be repaid what we could let them have. One man wanted tobacco so badly that he became nearly wild,— caught Mr. Rea by both arms and plead for it with tears in his eyes. Another one returned after bidding us good-bye, and pretended that he had lost a piece of tobacco on the floor. He got down on his hands and knees and crept all over the house, pretending that he was looking for it. Then he commenced to bewail his fate. We spotted all

such actions, and were firm in denying them at all times. I never used tobacco in any form, and would tell them it made me sick, and I was afraid to give it to anyone for fear it might affect them in the same way. Mr. Rea had learned a good deal of their language, and I soon learned some of the most important words; so that, with this knowledge, aided by signs, we could converse with them quite freely. The best interpreter we found among the Yellow Knife tribe was a deaf mute, little Emma, a girl about twelve years old. We could make known to her almost anything by signs; she would then convey our wishes to her family in her own peculiar way. Whenever we could not make ourselves intelligible to the Indians congregated in our cabin, we invariably asked for " Emma nachila " (Emma, little). Poor child 1 her lot was doubly deplorable. The story of her sufferings would fill a volume. One day, during a terrific blizzard from the north, I bundled up and went to the lake for water; just as I neared the bank, the child stepped up with a birch-bark pail full, when a mighty gust of wind caught and whirled her down the bank on the lake. The water flew all over her, and immediately froze. There she stood, with her arms stretched out, head bare, without shoes or stockings, with only a loose frock made of caribou skins to cover her nakedness. I picked up the pail, and by signs told her I would get the water and carry it to the top of the bank. She uttered a peculiar sound, and bowed in thankfulness. As quickly as I could, I handed her the pail of water, and she went swiftly to her father's teepee. The most provoking thing about it was, I knew her father and two full-grown brothers—all hale and hearty — were lounging in the lodge on caribou rugs, before a rousing fire, the wood for which had been chopped and hauled over a mile by an elder sister, only fourteen years of age, an ideal Indian lassie. This is only one illustration of the ways of those Indians of the North.

One night a great number of Indians pitched their teepees about a quarter of a mile from our cabin. The next morning on opening our door, there stood not less than thirty boys and girls in the snow. Most of them were barefooted and bareheaded. Their ages ranged from seven to fifteen years. The moment they caught sight of me, all turned and ran toward the village as if a pack of arctic wolves were in close jmrsuit.

It must be remembered this was the first white man they had ever seen, and having heard so many bloodcurdling stories about the dreaded white race, no wonder the\'7d" were frightened nearly to death. At last one of the boys ventured to look back, and seeing no one pursuing, stopped, and looked as wild as a reindeer. I beckoned him to come to me; he took a few steps, and then halted, not daring to venture farther. By this time quite a number had stopped, and they looked at me with the wildest expression I ever saw on mortals' faces. I beckoned them to come to me, but they stood motionless, except some of the smaller ones, who kept right on until they reached the wigwams, where they no doubt crawled under deer-skins to save themselves from the paleface.

I stepped back into the cabin, took two handfuls of sugar, and again appeared in the door, where I held out my hands toward them. They had not the slightest idea of the taste of sugar, although they had often eaten salt, which is found in great abundance in some of the marshes of that region. I took a lump in my mouth, smacked my lips, and said, " Nazou! nazou 1" (Good 1 good!) Finally, a boy of about thirteen years came to me shyly, and held out his hand. I gave him a lump. After putting it in his mouth, he turned to the others with the most comical expression. At last he managed to find his tongue, and shouted, "Hoppy shompooly! hoppy shompooly! " (Salt sweet I salt sweet!) Then I was kept busy supplying the little beggars with the " sweet salt." The boys, when the supply of sweets was exhausted, ran to the woodpile, and

seizing the two axes which were lying there, began to chop wood as if their very lives depended upon it. Perhaps they were looking for more sugar to follow this extraordinary feat, or maybe they were only showing their appreciation of the treat, but we were kept well supplied with wood for several days. Not being satisfied with their work, however, they began on the logs of the cabin, and I was compelled to send them on their homeward journey, to save a shelter for ourselves. No doubt their dreams that night were of the "sweet salt." At all events, my introduction into Indian society was made.

By the 20th of October, things commenced to look gloomy. The last cache^ had been invaded, and all the meat gone. Still more Indians kept coming; hundreds gathered around our cabin, all pleading for a mouthful of something. Several of them were sick; one nearly dead with the consumption, and we felt obliged to give him rations from our scanty store. Had it not been for Mr. Kea they certainly would have robbed me of everything. His experience on the Mackenzie river was of 'great value to us. He handled them without gloves; at least they thought so. One big burly savage attempted to run things his own way by kicking whatever came in his path. He having one day kicked over a bread-pan just to see it tumble, that was the last kicking he ever tried with us, as Mr. Rea struck him such a swinging blow under the ear that it laid him apparently lifeless on the ground. Mr, Rea then choked him until his eyes bulged out like peeled onions. The other Indians looked on with amazement stamped on their otherwise stoical countenances.

A few days afterward, another "smart Aleck" arrived at our camp, and brought with him fifteen or twenty more starving redskins. We were eating dinner when they all

^ Cache, a place for concealing or storing anything; as, a hole In the gn^ound or a cavity under a heap of stones ; also, provisions, ammunition, etc., stored In such a place. The custom of "caching" provisions Is a common one by travelers In the far North, to provide against the emergency of a scarcity of game, which frequently occurs.

IMPUDENT INDIANS C27

unceremoniously bolted in, and the moment we arose from our improvised table the leader walked up to it and exclaimed, "Dennie la tea, hula" (Indian tea, none), at the same instant seizing the copper bucket containing the coveted liquid, and swilling down about a quart. Thia was insulting in the extreme, but as we had several caddies of the article it was of little consequence. As sooii as he sat the bucket down,-he picked up a pot of meat at the other end of the table, thrust his dirty hand into the soup, and drew out a large piece of meat. This he held in his left hand and caught one end with his teeth; then picked up our butcher-knife and cut off a chunk so large it would scarcely go into his mouth, and began devouring it. This was taking rather too much liberty for me to tolerate, and I sprang like a wildcat at his throat, wrenched the savory morsel from his hand, and sent him headlong toward the door; then quickly made my way to the corner of our cabin where we kept our supplies, deposited the pot of meat, and stood between the eatables, Winchester in hand, until the Indians were gotten rid of. I said to Mr. Rea, that I was surprised he did not resent such "pure cussedness." He laughed, and replied he was waiting to see if I had any " sand." I told him I had a little left. " Then," said he, " let's clean them out," and commenced to knock them right and left. They went out like a flock of sheep, except three that lay on the floor. Mr. Rea swung them out by the heels. We were very thankful when the impudent crowd left, as they were next to the hardest set we had to deal with v/hile in the northern country.

Mr. Rea was frequently absent looking after his traps. He would be gone for hours, sometimes for days. On one occasion when I was alone, the night a dark and wretched one, suddenly six impudent Indians entered the cabin and demanded tea, tobacco, flour, and in fact, "wanted the earth." They offered nothing in exchange, and I promptly refused to accede to their demands, ex-

cepting for water, which was ever at their service, if they would help themselves, as I always refused to wait oii them. Finally one of them jumped up and exclaimed, " Con ! Con ! " (fire), upon which five of them rushed out and gathered their arms full of chips and dry sticks, at our woodpile, one of the number returning with two pieces. He deliberately helped himself to a brand from my fireplace, and with it he darted out into the darkness. The Indian that remained inside the room said, "Dennie mad! " I stepped to the door and saw them heaping up chips at the corner of the cabin, which they had already ignited, intending to burn us out.

It was an awful night, and I told the Indian who had talked to me in broken English, to stop them and we would have a pow-wow, and perhaps fix it up. He went to the door and spoke to them, and I went out and pulled the fire away from the cabin, when they all returned with me. I gave them two plugs of tobacco and a cup of tea each, at which they appeared satisfied. It was lucky that Mr. Rea was not there, or trouble would surely have ensued, and of such a character that the breach could not have been easily healed. I often think of that dreadful night and shudder, yet am thankful that I chose the right course at once. After that raid on me the Indians attempted to force us, but they were never as demonstrative again. We took a firm stand against any more of their foolishness, by knocking them down and dragging them out at the slightest provocation. We gave them to understand we " made medicine " so strong we could hurl such bolts of thunder and lightning upon their heads as would annihilate the whole tribe at one blow.

November arrived without the advent of a single caribou, and the Indians were in a starving condition; very few of them could muster half a meal. All left the neighborhood excepting about a dozen families. No sooner had the last of them gotten out of sight than a band of five caribou made its appearance from the

northwest, on the opposite side of the river, when we had really been expecting the'm from the northeast. I carried a Winchester rifle of forty caliber, using eighty-two grains of powder. The Indians had small single-barrel shotguns, with balls. They made things lively with their small weapons, trying to secure some meat, but became so excited that four of the animals passed through their lines and escaped. The renjaining one was a monstrous bull, that threw his antlers high in the air and attempted to go around them. I stepped behind a clump of bushes, and as he trotted within a hundred yards of where I stood, took my first shot at a caribou.^ The ball broke-his neck close to the shoulder, and he dropped dead. The Indians came up rejoicing, while I took a back seat. They helped themselves, saying, by signs and their own language, "We pay you back when we kill one!" The next morning I was out of my blankets and traveled two miles before daybreak. As the sun rose, a herd of twenty-eight caribou appeared on the opposite side of the river^ moving eastwardly to where I had secreted myself on the trail of the five that had already broken a path the day previously through the snow over the ice. They came within two hundred yards of me, then turned northwardly, trying to ascend the bank at another point, which was also low. I opened fire, and killed the leader at the first shot. I pulled the trigger eighteen times, but got only six animals. The Indians soon came over by

1 The caribou of the arctic region is a North-American variety of the reindeer, and is much smaller than his congener, the caribou of Maine. It has never been domestic cated. The caribou deer in America have to contend with the deep snow more than do the reindeer proper of the old continent; their horns are broader, and better adapted to the purpose. Besides, both varieties, In addition to these natural shovels, have broad feet, not only to sustain them better on the snow, but also to clear it away ; their legs are much larger than are those of the common deer; their hoofs are as broad and as large as those of a full-grown ox. A full-grown male caribou will weigh, when in ordinary flesh, four hundred pounds, while the common American deer weighs but little over half that amount; but the caribou loses much more in dressing, for the reason that his stomach is abnormally large, this condition arising from the fact that his principal food is moss. In which there is relatively very little substance. They will net when dressed about one hundred and eighty pounds, while the deer will net very near the same amount.

the dozen, and commenced to ridicule me for not killing more. I was so disgusted with myself I felt like breaking my gun over a rotten log. All the time Mr. Rea had been standing on the bank, half a mile distant, witnessing my miserable shooting, and was as much provoked as I. A fire was quickly kindled, and the Indians soon had all six of the heads roasting before it, without stopping to ask my permission. I picked up my rifle and walked to the fire, for it was dreadfully cold, where I commenced to make a close inspection of the weapon, and discovered that the raised sight which I always used had been lowered three notches; upon which I laughed aloud, and exclaimed, " Nazzula! " (no good), and then showed the Indians and Mr. Rea that the gun had not been properly sighted. Some one had misplaced the sights, and I had fired with a sight three notches lower than usual,— and that was the cause of my missing.

One old Indian then struck himself on the breast and exclaimed, "Dennie nazzula 1" (Indian no good), admitting that on the previous day, while I was absent at the cabin after the dogs and a sled to haul some meat home, he had placed the sights down to where he thought was the correct notch for them. His explanation exonerated me, and every one was astonished that I had even done so well. They had been pointing at me and exclaiming, "Nazzula," (No good); now they exclaimed, " Nazu; molar nachawI" (Good white man; big).

The next day I killed six more caribou, out of what we hoped was the main herd, but they proved to be but a few stragglers. It was a Godsend that thirteen had fallen before my unerring rifle,— more than double the number that had been secured by the whole band of Indians.

Days and weeks passed, but no further signs of the caribou could be discovered. We had eight dogs to feed, and all the Indians remaining with us, numbering about forty, with whom we would shortly be compelled to divide, to prevent them from starving. They possessed sixty-two

dogs, SO that if they fed them, the few caribou they had killed would furnish them only two days' rations. As long as an Indian has anything to eat he never stops eating, or gives any thought to the morrow. Some historians claim the Indians have no particular time for eating. I say they have, and that time is all the time, if anything to eat is to be had. As we had anticipated, they commenced to come to our cabin the second day after the killing of the last caribou, begging for meat. They plead most piteously, and when the older ones failed to receive anything, they sent their children; and when they too failed, the women made their appearance. When they found it was of no use to beg, they tried to buy, offering their garments and a few furs they had secured. But we never sold any meat; if we allowed it to go at all, it went freely, without money and without price.

On Saturday, the 9th of November, the Indians congregated in one wigwam; and of all the wailing, screeching, shouting, lamentation, and chanting, it was far in excess of what I had ever heard. We knew very well what it meant: they were conjuring the return of the caribou. They continued their incantations into the night; and the next morning, Sunday, it was intensified by the addition of tom-toms\ pans, kettles, and all manner of such discordant instruments, during the entire day. Just as the sun was about sinking into the great lake, which was only partially frozen over (the center remaining open until December), while I was swinging my axe preparing kindlings for the next morning's fire, my eyes caught sight of a dozen caribou crossing the bay, fully a mile away, going in an angling direction from me. I darted into the cabin, snatched my rifle from the rack, and was soon rushing over the ice (which was quite smooth) toward the leader of the herd. The animals would trot a little, then stop, and look in every direction. While they moved, I ran as

IA peculiar kind of drum, constructed of wood, covered with rawhide made from reindeer skins.

rapidly as possible toward them; when they stopped, I stopped too, in a crouching position. Seeing me in plain view, they gazed for five or six minutes at a time, to see if I moved. When no motion was observed by them, they appeared satisfied there was no danger, believing me, no doubt, to be a stump, or a clump of spruce bushes; then would again move cautiously over the ice. When they stopped, I stopped; when they started again, I moved swiftly on until I had gotten within three hundred yards of them: then turned my battery loose. Four large animals fell, and several others were badly wounded. I had not taken the precaution to get my belt of cartridges when starting from the cabin, and was therefore compelled to content myself with four, as the magazine of my rifle contained only eight loads. Besides, I was obliged, on account of the position of the herd, to shoot directly toward the setting sun; so it was more from luck than by science that I secured as many as I did.

When the smoke from my rifle had cleared away, I looked over the lake toward the wigwam, and to my dismay saw all the Indian women and starving dogs on a rapid run for the caribou which I had killed. I rushed in the opposite direction from the dead carcasses, and drew the attention of the dogs from the meat, starting them for the living caribou across the bay, as there would not have been a pound of meat left had they discovered the dead animals. But the poor canines were so miserably thin and weak they could not have caught one with two of its legs shot off 1

I could not fool the squaws as I had the dogs, and they, armed with butcher-knives, incontinently scrambled for the heads and limbs while I was slashing out the viscera. They had brought with them some birch-bark buckets, and scooping up the blood, poured it into the buckets and appeared very grateful to me for allowing them to get it. They very carefully saved all of the offal excepting what they themselves devoured raw on the spot.

The men were not so grateful. They really believed they had brought the caribou by their heathenish incantations and prayers to the Great Spirit, and gave me to understand by signs and words that they were entitled to the lion's share on that account. But it did not convince me, and they got nothing.

The old men regarded me with amazement, and were emphatic in their praise for a man that could walk up to a caribou on the ice and shoot him down in such an easy manner. They really believed I could command the animals to stand still and they would obey. We took advantage of their superstition whenever possible. They imagine themselves great hunters, yet never have learned the art of stalking in an open field; they are cunning and crafty in the forest and brush, among the hills and large rocks, but of little account where there is nothing behind which to secrete themselves.

When we study the habits of these reindeer,— how they always avoid the forest and hills by traveling on the ice and level plains, in order to avoid dangers from Indians and wolves that attack them in such favorable places, it is not surprising, in reading the history of Franklin's first expedition to the Barren Lands, to learn that the party saw plenty of reindeer on the lakes and level plains, but could not approach near enough to shoot them; and that all of that heroic band perished excepting four or five. Had there been a "killer," as well as a hunter or a military captain or lieutenant, the whole party would have returned safe and sound.

We plainly perceived that many of the women and children would perish from hunger, unless we denied our dogs, and divided what we had with them. We gave a little from time to time, but found it was apportioned to those who really needed it least. We therefore had to compel each family to send over one person each evening, to whom we gave just enough to keep them alive and able to move around.

CHAPTER XXI.

ARRANGING FOR A MUBK-OX HUNT — MR. REA AND TWO INDIANS MAKE THE JOURNEY CAUGHT IN A BLIZZARD

GRAPHIC DESCRIPTION OF THE GREATEST WATERFALLS OF THE FAR NORTH — SECOND NIAGARA — BANDS OF REINDEER EVERYWHERE DRIVING THEM INTO A CORRAL

INDIANS DETERMINED TO STAY AND EAT WHITE MAN's MEAT NOTHING COULD DRIVE THEM AWAY.

THE date we had determined upon, early in tlie fall, to leave on a winter musk-ox hunt, was the 16th of November. All the Indians in our vicinity who had learned of our presence and intentions were anxiously waiting for the time to arrive, as they always regard an event of that character as a "red-letter " day in their calendar. As the auspicious moment draws near they become as fidgety as a sixteen-year-old maiden when she is to take the initial excursion with her first beau. Everything is hurry and bustle: the men making sleds and snowshoes, collecting meat and fish, and running races to harden their muscles,—for they are well aware that if they fall by the wayside they must return from the hunt in disgrace. So everyone nerves himself to meet the responsibility of such occasions, and if possible, to "put the other fellow in the hole." The women, too, are not by any means idle: their fate is continual labor, and now they are doubly subjected to the yoke of their masters. Tanning skins, making moccasins, mittens, chopping and hauling wood, besides everything else in the nature of labor, falls to their lot, excepting the manufacture of sleds

(834)

and of the frames for snowshoes. During the limited amount of daylight in that remote region, their home, they are continually at work getting a supply of wood for the long nights that follow. In the prolonged darkness they are busy with needles, using the sinews of caribou for thread, lacing snowshoes, trimming the carryalls, and performing anything else that is beneath the dignity of a male Indian.

The term "carryall," as high-sounding as it may appear to some, is nothing more than a box made of dressed deer-skins, the framework of which is wood, placed upon a runner, which is simply a single birch board about twelve inches wide, hewn out with an ax and butcher-knife, and curved in front in the similitude of a toboggan. The narrowness of the sled (one foot in width) is necessitated by the fact that it is to follow in the tracks of snow-shoes, and pass through thick timber and brush.

Frequently bands of Indians would visit our cabin to trade musk-ox hides and other furs for tea, tobacco, ammunition and other goods; at other times they demanded credit, saying they were sure to kill great loads of animals, with whose furs they would repay. They declared they had fourteen sledges to go on the proposed hunt for musk-oxen, which would be sufficient transportation for one hundred and forty skins. We had no goods to part with on such an uncertain tenure. That we were correct in our estimation of their truthfulness, was verified shortly after, as will be seen.

When the Indians were convinced that we had no idea of letting goods go or parting with our flour and other eatables, at any price, they ceased troubling us, most of them taking to the lakes with nets; others with guns pulled out for the northeast, hoping to meet the caribou coming south. On these expeditions the women and children always accompanied them. The last band, just referred to, returned in about two weeks, in a starving condition. They then started for a point forty miles

south on the lake, where it was reported an abundance of whitefish were being caught with nets under the ice; and that was the last we saw of them until the following spring.

When the 16th of November arrived, we were ready with ten days' supply of dried meat in our carryall, expecting at least four more sleds to be on hand. The Indians congregated at our cabin early in the morning to witness the start. To our disgust, there was but one sled and two men in readiness to go, and they had managed to procure but four days' rations for themselves and their dogs ; and even then robbed their women and children of what little there was in store, intending to trust them to our generosity, knowing they would not starve during their absence. We promised to divide our meat with them, and furnish tea. A promise was also exacted from us that we would not attempt to take any musk-oxen alive; we were also to furnish the men with ammunition and tea. If the Indians had had the least idea of our real intentions regarding the capture of live animals, they never would have consented to move a step in the direction of the haunts of the musk-oxen, as they look upon them as sacred.

It was very evident to Mr. Rea and myself, that if we both left our cabin while the Indians were in such straits for food, there would not be a pound of anything eatable left on our return. Each wanted to go badly, but it was simply impossible under such circumstances; so we adopted the old Biblical custom of casting lots to see which should go and which should remain to guard our property, and to kill and store meat for future use. It was my luck to have to stay behind, for which I had no taste; but there was no alternative.

At nine o'clock Mr. Rea with a train of two dog-sleds — four dogs to each sled — and two shepherd dogs and the two Indians started on a long, wearisome tramp after the most remote northern herbivorous animal, the musk-ox.

There were already eight inches of snow, and more expected daily. Snowshoes were an absolute necessity from the beginning to the end of their journey. The elder Indian was an old-time hunter about sixty-six years of age, while the other, his son, was a mere lad of not over twenty-two snows, and hale and robust as can be imagined. It was the latter's duty to do the "tripping"; that is, to go on ahead of the sleds and break a road for the dogs. If any of my readers believes that he can outwalk an Indian on snowshoes, let him challenge La Pierre, jr., the champion of the Yellow Knife tribe. Mr. Rea in his itinerary says:

" Our course the first day was northeast, and we camped four miles from the south end of Artillery lake, near the river that drains it into Great Slave lake. I slept but a few moments that night, as we were near one of the most wonderful waterfalls on the continent, excepting Niagara. The roar of the great sheet of water can be heard for forty miles, and in winter the vapor rising from it can be seen at an immense distance. I am inclined to think that the origin of the name, 'Artillery' lake, is because of the column of mist seen rising from it as the lake is approached, and the dreadful roar of the fall, which sounds like a battery of artillery in action,— the vapor adding to the illusion.

"Many carcasses of caribou, bear, wolves and other animals are annually carried by the rapids to the falls, over which they are tumbled, to be dashed to pieces at their base.

"The neck of Artillery lake is quite narrow immediately above the falls, and its very narrowness is an inducement for wild beasts to cross at that point, after wandering fruitlessly elsewhere along the rugged and precipitous margin for some suitable crossing-place. The water is extremely smooth at this place, but very rapid, and once in its clutches the victim is doomed to certain — 22

death, for the distance in perpendicular height is about two hundred feet, and the water in its terrible descent strikes a series of pointed and jagged rocks, making death inevitable to whatever living thing goes over the cataract.

"Before the water was frozen, our dogs had plenty of food in the shape of the carcasses of caribou and bear that had met their doom at the falls, as at this point the volume of water emptying into the Great Slave lake forms an eddy which casts all the victims onto the shore.

"As I have stated, I caught but a few winks of sleep; so roused my traveling companions long before the first indications of the coming day, and by the time the sun was visible above the horizon we were fully ten miles on our journey. Our trail on the ice of Artillery lake was almost directly northeast. Here we discovered the first indications of the presence of game. A few tracks of caribou showed that the vanguard and leaders of the winter migration of these strange animals had already passed westward. We halted on the west bank of the lake, kindled a fire, and took a second breakfast. As soon as it was sufficiently light to distinguish objects at any distance, we discovered caribou on every hill and in all directions. It appeared as if the whole face of the earth were alive and moving. We killed five, enough to supply onr immediate wants; three of which we cached, so as to be certain of meat on our return trip. After that duty was performed we proceeded on our journey, our hopes renewed, and with freshly inspired vigor. Young Pierre swung off in the lead as tripper, at a * two-sixty-five * gait. When we halted for dinner I was wet with perspiration, and long before night it appeared to me that every step was the last I could possibly make; but I was too ambitious to acknowledge the fact, so it was my courage that kept me up rather than my muscles.

"At last we made camp on the west shore in a clump of good-sized spruce saplings, affording us an abundance of fuel of excellent quality. We had been among cariboa

all day, and the next morning we traveled more slowly, killing and caching our meat. The fifth day out we were to leave the lake and take a northwestwardly course to the shore of Clinton Golden lake, where we expected to find the musk-oxen.

"When we awoke in the morning a fearful gale was blowing from the southwest, with snow coming down rapidly. We had a regular wigwam in which to shelter ourselves, but had passed the ' land of little sticks,' ^ and all the material we had to burn was roots which stood high above the surface of the ground, from which mighty winds had blown away the sand and snow. Here we were absolutely imprisoned for four days and nights by the violence of the storm. Fortunately, we had loaded our sleds with wood to serve us further on our journey. To burn it now, meant a day's travel on the back track for more; so we put in all the little daylight we had in gathering the roots mentioned, managing by hard work to get enough to cook our meat and dry our wet clothes. The other twenty-five hours of the wearisome night we passed rolled up in our blankets.

" We expected to be back at our starting-place in ten days, consequently provided ourselves with only sufficient bread for that period, but before we broke camp the last biscuit had vanished. It was two days' more of weary travel to Clinton Golden lake, then the long journey home,— all of which must be endured with only meat for our entire diet. True, we had an abundance of tea, and a combination of these two articles must suffice for every meal during thirteen days' travel 1

" Our two days' journey overland was through a region quite level, a vast expanse of moss-covered granite with a little dead grass, appearing like an immense pasture tinged with the holocaust of autumn, which must be a para-

' liand of little sticks, the most northern region where wood can be obtained. Here the trees are so whipped and twisted by the wind from off the Barren Lands that they only attain a height of from three to ten feet. Thus, all Indiana know this country as the " land of little sticks."

dise in summer for vast herds of caribou and musk-oxen. The hills were relatively barren, whose principal carpeting was broken granite, their surface in turn covered by moss. In winter when the wind whirls the snow from these elevated places to the valleys and it lodges there, and in the gorges, the caribou and musk-ox live on the mosses of the bare hills.

" On the second morning out from the lake we came upon an old musk-ox bull's track, so recently made that our loose shepherd dogs became terribly excited and took up his trail, which we also followed for some distance. If we had killed him and two more, it would have made three, as the boy answered who was fishing one day, according to the ancient story. The trail of the huge fellow soon became obliterated by the drifting snow, and that was the nearest we came to killing the game we were after,— and it took twenty-three days of our precious time to do even that I

" The weather continued so stormy that there was little daylight; in fact, it was only twilight, and the winter was asserting its potency very rapidly. We turned southwest, making a-great detour in returning to our last camp on Artillery lake, where we had several caches in which were stored our caribou, needed so badly, for our dogs had been living on half-rations several days, and began to show the effects of it in a most deplorable manner.

"We arrived at the cache late at night, and when we opened it discovered to our sorrow that the wolverines had anticipated us and devoured the last scrap deposited there 1 We raked the bottoms of our carryalls, and were rewarded by finding a few pieces of dried meat, which were divided between ourselves;])ut the poor dogs were in tlie same fix as the traditional Mother Hubbard's,— 'had none.' We had two more caches farther down the shore, which we could reach by hard traveling the next night.

" When morning came the first thing we saw after getting out of our blankets was a small herd of caribou.

Young Pierre took my rifle and managed to shoot all the cartridges in the magazine, which contained eight, and succeeded in killing seven. Two would have been an abundance, but when an Indian sees game and has plenty of ammunition, he never stops shooting until it is exhausted.

"We selected two very fat young animals, and all of us, including our hungry dogs, had a great feast. We carried but little of the meat away, trusting to the supply in our caches ahead, which we had taken greater pains with in constructing, building them of green poles, which were frozen so hard that the most voracious wolverine with his remarkably keen teeth and powerful jaws could not gnaw them away, as we flattered ourselves. When we arrived where they were located, to our infinite surprise and chagrin both had been robbed by those ghouls of the Barren Lands, the irrepressible wolverines!

"We fortunately killed a caribou now and then. Finally, on the night of the twenty-third day out, we arrived at our starting-place. Fort Reliance, where I found Mr. Jones seated before a blazing fire in the comfortable cabin, and twenty-five caribou carcasses and half a hundred exceptionally large whitefish stowed away in our larder, the roof of the building. He also had plenty of biscuits baked, and a large pot of beans smoking hot, over the fire. What joy and real comfort all this afforded me, I leave to the imagination of the reader, who will kindly put himself in my place on that midwinter night in the arctic darkness."

The fourth day after Mr. Rea left, on the 20th of November^ my last pound of meat was exhausted, excepting what was in the pot for myself. The next morning the thermometer indicated thirty-six degrees below, and matters looked gloomy enough. Just as I was in the act of tying on my moccasins to start in search of something to kill, all the Indians in camj) came bursting in at the

door, crying, " Jones 1 Jones I atonl atoni" (caribou). I grabbed my rifle, and before I arrived at the shore of the lake a hundred yards distant I saw a herd of about twenty-five animals running for the opposite side of the bay, with twenty starving dogs after them, and had not one-half of their pack already perished from hunger, the same additional number would have been on their trail. I turned back into the cabin, the Indians beseeching me to follow, but I was too experienced a hunter to run on a cold trail. To me it was a "cold day," and it would have surely been a cold trail. I sauntered leisurely up the river, and found the caribou had been crossing by the hundreds. I luckily killed two fine bucks, and the Indians were saved from starvation, as I gave one to the squaws for dressing the other. The animals had made their appearance, sure enough, though about a month later than usual.

That day one of the largest bands of caribou of the season made its appearance on the ice, near where we had previously constructed a corral.^

I saw a fine opportunity to bag the whole herd, by turning them on the trail leading up to the corral. There was an Indian hunting with me that day, who was stationed at the only other point where the animals could ascend, while I was far out on the ice in their rear, driving them in the direction I desired them to go. I motioned for the Indian to come out from his hiding-place and show himself, so as to turn the caribou on the trail to the corral; in fact, I had told him before if the opportunity occurred,

^The corral was built of polee. In the style of an old Virginia worm fence, about eight feet high, with a capacity of one hundred and fifty animals. The gate of the corral was constructed after the manner of a wire rat-trap, and when the animals once entered they could not return. The corral stood back from the margin of the bay about a hundred yards, and from each side of the gate a flaring wing fence extended from the corral down to the bay, at an angle of about twenty degrees, forming a lane leading from, the ice to the entrance. There were only two places where the caribou could ascend the bank, and the wings encompassed one of them. When the animals left the ice for the high land, some one was always secreted on their leeward side, and the moment they entered the wing all he had to do was to jump out behind them, give a yell, and they went pell-mell Into the trap.

to do exactly what I was signaling for, but he was so anxious to get meat he refused to obey, and the caribou rushed past him so close that he could have touched some of them with the muzzle of his shotgun. The fool of a savage fired both barrels of my shotgun loaded with buckshot, without touching one of the herd, which I discovered by inspecting its trail afterward;

there was not the slightest semblance of blood on the snow. Through his excitement the chance for procuring enough meat to last us and the Indians all winter was lost, and did not occur again that season, though Mr. Rea and myself afterward succeeded in capturing a few in the corral.

They continued to pass in small bands for two or three days, and when the slaughter was ended I had piled up on our cabin twenty-five choice carcasses of the reindeer. The Indians managed altogether to kill nearly the same number, and I had a little rest from their constant importunities for meat,— aggregating only about ten days, unfortunately.

Mr. Rea was unluckily absent during the hunt, or we would have secured as many more. He was out prospecting for musk-oxen on the shores of Artillery and Clinton Golden lakes.

During Mr. Rea's absence one of the Indians to whom we had rented a net came sixty miles, bringing us sixty-two whitefish as our portion of payment out of his catch. These, together with the twenty-five caribou, were to constitute our winter's supply of meat, as there would be no opportunity of obtaining more until the middle of March, at which time the female caribou pass on their way to the shore of the Arctic ocean to rear their young.

The Indians commenced to again beg for our supplies, until we plainly told them, " No more 1" They stayed until the last morsel of offal was gone, and I actually saw children eating the frozen contents of the paunches and intestines I They might have done this simply to excite my sympathies, but it only resulted in intense disgust on my part.

On the 17th of December the last wigwam was lowered and the occupants were strung out for a mile or more, wending their emaciated forms toward the setting sun (which had only peeped through the hills in the south). I was across the bay opposite our cabin, cutting wood. On seeing the long line of march, I was so rejoiced I could not cut another stick, but put on my coat and started for the cabin to have a general time of congratulation with my partner, Mr. Rea. But on arriving there, I was terribly disappointed, and all my feelings of relief were turned to anger. They had not all gone 1 In the center of the cabin sat a squaw and her child, a little girl about seven years old, that I at one time had saved from a lingering death by the administration of the proper medicine at the right moment. She had been caught in a burning wigwam and her greasy clothes were nearly consumed on her. Had she been a white child there would have been no hope of cure, but an Indian can submit to almost anything. I asked Mr. Rea what their presence there meant. His reply was, *' I do not know." The squaw was a widow, and her dogs had starved to death, excepting one, and it could scarcely stand alone. I opened the door and told her, " Towtee 1 " (be gone). I exclaimed several times in such an emphatic manner that she knew what I meant. She laid her head on her hand once, and motioned that she would go. That meant one sleep, and then she intended to leave. We sent them to our teepee that we had pitched to shelter our dogs. The next day I again ordered her to go; she made signs indicating that after five sleeps the Indians would return for her. I knew she was lying to me, and told her so in the best signs and language I could command. There she was, and what to do with her and the child was a grave problem, indeed. We could scarcely live and keep our dogs, let alone keeping two Indians and their dog. We finally agreed to allow her to occupy the

teepee until the Indians came. The five days soon passed, but the Indians did not make their appearance. We determined that it was very imprudent to keep her any longer, our storehouse being so near depletion. In fact, we feared that we should even be obliged to kill our dogs in order to sustain ourselves.

On the tenth day Mr. Rea had the dogs hitched up bright and early, to take her and her outfit to the Indian camp sixty miles away. I told her then to pack up her traps and go. She was completely dumbfounded, and absolutely refused to move. When I made her understand, however, that we would give her no more meat, tea, or wood, she agreed to get ready and go, provided we would bring her back if we failed to find the Indian camp,— all of which we agreed to. Then, with four days' rations for every one, the dogs included, Mr. Rea started on the tedious journey. The thermometer registered forty-two degrees below zero. The little seven-year-old child rode in the carryall, while Mr. Rea and the woman were obliged to go afoot, with snowshoes.

To say that I was happy when they pulled out, does not at all express it.

As the sun was going down, on the fourth day after their leaving, I took my field-glass and swept it across the lake southward. In the distance I could see a train of dogs and a man walking ahead of it. I was worried, as I knew that if Mr. Rea were alone, he would be riding in the carryall. Presently a dog rushed out at one side. Then I was convinced that Susann (the squaw) was returning, with the miserable cur that belonged to her. He was of no possible use except to rob us of our subsistence. Long after dark they arrived at the cabin, cold and hungry, as may be imagined. I had a hot supper prepared for them, which was fully appreciated. They had traveled two days through soft snow, and had made only a little over half the distance to the Indian village. Realizing that if the Indians were not there, it would require three days' journey to reach home, as the distance was much greater than was expected, Mr, Rea turned his face homeward, where he knew there was at least a small store of eatables. Supper was soon served. The woman, child and dog had gone to the teepee, and we were resting ourselves before the fire, discussing the deplorable state of affairs, when suddenly our dogs broke loose, barking, and running toward the lake. On looking out, there we discovered a train of dogs and two young Indians advancing toward our cabin. They proved to be from the lodge Mr. Rea had been trying to find, and had broiight a small supply of dried meat, to exchange for powder and balls, which we secured with gladness.

CHAPTER XXII

INDIAN TRIBE LEFT WOMAN AND CHILD TO PERISH — THE SCANTY
SUPPLY DIVIDED WITH THEM—DROVE THEM OUT

MERCURY AT FORTY-EIGHT DEG. BELOW ZERO — LITTLE
ELLEN COVERED WITH ICICLES WOMAN CUT HER FOOT
WITH AX AS AN EXCUSE TO REMAIN—COLONEL JONES's
LONG JOURNEY IN THE DEAD OF WINTER CLOTHES FROZEN
STIFF FAILED TO FIND INDIAN VILLAGE — SAVED SUPPLIES BY SCARING
THE INDIANS—ATTEMPT TO SECURE
REINDEER INDIAN WOMAN SCARED THEM AWAY — TOO
"mad" TO SWEAR — SECURED A GUIDE FOR A MUSK-OX HUNT.

THE good fortune we met with in receiving the small supply of dried meat brought in by the two Indians on the night of the new year revived our drooping spirits, and that night delightful dreams of plenty pervaded our slumbers. The idea had never entered my mind but the Indians had come purposely for Susann, as she had insisted they surely would. The next morning, after the Indians had feasted on the meat we had purchased of them and begged about one-half the remainder to last them on their journey home, they harnessed their dogs preparatory to leaving. Susann still «at flat upon the floor, as was her custom when at our cabin, not making a single sign indicating a purpose of ■departure. I asked the men if they intended taking her with them, which was answered by a most emphatic " Ela 1" (no). I knew then that I must act very decidedly in the premises, as the squaw with her "outfit"

(347)

would devour everything remaining of what we had bought from the men. I plainly told them that Susann must go; that we would give her no more meat, tea, wood, or shelter ; that she had promised to leave one day after her arrival, then in five, now she had been here fourteen days; — she must go at once.

The woman's eyes flashed fire during our conversation, and she begged piteously to be permitted to remain five days longer, when the father of the young men would certainly come for her. I told her and the men that I would listen to no more of their libs; she must go 1 The woman still sat in her place, determined evidently, not to move; so I gathered up her leather hand-bag, with the fur coat she had pulled off, tossed them out of doors, and told her at the same time, " Towtee 1" (be gone).

She finally agreed to the proposition, but the men were to go ahead about five miles to a piece of timber, prepare tea, and await her arrival.

Finally all had left, and my soul rejoiced over their departure, although I had turned a widow and orphan out into the cold world, without shelter. The wind was whistling through the trees, and the thermometer registered twenty-four below zero, and still falling. When night came it was forty-three below, and the next night five degrees colder. Mr. Rea remarked that if the temperature continued to lower, the child would certainly perish that very night. I answered, "If ' God can temper the wind to the shorn lamb,' will He not stay the storm and temper it to an innocent little waif ? " *' But," continued Mr. Rea, "the devil has control of matters up here." And it really apjjeared to me Mr. R. was correct.

I was well aware that Susann and her little child were somewhere on the lake-shore, with nothing but dried meat and tea to eat and drink; without shelter of any kind, excepting that of the heavens. True, they had a blanket and a caribou robe; but these were cold comfort. Thinking the matter over, I really regretted my action,

subann's self-mutilation ' 849

and was worried concerning their deplorable condition, especially when I thought of the rugged road they were compelled to travel. The Indians had moved their quarters forty miles northeast, and it would require at least four days' journey for them to reach there.

It was late at night. I had recorded the temperature, which indicated by the thermometer forty-eight degrees below zero, and had gone back into the cabin and was enjoying a rousing fire. All at once the door opened, and there stood Susann with little Ellen by her side, the frost covering them both, from head to foot. The face of the child was complety obscured by the ice that had formed from her breath on her capoo (a combined hood and frock), while icicles appeared to hang from every hair of her head.

I reluctantly bade them come in, and learned from Susann that the Indians had not waited for them at all, and that she had cut her foot with a small axe, which she carried for procuring firewood. As soon as both had swallowed some tea and a bowl of soup, I examined Su-sann's foot. Her moccasin was terribly cut, but the wound proved to be very slight. I had mistrusted something, as she only wanted me to look at the great rent in her moccasin and not at the gash in her foot. I examined the moccasin carefully, and discovered that the axe had gone entirely through the sole, as well as the top. That was enough: she had determined to remain at our camp or die in the effort, and had deliberately placed her moccasin on a log and cut it with the.axe, then used her butcher-knife, gashing her foot to correspond, which she thought would excite our sympathies, and she would be allowed to remain and continue to feast off our scanty supply as she had been doing.

I said nothing to her about my decision regarding the wound, but applied carbolic acid, then some iodoform on medicated cotton. On the fourth morning, when taking off the bandage, I found it entirely well. It was a great

surprise to Susann, as she had never before known a wound like hers healed in less than a fortnight.

I then told her to get ready; that I was going to take her and her child to the Indian camp, sixty miles distant, on the sled. All she did at this intelligence was to grunt and gasp. I was obliged to take summary measures, for our meat was nearly exhausted, and it was impossible to feed them any longer. She tried all sorts of excuses to awaken my sympathy, taking hold of her foot and pretending that it was very painful; but I insisted that she must go, " Hurra 1" I picked up little Ellen; she kicked and screamed like a wild Indian, but I finally had her in the carryall, and at last Susann hobbled to the door and tumbled in also. Susann was at least forty years old, and weighed about 180 pounds, which made a big load for our dogs in their half-starved condition; besides, there was the little girl and three days' provisions, my gun, ammunition, and robes.

The thermometer registered thirty-two degrees below zero when we started, and I acted in the role of " tripper." All day I plodded along, until late in the night, having made fully forty miles. I was completely worn out; my stockings and moccasins as well as my trousers were saturated with perspiration, and were frozen stiff,— so it seemed to me I was in splints, as I could scarcely bend my limbs.

A fire was soon kindled, and until it was burning briskly I kept up the circulation by wading throilgh the deep snow, cutting dry sticks in the darkness. We piled up brush and spruce boughs on the north side of the fire, which served us very well as a shelter for a while, until the wind changed to the southeast, and made matters disagreeably uncomfortable, as the wind, smoke, sparks, ashes and snow were flying over us, all at the same time. The Indians did not seem to mind such trifling play of the elements. They rolled themselves up in a blanket, pulled the caribou robe over them, and were soon sleeping soundly.

I had a robe and blanket also, but it was so windy and cold I could not sleep a wink during the whole night; it was an impossibility, I lay as quietly as I could, watching the Big Dipper as it apparently circled around the Polar Star, and when it was half-way around from where I had first noticed it, I knew that twelve hours had passed. My watch had long since become disabled, and I only knew how time was fleeting by watching the constellations at night and a sun-dial during the day.

The kettle was boiled, Susann suddenly ceased snoring, and after a scanty lunch we were once more on our lonely way.

About ten o'clock I discovered sled-tracks running in all directions, where the Indians had been hauling wood, and I knew we were near their camp. Another half-mile brought us round the sharp point of a cliff, and there, a short distance away, the skeleton poles of three teepees stood, indicating where the village had been. Their inmates had acted the part of the Arabs,— " quietly folded their tents, and as silently stolen away."

Did they flee to avoid Susann ? was my first thought. I then tried to solve the problem, and remembered that we had not come across a single caribou-track made since the last snow, more than a week previously. This told the story: they had been forced to march to where there was game, or all perish from hunger. They had blazed trees and placed sticks along the route,^ which they knew Susann or anyone else could easily follow. They had also provided against her starving, by carefully hanging the carcass of a fox on one of the teepee-poles.

By indications I decided they must have left three days before our arrival. I was sorely disappointed. My feet

^ Whenever the northern Indians break np their camp they Invariably place In the ground or snow two sticks at an angle of about forty-five degrees, one immediately behind the other, pointing in the direction they have gone, and at Intervals on their march set single sticks, excepting when in the timber, where they blaze the trees for the same purpose. Whether on bare ground or snow-covered ice, the same method Is employed.

were sore from the long walk, and my journey back must be performed as I Had made it, by walking, unless the load which so hampered me could be disposed of; I could then ride in the carryall.

To attempt to follow an Indian trail to the end in the winter is a dangerous undertaking, unless one is well fortified by a good supply of provisions, of which we were very short; and besides, I had only one small feed for the dogs, and enough for myself to take me back to our camp, but no more. Now this must be shared with the Indians. I determined, therefore, to follow the trail, to find out, if possible, what direction the occupants of the deserted camp had taken. Away we went for four hours in an exactly southeast course directly from my way home. Finally we came to their first night's halt, and here we stopped, boiled the kettle, took a lunch of dried meat, tea, and cold biscuit. I knew their destination must be far beyond, or they would not have stopped and camped for the night; so I turned the carryall around, and about three o'clock commenced the weary journey back to our humble cabin.

Darkness coming on, we stopped and made tea, after which we plowed our weary way through the wilderness of spruce and birch trees,— or rather, bushes, for large timber is not found away from the margins of the lake; and even there the trees are not more than eighteen inches in diameter. I tramped along far into the night and until completely fatigued, then halted for a little rest. It was bitter cold, and my clothing was frozen stiff. By good luck we stopped in a group of dry tamarack, and shortly had a brisk fire under way. I fed the dogs the fox's carcass and took their food for ourselves, which made a scant supper.

I partially dried my garments, rolled up in a blanket, and had a short nap. When I awoke, shivering with cold, the fire was still burning, and we soon had the kettle boiling. After eating a few scraps, at about four

o'clock we were again toiling on our way home. I did not walk, but took a swinging gait between a fast walk and a run, at the rate of about four miles an hour. When noon arrived we were within twenty miles of our cabin, and I felt sure I could hold out until safely there. We had two small biscuits for supper, which I needed badly in order to keep my strength. Susann, apparently realizing the fact without any suggestion from me, refused to eat any. This was the first charitable act she had ever shown me, as we had not been at all congenial since the day she came to our teepee. When within seven miles of home I ate the last morsel, and by ten o'clock was sitting before a brilliant fire in our comfortable cabin — something I appreciated as never before, especially when I discovered that the thermometer registered fifty-two degrees below zero.

The best and most cheering thing of the season was soon revealed to me by Mr. Rea: that he had killed two caribou, stored the meat away on the roof, and plenty was to be our portion for some time at least. My heart was gladdened by the intelligence, for now we were sure of subsistence for three weeks more, at which time the caribou were expected. Another gratifying thing was, we could save our dogs also, which were indispensable for our musk-ox hunt in March.

Wood became very scarce, as the Indians had gathered every dry stick in the early part of the winter, and we were obliged to haul all we burned from a point over a mile away, through deep snow and over rough roads.

Our dogs were so poor it became a vital question whether we should remain at the cabin or be compelled to use our teepee and move to dry timber. On account of the scarcity of wood, we were obliged to deny Susann any for her wigwam, as it required much more to keep it warm than it did the cabin. So we moved her and the teepee across the bay, where plenty of fuel could be procured, and from that on she had very little trouble in keeping herself and — 23 . ,

S54 FORTY YEARS OF ADVENTURES

child comfortable. We set her to lacing up snowshoes, making moccasins, and repairing those nearly worn out, as no Indians were near, and it was an art with which we were not familiar.

A week passed, and the father of the young men arrived with a sled-load of meat, which assuredly we were glad to receive. He brought a good supply for Susann also, as they had moved forty miles to the northeast, and had discovered the feeding-grounds of vast herds of caribou.

"We gave the dogs a reasonable allowance of the flesh, as we were now sure the danger of our starving was past; and if necessary we could go to the Indian camp, provided no game made its appearance by the time our meat supply became exhausted. It was impossible for us to hunt caribou, as the snow was very deep, and required snowshoes at least five feet long to hold us up. We could not induce the Indians to make us any large shoes, for they were afraid we would get all the game.

The Indian did not take Susann with him, but promised to return in one half-moon with his family and go with us on a musk-ox hunt. Several half-moons passed, however, but no Indians made their appearance. On the 4th of February, Mr. Ilea took the dogs and sled and went to the Indian camp. It required four days to make the journey. He did not find the Indians. Fortunately, however, he discovered a cache well supplied with meat, and loaded on three caribou carcasses, leaving tea, powder and balls in their place. As the weather was good, his return trip was a pleasant one.

On the 9th of February, while looking through my field-glass, I discovered nine caribou in the distance, coming on the ice of the lake. They took a different route from any others, bearing farther to the east of our cabin. There was no trail broken by which I could head them off in that direction. As we needed meat very much, to secure it I must hasten on ahead of them where they would enter the timber. It looked almost hopeless to try to

wallow through the snow with small snowshoes, and the snow was very deep for a mile and a half. Yet there might not be any more game coming our way for a month, so I plunged into the drifts, which were nearly three feet deep. The snow was so light that I sank about eighteen inches at every step. I kept plodding along while breath and muscle held out, then halted under the shelter of a spruce tree.

There was a bare chance that the animals might swerve a trifle toward me and come within range of my rifle. Sure enough, the angle was made by them that I had hoped for, and they were about to pass three hundred yards to the east. Deliberation was not necessary: it was shoot or no meat. I pulled the trigger and away went the nine caribou over the lake, on the back track. I knew that if I sat perfectly motionless they would stop to investigate the cause of their fright, before running very. far. Soon they all halted in a bunch. I then raised my rifle and sent a ball into the group, and was rewarded by a sound that convinced me that my calculation of the distance had been correct. Away the herd dashed, leaving two of the coveted animals, each limping on three legs. The ball had not carried quite high enough to hit their bodies, but fell to their knees; it had broken a leg for each. They hobbled off quite lively, and were soon out of range again. Satisfied I should lose them if they ever sighted me, I retreated under the shade of a sapling, and from there went to the cabin. I now took two of the shepherd dogs to the trail of one of the wounded caribou, that was hit in the hind leg. As soon as the dogs caught scent of it, away they went, and after a lively race for a mile or more, brought a fine doe to bay. Mr. Rea started after it, and succeeded in knocking it in the head with an axe. It was a fortunate circumstance there were no Indians near to witness the killing, or they would have been wild with rage, as the first thing they cautioned us against when we met them was never to

knock a caribou in the head. It must either be shot, or its throat cut, for to knock them in the head would drive all caribou from that part of the country, never to return. This they in their superstition religiously believe. They claimed that the reason Mr. Rea and the Indians failed to secure musk-oxen during the winter, was because the former wore a leather belt, which they believe is disastrous to success on such hunts.

Although this caribou was secured by their disapproved method, we found others came along just the same.

The next morning I took the trail of the other crippled one, overhauled it about two miles from the place of shooting, and settled all its trouble by a well-directed ball.

On the 10th there were brought to us by Indians, to trade for powder, two sled-loads of meat. The Indians also desired bullets with which to hunt musk-oxen. It was gratifying to make the exchange.

Our dogs were soon able to haul wood, and Susann saw how, while absent after musk-oxen, we intended to leave the cabin. I fastened my revolver to the center-post, tied a cord to the trigger, ran it through a pulley attached to a beadstead beyond the other post, thence through a pulley in the door casing, and fastened the cord to the doorlatch. Then I attached another cord to the doorlatch, passed it under a bent nail just above the latch, then stood behind the revolver and pulled the cord. This had the effect to raise the latch and pull the door open, thus tightening the first cord so that it cocked and discharged the revolver, it being a double-action piece. The ball struck the door-casing and made the splinters fly. In order to discharge the weapon, all required was to pull the cord as many times as there were loads in it (five). I pulled the string and the ball struck the door-casing. I then readjusted the revolver, and pulled three times, and at each pull a ball passed through the open space. The little girl was so scared she crawled under the bed, and

only came out after the weapon had been taken down. Susann watched my operations with amazement, and actually believed the weapon would shoot as many times as the string was pulled! She was so frightened that she trembled like an aspen. I then took one of our surplus rifles, placed the muzzle of it at the bung-hole of a powder-keg, and arranged a string to the trigger so that if any one knocked off the boards from the windows, raised a rafter, or opened the door, the rifle would be discharged, the powder ignited, and everything blown to atoms. I did not attempt to explain matters to Susann in any way whatever, but would occasionally, after testing these methods, exclaim in an audible tone, " Nazu! " (good).

When I went to my traps soon after, Susann took occasion to visit Mr. Rea, to learn if I had not gone crazy. She was terribly frightened, and begged him to take her and the child immediately to the Indian camp, seventy-five miles distant. He explained to her, however, that as long as no one attempted to disturb things, hammer on or open the door, or raise the windows or rafters, there was not the slightest danger, but woe unto the Indian that molested anything whatever in our absence after musk-oxen. He also explained to her that her teepee was a good distance away from the cabin, and no harm could come to her and her little Ellen. This seemed to somewhat calm her. She spread the report of what I had done, as soon as she got within hearing distance of the Indians on their arrival,— which was just as we desired, in order to protect our property from the prowling, starving thieves of that region, who never lose an opportunity when hungry to steal whatever they can lay their hands on in the way of eatables. In all our dealings with those heathen, we made them understand that we possessed the power to destroy every Indian in existence at our will, and by so doing, saved ourselves from starvation.

In four days the Indians were expected to arrive on their way to the musk-ox hunt, some four or five hundred

miles to the northeast. The time had expired, but no Indians came. Day after day dragged its weary length along, and our supply of meat was being rapidly decreased.

We were well aware that it would be the height of foolishness to leave for a trip of such proportions without at least ten days' rations for the dogs and ourselves, therefore it became evident we should have to make a trip to the Indian camp to get meat or game. It was agreed that if no caribou made their appearance in the vicinity by night, the next morning Mr. Rea would niake the trip.

That morning it was very stormy, the wind blowing a gale, which precluded the possibility of seeing any great distance in advance. The caribou have three trails leading from Great Slave lake to Artillery lake, their thoroughfare to the north: one by way of a small stream a mile and a half east of our cabin ; one by way of a draw half-way to the stream; another via the large stream just west of our camp. It was quite early when I started out and plunged into the storm and deep snow toward the small stream mentioned, to find out whether there were any signs of the anticipated animals. Arriving at my objective point, I failed to discover a single track. On my return to the cabin I saw, through the almost blinding storm, eight of the coveted animals out on the lake, evidently directing their route up the little stream. No snow melted under my feet as I struggled toward the cabin, and upon reaching it I apprised Mr. Rea of the cheering news of the animals' presence. At once we were both on our way to head them off. The wind was blowing hard from the southwest, and we were obliged to keep under cover, as the eye of the caribou is exceptionally acute. The snow in the timber was very loose, and about three and a half feet deep. To run was impossible, to walk was almost as difficult, and we were compelled to wallow on as best we could, which was effected by taking turns and breaking a trail through the snow. When we

reached the little river, both of us were completely saturated with perspiration.

The .animals approached within five hundred yards of the mouth of the stream, and then laid down. Mr. Rea and I regretted that we had not taken it more easily and not overheated ourselves, as the terrible wind with the thermometer at twenty-six deg. below zero made us very uncomfortable, indeed, now that we were compelled to stop so suddenly. All left for us to do under the circumstances was to break a trail through a thick clump of pines and keep walking under cover until the caribou had concluded their noonday nap, which lasted fully two hours. At the end of that time they all rose, and proceeded on their course until they arrived at the trail I had made early in the morning. There they appeared to sniff danger, and turned their heads up toward the draw. We hurried back to that point, and were ready waiting for them. Before caribou enter a piece of timber they invariably pause to look and listen for any danger ahead on the route they intend traveling. While the herd was thus cogitating, a raven suddenly flew up the draw, and on seeing us uttered a series of shrill notes, which I interpreted to be a rendering of Poe's refrain, " Nevermore " ; but the caribou appeared to have a translation of their own, of the bird's croak, for they immediately wheeled about and made a long detour toward the big river west of our cabin. Their movements suited us perfectly, as there we had provided blinds so that we could easily kill the last one of them, thus saving a wearisome journey of a hundred and fifty miles for meat. We hurried westward, knowing there was nothing to alarm the animals. Susann had come over that morning, and we had left our dogs in the cabin, cautioning her to be sure to keep them perfectly quiet until our return. Just as we had fixed ourselves in position to secure the game, we heard the report of a gun from near the cabin, about where the caribou were passing it. We instantly divined what it meant:

Siisann had taken the small twenty-eight-caliber shotgun, loaded with nothing but small shot (which we used to shoot ptarmigans^), and discharged it at the animals while passing. Stepping out from where we had been concealed, to an elevation close by, to our intense disgust we saw Susann standing on the bank of the lake, and the caribou running at full speed half a mile away, in the direction whence they had come. Thus ended our hardest day's hunt of the season. On our return to the cabin I stepped the distance from where Susann had stood when she fired at the animals, to where the nearest had been, and found it to be three hundred and twelve good long paces. If she had been within ten feet of them, she could not have killed one by any possible chance 1

To say that we were disappointed would be flattering the English language. No words can express our feelings at the turn matters had taken, but we could do nothing to help ourselves.

The next day Mr. Rea started on his long journey for meat, with the mercury at forty-eight below, and returned the fourth day without anything, as the Indians had moved their camp, and the great storm had so drifted the snow as to entirely obliterate every semblance of a track to indicate which way they had gone.

Susann informed us that the Indians were to move to a small lake at the head of a little stream, emptying into Great Slave lake; so all that could be done was to take her and the child as guides to their whereabouts. The next morning Mr. Rea started again with his guides, determined to find the Indian camp or some game; both, if possible. After two days' absence Susann and the girl came tramping over th-e big lake and reported no Indians at the little lake, and that Mr. Rea had gone in the direction of their old camp, hoping to find some trace of them,

1 Ptarmifianf a bird belonging to the partridge family. They are yery plentlfal in the far North. In winter they live on the buds of willows and other trees. While their color is a pure white in winter, as the snow leaves they shed their white feathers, which are supplemented by a brown plumage, the color of arctic mon.

or caribou, as plenty of tracks had been discovered in that vicinity on his previous trip.

That same night, two Indian boys came to the cabin from the village to have me dress a severe cut on the leg of one of them, occasioned by the cut of an axe. They reported meeting Mr. Rea that morning; then I knew he would be guided to their village by their trail. They brought with them a small supply of meat and a dozen caribou tongues, the sight of which cheered my despondency, especially the tongues, for they were certainly delicious enough to set before the greatest epicure. Caribou tongues are entirely different in their flavor from those I have ever eaten of any other animal. Summer-cured tongues are prized by the Indians for the amount of fat they contain. In winter they are spongy, and lacking in oil. The Indians claim, and insist upon it, that in summer the marrow leaves the bones and flows to the tongue, and that in winter the reverse is the case 1 But I know for a certainty, that there is a vast difference in the amount of fat, both in the tongues of the caribou and in their bones, at the times specified.

The gash on the boy's foot was a horrid-looking sight. His leg had been wounded two weeks previously; " proud flesh" (excessive granulation) had already made its appearance, the whole foot was terribly swollen, and it had an angry phase about it I did not like. I first made him bathe it in hot water, then bound on burnt alum, letting it remain until morning. It was then again washed out with warm water, to which was added one-twentieth part of carbolic acid. After drying, medicated cotton well sprinkled with iodoform was bound on. He then took his leave in the carryall for the village. I learned afterward that he reported that I had made " strong medicine," as he was entirely cured in six days.

During the sojourn of the two boys I kept track of them pretty closely. They were just as likely to sit down in a bucket of water as on a box; sometimes stirred the fire

with the wrong end of the poking-stick; would lounge on our bed, which was certain to infest it with vermin, much to our discomfort.

I bought the meat the boys had brought, and when they were ready to leave discovered they had reserved none for themselves (their invariable custom); they appealed to me for enough to last them until they reached home — a two-days supply. I asked them how much it would take, and kept on laying it out until they said it was enough. I had piled up more than half purchased of them, before they would admit it to be sufficient. I then placed it all together, and told them they could not have any unless they surrendered the tea, ammunition, and other things; that I had paid them sufficient for all that I had received. Susann was present, and began to chide me for my refusal to give them "meat su" (a meal of victuals). I ordered her out of the cabin, after which she gave me a respectful letting alone. The boys would not buy back a scrap of meat, and were starting on their long journey without anything, either for themselves or dogs. After they had gone nearly a quarter of a mile, I called them back^ and gave them a dozen biscuit, which I knew would be ample for themselves; the dogs I thought could stand a two-days journey without food.

On the 24th Mr. Rea returned with a load of meat, having taken the trail of the boys to the village, as I had imagined he would, and experienced no difficulty in reaching his destination. While at the lodge he had hired two Indians with sleds to go with us after musk-oxen, and we were to start the next day. They had no idea that we wanted any young animals, as they are not born until about the month of May. Mr. Rea had merely told them that we were after bull-heads. Had they suspected that we were really after young animals as well as heads, they

^ It is a well-known principle of acoustics, that sounds can be heard In the higher latitudes at a greater distance than elsewhere. It Is a very easy thing for a man to make himself heard, In loud conversation, fully the distance of a mile.

would have refused to go a step with us. Late that evening one of the Indians he had employed arrived with his sled; the other arrived late at night. But at the last moment, suspecting the real purport of our mission, and angry at me for garrisoning our cabin in such a manner, they refused to go.

The Indian who had thus far fulfilled his contract was Sousie Barromie — Sousie in his own language meaning Joseph. He was about thirty-five years old, small in stature, weighed nearly 125 pounds, and was very lithe and powerful for his size.

CHAPTER XXIII
MUSK-OX HUNT

A 8TABT FOR THE FAR NORTH WITH DOO-BLEDB CR0B8INO

MOUNTAINS — ON ARTILLERY LAKE CUTTING TEEPEE-POLES—TERRIFIC BLIZZARD LYING IN BLANKETS THIRTY-SIX HOURS FACING THE WIND AT FORTY DEGREES

BELOW ZERO ON CLINTON GOLDEN LAKE—CAMPED IN

LAND OF " LITTLE STICKS " — DOG CARRIED OFF BY ARCTIC WOLVES — COLONEL Jones's narrow escape — pressing TO THE FAR NORTH, FOLLOWED BY THE WOLVES

DISCOVERY OF NEW RIVERS AND LAKES — MUSK-OX AT LAST

KILLS BIX MONSTERS WOLVES TAKE VENGEANCE

MINUTE DESCRIPTION OF A MUSK-OX INDIAN TALKED TO

THEM, AIND BELIEVED THEY OBEYED HIS COMMANDS

CROSSES GREAT FISH RIVER AND ARCTIC CIRCLE — OUT OF

WOOD, HE RETURNS GUIDE BADLY LOST — COLONEL JONES

DEPENDED ON HIS OWN JUDGMENT, AND ARRIVED IN THE

OLD CAMP PREPARING TO MAKE ANOTHER TRIP FOR

MUSK-OXEN GUIDE LEARNS INTENTION OF HUNTERS

IS HORRIFIED, AND ABANDONS THE TWO NIMR0D8

ON the morning of the 25th of February, 1898, just as the sun peeped over the high range of hills east of Fort Reliance, we started with our two dog-trains across a portion of the lake and up a small stream northeast; then commenced to climb the steep hills, the route so graphically described by Capt. Back, of the Royal Navy, sixty-five years before. The hills really turned out to be mountains before we reached

(864)

their summit. The day was passed in breaking trails through the thick birch thickets and in crossing many-small lakes. When the sun was sinking in the west, we had arrived at a point ten miles up the west shore of Artillery lake. The weather was as fine as could be desired, excepting the extreme cold, which caused us to shiver. We made our first night's camp in a clump of timber, and the early morning found us again on the road, taking a northeasterly direction to the east shore of the lake. At noon we arrived at a small grove of spruce trees; and here Sousie gave us to understand that we must cut our teepee-poles, as this was the last wood long enough for that purpose ; there were " plenty little sticks " that would serve us for fire on the next " big water."

Here, in order to get poles long enough for our teepee, — and it was only a small one,— we were obliged to cut down the scrubby dead timber, which was fully seven inches in diameter, score and hew them down to about three inches, so as to make them as light as possible. We placed five on each sled, but unfortunately broke two that night,— or fortunately, as it turned out, as eight were as many as we cared to haul.

We made a light drive that afternoon to a canon where we found wood enough for a fire, and where Sousie succeeded in killing four caribou, while Mr. Rea and myself pitched our tent and cooked supper. One of the animals shot proved to be a barren doe; was very fat, and we fully appreciated its delicious flesh. It was the first meat fit to be eaten that we had tasted for four months. True, we had plenty of dried meat in our sledges, but it was nearly as tough as rawhide.

The next morning a fine buck caribou came trotting across a small bay, and before we realized it one of our shepherd dogs broke away and gave it chase. That was the last we saw of poor " Shep " until our return to the cabin, where we found him camping with Susann. He had traveled over sixty miles alone, on his return home.

In the afternoon we pulled off for the bluffs, found a few small dry sticks, and loaded them on our sleds, for cooking supper and breakfast, Sousie said, "Teweyna-chaw, ditchen slaw" (big water, wood plenty), which we knew had reference to Clinton Golden lake.

The weather was quite warm and sloppy. Shortly before night, snow commenced to come down thick and fast. We had left the lake, and were ascending the small river that connects the two large lakes. We pitched our teepee on a large knoll just west of the river, where the wind had swept off the snow, but it was covered with jagged rocks, and made a very uncomfortable bed; yet anything was preferable to lying on the wet snow. The wind soon changed to the north, and blew a gale. We piled large stones on the lower walls of the teepee, and with a guy-line from the top, anchored it to a large stone.

All night the teepee kept flapping and jerking with such terrific force that we expected every minute it would be rent from top to bottom. When morning arrived the wind was still blowing, the snow sifting through every place where even a single stitch had been broken in our heavy duck-cloth teepee. It was already three or four inches deep over our covering. We did not dare to stir, or the uncomfortable element would fill our bed. All we could do was to lie still. Toward night we realized it would be best to eat a lunch at least, but Sousie was too smart to uncover himself, and we were emulating Indian habits in a commendable style. Finally I reached into the carryall (that of necessity was always inside the teepee, to prevent the dogs from eating the rawhide strings with which it w^as lashed up), and fished out of the snow a small sack of frozen biscuits, which I passed around under cover; and that was all we had to eat until the next morning. The wind raged all day, and as night came on it increased, and, combined with the jerking and flapping of the teepee aind the howling dogs outside, made the long, dreary night hideous.

At the first streak of dawn, Sousie peeped out and gave an Indian whoop; then said, in a cheerful tone, with much emphasis: "Nazu! Nazul " (good).

Mr. Rea and myself had been in our blankets for two nights and one day, therefore were in a good frame of mind for such cheering news, not having eaten anything for thirty-six hours, excepting a frozen biscuit. We had barely enough sticks to make fire sufficient to bring the kettles to a boil, and were very glad for the opportunity of i^roceeding on our journey.

By the time the sun was up we were ofif for the " big water." The thermometer registered forty degrees below zero, the wind was sharp, and our faces were more or less frosted. About noon we were gliding over Clinton Golden lake in a northeasterly direction. At 8 o'clock in the afternoon we saw a clump of bushes far to the east, up a deep ravine. When we arrived and inspected it, found nothing but green sticks, but discovered another grove with some dry wood (very limited). Here we pitched our teepee. That night it snowed and blew furiously.

Mr. Rea and Sousie had killed three caribou before the storm set in, and we were well supplied with meat. Next day was so stormy we were obliged to lie in our blankets most of the time. That night the arctic wolves made their appearance. They made no noise, but came for business. It was the sneaking, silent devils that did the mischief. The " calamity-howlers" we did not fear; all we had to do was to stop the calamity (by killing them plenty of meat); then they always stopped their howling.

Long after the midnight hour had passed, our dogs commenced to make a great fuss around the teepee. Finally we made up our minds that the Indian dogs were trying to eat up our dogs, or vice versa. We knew they could not be hungry, as we had supplied them liberally with meat. I heard my faithful shepherd dog, Don, screaming as if about to be killed. It was so stormy we

well knew that if we stirred, our beds would be filled with snow. The dog cried pitifully. I could not refrain from rushing out, and as I slipped under the flap door of our tent, I grabbed an axe, and before my feet were out, a dog ran against me and I went rolling in the snow. As soon as I could collect myself, I discovered all the dogs were going around the teepee at a terrific speed, and behind them came nearly as many white objects, which sent a thrilling sensation over me, as it reminded me of the "white-winged messengers of death." I knew what it all meant, and called to Mr. Rea to hand me the gun, crying, " Wolves 1 wolves 1 " Before he could pass it out, a monstrous wolf dashed at one of the little shej)herd dogs that had taken refuge between my legs. I struck at him with the axe, but missed. "Don's" courage was still with him, for he caught the wolf by the hind leg, but the monster seized him by the back and started toward the brush a few rods to the east. Just then Mr. Rea handed me my Winchester. I ran up to the enraged brute, almost close enough to touch him with the gun, and fired. He let loose his hold and dashed at me. I warded him off with the gun. He grabbed the barrel of the Winchester so tightly that he broke several teeth; he held it till death relaxed his grip. The ball had passed through his lungs. I cut off his head and skinned it for mounting. As soon as I had disposed of the dreadful brute, the others skulked into the brush. We took the dogs into our teepee, and at daybreak pulled out for the north.

The storm had not fully abated, yet we could make fair time; in fact, we were obliged to make time or freeze. All day we plowed through the soft snow until nearly night, when we came to an immense band of caribou. Mr. Rea, Sousie and I killed one each. We then went into camp about two miles north of where we had killed them. We took particular pains to take the fattest animal and leave two for the howling wolves, so as to get rid

of them if possible. We took the dogs into the tent, and Jiad a good rest until near daybreak, when we were awakened by the snapping and growling of the miserable brutes. There were so many they no doubt had devoured the caribou, and wanted our portion of the fresh meat.

Again we were out bright and early, keeping up our old gait. The wind was still blowing a gale from the northeast. " Bucking " a gale on the Barren Lands is no boy's play, and by night we were in good condition to rest; as we had no fresh meat that night, the wolves gave us no trouble.

We kept close-watch all day for signs of musk-oxen, but saw nothing to indicate their whereabouts. The limit of the range of these animals is as far south as the north end of Artillery lake, yet they rarely pass south of Clinton Golden lake. We were now about seventy miles north of the south line of their range. Clinton Golden lake lies at a high altitude, about twenty miles north and some three hundred feet above Artillery lake, while the latter is fully seven hundred feet higher than Great Slave lake. The altitude and latitude make it ten to fifteen degrees colder there than at our cabin home. Clinton Golden lake is connected with Artillery. lake hy a small river. The latter lake empties about the same amount of water as it receives, into the Great Slave lake, through another river, of about the s(ime size, sixty miles long.

We discovered a river nearly or quite as large as either of such rivers, emptying into the Clinton Golden lake at its northeast corner. The river was open in places where the current was at all rapid, indicating that it came from a deep lake near by. This river we trJiced in a north-by-northeast direction about ten miles to where it emerges from a small lake. The small.lake was connected with larger lakes to the northeast, as we could see them from elevated places, stretching out as far as the eye could see. On the return we crossed a lake eight miles wide by twenty long. — 24

FORTY YEARS OF ADVENTURES

On the morning of the 4th we pulled northward, with the wind more in our favor, blowing from the west. About noon we discovered tracks of the mighty musk-ox, and went into camp.

Mr. Rea and Sousie took a reconnoiter, and soon located a herd of six very large bulls. I was apprised of the fact, and soon hastened to the scene. When we ap-■ proached the black monsters the contrast betwe*en them and the surrounding white landscape made them appear much larger than they really were. Sousie commenced to talk to them in a loud tone of voice, and on hearing him they ran into a compact group, looking in all directions for the strange noise. We were well sheltered behind a pile of large rocks, and lost no time in getting in proper position. All the time our guide led the way, and told the animals to keep quiet; that we intended to kill them, just as the Great Spirit wished them to die, and that we would not kill any more than He had determined upon; that it was much more honorable to be killed by shooting than to be devoured by the wolves, as they would surely come soon and destroy all if they disregarded the warning he was giving them. We did not understand fully what he said at the time, as our excitement and the creaking of our snowshoes had prevented it. We questioned him that evening all about what he had said, and why. He believed that if he had not told them to stand still, they would all have escaped and we should have lost not only them, but all others, on that particular trip.

We had no trouble in getting within a hundred yards of them, as the country was all piled over with stones, some as large as a farm-house. Each one picked his animal, and in less time than it takes to write it they were all dead among the stones excepting one, that darted behind a large rock. When we walked around so as to look at him, the poor fellow was tottering on his trembling legs.

Sousie raised his gun to shoot, but I shouted "Ela!" (no), "let him die peacefully;" and he dropped the gun at his side without firing. The animal lived but a minute, then laid down, and rolled over on his side. We had anticipated great sport in shooting the musk-ox, believing it to be a game animal, but in this we were sorely

disappointed; it was like slaughtering cattle in a corral. We then inspected our dead quarry. They were much larger than I had expected to see; they are relatively diminutive while standing, as their legs are so short that they do not appear as large as they really are. Their bodies are as large as a good-sized bullock, and had those we killed been in good condition, I believe they would have compared favorably with a fair-sized three-year-old fat steer. Their bones were massive and firm, which indicates wonderful strength. The bone between the ankle and knee, from joint to joint, was exactly the length of the width of my three fingers; their other bones were not in proportion.

They must possess wonderful vitality and endurance, as they are so large around the girth. Their breasts are as broad and as well developed as that of a Norman horse. Their hinder parts are unlike that of the buffalo; they are as squarely built as a Galloway steer. The meat on the ham extends well down to their hock, and lies in rolls. When fat, a square cut across the buttock resembles variegated marble. The under fur is very long and compact; as fine as silk, and when twisted into a small thread tightly, a man can scarcely break it. Doubtless it would produce the strongest fabric known, if properly manufactured. The tail is not at all worthy of the name — merely a small tuft of hair at the end of the spinal column. The hair on their necks and sides nearly sweeps the ground as they walk. It is jet black, except that around the nose and feet, and a large spot on the back, which is of a gray cast. The dark hair is of a glossy nature, rivaling the locks of a Mexican senora, which have been bathed in bear's oil for half a score of years. On dissecting the stomach we found a little dead grass and a great amount of moss, well mixed together, which convinced me they would thrive on good hay or other forage. Their feet very much resemble those of our domestic cattle, excepting that the heels are a little broader, and

are as soft as the frog of a horse's hoof. They roam very-little, as their hoofs would rapidly wear away on the rocks and pebbles covering the nigged region of their habitat.

We pitched our teepee near the dead carcasses, and spent the afternoon in skinning and preparing the heads for mounting. On dissecting their bodies we found their anatomy resembled the bovine genus ^ in all particulars, excepting the stomach and intestines. These are formed like those of the sheep; their droppings resemble that animal's, but are larger in proportion to the size of the beast. In consequence of such a marked contrast between these organs and those of the bovine, it is hardly probable they could be crossed with domestic cattle or buffalo. Having had so large an experience in crossing the latter, it was a very interesting study to me, and I was well repaid for our trouble thus far.

That night it appeared as if all the wolves in North America had congregated around our teepee to take vengeance on us for slaughtering these dumb brutes. At early dawn I peeped out. Every elevation, every depression, and every slope between, was literally covered with wolves. Some stood within four rods of the teepee. I slipped my Winchester through the door, and selecting a large, pure-white animal, held my gun rather low, as it was quite dark, and I feared I might overshoot the mark. At the crack of the gun, the wolf went hobbling off, but soon fell dead, as I supposed. I lingered a moment, hoping to get another shot, but the others took the hint and skulked away. I then went out to examine the one I thought already killed, but the moment I came near it, up it jumped and started to run; I gave him another shot and he came down. When I approached him I found both a fore and hind leg broken; I shot him again, and he soon expired. He was a magnificent specimen, so I set myself at work to skin him for mounting. After

' Many anatomists claim that the musk-ox belongs to the order of goats, but it is generally classed with the bovine.

I had proceeded well with the work, I was astonished to discover that the brute had eaten off his foot below the place where his leg had been broken by my first shot. No doubt, on smelling the blood that saturated his leg, his appetite could not be restrained. The foot gone, I regarded the animal as worthless for the purpose desired, so abandoned it. I had often seen wolves, when wounded, devoured by others of a hungry pack, but this was the first time I had ever witnessed or heard of any animal eating itself. (I have inserted this remarkable instance, despite the protest of Mr. Rea, for while he declares that he personally knows it to be true, yet says no one will believe it. I am determined to give facts, regardless of the opinions of the public.) We were astonished, when we inspected the six musk-ox carcasses, to find they had not been disturbed in the least by the numerous hungry wolves.

The wolves of the far North are as white as the arctic snow, excepting a jet black one is occasionally to be seen, and a few gray,— exactly the color of the prairie "loafers," or buffalo wolves, so numerous during the days of that great ruminant. It is a mystery to me why the hordes of arctic wolves have not long ago exterminated the musk-ox and reindeer, yet the deer were so numerous that we saw tens of thousands every day. The whole country had been literally trodden down by them since the last snow, until it resembled a sheep corral. Those who have not seen the immense herds of these graceful creatures cannot realize their magnitude; and language fails to convey the idea.

Of the vast number of these animals we saw on that trip, all were females on their way to the Arctic ocean regions to bring forth an equal number to themselves during the summer, now rapidly approaching. The males were still lingering in the forests far southward, which they visit in November, leaving them during the months of August and September on their northern migration, to meet the does in October.

The wolf appears to be their only enemy, as the Indians do not kill a number sufficient to be noticed, any more than the falling of a single needle in the mighty pine forests of the Pacific coast. These arctic wolves are very cunning animals. They must be very hungry, to be induced to eat meat they do not themselves kill; that is why they fought so viciously for our live animals. For the reason referred to, it is very difficult to poison or trap them. The arctic wolf is a swift animal, and the Indians claim he can catch a caribou whenever he chooses; but I doubt that statement very much, or they would be in much better condition, and not so persistently ferocious in their eagerness to get something to eat. I have often seen them chasing reindeer, but they never came anywhere near catching them. They lie in wait for their prey, and rush after it with tremendous speed; but the deer, seemingly ever on the alert, elude the fangs of the hungry devils. I am convinced it would take a mighty fast wolf to overtake even a poor old reindeer. Some of my shepherd dogs were regarded as excellent runners, yet it was rarely that they went fast enough to make a deer break his trot. Talk of Nancy Hanks 1 Through a field-glass I have watched my dogs flying over the Great Slave lake after the trotting beauties, but have never seen a horse in the United States that could glide along with such ease and grace as the reindeer,— and I have been present at some of the most prominent races that ever occurred in this country. While, of course, wolves cannot catch a caribou in a fair race, yet when they have exhausted all other means of obtaining food; when actual starvation compels them, and not before, they start after a caribou, chasing it day and night without ceasing, until, completely worn out, the poor creature succumbs to its ravenous enemy. It does not make the slightest difference how

many herds of its fellows the chased caribou runs through, the wolves keep on its track, paying no attention to anything but the capture of their prey, which event they know is just ahead.

After I had spent an hour shooting wolves, Mr. Rea called me in to breakfast. That suited me, for I was hungry; and we ate the flesh of the musk-ox. One of the animals killed appeared very old, but was quite fat. We saved a jjorterhouse steak from him, and the ribs; the latter, when boiled long enough, were very palatable. I could neither smell nor taste any musk, though Mr. Rea declared he got a whiff of it while skinning the superannuated bull.

After breakfast we took up our old course, north by northeast, and kept it for two days, when we reached the Great Fish river. Here we reconnoitered diligently, but found no signs of musk-oxen. We then crossed over, and traveled two days more in the same direction, but discovered nothing. Even reindeer were left far behind.

On the 8th we swung around to the east, and took an almost southerly direction for three days. We saw old signs of musk-oxen, but nothing fresh. On the 10th it snowed, and the wind blew furiously,— so much so that our guide (Sousie Barromie) became perfectly bewildered and lost. He was considered the best posted and best hunter of the Yellow Knife tribe. We had a terrific wind at our back, and the very fact of being lost was such an incentive to find some place that Sousie would recognize, that it sent us to a high rate of speed. Having started at four o'clock in the morning and kept up our pace until seven in the evening, with only one hour's stop for dinner, we must have covered fully fifty miles. Three and a half miles an hour, I am sure, was the slowest rate at which we traveled that day. We felt the effects of our march all that night and the following day; in fact, the muscles of my legs were so stiff and cramped that it was

impossible to sleep. I bathed them in strong cayenne pepper tea, or I should have suffered much more than I did.

Mr. Rea and Sousie each drove a train of four dogs, and I did the tripping ahead. I felt perfectly safe, knowing that by going far enough south, then turning westward, we were sure to strike one of the great lakes, or the-river between, which was partly open water, and we could not get lost,— which would have been the case had it been frozen over and covered with snow. The greatnvorry was that our wood had nearly been exhausted, and we must have something to melt snow or die of thirst.

Sousie kept urging me to lead off westward, but I would sway to the southwest in spite of his protestations. I was sure if we went west, we should leave Clinton Golden lake to the south of us and surely perish, as no wood could be found for two hundred miles in that direction. On the morning of the 11th Sousie became furious, and fairly danced with anger, because I would not lead where he directed. I felt quite safe then in going more to the westward, and at noon noticed a long mark on the crust where-the wind had cleared the new snow from the old. By careful inspection I could plainly see the imprint of our dogs' toenails, and the long mark was that of one of our sleds. It was our old trail, and we discovered it by the merest accident. We might have crossed at a hundred other places and should never have noticed the fact.

By taking exactly the direction whence it came, we occasionally saw some mark or scratch, and its course was: followed up for several hours. Finally Sousie recognized a stone laid by him on top of another, seven snows (years) previously. Then he was happy, and pointed nearly souths exclaiming, " Ditchen 1 ditchen I " (timber.) In about three hours we came in sight of the " land of little sticks," where we had our first wolf-hunt. Luckily, I trusted more-to my compass than I did to Sousie. Had we taken a west-

-wardly course the i^revious day, we should have gone far to the north of Clinton Golden lake, and should have perished.

The first bush I came to, I cut for a cane. I still have the cane, and prize it very highly as a souvenir. It was a green spruce, about four feet high. I counted the years it had been growing by its rings of knots, and they numbered thirty-eight.

To say that we were rejoiced once more, does not express •our emotions in the slightest degree. We quickly cooked our meat, as meat was all we had, and then continued fifteen miles farther, to Artillery lake, where we camped for the night. Here we made known to Sousie that our hunt was not ended — only commenced; that we would pull a little farther down the lake on the morrow, get some good dry wood and then go to the northeast for musk-ox. Sousie's eyes rolled in their sockets, for the Indians all believe that if any musk-ox is taken out alive, all other animals will follow. They also worship the musk-ox as a god, believing it an unrighteous act to catch them or dispose of them in any way except to shoot them. They talk to them as if they were human beings.

Sousie looked wild and perplexed. He said: "Why, O white man with long legs, why do you wish again to freeze, and be devoured by wolves ? Have you not already killed more and larger musk-oxen than any of your family who ever hunted them in this far-away country ? You have already left three heads and as many hides to be eaten by the wolves. The Great Spirit don't approve of that kind of work. I told a lie already for you, as the musk-oxen understood me that we would only kill what we needed, and I can't fool any more that way."

He was much distressed over our intentions, and he would say no more, except " Xazzula 1 Nazzulal" ("no good " or " awful bad "). We gave him our ultimatum, and he knew there was no use to protest. He could speak a few words of English, and we had learned the language

of the Slave tribe very well; so that with signs and words, both of which he understood, and the English language together, we could understand and make known to Sousie any ordinary subject. He was quick-witted, and "caught on " without difficulty. Next day we pulled to the timber, and Sousie said he must go home: " Jackwee bur hula " ^ (" squaw-meat none ").

We could not prevail on him to go a step with us. We were now far south of the arctic wolf range, and his courage came back to him. We did succeed in persuading him to take our musk-ox heads, wolf-scalps and other trophies to our cabin, thus relieving our fatigued dogs of a great burden. ■ We ate dinner together, after which Sousie started down the lake, and we went northeast.

'In all the words of the Slave language with which I am familiar, the accent Is placed on the ultimate, which gives a sad intonation. Their language comprises very-few words, and upon the emphasis depends the meaning. For instance, a word mean-in(j a short distance will be soft, without any accent; while If meaning farther away, the same word is accentuated,—so that by varying the accent, all known degrees ■of distance may be conveyed by the same word.

CHAPTER XXIV

COLONEL JONEB AND JOHN R. REA START FOR CHESTERFIELD INLET, NEAR THE MAGNET POLE, ALONE MEET

A BAND OF ESKIMOS ON DOOBAUNT RIVER — DISCOVER YOUNG MUSK-OX NEAR THE ARCTIC OCEAN — SHOOT ALL BUT THE CALVES—FIVE ARE LASSOED —" WILD WEST show" in THE FROZEN ZONE—WOLVES DEVOUR A SHEPHERD DOG MAKE NIGHT HIDEOUS—rA START FOR HOME

— POOR PROGRESS ANOTHER NIGHT OF DREAD — CARTRIDGES GIVE OUT, AND DESTRUCTION BY WOLVES SEEMS IMMINENT — TOILING WITH THE CAPTIVES BY DAY AND FIGHTING THE ARCTIC WOLVES BY NIGHT — INDIANS OR ESKIMOS CUT THE THROATS OF THE MUSK-OXEN WHILE

THEIR CAPTORS ARE BLEEPING OBLIGED TO ABANDON

THE HUNT FOR LACK OF AMMUNITION — A HUNDRED MILES FROM CABIN, AND OUT OF PROVISIONS — COLONEL JONEB FIRES THE LAST CARTRIDGE AND KILLS A REINDEER A HAPPY NIGHT — BEACH THEIR CABIN. HOME IN

DEPLORABLE CONDITION.

THE first night after parting with our guide we camped near a small clump of dry sticks, which saved the wood we were hauling. The next two days we traveled east by northeast through a blinding storm. The next day was fair, and we made good time until about noon, when we struck a tributary of the Doobaunt river, and found plenty of wood. We followed the stream in a northeasterly direction until night, and camped in a large canon at the mouth of the Doobaunt proper, just north of the lake of the same name. Here were dead spruce trees, some a foot in diameter. Next day we found the river trending to the east,

(380)

and abandoned it where it empties into Chesterfield inlet, taking a northerly direction.

Just before leaving the river we came to a camp of Eskimos containing twenty men and three women. They were dressed entirely in furs, and looked robust and healthy. I supposed they were Indians, until I came in close proximity to them; but when I saw holes in the under lips of the men, with ivory buttons inserted, I knew they were not Indians, but Eskimos. I attempted to pass around them, at which one of the old men struck himself on the breast and uttered some words which I interpreted to be, "Me good Indian! " He had evidently been among the whalers of the Arctic ocean. I stopped, and repeating the signal, turned toward the little fire they surrounded. As soon as Mr. Rea arrived he remarked, "Well, I guess we have run into a hornet's nest." I answered, "Yes, no doubt." We had a pot of tea made, and invited them to drink, and to eat meat. They certainly drank tea, but touched the meat lightly, as they had an abundance of their own. Apparently they seemed determined to drink tea all the afternoon; so, to rid ourselves of them, we gave them about a pound of it and a sheet-iron bucket to boil water in. This seemingly satisfied them, and we hastily drove away. They ran after us, but we paid no attention to their chatter, not stopping until late at night. While among them I noticed shotguns and a few small breech-loading English rifles. That evening we found where they had made walls of blocks of snow to shelter them from the piercing storm that held us so close to our teepee.

On the 16th and 17th we passed through some of the most rugged and God-forsaken country that I have ever seen. The caribou were abundant, and we never lacked for meat. We saw a few jack-rabbits, and numberless wolves; several black wolves were also seen, and many tracks of the arctic fox, but that animal is so shy we never saw one. On the 18th we saw droppings of the

musk-ox, and late in the evening saw three old bulls, but did not disturb them.

The 19th came, clear and warm. Before we had proceeded three miles we crossed the tracks of about a dozen musk-oxen, made that morning. We halted, and Mr. Rea followed the tracks, soon returning, and reported the herd just ahead, behind a large peak of rocks. We took our guns and slipped up closely to them; counted six cows, five or six young animals, but only one yearling, and as yearlings were as large an animal as we cared to tackle, we rose up and walked directly toward them. They also advanced to meet us, approaching so close we could see their eyes bulging out, not to exceed seventy-five yards away. Finally one of the cows gave a snort, and away all went, running southward against the wind.

We returned to our sleds without shooting, and drove to the shelter of a high range of stone a mile to the east and went into camp, deciding to circle around for game. While we were pitching the tent our shepherd dogs kept barking and trying to get loose; (we always kept the shepherd dogs chained to the sled.) Finally I climbed to the crest of the ridge, and there stood, or rather lay, a herd of musk-oxen just beyond, on the sunny south slope. And now we knew what had caused the dogs so much worry — they had scented the strange beasts.

I saw the herd contained animals of all sizes, and retreated to the teepee without their observing me. Mr. Rea had tea boiling, which we soon hastily drank, and swallowed our dinner of meat. AVe then opened the bag of ropes, swivels, hobbles, etc., and put them in shape. Our lassos were swung around our necks, also a long half-inch rope intended for an anchor-line. Our gun magazines were filled with cartridges; our pockets also: everything was now ready. When we reached the crest of the divide I must confess my heart beat a little quicker than usual — perhaps owing to the high altitude, or from exhaustion in climbing with such a load of ropes, guns, ammunition, and hobbles.

I said to Mr. Rea, " Let's take it coolly, and have a little rest." He smiled, and said, "All right."

I had supposed he would get very much excited, not having had the experience of myself in catching buffalo and other wild animals, but I could not detect in him a motion that evinced the least nervousness. Long before leaving our cabin on the Great Slave lake we had our plans well matured as to the manner in which we were to capture the animals we were after. We were to run up to within a hundred yards of them, under cover if possible, and shoot down all but two cows and the yearlings. We were then to break the hind legs of those cows, so they could not run, but stay and fight. We expected the yearlings would keep close to their mothers until we could lasso and tie every one.

There were in the herd seven cows, two two-year-olds, and six yearlings. It being unlawful to hunt musk-oxen with dogs, we left our shepherds tied to the sleds; the others we could rely upon staying with them; of course we didn't intend to violate the lawl My shepherd dogs knew that musk-oxen were near, and they were to be cheated out of a very good time; but " Scrapper" had made up his dog's mind to be in at the killing if possible. We were creeping up behind some rocks for final position, when to our surprise five dogs went thundering past after the musk-oxen. . "Scrapper" had slipped his collar and led the way; all the others not tied followed at his heels.

The herd rounded up close together at first, as if to fight wolves,^ but they soon separated, and escaped from us, excepting two cows, a two-year-old, and five yearlings,

1 Musk-oxen always move In herds ; very seldom Is one seen alone. When pursued by wolves they invariably form In a circle, heads outward, the young animals Instinctively taking their place in the hollow center, remaining there until all danger is past and the formation of the herd broken up. The Indians assert that a single full-grown musk-ox can defend Itself against any number of wolves, provided It finds a large rock or ridge to back against. I very much doubt the statement. They never depend upon running from an enemy for safety, however. Their horns are very long and sharp, formed In the most suitable curves for defense, and are so massive, and set Into the head so firmly, that no force, even should they strike a rock, could knock them loose or break them off.

— which was a most fortunate division for us. Our plans were carried out to the letter, with the exception of shooting under cover and breaking the hind legs of two cows. We both shot, when one cow and the two-year-old sank on the snow. I called to Mr. Rea, " Break the hind legs of the cow! " It required fine shooting to do it, .and I knew Mr. Rea was the best shot; at least he was while I was obliged to wear smoked glasses, as I had a slight touch of snow-blindness. He complied with my request, and at the second shot she dropped down on her hock-joints, a fixed object instead of a runaway. True, this was cruel, but such acts are always pardonable in the interest of science. My lasso was soon in shape, and I moved forward to take the little ones " out of other dangers into which they might fly." The pretty, black, glossy creatures were terribly excited, and hovered around the old cow like a brood of goslings around a fighting gander when danger surrounds them.

When I arrived at throwing distance one yearling stood alongside the old cow, his head close to hers. I whirled the noose in the air till it fairly hissed, and let it fly for the prize. The rope went fairly well to the mark, but a little too far, and hooked over the point of the old cow's right horn, where it hung up. The little dog was biting at the heels of the animals, which kept them twisting around in all directions, while our sled-dogs stood in front of the old cow, keeping up such a continual barking that it held her steadfast facing them.

I paused a moment; just then " Scrapper " nipped the heels of the yearling that I was after, which caused it to make a bound forward right into the loop, knocking it from the cow's horn, when with a quick jerk I fastened it safely around its neck.

Mr. Rea was on hand, and we commenced to pull the rascal in, in about the same style as if there were a hundred-pound trout at the end of our line. Now came the danger of the others escaping, as all the dogs left the old

COW and made for the animal we had caught, as we anticipated they would; and for that reason we had spiked the old cow to the very earth by breaking her legs. She made several lunges in her frantic effort to escape, but finding she was doomed, she suddenly stood still.

The other four yearlings, relying entirely on her generalship, waited and lingered with her. We drove the dogs off as quickly as possible, but not until they had made several bleeding wounds on the legs of the one we had on the line.

Mr. Rea held the rope while I threw a lasso on one of the animal's hind legs, by means of which we soon stretched the stubborn little brute on the snow. We hastily tied all four legs together in the same style I used to tie a hog when a boy on my father's farm. Then I took the lasso and walked up until quite close, and as soon as one of the yearlings came darting around the cow, I gave my rope a whirl and threw it over another, but the little beast went right through the loop, excepting its hind legs. By a quick pull I caught it just above the ankles, and soon pulled it out in sled fashion. The dogs did not trouble it much, as they had learned in the melee with the first one caught what was expected of them.

One by one we dragged the little beauties out and tied them, until we had four safely in the toils. I was so nearly exhausted that I could scarcely stand, and the dogs were making things " red hot" for the last yearling. Sometimes it would be fighting them; sometimes running around the old cow, becoming so frisky that I made several throws at it, but missed. Finally Scrapper nipped it so sharply, it sought other protection, and came bounding over to me. I was sure it had selected me to take vengeance on, and made ready to jump aside to let it pass, but it ran to my left side, and as it did so I whirled around and laid the noose over its head without throwing it at all.

As soon as it winded me, it darted toward the old cow, — 25

jerking me headlong in the snow; but the dogs were after it,— so it came bounding back. Mr. Rea grabbed it as it endeavored to pass between us, and threw it. I was soon on its neck; its legs were quickly bound, like the others. Our dogs were then whipped off and made to lie down. I was completely exhausted, and was obliged to ask Mr. Rea to go to the camp, half a mile away, and bring some water. He brought a small pail of cold tea, which revived me very much. Before leaving for the tea, however, he put an end to the cow's misery by sending a ball through her vitals.

We had not taken time to size the animals up, and it was a very interesting hour of my life, when I could quietly stand and see every twinkle of their eyes. The long shaggy fleece that covered the little creatures was of a browner color than that on the old bulls. They looked more like doll animals than like real live musk-oxen. Their short legs made me liken them to a little Shetland pony colt, as compared with a race-horse. They had a tuft of long hair on the shoulders and also on their necks. The males had small sharp horns that pointed straight out from the side of the head and protruded about an inch through the thick mat of hair; while the females' horns were not visible at all, yet could be felt beneath the clump of hair. Though they seemed diminutive, they were deceiving in size and the weight of their bodies. I had seen several of different ages, mounted in museums; but it is evident the taxidermist never had seen one alive, or these specimens would have been filled out more plumply, and their bodies taken almost exactly the shape of a barrel. The very little nutrition contained in the moss compels them to gorge themselves until they have assumed an abnormal shape. These we captured really resembled a domestic yearling calf in the springtime, that has been wintered at a strawstack.

We now commenced to gather up the captives. We first took our long hemp rope, and tied five loops in it about

twelve feet apart; we then fastened each end of this rope to large rocks, and drew it quite tightly. From the loops a small rope was attached, at the end of which was a swivel, which in turn was fastened to the small rope around the animal's neck, in order to prevent tangling, or choking to death. While marching our yearlings up to the anchor-line, we loosened only two of their legs, but when they were securely fastened to it, gave them the freedom of all their limbs, and the way they made the long line jerk and whirl for an hour or more was amusing. It was so long, however, that it relaxed at every surge of the animals, thus preventing the possibility of injuring, that would have otherwise occurred, as it yielded to every effort in their attempt to escape, I had handled buffalo so often that my premeditated plans for the capture of musk-oxen were very easy for us to put into execution.

We moved our teepee over to the south side of the hill, within about a hundred feet of one end of the anchor-line, and watched the frisky little captives endeavoring to regain their freedom, until the sun had sunk in the west.

No sooner had the king of day passed beyond our vision, than we heard a pack of wolves just over the ridge. We knew what it meant — no sleep for us that night. As there was plenty of meat lying a little to the southeast of us, we had hoped they would be content to let us alone. Not so, however. It appeared as if they had not found the carcasses of animals we had killed, but drew nearer and nearer our little live ones, evidently wanting meat they had themselves killed.

As night advanced, the ravenous messengers of death came on. Our dogs were loosened upon the supposition they would be in no danger as long as we remained outside with them, but little "Scrapper," one of our best shepherd heelers, anxious to measure his strength with them, dashed over the divide after one, where he had a "scrap" that the poor fellow hardly anticipated; that was the last we ever saw of him. Doubtless he was devoured in a minute by the pack we knew he had encountered.

It was warm and pleasant that evening, compared with others we had experienced; so I took my stand at the end of the rope farthest from our teepee; Mr. Rea at the other. We both had our guns and plenty of cartridges, and one by one we rolled the white monsters over as they appeared. We never pretended to shoot when they were more than forty yards away. Sometimes they would come singly, then in howling groups, two to a dozen in the pack.

All night long — about nine hours of darkness — the crazy fools would trot up to be slaughtered; most of them running as soon as shot, unless we put a ball in their head or breast. Those wounded would drag themselves away, to be instantly devoured by the others. When morning came they were just as numerous as during the night, and the sun was high in the heavens before they commenced to skulk away or attempt to get under cover. About noon we determined to try to get out of the horrid place. We had killed twelve wolves outright, and twice as many more, wounded, had gone off, to be devoured by their companions.

We tied one end of our anchor-line to the carryall, I walking behind, holding the other. We set our only shepherd dog at heeling the yearlings up, as they were very stubborn at first, refusing to be led; but within an hour we succeeded in cooling them down somewhat. We fixed hackimos^ in the mouths of our animals, so they could not pull very hard on the line, which saved me many upsets.

The day was warm, the snow melting rapidly, with the thermometer registering forty-eight degrees above zero at noon. We set our compass, marked our line of retreat,

1 Hackimo, a headstall made with the rope after one end Is fastened around the neck, so that It passes through the anlmaPa mouth, whereby It can be held with but little eSort.

and started off, desiring to get along as fast as possible, as it was four o'clock in the afternoon before we got fairly under way.

When the start was made, some of the animals pulled back on their haunches and stopped the whole train. At this juncture all I had to do was to point my finger at the refractory animal, when Don would fly at them, nipping their heels, at which they would take a spurt forward and I be pitched headlong in the sloppy snow; then they would change ends in order to fight the dog. Sometimes the animals would become tangled in the line; the hind one in front and the front one behind. It was certainly discouraging. If we undertook to untangle them we were sure to receive a butt or two that would send us rolling over and over. My shins that night were "as black as the ace of spades."

Musk-oxen are unlike the buffalo in one respect: that is, they do not kick like a mule, while the buffalo kicks like two mules — only much harder and oftener. The cows are of about the size of a thorough-bred Jersey, but not so tall. Their legs are so short, they look as if standing on their knees. They have four teats like a cow, but they are short; have a round, compact udder. They apparently drop their calves about the middle of May.

We went into camp the first night of omr homeward journey about three miles from where we caught our animals. The wolves appeared, and were as numerous as on the night previous; indeed, more so. They were determined, apparently, to have dog, musk-ox, or human flesh: sometimes it seemed they would get all. Our ammunition getting scarce; we did not dare waste a single shot. We were compelled to employ our dogs to help start the ravenous group off, but they soon tired out, and skulked back to the tent. We threw stones, and even resorted to clubs as weapons, taken from our wood supply. We shot only the foremost one of the pack, which was always an old white male. If we drew blood on one, it retreated to the

main puck in the rear, where it was instantly devoured without ceremony — every morsel eaten excepting the skull and skin.

When morning arrived we again started on our homeward march. All that we had taught our musk-oxen on the day previous we discovered to our disgust had been forgotten, and that they possessed more "cnssedness" than we had imagined possible. They were as bad, if not worse, than when we first broke camp. All of them were gaunt, not having eaten anything since their capture; at which we felt alarmed, fearing they would refuse to eat, and die. We worked carefully with them until about ten o'clock, then pitched our tent; and as there were no wolves bothering, we laid down and slept soundly till awakened by the barking of our dogs. On looking out, there stood a herd of reindeer not two hundred yards away; apparently inspecting the small herd of musk-oxen and dogs, as well as our tent. Our dogs were as much worn out as ourselves,— so much so that they hardly knew whether to run out and catch a deer or not, after we had broken both of its fore legs. We secured two fine fat animals, and, after dressing and taking the best part, gave the dogs all they wanted, and proceeded on our journey. We made fully ten miles that day, and felt encouraged. When we stopped and anchored the animals, two of them commenced to paw up the moss and grass, and ate freely. We felt highly elated, as almost the last cause of fear had been cleared away. The wolves were prowling around on all sides. That night was a repetition of the two previous nights.

To our delight, we noticed all the musk-oxen diligently pawing up the moss and eating it, excepting the first one we had caught. It appeared stiff and sore from the wounds made by the dogs. As soon at daylight arrived, we struck our tent and continued the journey, swinging a little more to the south, as it was evident we must procure another supply of wood before crossing the divide between the Doobaunt river and the great lakes.

We again slept during the middle of the day, and about three o'clock started on our journey. We reeled off from fifteen to eighteen miles during the day, and had the yearlings so subdued that they gave us much less trouble than on the previous days. The day had been dark and cloudy, and the wolves appeared much earlier than on the days previous, having no doubt followed us from the last camp. We did not have more than a dozen cartridges left, and depended upon our guns alone for meat for ourselves and dogs. The situation began to look serious. Our bread had been all gone for two weeks. We battled all night with the wolves and managed to keep them "from the door," and from devouring our animals. The weather turned quite warm during the night: we were having an old-fashioned January thaw, and all the musk-oxen worked diligently filling themselves with such provender as they could paw out. The wounded one appeared convalescent and refreshed. We had secured two bulls and three heifers, and were now in high spirits over our golden prize; yet dreaded our possible fate, on account of the constant pursuit of the wolves and our short supply of cartridges.

We were off early that morning, bearing directly south for Doobaunt river, as only a few sticks of wood were left with which to cook meat, and to melt snow for water to quench our thirst and refresh our exhausted bodies. W3 expected certainly to reach timber the next day. About eleven o'clock we halted, having worried along fully ten miles that morning. Here, after taking a slight lunch and drinking cold tea that we carried in a rubber bag (the life preserver I bought at Edmonton), we rolled up in our blankets, and I was soon dreaming of my far-away sunny home in Oklahoma. About three o'clock Mr. Rea woke up and went out to look after our animals. He returned, and said, "Jones, we are ruined! some one has killed all our musk-oxen. They have cut their throats 1 " I awoke from my happy dreams, and thought him only

joking. I raised the side of the tent, looked out, and saw it was too true 1 Then my heart that had been throbbing so buoyantly with joy in the past few days sank within me; a dizziness seemed to come over me, and I fell back on my blankets and was soon lost in a deep slumber. Mr. Rea said afterwards, it was quite difficult to arouse me again.

We went out and inspected the situation of affairs. There had been twelve or fifteen Eskimos or Indians there on snowshoes, and they had cut the throats of all of our animals, leaving them lying dead with the ropes around their necks. We had only one dog (Don) left that would bark at the appearance of Indians, and he was so badly mangled by the wolves he could scarcely heel up the animals on the marches, and we had allowed him a caribou-skin inside the tent to sleep on. Had he been outside, doubtless he would have given the alarm, and we would have saved the yearlings, or shared their fate ourselves. The marauders left a peculiar-looking knife on the snow near the animals, having a handle about eighteen inches long, made of caribou or some other animal's rib, or tusk, with a blade four inches long, riveted to the large end of the bone. If we had known whether this knife-handle was from a land or sea animal, I could have decided who had committed the dastardly deed — Indians or Eskimos. If it belonged to a sea animal, it would implicate the Eskimos; if to a caribou, more than likely the Indians.

We followed the snowshoe-tracks for nearly four miles, and discovered that the party had been following our trail, and had retreated by the same route. We returned to our camp sad and weary, not able to tell if they were Eskimos or Indians. Apparently we were on the neutral grounds between the hunting-fields of these two savage tribes. We had been warned time and time again by the Indians not to take any musk-oxen alive, but had paid no attention to them, as we were well armed, and knew they were cowardly and dare not open fire on us. We expected

HOPE OF BECURIXG LIVE MUSK-OXEN ABANDONED 893

to guard our animals day and night while passing through the enemy's country. It did not enter our minds that there Avas an Indian within two hundred miles of us, and we did not suspect the Eskimos of such treachery. We were so worn out and depressed in spirits that we rolled up in our blankets and slept until night was fully on, when we were awakened by the dogs barking and running around the teepee, occasionally screaming as though they were being devoured. We soon saw the wolves were closing in on them, and called all the dogs into the teepee. Then we took turns in keeping watch, in fear of being destroyed, as we had no cartridges to waste.

When morning arrived we unloaded everything we could possibly spare; threw away all we had left of the sack of ropes, swivels, hobbles, etc., as well as a small sack of salt and other unnecessary burdens. Before leaving the dead animals we went out, hoping to save one or two of the heads for mounting, but found the wolves had devoured everything, excepting the hair, which convinced us they must have' been desperately hungry. We had been so worried and perplexed the day before, that it never occurred to us that we would want to see even any part of the remains of our dead animals.

We abandoned all hope of securing even a single live musk-ox. We would have returned to their haunts and tried again, but knew that such action would be suicidal, as our ammunition was almost gone, and it was a serious question whether we could reach our cabin without taking great chances of starvation.

So, with sad hearts and profound regrets, we relinquished all our high hopes, and turned our faces southward.

The snow was melting rapidly, and we were obliged to pull across the ridges on bare rocks. The sledding was good on the little valleys and lakes, which cover about one-fourth of the whole area of the country.

We reached a canon of Doobaunt river that evening,

and supplied ourselves with enough dry wood to last during several days while resting, and for the three-days journey to Artillery lake. The wolves were not nearly as numerous after we lost our musk-oxen. They had doubtless been attracted by them, and as we had traveled slowly they followed us, and probably were joined by others every day. We killed plenty of meat at the canon where we found wood, and finally made a bee line for Artillery lake. When we reached the latter place, I had just one cartridge left in the magazine of my gun. We had barely meat enough for supper, and there was yet a three-days journey ahead. The great herd of reindeer had already passed to the north, and only occasionally could we see a stray one, and they were very shy.

We had directed our course so accurately that we struck Artillery lake about two miles north of where we had left it. When nearly down the divide, two reindeer ran out of a draw ahead of us, and circled around to the north. They came within about four hundred yards, and one stopped nearly facing us. I had my gun ready, and no sooner had it halted than I had "a bead" on it. Mr. Rea shouted, *'Shoot the other onel It stands broadside to us;" but I did not see "the other one," and was determined not to give up my chance, to look for it. This was our only hope. If ever I took aim carefully and held my rifle with a steady nerve, it was then. I judged the distance quickly, knowing the animal would pause but a moment and then be gone. I elevated my gun .about four inches above the top of his shoulders, and touched the trigger. " Bangl" went the gun. A puff of smoke, the recoil of my Winchester, and at almost the same instant the sound of a sudden "spat" reached my ears, which assured me that the deadly bullet had been well directed. As the smoke cleared away, I saw the coveted prize lying on the snow, and the "other one" flying northward.

" Thanks 1 thanks! my worthy friend," sang out Mr. Rea, from where he stood.

We went to where the dead deer was lying, and upon examination, found the ball had hit exactly where I intended, at the point of the shoulder, coming out on the other side near the flank, having pierced the animal's vitals. We were almost overjoyed at our good fortune in having secured such a magnificent doe. It lasted us and the dogs until we reached our cabin, where we had left an abundance of dry meat. We journeyed down the caiion, where there was plenty of wood, and enjoyed a royal feast.

The next day we reached Artillery lake, where we found fine sledding until we arrived at the portage which carried us over to Great Slave lake. The country there was almost bare ground, and we had about thirty miles to lug our sled across. We were obliged to pull along with the dogs in order to make any progress whatever; some days we did not exceed ten miles. But we worried along, and finally reached the cabin on the afternoon of the 10th of April, having been absent forty-four days, traveling on an average not less than twenty-five miles per day, through storms and blizzards, over ice, rocks, and plains; making in all fully thirty-nine days' travel, or a distance of 975 miles, on snowshoes. So the reader must concede that we had a foretaste, at least, of real Arctic exploring.

When we reached the low altitude of the Great Slave lake, nearly all the snow had disappeared; the birds were singing as sweetly and warbling their carols as joyously as those of the far south.

CHAPTER XXV AT THE CABIN HOME

HYDROPHOBIA AMONG THE DOGS — ONE DOG SEVERS A STEEL CHAIN WITH HIS TEETH, AND DISAPPEARS — MR. REA'b

NARROW ESCAPE WAITING FOR SUMMER HOW TO REACH THE NORTH POLE COLONEL JONES's PRACTICAL METHOD — A START FOR THE SUNNY SOUTH — SLOW PROGRESS, LESS THAN A MILE A DAY LAKE FROZEN FROM SHORE TO SHORE ON THE FOURTH OF JULY LIVING ON BREAD ALONE — ARRIVE AT FORT RESOLUTION IN THE MIDDLE OF JULY FIRST NEWS OF THE WAR WITH SPAIN — MUSIC IN THE FAR NORTH, THE " SWEETEST EVER HEARD " — COLONEL JONES BO BEWILDERED, FANCIED HIMSELF IN THE " SPIRIT LAND " FEASTING ON THE FRUITS OF HIS NATIVE COUNTRY ONCE MORE — GRAND RECEPTION AT THE FORT.

WHEN we arrived at our cabin, after our musk-ox hunt, both of us were completely worn out. My feet were swollen to twice their usual size; where the snowshoe-straps crossed, the blood oozed out and saturated my socks. Of course we were compelled to wear moccasins in that frigid country, and they could stretch to the size of a gunboat if necessary.

We found the Indians congregated about a mile from our cabin in large numbers. They had picked up every conceivable thing left outside of a radius of two rods from the building. The knowledge that the revolvers and

(396)

gun were inside, and the assurance that the keg of powder would explode in the cabin, kept them all at a respectful distance from it. Had it not been for these facts, every vestige of our supplies left behind would have been carried away by the thieving band, and our experience would have been that of all others who ever trusted to the honesty of hungry Indians. To their credit be it said, however, that when not hungry (which is rarely the case) they can be trusted implicitly, for the property of others is then regarded as sacred, particularly caches where food is deposited, and only when upon the verge of starvation will they touch it. Our supplies no doubt would have been an exception to the rule,— at least we believed so.

Shortly after reaching our cabin we noticed that one of our large dogs ("General ") next to the lead in the team grew very quarrelsome, and was continually fighting his comrades. He was quite old, and his tusks were worn off until very blunt. We had observed his strange actions while on the last of our homeward trail, but knowing he could do little harm we paid but little attention to them. He had always been peaceable, and we trusted him more than we ought; at least Mr. Rea did. I was convinced from his strange actions and the froth from his mouth that he had a genuine attack of hydrophobia. He would bite his tongue until the blood and foam would run out of his mouth in a stream, and was continually snapping at everything that came near him. When we tied him up he would howl so pitifully we could not sleep. Several times Mr. Rea got up in the night and let him loose. During the day while hauling wood, he would pull all the load himself, trying to get to the dog ahead to fight him. It made no difference how many joined against him, the more there were the better he liked it. His teeth being so dull was all that allowed a single one to escape. He was very vicious when once aroused to anger, and had been the most faithful of our train-dogs in guarding off the wolves;

but the wolves had wounded him severely at various times. His nose had been badly split, as well as his under lip, while other wounds on his head plainly showed he had always been "in at the finish." He constantly grew worse. One day when we were out with the sleds on a hunting-trip, "General" stopped about every half-hour, turned entirely around in the harness, and fought the other dogs viciously. As soon as unharnessed he would pounce upon the first dog he met, upon which, all the train would set upon him; but it did not daunt his courage in the least,— it only stimulated him to greater effort.

I suggested to Mr. Rea that the dog was surely mad. He scouted the idea. Then we fastened him with a steel chain, and in less than an hour he had severed it with his teeth and immediately attacked the other dogs. Twice he was thus fastened, and as often severed the chain with his teeth. I do not wish to convey the idea that he cut a steel chain as a smith would do with a cold-chisel, but he crushed the links so hard they snapped apart and set him free. Probably no one who may read the above will credit the statement, but it is absolutely true. The dog was undoubtedly endowed with this abnormal strength of jaw, under the influence of the terrible disease from which he was suffering.

Finally he attacked Mr. Rea, and but for his thick buckskin mittens and the blunt teeth of the dog, he would have been inoculated with the poisonous virus. Mr. Rea grabbed his gun, and instantly put an end to old " General's " sufferings.

We were convinced that he had a well-developed case of hydrophobia; that he had been inoculated by the bite of the wolf which came so near to me that night at the tent while I was out on the musk-ox hunt. The wolf, doubtless, was passing through the last stage of the dreadful scourge itself. I firmly believe it is that disease which keeps the wolves of the Barren Lands reduced in number,

or they would increase so rapidly as to exterminate all ruminant animals, for they propagate fully five to six times faster than either the caribou or musk-ox; besides, they have no enemies to lessen their number, for the Indians will never kill a wolf except in self-defense, believing that after death, one who kills a wolf will be transmuted to that animal in the Happy Hunting Grounds.

We chained up all our dogs, for fear they too would take the dreadful disease. The third day after disposing of "General," our faithful little "Don," that had been BO badly torn by the wolves, showed symptoms of hydrophobia ; and within twenty-four hours he became so vicious that we considered it unsafe to allow him to live any longer, and ended his troubles by a shot from my Winchester. In about twenty days thereafter, " Franklin," another train-dog, became very quarrelsome. We neglected to chain him, as his good-nature, as we supposed, would prevent him from doing any harm. The next day, while we were out setting a fish-net, " Franklin " took to the woods, and was never seen afterward.

After resting for a week from our visit to the Barren Lands, we fully realized how embarrassing it would be, after spending a year in that region, to return without having secured at least one pair of musk-oxen. We would gladly have waited until May or June and captured some young calves, but having no milk, it was out of the question. We had depended for a supply of milk upon a Mr. William Armstrong, a partner of Mr. Rea who had been on the Mackenzie river trading for furs. I met him at Fort Smith, and made a contract with him to go after musk-ox with Mr. Rea and myself. While Mr. Rea and I proceeded to Fort Reliance, Mr. Armstrong was to go to Edmonton by open water in a boat, and return that fall by the same route to Fort Resolution; then to proceed to Fort Reliance on dog-sleds, and join us. Among other things he had promised to bring from Edmonton was a large quantity of con-

densed milk, ^itli which we would be able to sustain any calves of the musk-ox we might catch. But when he arrived at Edmonton, the Alaska gold excitement was at its height; he then forgot all about his partner, Mr, Rea, far off in the Barren Lands, and turned his face to that new El Dorado. Long did we watch and wait for his coming, but received no tidings from him until the 25th of February, when Mr. Rea received a letter by an Indian carrier who had just returned from Fort Resolution. It was not from Mr. Armstrong directly, however, but from a friend at Edmonton, informing him that Mr. Armstrong had gone to Alaska. This was cold comfort for us, and the only thing remaining to do was to undertake to bring out some yearlings instead of calves. The plan would have worked successfully had there been one or two other men with us, so that we could have established reg^ ular watches and all have secured sleep enough to warrant a continual guard until we had passed beyond the line of danger. Even after our yjearlings had been slaughtered, if we could have procured milk we should have remained and brought out some small calves, which could have been accomplished by the aid of canoes for a greater part of the distance, while it would have been impossible for us to transport yearlings or older animals in this manner.

Before leaving Fort Reliance we decided not to return up the rivers by the route we went into that country, but chose rather to come out by way of Alaska, as it is all down-stream by that route excepting about twenty miles on the Peels river and sixty miles up the Rat river.

I made a fair catch of furs during the winter, such as wolves, wolverines, fox, marten, lynx, etc. I had caught three silver-gray foxes, and saved them alive, and bought two at Resolution, making five; had saved ten marten alive, and was getting along very nicely with my charge. These, unfortunately, I was obliged to leave with some Indians on the Great Slave lake when we determined to change our course around by Mackenzie river, the Arctic ocean, and the Porcupine and Yukon rivers. I hope to have quite a number of the marten and fox brought out sometime during the winter or next spring, and place them on an island in the North Pacific ocean, for breeding purposes.

We had been in darkness so much during the previous winter, I was almost wild to reach the land of eternal day. Yes, I felt as if I would like to reach ;the North Pole, in order to realize the largest possible amount of daylight.

Speaking of the North Pole, I desire to say:

After my experience in the far North, I have come to the conclusion that the man who reaches the North Pole must be made of sterner metal than anyone who thus far has attempted the perilous journey. No "tenderfoot" will ever hang the flag of his country on the mythical pole, or on a real one, at the northern extremity of this terrestrial globe. When I say "tenderfoot," I mean anyone who has not had experience in all the arts required to meet every contingency necessary to such an undertaking. In the first place, he must be an expert hunter, or rather, an expert " killer." There are thousands of men who can shoot glass balls, kill birds on the wing; also many who can stand on the trails or runways of deer and shoot the majestic stag as he gallops by. He maybe a skilled hunter, who has pitched his "A" tent in the " Rockies," and been fortunate enough to have slain the stately elk, mountain sheep, caribou, and even the grizzly bear; but all these accomplishments will not, alone, perfect him for the great feat yet to be accomplished.

The man who can not only kill game in favorable locations, where there are plenty of blinds behind which to conceal himself, but has learned the secret of creeping on all kinds of animals, equal to the white bear when it stealthily approaches the seal on the smooth ice, is only partially prepared for the adventurous undertaking. He should take lessons of the animals which prey upon others — 26

for food, and not only closely observe them, but put into practice the lessons learned, until he is as skillful as the creatures that have unconsciously taught him.

Did the reader ever study the cunning of a cat endeavoring to secure a meal? If not, watch her when she discovers a mouse, rat, or gopher. She crouches close to the ground, never moving a muscle or winking the eye while the little rodent is still, but the moment the tiny creature moves, or lowers its head to drink or eat, she moves closer and closer, for while the victim-to-be is thus engaged, it does not discover or detect the action of the pursuer. While thus following her methods, she does not take her eyes from off the creature whose dainty flesh is to furnish her food; every movement must be weighed and measured accurately, and thus not allow her quarry to detect a single motion or it would be fatal. When the right moment comes, she is on her victim with a single bound, and the watch is over. What is true of the cat also applies to the panther, lynx, wildcat, mountain lion, and other animals of the feline species, and should also apply to the hunter.

During my twoscore years of hunting, on the Plains and in the Arctic region, I learned to kill animals on the open prairie, ice-covered lakes, and barren lands, where there is no shelter behind which to hide, with as much ease as in the forests of the middle States, or among the rocks and hills of the Rocky Mountains.

The reindeer and seals are very difficult to approach, owing to their acute sense of sight and smell. The Indian never attempts, like the Eskimo, to measure cunning with the reindeer in the open country, or on the ice, but relies upon waiting behind trees or rocks, near their trails, or spears them as they cross large rivers or small lakes. The curiosity of the Indians was aroused to a high pitch, when they witnessed my attempt to kill four large reindeer bulls on the ice without a blind behind which to hide. This, to them, was an unheard-of exploit, but to

me it was an every-day occurrence. I had learned to walk up to that most wary of beasts, the antelope, on the open prairie, with as much ease as did the hunter for buffalo Avhen he stalked those dumb animals in the early'TOs, and could shoot them with all confidence and certainty. And unless the would-be Arctic explorer is skilled in all the arts of creeping onto and killing game in the open fields, he had as well stay at home.

There is another requisite which is just as important to success as the game question. I refer to the will-power and willingness to do or die, without which the explorer will fail in his j)urpose. When he starts on his perilous Journey, he must have made up his mind he has lived long enough, resign himself to any fate, and be ready to "give up the ghost" in that land of darkness, rather than have written beside his name, "Failure! "

Andree, who started to the Pole in a balloon, possessed this determination to such a degree as in one sense to be commendable, and if the expedition had been judiciously planned, he might have been successful. His method of locomotion, however, was simply suicidal, and should have been prevented by his Majesty King Oscar of Sweden, instead of receiving encouragement from him.

No one has any conception of the terrible solitude of a country where the foot of man has never trod, and even animal life ceases to exist. Here the tiny ant, the annoying fly, and even the horrid spider, would be welcome visitors.

If the winter darkness prevails, one is almost convinced it is the "everlasting darkness " of which we read, minus " the fire which water quencheth not," and is all that is needed to make it a veritable "hades." On the other hand, when the summer sun shines continuously, it causes serious belief that you have reached the portals where "eternal day excludes the night," and were it not for the pangs of hunger, certainly "pleasure would banish pain."

The solitude causes one to become bewildered and lost, and only the strong-minded man, with an indomitable will, should ever attempt, or give serious thought to the undertaking. When Death, the "last enemy," appears to be right ahead, the hero must press on harder than before, even to the very end.

I firmly believe the North Pole can and will be found, if such a character or characters as I have attempted to portray, start w^ith a well-planned expedition and line of march.

Of course, dog-sledges are indispensable. Were I organizing an expedition, I would not take more than two companions, on the last four hundred miles. I would start with three boat-sleds of five dogs each, with as many reindeer and loose dogs, working them every other day. Upon one team I would depend to bring me back, and would feed it fairly well, on dogs and deer killed for that purpose. The others I would keep on half-rations, while about one-third of the animals would receive very little food. When the first animal gave out, I would kill it and feed the flesh and bones to my dogs, or cache it; and as the others became exhausted, would treat them in the same manner. Thus I would go to the Pole and return, with only one sled. By taking dogs and reindeer for rations, for the return team, it would relieve us of a great burden, and lighten our load of provisions. If game were sighted, I would secure it, whether there were blinds or not, and thus save all the dogs possible.

It is all-important that one be properly and lightly equipped; also, just as important not to be overburdened with heavy clothing, which is detrimental to locomotion. Worst of all, too much clothing causes the body to become heated to such an extent in that climate, where the humidity of the atmosphere is greater than in any other part of the world, that it thereby causes perspiration so profuse that one's garments become entirely saturated. The sun's rays are almost powerless to cause evaporation ;

consequently, when at midnight the sun sinks near the horizon, the clothing is frozen stiff (and this too, in summer-time), which robs the explorer of the rest he so much requires.

There is a way to accomplish anything and everything, and after it has once been learned, the journey to the North Pole will be comparatively an easy one. The only person I have ever had the least confidence would reach the Pole, is the gallant young Italian Prince, Luigi, who is now on his way in that direction. We all know he is a great hunter, and no doubt knows the art of "creeping up" to-game. He is reported to be a very successful game-killer, and is courageous, with great will-power, which, unless judiciously used, may send him to his death; but if he plans with a discretion equal to his valor, all will be well. When he kissed the hand of his aunt, the gracious Queen of Italy, accepted the flag made by her own skillful hands, and said, "I will place it on the North Pole or never return," I felt persuaded he would succeed.

During the long nights of the previous winter the ice had frozen to a depth of six or seven feet on the Great Slave lake, and we must wait for open water or go to Fort Resolution on dog-sleds. My freight was somewhat limited after a stay of eight months; as both of us had been blessed with a good appetite, our raids upon the original stock of provisions had reduced it materially. I could therefore have hauled all I had left with one dog-sled. Fortunately I had cached at Fort Resolution the previous year a goodly supply of flour, bacon, and other eatables with my friend Mr. Nagle. Mr. Rea was differently situated: he had brought a boat-load of goods, hoping to trade with the Indians for furs, but the savages had been so dilatory they were almost destitute; having failed to trap any animals, they consequently had no skins. Failing in the fall to kill any musk-oxen, and not having made their other semi-annual hunt in the spring,

doubtless fearing we would follow their trail, they had not even a single robe of that animal, which is their principal dependence, with which to trade; so Mr. Rea still had all his goods left, with nothing to trade for.

Here was a dilemma for which no provision had been made, for it would have required at least four dog-trains to transport Mr. Rea's goods to Fort Resolution, which it was impossible to secure, as, though the Indians had plenty of dogs, these dogs were in a starving condition, therefore the Indians could not go. The Indian dog cannot live upon Arctic snow and do hard work; he appears to do light work around the teepee on that provender 1 So Mr. Rea was obliged to travel by open water. I was aware that if I could only reach the Mackenzie river on ice it would put me at least a month ahead on my journey, as ice always breaks up on the rivers a month before it does on the lakes.

What to do was the problem that confronted me. Mr. Rea consented that I should do whatever I deemed best; that is, go on a single dog-sled, with the two dogs still remaining, or remain until open water, when I could go with him. After lying awake several nights, rolling and tumbling in my blankets, I remembered the golden rule. Realizing what a dreadful thing it would be for me to live in that horrid country alone, three or four wearisome months, I decided at once not to treat Mr. Rea as others had, and told him my intentions were to stay with him "to a finish."

Whether or not he was pleased in having my company in that God-forsaken country, i.t is not for me to say; the reader can be the better judge.

When June came, the snow left—also our eatables, as we were obliged to divide our scanty supply with a band of starving Indians who arrived at Susann's wigwam on their way to the Barren Lands after reindeer. We divided equally with them, altliough we needed every scrap badly. They ate it all at one meal, and then left, trusj;-

ing to the Great Spirit for their next. Susann and little Ellen joined them to share their fate, on a vague possibility of living. Before leaving, the little girl came far out of her way, and with tears streaming down her cheeks reached out her little hand and said, "Molar, mecha," (white man, good-by). I gave her many little presents,^ such as knives, forks, spoons, a blanket, etc., which cheered her despondent soul, and she wended her way oa the trail of her mysterious kindred. Susann did not even say good-by, and I was not aggrieved by her action. The female caribou had long since passed to the north. The males still lingered far to the south, and we relied entirely upon catching fish and shooting ducks, but found the fish did not abound in that end of the lake, or at least we failed to catch them in our net, or with hook and line,— no doubt on account of the transparency of the water, which allows the net to be seen from a great distance. We succeeded in shooting a few ducks, but cold weather Bet in again, and froze the lake completely over. We could see geese and ducks occasionally flying high in the air, but none came down. For eleven days we eked out an existence on half a biscuit each, three times a day, which was the hardest living that ever fell to my lot. I am certain of one thing: our Saviour knew of what He spake when He said, " It is written, man shall not live by bread alone," for I was so weak and emaciated, after my dreadful experience, I fully realized the truth of the statement. I could not see where to step, or distinguish one direction from another. Living for twenty-seven days on meat alone, as I did at one time while on this Northern trip, was continual feasting compared to slowly starving on bread alone.

On the 20th of June we determined to abandon our horrible quarters, which were but a prison, and make as fast time as possible toward Fort Resolution. There was about fifty feet, on an average, of open water next to the shore, when the wind was in a favorable direction; but an ad-

verse blow would drive the ice up on the margin of the lake and cut off navigation, especially when it blew fiercely, which in this close vicinity to the Barren Lands was nothing unusual. Later on, the ice came across the lake in such great force that we were compelled to haul our boat far up onto the shore; and often floes of ice, many rods square, four and five feet thick, were sent thirty to forty feet upon the shore, by the great volume of ice that had gained such momentum that its force was almost irresistible. It took good generalship and plenty of muscle to prevent our boat from being ground to powder by the great floes of ice that came together with terrific force at each unfavorable turn of the wind. Often we were obliged to jump out, one on each side of the boat with long levers, and as the great floes came together we would pry the boat out of the water and it rode high on the ice until a separation was effected.

It took us just eight days to make six miles in the direction of Fort Resolution. After all our hard work we were again frozen in solid at the end of our short progress, and were compelled to remain until the 6th of July, when a north wind with the velocity of a hurricane came, which broke up the ice and ground it to slush.

The next morning we set a net across the mouth of a little stream, where, by taking poles and thrashing the water above, we so frightened them we secured twenty-four fine, large trout by that method. That was a happy day for us as here, seated on a large stone, we ate boiled fish and drank tea,— the best meal I ever enjoyed in my whole life. It was a happier day for the dogs, for they had not had a bite to eat for three long weeks, excepting what they may have foraged for themselves, which must have been almost nothing. It seems hardly credible that any animal could exist so long on the verge of actual starvation, but such a condition is common to the arctic dogs, particularly those owned by Indians.

Again that dreadful scourge, hydrophobia, made its ap-

pearance in our camp. That night our favorite leader, the dog " Sandy," became raving mad. He was a great favorite, and very valuable in that northern country. He was much more intelligent than any of the native dogs. Mr. Rea had been much attached to him for two years, and I knew he could never muster up sufficient courage to put him out of his misery. After the poor animal had howled all night long, preventing us from sleeping at all, I suggested to Mr. Rea that Sandy was certainly doomed, and asked him if I had not better take care of him. For a moment he was silent, but at last said, "Use your own judgment." I took my Winchester, went outside, found the dog lying down with his front legs stretched out before him, and his head in the air, howling most pitifully. I shot him just back of the ear. He did not struggle, but simply dropped his head on hia paws, and in a moment he was dead.

After breakfast, as we passed the body of the poor fellow on our way to the boat, I said to Mr. Rea, "We'll allow old Sandy to take a long 'spell,' " for we saw he was in the position he always assumed while resting. At my words Mr. Rea took a last look at the faithful animal,, said nothing, but merely nodded his head. Sandy's death, left us with only one train-dog and our last shepherd.

After arranging our sails we launched the boat into the rough waves, and with a favorable wind went spinning through the water in earnest in the direction of Fort Resolution. After having proceeded a hundred miles down the lake we arrived at an Indian camp, which was well provided with dry meat. We traded with its occupants for several hundred pounds, but the men all tried to discourage us from proceeding alone on our hazardous journey. The politic fellows evidently expected we would hire guides, but as we had been close observers on our initial trip, we were determined to be our own pilots, as I had drawn a very accurate chart of the route. There are so many "blind pockets" and sunken reefs and rocks.

that boats are easily dashed to pieces upon them. Perhaps, after all, the Indians were justified in their apparent concern for our safety, for there are thousands of islands between which a boat must make its tortuous passage, and it is a very difficult matter to get through them if one is not well acquainted with the proper channels.

On these islands, and in the marshes between, as well as in the whole of that northern country, the mosquitoes and sandflies hold high carnival. The air is literally filled with them; it is impossible to open the mouth, or take a long breath, without inhaling swarms of them; and with no mosquito-bars, sleep is impossible. They even crawled under our blankets, up our sleeves and trousers-legs. They were certainly the most persistent insects of their kind I have ever seen anywhere, making life one continual torment.

Referring to the clouds of sandflies and mosquitoes which annoyed us at times almost beyond the point of endurance, I cannot refrain from quoting Capt. Back again. He gives the following vivid account of his experience:

" We suffered dreadfully from myriads of sandflies and mosquitoes, being so disfigured by their attacks that our features could scarcely be recognized. Horseflies, appropriately styled 'bull-dogs,' were another dreadful pest, which pertinaciously gorged themselves like the leech until they seemed ready to burst. It is vain to attempt to defend ourselves against these puny blood-suckers; though you crush thousands of them, tens of thousands arise to avenge the death of their companions. . . .

"How can I possibly give an idea of the torment we endured from the sandflies 1 As we dived into the confined and suffocating ravines, or waded through the close swamps, they arose in clouds, actually darkening the air; to see or to speak was equally difficult, for they rushed at every undefended part, and fixed their poisonous fangs in

an instant. Our faces streamed with blood, as if leeches had been applied, and there was a burning and irritating pain, followed by immediate inflammation, and producing giddiness, which almost drove us mad, and caused us to moan with pain and agony."

The above is a truthful picture of our own battles with the insects described; but Captain Back does not refer to the unutterable torments the animals of that region are subjected to, for his mission was entirely different from that of ours. We were necessarily brought into contact with nearly every variety of mammals in that country, and despite our own sufferings in the particular referred to, we pitied the reindeer and moose, whose sufferings were only relieved at times by frantically rushing into the water, thus gaining a little respite from the attacks of the swarms of blood-suckers. The south shore, lined with the driftwood, dead grass and vegetation of the lake, seemed to be an ideal breeding-place for these insects.

There is one thing very striking in the Northern country: it appears like a newly made world. There is nothing that indicates age, excepting the stones, and even they look as if of recent formation. The trees north of Fort Smith and south of Great Slave lake all appear young and thrifty; none indicate old age, or dilapidation caused by the storms of time. Wherever the rivers cut through and make new channels, the banks show logs and sticks deposited thickly through the whole region, to a depth of twenty to thirty feet below the surface; while north of the lake there is little or no soil. The surface is nothing but moss-covered rocks scattered over the country, except that occasionally in the valleys a little soil borders the edges of the streams and lakes. My opinion is that within a thousand years the Athabaska and Great Slave lakes will not be half as large as they are to-day. From the best information I could obtain, and judging from re-cent marks at the water's edge of Great Slave lake, the lake has lowered fully three feet in the past ten years. Water-marks of relatively modern time can be plainly traced from twenty to thirty feet above the lake's surface; that is, east of the narrows, which once was a high ridge clear across. The logs, sticks, dirt and silt, that are hurled down the mountains and precipitated into the dashing waters throughout the vast expanse of country tributary to the Peace, Athabaska and other rivers, all go to the Athabaska and the south half of Great Slave lakes, whose waters are very muddy. This great accumulation of sediment is then cast ashore or settles to the bottom. This process is all the time building up more land. In fact, each year's encroachment of the land upon the great lakes' area is plain to be seen for many miles before reaching these lakes, evidenced by the age of the trees, by saplings and little sprouts and newly made land. The same is true of the Arctic ocean at the mouth of the Mackenzie river only; while on other parts of the coast and shores of the inland lakes, as Artillery, Clinton Golden, Bear, and others, there has been no apparent change for ages. There is not an indication of the "made" land around their borders,— nothing, as a rule, but clean, sharp rocks, where the ever-dashing waves are always rolling.

The territory between Edmonton and Great Slave lake is one great wilderness. The forests are so dense that one can scarcely pass through them, owing to the fallen trees and underbrush. In many places a person is compelled to cut his way through with an axe. The country is hilly, rising in many places to the height of small mountains. The forests are largely composed of spruce-pines; they often grow to three feet in diameter, are very straight, and would make fine lumber. White poplar comes next in amount. It seldom reaches half the diameter and height of the spruce. From the leaves and twigs of this tree the moose gather most of their provender, and the beaver thrive on the bark cut from the trunks with their long sharp teeth. White* birch is found throughout this region, and often trees grow two feet in diameter. Tamaracks abound in limited numbers in the swamps. They are small, and scarcely ever reach a foot in diameter. Where the shade from trees is not too dense, red raspber> ries, red currants, gooseberries, strawberries and siisca-toons grow to perfection. I gathered all these fruits as far north as Great Slave lake, and red currants and cranberries two hundred miles north of the Arctic Circle. The cranberries are found on a delicate vine that grows in the moss, and are so plentiful in some localities that they can be gathered by double-handfuls.

We were now living like lords upon the dried meat which we had obtained from the Indians, and the weather continuing fine, we experienced very little difficulty in our progress until the evening of the 18th of July. At that time, when only a short distance from Fort Resolution, a fearful tempest rose that drove our frail craft at a terrific rate, the white-caps of the angry waves pouring into it. Mr. Rea held on to the rudder with a firm grip, while I bailed vigorously, until we rounded a point and were in the lee -of the land; then the fort was in sight. The two or three buildings which constitute it were a wonderful exponent of civilization to us, when compared with the total absence ■of anything to which the term applies, during our long and sequestered absence, seemingly out of the world. In addition to the regular buildings, all of which are whitewashed, we could see through our field-glasses a large number of tents close to them, which reminded us of the ^'White City " at Chicago in 1893 (World's Fair).

We sailed into the harbor, where were boats of every style and shape. On anchoring and going ashore we found a large delegation from the "White City," sure enough, some of whom proved to be members of the Yukon Valley Mining Company, besides hundreds of others bound for Alaska. George Enderly was captain of the mining com-

pany; T. V. Cannon, the commissary, and when upon their invitation I dined with them, I was convinced that those under his charge lived sumptuously. Charles B. Tapp, another of the members, was a musician, and had organized a fine orchestra. They were a jolly set of fellows.

At this outpost we obtained all the news of the year past. The particulars of the recent gold discoveries in Alaska were here revealed to us. Our first talk was with a party from Nova Scotia. We asked them to tell us the principal events of the year.

They answered, " Certainly. You know of the war between the United States and Spain ? "

" No. "What is it ? " was my reply.

"Well, the United States has been in a great war with the Spaniards, and licked them good."

I asked who did the fighting for the United States, meaning, was it the regular army or volunteers ? Their answer was, "Oh, Dewey did the fighting."

" Well, who is Dewey ? " was my eager inquiry.

"Oh, Dewey is the fellow that whipped the Spaniards,'" was the reply. And that was about all I could find out until I met the Chicago boys, when I learned the particulars of the war up to May 15th.

We made the acquaintance of many others bound for the new El Dorado; among whom was an interesting^ party from Paterson, N. J.,— Herbert Davenport and brother, and Wm. Deane. The younger Mr. Davenport played the autoharp with exquisite taste, and otherwise entertained us with songs and music in right royal style.

The sun had already dodged behind a small island in the far northwest, for the night. I knew it would soon slip out from the other end, and morning would be with us before we had time to sleep. I had scarcely closed my eyes for three days and nights, as the mosquitoes had been singing to me persistently, and insisting in "putting in their bills " for payment. Tired and weary, I soon sought my

blankets, dropped a new mosquito-bar just purchased, and was just dozing off into dreamland, when Messrs. Tapp and Davenport started their orchestra, beginning with a little Sunday-school song I had often heard, the chorus of which ran, " Sweetest music ever heard," etc. Just imagine the contrast in the music we had been compelled to listen to for a whole year I The sounds that had greeted our ears during that time were only those of the howling wolves, the snarling arctic dogs in their life-and-death struggles for the bones their masters had cast away simply because they themselves lacked maxillaries sufficiently powerful to crush them, and the diabolical, discordant yells of the savages at their incantations. Mr. Tapp played the cornet, and his selections were of the highest order. The calm, cool air wafted the music across the bay, then returned it in a thousand melodious echoes. I can truthfully testify that to me, under the circumstances, it was in reality "the sweetest music ever heard." It so startled and affected me that I was obliged to gather my reasoning faculties in order to determine whether or not I had been transported into that other world "where the wicked cease from troubling and the weary are at rest." I never before realized the vast difference between barbarism and the culture and refinement to which a civilized people are susceptible, until that music, in such a barbarous country, met my ears.

We remained at Fort Resolution until the 17th, receiving, every day of our stay there, more invitations to breakfast, dinner, or tea, from the different mining outfits and from Mr. Nagle (the trader at that place), than was possible for us to accept. We never declined,excepting when previous engagements compelled us. We frequently dined with the young gentlemen from New Jersey, who had brought with them an abundance of preserved peaches for which their native State is noted, together with California canned fruit, which, after our monotonous diet, we realished beyond expression.

While we were at the fort, several delegations en route for the gold-fields of Alaska arrived from the States, and were heartily welcomed with appropriate songs and orchestral music. Whenever a boat arrived at a point where it should turn into the harbor, the cornet played that beautiful refrain, "Pull for the shore," and then everybody present would join in and make the very hills ring with the chorus. The effect on those in the boats approaching was inspiring, and the brawny arms of the oarsman rowed in time to the music. On the evening previous to our departure a grand banquet was given us, by the miners and citizens. We had a delightful time, with the exception of a call upon me for a speech, which was impossible for me to decline. I was like the beaver that "had to climb,"—I had to speak.

Fort Resolution is the first place on the route where miners' laws are in force (as they make their laws themselves), because the place is beyond the jurisdiction of the mounted police or of any other civil or military tribunals. While we were there an interesting suit was submitted to a jury of six, and was disposed of satisfactorily. The miners'code is, "Equality before the law." This "high court of justice" is always ready, in all the mining districts beyond courts of justice, night or day, to listen to any grievance that may exist in the community. Although harsh to the offender, the effect inspires evildoers to deeds of righteousness, and might be adopted with good effect in many localities where the laws are administered in a farcical manner.

CHAPTER XXVI METEOROLOGICAL PHENOMENA

" TOTAL DARKNESS " AND " EVERLASTING DAY " — EXTREME TEMPERATURE OF EACH MONTH — PRECIPITATION — TWELVE DEGREES BELOW ZERO IN THE CABIN BEFORE A ROUSING FIRE—IRON OR STEEL WAS SO COLD IT COULD NOT BE TOUCHED WITH SAFETY — BRILLIANT DISPLAYS OF AURORA BOREALIS — TWO VARIETIES GRAPHICALLY DESCRIBED

WONDERFUL PARHELIA (MOCK SUNS) — ICE UPHEAVAL ON THE GREAT LAKES.

THE meteorological phenomena of the Arctic region are its most interesting feature. The intensity of the cold in " The Land of the Midnight Sun " is something hardly conceivable by those who live where the thermometer never falls more than forty degrees below zero. During the short summer of nearly three months, when the sun for nearly half that time is constantly above the horizon, the mean temperature is about sixty above zero; sinking to thirty-five above when the sun reaches its lowest point. During three months of the long nine months of winter, nearly one and a half months of that time the sun is constantly below the horizon ; then comes the intense cold of the Arctic night.

Excepting the period of the constant appearance of the sun above the horizon and its disappearance below, it rises and sets every day. The time from the first appearance (or sunrise) above the horizon, after the long night, to that point where it disappears (or sunset), is so short that the change from daylight to darkness is very rapid.

—1?7 (417)

As the distance of the point from sunrise to sunset increases or decreases from day to day, the continuance of sunlight or darkness of course increases correspondingly; so that the day or night proper varies gradually from one minute in length to forty days of twenty-four hours each.

The above phenomena of the varying length of the day and night apply to the most northerly region we attained (two hundred miles within the Arctic Circle). Of course, north of us to the very Pole the day and night materially increase in length, while south of us the reverse is the case.

The lowest temperature experienced by us during our sojourn in the north was at Fort Reliance, on the morning of the 9th of January, when the thermometer registered sixty-eight degrees below zero.

It would require too much space to present in tabulated form all the variations of temperature during the whole period of my absence from the United States. I therefore submit only that of the coldest and warmest day in each month, for a period of eight and a half months of winter. I commenced keeping a meteorological record at Fort Reliance, on the 1st of October, 1897. My instrument was a spirit Fahrenheit thermometer, registering to eighty below zero. It was hung against the logs on the south side of our cabin, the only place in which it could be put, there being not even a tree in the vicinity from which to suspend it. It could not be detached from the building, on account of the wind. Of course there must have been considerable radiation from the heat inside the building, and my figures are merely approximate to the real temperature.

When on our hunt after musk-oxen we carried a thermometer suspended under the curved neck of our carryall.

The first time the thermometer indicated zero was at Fort Reliance, at sunrise on the morning of the 10th of October; at noon on the 2d it registered forty-two above, the warmest day of the month. On the morning of the

80th, twenty-one below; November 29th, forty-eight below; the 9th was tlie warmest day, sixteen above at noon. December 14th, fifty-three below; the warmest day the 10th, nine above. The coldest day was January 9th, sixty-eight degrees below; the warmest day, 28th, ten below. February 16th, fifty-nine below; the warmest day the 2d, six.above. March 17th, forty-one below; the warmest day the 20th, forty-nine above at noon. April 18th, twelve below; the warmest on the 5th, fifty above. May 10th, nine above; the warmest on the 29th, seventy-five above. Here my record ends, with the exception of fifteen days' observation in June, the coldest day of which w'as the 14th, thirteen above; the warmest on the 5th, seventy-three above. I have thus covered the larger portion of the year, which to those interested will furnish-an approximately correct record of the temperature of that region.

The total amount of snow which fell during the eight months and a half, in which I kept as careful a record as possible, was four feet seven and one-half inches; and the greatest depth in any one day was seven inches, on the eleventh of June.

Referring to Captain Back's journey again, he says, alluding to the subject of temperature: " Such, indeed, was the abstraction of heat, that with eight large logs of dry wood on the fire, I could not get the thermometer higher than twelve degrees below zero. The skin of the hands became dry, cracked and opened into unsightly and smarting gashes, which we were obliged to anoint with grease. On one occasion, after washing my face within three feet of the fire, my hair was actually clotted with ice before I had time to dry it."

Captain Back further states that " the hunters suffered severely from the intensity of the cold, and compared the sensation of handling their guns to that of touching red-hot iron; and so excessive was the pain that they were obliged to wrap thongs of leather around the triggers to keep their fingers from coming in contact with the steel."

Mr. Rea and myself experienced the same sensation in handling our weapons during the intensely cold weather, as that related by Captain Back. Not only was this confined to metal, but our wooden axe-handles, which had been lying out of doors, seemed to burn us. In touching the trigger of my rifle, the same feeling was experienced. Several times while out hunting, my trigger-finger and those by which I grasped the trigger-guard were badly frosted. In order to prevent such an occurrence again, I constructed a finger on my mitten, wearing another mitten over it, which I pulled off when I fired. We were obliged to keep our hair and whiskers cropped short, as icicles formed on them in great masses, caused from our breath, and steam from the heat of our bodies.

There is a variety of celestial phenomena in the far North. I had often witnessed displays of the aurora in lower latitudes when a boy in my eastern home, and imagined that it made its appearance only during the coldest weather; the more intense the cold, the more brilliant the phenomenon. In the high latitude where we were, it was not at all at the time of lowest temperature that the display was the finest; in fact, during some of the coldest nights, there was not the faintest "streamer" visible.

The most brilliant and wonderfully beautiful visitation of the aurora that it has ever been my fortune to witness, occurred on the evening of the 15th of August, 1897, while floating down Slave, river in my boat, about fifty miles south of its entrance into Great Slave lake. The spectacle was so sublime and awe-inspiring, language fails to properly convey to the reader an idea of its magnificence. It commenced about eleven o'clock at night; the wind blowing freshly from the northeast. I almost fancied that this gorgeous display in the heavens, so glorious in its sublimity, was made for my special vision.

Suddenly, brilliant and many-hued "streamers" began to form in the southwest, gradually expanding in length until they reached the zenith; laterals at the same moment stretched across the whole breadth of the firmament. The great cloud of red glowed with the intensity of incandescent hydrogen. As I gazed on it I could not help comparing it to the traditional pillar of fire recorded in Holy Writ, which guided the children of Israel through the desert. Not only did the color simulate the brilliancy of the glow of the ignited gas above referred to, but there was a constant play running through all the shades of the solar spectrum. The compact form of the phenomenon did not last more than thirty minutes, when it gradually unfolded in graceful festoons, one below the other, at a distance of about two degrees apart, stretching across the whole heavens like the most exquisite drapery, which gathered in a plaiting at the top, drooped into radiating folds at the bottom. These beautifully variegated curtains appeared in three separate pieces: the top of the first was tinged with gray, blending gradually into all the colors known to art; the second increasing in its marvelous play of shading; while the lower one, if possible, exceeded the others in brilliance. They moved rapidly against the wind, passing directly over me as I stood entranced by the glorious spectacle, seemingly so near that I might have touched them. The rapid change of the many colors which marked the folds as they passed over, simulated a rich changeable silk dress of some society queen, as its wearer passes under the most brilliant electrical illumination of the ball-room. For more than an hour the glorious vision floated in the air, in swift motion like the most graceful figures of the serpentine dance.

I frequently witnessed other displays of the aurora during the long winter of 1897-8, but their appearance was marked in its difference from this. They usually appeared like molten fire at the center, then radiated off like a thin cloud extending across the heavens, with flashing points in all directions, which quickly receded to a common center. They were beautiful, it is true; but nothing comparable to the one I have attempted to describe, had ever before or since been seen by me.

Frequently the most brilliant "sun-dogs," or "mock suns," (so-called colloquially, but known as parhelia in scientific parlance,) occurred. I witnessed one of these phenomena on the 4th of December. This was one of the very rare double parhelia — four "mock suns," instead of two. They were so brilliant that it would have been a difficult matter to distinguish the false from the true, did not one know that the mock suns are always on each side of the real.

Referring to the aurora again: It has been asserted by some explorers that there is sometimes a crackling noise accompanying its display, but I have never heard it. I have, however, distinctly heard a crunching sound at the time of its appearance, but I am certain it was caused by ice forming on the lakes; it was so loud that frequently it resembled distant thunder. That it proceeded from the ice, I am satisfied, because I often saw, during the absence of the aurora, great masses of ice, sometimes extending for twenty miles, thrown up in the similitude of the roof of a house, ranging in height from five to seven feet; and the accompanying noise was like that heard at the time of an auroral display.

CHAPTER XXVII
INDIANS AND ESKIMOS OF THE FAR NORTH.
GREATLY DIFFERENT FROM THE INDIANS OF THE UNITED STATES — MODE OF LIVING IN THE LAND OF DARKNESS
THE WOMEN ARE SLAVES — THESE INDIANS NEVER EAT FRUIT, VEGETABLES, OR BREAD — MEAT AND FISH THEIR ONLY DIET — THE MARRIAGE RELATION — NUMBER OF TRIBES IN THE FAR NORTH, AND THEIR LOCATIONS — THEIR HABITS AND DWELLINGS — DEGREE OF INTELLIGENCE — ENORMOUSLY SUPERSTITIOUS — THEIR TRADITIONAL HISTORY OF THE FLOOD SKILL IN FORETELLING
STORMS — NO DISEASE AMONG THEM UNTIL THE WHITE MAN CAME — THE "HAPPIEST PEOPLE ON EARTH "—EDUCATION RUINS ALL THAT TRY IT.

TH^RE is the widest variance in the characteristics, both mental and physical, of the northern Indians from those of their race on the great Southern Plains. The former, like the inhabitants of Siberia, are exiles, having been driven by force into the desolate region they now occupy. The northern tribes are lacking in that defiant and warlike spirit which prevails among their southern kinsman. They are neither naturally vicious, delighting in bloodshed and brave in battle, nor imbued with that pride and independence which is such a marked trait among the savages of the interior of the continent. They are the most consummate beggars, elevating it to an art, as sympathetic' as that

(423)

which characterizes the methods of the professional mendicants of the advanced civilization of our great cities. They are ever humble in the presence of the dominant white race, never attempting to arrogate to themselves that spirit of superiority always assumed by the Sioux, Cheyennes, Kiowas, or Comanches.

They are always asking for food from the whites with whom they come in contact, no matter how much they may have stored in the shape of provisions. They commence to beg, the moment the ceremony of shaking hands is gone through with, which is invariably accompanied by the assertion: "Dennie, bur hula" ("Indian, meat none "). If they have reason to believe you have tobacco or tea, which they inordinately crave, they always declare they have none. Giving to them does not by any means end with the act: you are sure to be visited by the whole of the tribe who may happen to be in the neighborhood of your camp, and these are more persistent in their claim for alms than were the original callers.

They possess, however, some commendable traits, which could be emulated at times by the dominant white race to its advantage. They will divide their last morsel of food with each other, and none are allowed to go hungry so long as there is a bite left in the village. I have seen them so fearfully in want of something to eat that they would watch for a dog to scratch up a bit he had buried for future use, and choke him until he dropped it on the ground, when they would divide it among those who stood about them. If one Indian has anything, they all have, which proves that they are as free from selfishness as they are from cleanliness.

They do not live in houses, but in teepees, made of tanned hides of reindeer. These hides are usually perforated, the holes being about the size of a large lead-pencil, made by a grub that hatches from eggs deposited just under the skin on the living animal b\'7d" a fly, as is sometimes the case with our domestic cattle. These holes

in the covering of their lodges provide excellent ventilation,— which, however, is not at all necessary in that cold country. Their fire is built in the center of the teepee, the. same as in the lodge of a southern Indian, but they do not appear to have a proper idea of a draft as do the latter, by an apparatus affixed to the top; the northern Indians effecting it by raising the lower ends of the skins forming the walls of their houses. Their seats are boughs of trees, or the natural floor of earth; but they sometimes use reindeer-skin mats.

The mode of reclining, on the part of the men, is to double up their legs like a tailor on his bench; while the women throw theirs back, as did the Romans while eating. None of the inhabitants of a lodge stand up for any length of time; as the smoke which rolls above in clouds about four feet from the floor would asphixiate them. As & means of entrance and exit from the teepee, a hole is made at one side, and covered with a large deerskin, at the bottom of which a stick is sewed to hold it in position ; its top merely fastened by a hide string from the wall of the teepee above the opening. In these rude lodges they dwell, even when the thermometer ranges from sixty to seventy degrees below zero.

Those who have been successful in hunting and are possessed of a sufficient amount of furs, clothe themselves similar to white people, often traveling many hundreds of miles to trade their furs to the white men for such goods as they bring into the country. In winter they wear capotes, or frock coats made of the skin of the reindeer with the hair on, having a hood attached to cover the head, all in one piece. The children under eight years old have long sleeves, which are sewed up at the ends so they cannot get their hands wet and freeze them during the long marches they are sometimes compelled to make in moving from one place to another. The poorer classes, however, have to content themselves with the same rude fiarb of skins in the summer which they wore in the win-

ter; but by that time, the hair having been completely rubbed off, the garment is a trifle cooler.

It is a common thing for the people to take down their lodges in the dead of winter and march one or two hundred miles to where the deer are more plentiful.

The women are virtually slaves. They do all the work, as well as drive the dog teams; while their lords do nothing but pretend to look for game. When the village is moved, the men are promptly on hand the moment the women have erected the lodges and a brisk fire is burning inside.

The children are carried, wrapped in furs, on the backs of their mothers, until they are three or four j^ears of age. Often I have seen them as large as some of our American school children, being carried in such fashion. They sometimes make life hideous, as they resist being loaded and carried in such a cramped position; and kick their mother until allowed to nurse at her breast. They are so unruly, the mothers are often compelled to crawl over slippery ice on their hands and knees, for fear of losing their balance from the struggling of the children, in their fits of anger. They reminded me of a large pig which I once endeavored to carry on horseback.

These Indians seldom, if ever, get a taste of bread, fruit, or vegetables, and when they do, regard them as the greatest luxury. A simple biscuit is a rare treat for them.

In religion they are generally claimed by the Catholics, but some have been taught the Protestant faith. I am inclined to think, however, that they have but a limited idea of holy things, save what has been impressed upon them by the traditions of the tribe,— that after death, for good Indians, there is a "Great Spirit" and a "happy hunting-ground." Many of them may be seen to cross themselves and mutter some "pater" or "ave" on a Sabbath morning, after which the men take their guns and go hunting, or occupy the remainder of the day

in their usual routine of idleness. Many of them pay an , annual visit to the Catholic priest stationed at some Hudson Bay Company's post, to have their record of wickedness for the past year wiped out. They marry and are given in marriage, but are never divorced, and as far as I can learn are considered virtuous; but this applies only to those who have remained in their primitiveness and remote from civilization. There are many widows and orphans among the tribes. The widows never marry again, and it is the duty of their relations to take care of them; but I noticed they were compelled to perform most of the menial work required.

These people seldom wash themselves, and are therefore exceedingly filthy, greasy, and swarming with vermin. They are very deceitful, and never pay a debt if they can by any means avoid it. They are very cunning in their transactions with the whites, and unless one is familiar with their methods, he is certain to be outwitted in any compact entered into with them.

A half-dozen or more tribes occupy the frozen region beyond the Athabaska lake, as follows: The Chippeway-ans, who range as far north as Great Slave lake; the Slave tribe, located along the western shore of that sheet of water and the Slave river; the Yellow Knife tribe has possession of the east end of the lake, and they range as far in that direction as the river Doobaunt, and northward to the Clinton Golden lake. The Dog-rib tribe roam at will over the country east of the Mackenzie river, and between the Great Slave and Great Bear lakes. All hunt the musk-ox east and west of Clinton Golden lake, while some have ventured as far north as the Great Fish river. All the tribes fear the Eskimos, and always avoid them if possible,— especially during the summer, when the Eskimos come farther south than at any other season of the year. In winter the Indians roam everywhere at will. All understand the Slave tribe language, and converse in it whenever people of different tribes meet.

Strange as it may appear, these Indians have no chiefs among them, but there are always to be found men of superior ability to the masses, who are looked up to for counsel. The Dog-rib tribe has a pretended chief, but his power is so limited he has little claim to the title.

The bark of the birch tree is quite an important article in their domestic economy. Buckets are made from it, in which to carry water, the seams and knot-holes being sealed up with gum from spruce trees; and their beautiful canoes and many other articles are constructed from the same light material.

Their habits in eating are most disgusting. The meat and fish, their only food, are usually boiled, in which pro-<;e8s they use sheet-iron pots. The flesh is allowed to cook until the blood no longer runs from it; it is then emptied on a tin or birch-bark plate, when each individual seizes a large piece with the left hand, placing one corner of it between the teeth, and mouthful after mouthful is cut off with a huge butcher-knife until he is gorged. This is the customary manner of eating which all Indians, whether northern or southern, with whom I have come in contact, employ. They are capable of consuming twice as much meat and drinking three times as much tea ^ as a white man, at a single sitting. Some writers claim the Indian has no particular time for eating: this is a mistake, as they do have a time, and that time is «// the time, so long as they have anything to eat. Both men and women are inveterate smokers, after once having learned the habit, providing tobacco can bo had. They often use willow bark (" kinnikinuick "), when tobacco is not obtainable.

The principal weapon of these Indians is a small 28-cal-iber shotgun, using a ball for large game; a few possess

^ Coffee Is unknown to the Indians of the far North, but they all know what tea is, and drink great quantities of it when they can get it. I often gave them a cup of coffee, and they almost invariably would say, "Nazzula" (no good). On inquiry at the Uudson Bay Company's posts on my return home, I was Informed the company never sent coffee to that country, but always send abundance of tea, as It is light, and more easily transported.

small 44-caliber Winchester rifles. When meat cannot readily be procured, they resort to the lakes and set nets for fish. In winter they are frequently compelled to cut holes in the ice (which is often four to seven feet thick), in ordef to permit the introduction of a net into the water below. They also catch an immense number of trout during the winter with a simple hook and line, baited with morsels of whitefish.

In summer the male reindeer becomes very fat. The Indians lie in wait at the accustomed crossing-places of that animal, at the rivers and lakes, where from their birch-bark canoes they spear them in great numbers. The redskins regard this as right royal sport, while in reality it is most barbarous, simply showing the innate savage instinct. A true hunter would scorn any such brutal method. In accordance with a superstitious tradition of the tribe, their first act after killing a deer — or any other animal, in fact — is to split open the breast. If a bird is shot, a handful of feathers is plucked from the same part of its anatomy, and tossed into the air. I could never clearly divine the reason for this, but believe it to be for " good luck."

Among the Yellow Knife tribe I met one aged squaw who must have been over a hundred years old. Her figure was bent half-way to the ground, and she always lagged for hours behind the rest of her people, when on the march. Some day, not very remote in the future, she will fail to reach camp, and perish miserably by the wayside.

Some of the men are able to write so as to be understood by other Indians, but their chirography is merely a system of pictographs or hieroglyphics which an ordinary white man cannot decipher.

They are rather epicurean in their tastes, viewed from a savage standpoint. Their most luxurious dishes are the heads of birds, beasts and fishes, and the unborn young of animals. The women and children are rarely

permitted to indulge in these savory morsels, the men reserving them for themselves.

I often invited them to partake of dishes served at our table, consisting of vegetables, canned fruits, puddings, etc., which they would eat, of course; but it was very evident they did not like them, for when I would ask them what they thought of these varieties of food, they would flatly say, " Nazzula " (no good), and ask for grease with which to complete their meal.

It is not astonishing that the appetite for fatty substances is so great in the remote North, for, as is well known, the human body is but a furnace, whose heat must be kept up, and requires that food which contains the greatest amount of carbon.

It makes little difference to the natives whether what they consume is half dirt and sand, or not, and meat turned partially green is seized with avidity.

The superstitions of the Northern Indians are as firmly rooted in their nature as are the giant redwood trees of California to Mother Earth. It would be useless to try to teach them otherwise in one short year, so I never attempted it. If the children were isolated from their parents, these traditional ideas would soon be eliminated from their susceptible minds. I have seen parents gather a group of their little ones and half-grown Indians around them, and for hours at a time relate stories concerning the origin of the different animals; that they were compelled to eat several kinds of food; and the extent to which man was permitted to kill the various beasts and birds of their country. They have been taught by tradition many things which in a measure corroborate history, both sacred and profane; yet the details are in wide variance from those of our own language and belief.

One lovely day in May I heard an old Indian, La Pierre, who was considered the head of the Yellow Knife tribe, teaching a group of children, who were seated on a beautiful carpet of moss. He was narrating to them a story, similar to that of the flood, yet vastly different in characters and circumstances. As near as I could understand, the story ran something like this:

Many, many years ago, the birds and beasts were fighting for supremacy. They fought great battles, and the beasts were always victorious. Finally the birds had a big talk among themselves, and agreed to adopt a new method of warfare. The eagle and the crane were sent to intercede with the Great Spirit, and implore him to withhold the rain until vegetation was all dead, and thus starve the beasts into subjection. They made the ascent by continually circling upward, for one moon. From that time on, the rain did not fall until all the vegetation had died, and the animals were without food. They too would have died of thirst, had not the Great Bad Spirit caught a beaver, and, laying its tail on a flat rock, took another rock and pounded it until it was flat. And from that time until this, the beaver's tail has retained that shape.

The Great Bad Spirit told him to make a dam, from sticks and stones, and to use his tail as a trowel and plaster it with mud. This he did, and thus a reservoir was formed that furnished water for the beasts. But the animals could not live on water alone, and many died of hunger. The fish were all dead excepting those in the reservoir, and the animals would not let the fish-eating birds come near it. At last things became desperate, and the loon rebelled, and cried mightily for rain. The Great Good Spirit bent his ear to listen. Then came the rain in torrents. It was in the spring of the year. The ice on the reservoir had melted from the shores, and as the rain came down, the water washed from the hills, great stones upon the ice. As soon as the beasts saw that a great flood had come, some of all kinds congregated on the ice, and thus floated without seeing land, for two moons. The rocks were so wet that moss grew on those that had lodged on the ice, and the animals ate it and lived. Finally the raven left the ice for one whole day, and came back with a piece of reindeer meat in his mouth. Then the animals knew that the flood had nearly subsided. Finally the ice, on which the beasts and birds had lived together with all differences forgotten, lodged against the rocks, on which there was only moss, and from that time to this, that land has been a barren waste, with only moss as vegetation. While the animals and birds were upon the ice, the musk-ox was chosen king of all, and where it goes, all the other animals are in duty bound to follow for protection'. The musk-ox understands all animals, also the Indians, who must always address that animal if they are compelled to kill one for food, as it can intercede with the Great Spirit for or against them. Therefore the little Indians ("yahzas," as they are called) are taught to reverence the musk-oxen, and to speak gently to them. That when an Indian observes this rule, no harm will ever visit him or his children.

He told them that the loon's cry was a sure prediction of rain, and when it was heard they must put up the " napola " (tent), as the rain was at hand; and when the eagles and cranes soared high, dry weather would certainly ensue.

Those little savages listened with awe, their eyes wide-open in wonder, and they stood like statues as the old patriarch related his marvelous story, much as do our own children, cast in a more refined mold, when listening to the nursery tales of Cinderella, Jack the Giant-Killer, or Aladdin.

I regret that I did not record more of the details. As silly as the recitals were, underneath all there may be much that would do for comparative philology what the folk-lore of other barbarous peoples has, and in the far North there is a field in this particular worthy of investigation by the philologist. Could I have understood all the details of their narrations at various times, I could fill a volume of most interesting folk-lore.

It is wonderful how accurately the Northern Indians are able to foretell the weather by the actions of birds and beasts. They would tell us what the weather would be, some two or three days in advance, and I never knew them to fail in their predictions. The loon's cry, we found, was a sure barometer, when rain was to be ex--pected. Dry weather is indicated by the flight of cranes and eagles, when they soar high, in circles. Before a storm, in winter or summer, the reindeer are continually on the move in the valleys, but in dry weather they are seen resting contentedly on the hillsides.

I met many Eskimos during my journey in the North. They are a very short, heavy-set race, with flat noses and high cheek-bones. They resemble the Chinese in many particulars: in size, color, appearance of the eyes, and other racial features. They very rarely see a white man, therefore such as never mingled with the palefaces have never learned what whisky and tobacco are. They are acquainted with but few of the deceits practiced by those Indians who have been associated with the whites. They are the very impersonation of robust health, never having been contaminated by those diseases common among the Indians who have come in contact with unscrupulous white men.

The mortality among the tribes seems to be evenly balanced by the births; so there is no increase, or it is at least scarcely appreciable for a long period. The general health of the tribes, notwithstanding the filthy habits of individuals, is excellent. Until recently there were no contagious diseases, and were it not for their insufficient shelter, lack of proper clothing, and scarcity of food, they would probably increase in a ratio comparable to other peoples. Since the great inrush to the gold-fields of Alaska, the grip, measles, whooj)ing-cough and mumps have been carried there, and no doubt will spread throughout that whole Northern country; and owing to their lack of medicines, comfortable shelter, and cloth-— 28

ing, many will be carried off by these diseases in that fitful climate.

Heretofore they have never been troubled with disease, and their lot has certainly been a happy one, excepting when out of food,—for to them, "where ignorance i» bliss, 'tis folly to be wise." They are as simple as were Adam and Eve in the Garden before touching the forbidden fruit. It is a falsely directed sympathy that suggests the sending of missionaries among them. While the advocates of such measures are entirely honest in their intentions, yet in their ignorance of the real status of those remote Northern people, they do not realize that such action would only bring misery and trouble where absolute happiness reigns supreme.

Let them alone 1 Do not disturb them in their innocence. They are infinitely happier than the Indians in some other portions of the far North, where they have been broken up into different grades of civilization by missionary schools. It is almost universally the case that the partially educated Indians there have come to be lazy, good-for-nothing, starving beggars; while the girls are of the same disposition, and almost invariably become prostitutes. There is no opportunity for them to obtain a subsistence, excepting they join their tribe again, which they never do. They appear to be too good or too tender to associate with their kindred. They neither hunt nor fish for a living, but lie around the posts, starving themselves and their families. An Indian or Eskimo who has never been spoiled by missionary educators, is a thousand times better off than those who have been petted and taught some of the white man's cunning ways.

I do not write this from any prejudice toward any sect or church, as I always encourage missionary work with my dimes and dollars. But I would say to all lovers of Christianity, invest your money and exercise your talents in some other direction ; and let all the Indians and Eskimos that governments are not ready to entirely support,

go their way in peace,— excepting those tribes that are able to at least help sustain themselves in a country susceptible to agriculture. If Indians and Eskimos have existed, as we certainly know they have, from a period which antedates the white man's advent into North America, they can and surely will, if let alone, take care of themselves in the future as in the past. When the last of the reindeer and musk-oxen have passed out of existence, and the fish have disappeared from the lakes and oceans; when the whale, walrus and seal are no more, and the governments gather in the waifs to feed and clothe them, or they have been deported to a more sunny clime to follow civilized pursuits, then and not before, will it be time to school and preach to these far-away happy souls.

To be sure, there are times when starvation stares the Indians and Eskimos in the face, and then they are of all men most miserable. At such times missionaries and education are to them of no avail. To ameliorate the condition of these poor creatures, I would suggest to those who desire to help them, send them good guns and ammunition. If they were thus provided and equipped, such occurrences as we witnessed in November, 1897, and the condition described by Capt. Back, would seldom be known.

Capt. Back, whose admirable journal I have referred to above, says, in writing of the miserable condition of the inhabitants of the region after their eatables had become exhausted:

"As the winter advanced, bands of starving Indians continued to arrive, in the hope of obtaining some relief, as little or nothing was to be procured by hunting. They would stand around while the men were taking their meals, watching every mouthful with the most longing, imploring look, but yet never uttering a complaint.

"At other times they would, seated around the fire.

occupy themselves in roasting and devouring small bits of their reindeer garments, which, even when entire, afforded them a very insufficient protection against a temperature of 102° below freezing-point,

" Famine, with her gaunt and bony arm, pursued them at every turn, withered their energies, and strewed them lifeless on the cold bosom of the snow. Often I did share my own plate with the children, whose helpless fate and piteous cries were peculiarly distressing. Compassion for the full-grown rnay or may not be felt, but that heart must be cased in steel which is insensible to the cry of a child for food."

I have interpolated thus much of Capt. Back's report, to confirm my own statements. Our experience among them was the same as his in every particular, excepting that anything he asked from the Indians was cheerfully granted if possible; while to us it was denied in almost every instance, and we were opposed at all points by their hostility to our mission. Capt. Back doubtless suppressed, as I have, a great deal that would be too revolting and shock the sensibilities of a refined civilization. The facts, however, prove that history repeats itself, as well among the savages as in the most enlightened race, and that the unerring law of heredity is as strongly marked in the one as in the other.

CHAPTER XXVIII

HOMEWARD BOUND

CAUGHT IN A 8T0BM ON THE GREAT INLAND 8EA EUDDER

BREAKS AND WAVES ROLL OVER THEIR SMALL CRAFT — AN ACCOMPANYING BOAT IS CAPSIZED AND DASHED UPON THE ROCKS — ON THE GREAT MACKENZIE RIVER — FORT PROVIDENCE — CATHOLIC PRIEST WHO NEEDS ATTENTION

VISIT TO FORT FRANKLIN ON THE GREAT BEAR LAKE

— A DESOLATE SPECTACLE — PICTURE OF SIR JOHN FRANK-LIN'b old cabin — HURLED THROUGH THE RAMPARTS — CROSS THE ARCTIC CIRCLE — PHOTOGRAPH OF THE CHURCH AT FORT GOOD HOPE — A SAIL ON THE ARCTIC OCEAN — UP reel's river to rat river, WHERE HUNDREDS WERE CAUGHT IN A HUMAN DEADFALL — MOUNTAINS CUT THEM OFF FROM THE GOLDEN EL DORADO — NEW ROUTE ACROSS THE DIVIDE — SHOOTING DOWN THE CASCADES ON THE WATERS OF THE PACIFIC — BOAT SMASHED ON A

ROCK — LONG JOURNEY DOWN THE PORCUPINE RIVER

JOURNEY TO ST. MICHAEL's — EQUINOCTIAL STORM ON BERING SEA — SEATTLE REACHED — GRAND RECEPTION — EVERYBODY SANG, " MY COUNTRY, 'tI8 OF THEE " AND "home, SWEET HOME."

ON Sunday evening, July 17th, the sun was far around to the northwest; the wind changed from north to northeast, blowing a stiff breeze, yet not too hard for expert sailors with good boats to make a safe voyage across the Great Slave lake. Three fine boats with good seamen, which arrived the previous

(437)

evening, hove off shore and darted to the southwest in the direction of the great Mackenzie river.

Our little yacht or skiff was quickly loaded and pushed from its moorings. Mr. Rea seated himself on the pilot-box and I unfurled the broad sail. The boat nobly responded to the stiff wind, and shot into the "great inland sea."

A mighty shout of three cheers from those on shore, appeared to rend the skies. I waved my hat in response and Mr. Rea threw up one hand,— all he could do, the other being engaged at the rudder. We were now off for our far-away homes, by way of that El Dorado of so many anxious hearts. When the orchestra started up a very appropriate refrain, "There's a land that is fairer than day," etc., it appeared to carry my soul beyond that dreary, desolate region, and to my native land once more. I stood swaying from side to side, holding to the mainmast with my left hand and beating the time with my right arm, so those on shore might know we distinctly caught every vibration of the melodious cornet. When they had finished, another boat hove off, and endeavored to follow us. It was one of the best boats in the harbor, and the occupants made up their minds they could cross the mighty billows and stem any storm that might occur. We were now under good headway, our boat plowing the rolling waves. Then, softly were the notes wafted toward us of that most pathetic of songs, " God be with you till we meet again." We were too far away for me to beat time, but I waved my hat in harmony with the touching melody. When the tune ended, I sank on the cargo, a tear rolling down my cheek for the first time since my absence from the loved ones at home.

The boat which followed us carried four persons — a Mr. and Mrs. Hoffman, A. J. Hoffmeier, and a man from British Columbia. They were particularly anxious to accompany us on the most hazardous portion of the lake, as Mr. Rea had previously crossed, and was familiar with

all harbors and places of safety. We gained steadily on them, yet they kept in plain view, and we headed for a small island five miles away. When we reached it the wind was still blowing favorably, and we glided to the left, heading for another island seven miles beyond. We had scarcely made a quarter of the way, when the wind suddenly veered to the north and a brisk gale sprang up from off the sea. It increased in velocity and severity every minute; the great billows became mountains; their white-caps, breaking, sent their spray in showers over us. The large scow kept right on, when it should have turned back at the small island. We had passed so far beyond the island that it would have been impossible for us to return. We must reach the one ahead or drift to the southern shore of the lake, to be cast upon its rock-bound coast or go to the bottom in the open sea. Mr. Rea was no longer able to guide our boat by pulling the ropes which held the rudder in its place, and was obliged to grasp the cross-piece on the top in order to guide the bark over the heavy swells. When two-thirds of the way across, a huge wave struck us, and Mr. Rea shouted, " Jones, the rudder's broken ! " This was a startling declaration. It meant drift ashore, there perhaps to be dashed to pieces, or sink,— with ten chances to one in favor of the latter. At this awful moment there came vividly to my mind the sweet strains we had just heard, "God be with you till we meet again;" but it was no time for sentiment 1 I grasped an oar, hoping to be able to keep our helpless craft out of the trough of the terrible sea, or at least float-ting. Mr. Rea threw himself far over the stern, and with his right arm thrust down into the water discovered the rudder had been split off, but a strip of wood nailed along its bottom was still holding it together. He grasped the upper portion of it with his strong blacksmith's arm acting as a vise, and held it firm while with his left hand he guided the boat in the direction of the island. Every minute while we were in this critical condition, seemed

an hour 1 The sun was already sinking below the horizon; the wind was increasing at a fearful rate, and I hardly dared look up, as the boat was shipping water at an alarming rate. I occasionally, however, glanced quickly at the sail behind, for I felt alarmed concerning its safety, as well as for our own. I continued to encourage Mr. Rea, who would shake his head in order to clear off the water so as to catch his breath before another wave rolled over him. I told him to hold on, as it was only a short distance to land. "Two miles! one mile morel half a mile! we're almost there! a few more rods!" Thank God, we were safe at last.

Anxious for the lives of the inmates of the boat behind, I looked earnestly for its broad sail, but could discover only a small portion of it, about two miles in the rear. I looked again and it was gone I Then I exclaimed to Mr. Rea, "My God! what has happened? Have they given up the island, and are they out on the lake at the mercy of this angry gale? "

The island where we had landed was long and narrow, in consequence of which the wind swept down each side the whole length, and made the harbor a poor one. Our landing was exceedingly hazardous. The boat repeatedly dashed against the rocks, but we soon tossed out the freight and dragged our bark ashore. In my anxiety I took my field-glass and swept the lake for some sign of the boat in which were our friends, but could see nothing but an angry sea. If it had been within the limits of possibility to assist them, we would have done so, even at the risk of our lives, but unhappily all we could do was to watch for some indication of the ill-fated boat. The wild waves and clouds of spray were all that appeared to our vision.^

' After returning to civilization I received a letter from parties at Fort Beeolutlon informing me that the boat was capsized and Mr. Hoffman lost, while the other two men and Mrs. Hoffman managed to cling to it until they drifted twenty miles on the southern shore of the lake, where it hung up for three days and nights on the rocks, during which time they were entirely without food or shelter. And just before going

PROTESTANT MISSION ON GREAT SLAVE LAKE.

CATHOLIC PRIEST OF THE FAR NORTH.

Oh, how deeply we regretted that our own boat was disabled, as, if its rudder had not been broken, we would have started at once and attempted the rescue of the unfortunate people.

The 18th of July was a blustery day. The morning was devoted to mending the rudder of our boat and drying the cargo of the skiff, which had received such a drenching the previous day. At noon we set sail for another island, five miles distant. We continued on until a fine harbor was reached, at a point where we first touched the mainland. Resting there that night, we started early the next morning, using our oars until about noon, when a favorable wind sprang up, which sent us rapidly across large bays and along the shore. About sundown the wind changed again to the north, pressing us hard toward the land. We made fifty miles that day, and were contented with our progress. We did not dare go ashore, for the coast was very dangerous, and there were only three harbors between the islands and Hay river. Woe to the craft that might collide with any of the treacherous rocks that form the coast, so desolate in its aspect.

We were compelled to beat against the wind until within five miles of Hay river, then turned into Sand creek, one of the harbors previously mentioned; an excellent anchorage in a drifting storm, but the channel is very difficult to follow, on account of the numerous sandbars.

The next morning we rowed into Hay river, where is located the Protestant mission, conducted by Rev. Mr. Marsh, who was one of the best men I met during my long sojourn in the North. He is a hard worker, and his wife and sister assist him, as does also a Miss Tims. There is quite a flourishing school here, composed of the

to press I received a letter from Mr. HoSmeler, dated at Sandon, B. C, corroborating the foregolDK facts. His first words In the letter were, "Dank Gott, I am live jet." Mr. Hoffmeier Is an intelligent Oerman, who has not yet mastered the English Inn-goage, bat his declaration vividly expresses all our feelings after that awful night.

Indian children of the neighborhood. They were fairly well dressed; were clean and neat in their appearance, which is a rarity among the Indians of this country. But their final destiny, I fear, will be deplorable. We were invited to partake of a second repast, and sat down to an excellent meal, which we indeed appreciated.

We informed Mr. Marsh of the mysterious disappearance of the boat and its crew, that had attempted to follow us, upon which he promised to go to Fort Resolution and make inquiry in relation to them.

In about an hour after our arrival, a favorable breeze sprang up, and we were again off for the Mackenzie river, forty miles distant, reaching its mouth at sunset, and there anchored for the night.

The following day was calm and relatively warm. By hard rowing, and a slight current of water assisting, we managed to pass through forty miles of what might be termed a very wide stream, or a narrow lake, which forms the mouth of the river. At six o'clock we entered the river proper; found the current very swift, averaging six miles an hour.

Soon we came in sight of the Hudson Bay Company's post. Fort Providence, where we remained that night. Here the Catholics have established a large mission, presided over by Father LaCore. There are four or five nuns connected with this establishment, and as many "Brothers." These monks are celibates, of course, living for the good of the church alone; they are, when under the control of harsh authority, mere slaves, but if the reverse is the case, live a comparatively happy life. The nuns and brothers at the mission labor six days in the week without ceasing, excepting the time they pass in sleeping, which is precious little. They live on fish almost exclusively, but sometimes are allowed potatoes, when they can be raised there. The priests at these Catholic missions fare much better: they have bread and butter, and in fact many of the luxuries to be found in the Edmonton markets,— even canned fruit. It is rumored that Father LaCore is not an exception to this rule, living sumptuously every day. He sits at the head of his table with rich food about him, the brothers and sisters eating at the same board; but their fare is limited to fish. All the food is blessed, preparatory to eating, by the good (?) father, and is very healthful, I have no doubt.

Fifteen or twenty men en route for Alaska were icebound near Fort Providence, and were compelled to pass the winter of 1897-8 there. Toward spring the scurvy made its appearance among them, and those who were very sick when the ice broke up could not continue their journey, while those who were not in so sad a plight were compelled to go on, or remain and perish from the same scourge. Father LaCore was applied to to take care of the sick until they recovered, or at least were able to travel. They were without money, but had plenty of provisions, which they offered in payment for the care of their comrades. The good father replied, "No! I will not take them unless you pay me, in advance, thirty dollars in cash for each man." They offered him beans, flour, bacon, and other staple goods. But no — he must have the cash 1

Such Christianity is a mockery, and I felt like taking a vow that no more of my dimes should find their way into the mission-box. Upon inquiry, however, I learned that this was an exceptional case, and that at Forts Simpson, Norman, Good Hope, McPherson, and Yukon, a different state of affairs existed, and many acts of kindness were shown to weary travelers during their sickness while at those posts during the same winter and the following spring. I met several of the fathers and missionaries of both the English and Catholic churches, who were ever willing to administer to the needs of those who required assistance. At Fort Norman, particularly, Fatlier Guoy frequently incommoded himself in order to help the

needy and those who were suffering, and everybody that knows him speaks in his praise.

I think that the head of the Catholic Church should investigate two or three of their remote missions, and replace them upon the foundation originally intended.

The next morning we left for Fort Simpson, arriving there in three days, where we found a vast number of gold-seekers with all kinds of boats, waiting for the Liard (Lear) river to go down, so they could ascend to its source, high up in the mountains, by water, and cross the divide to Alaska. I learned afterwards from the Indians that they were simply wasting their time, as the Devil's Canon, through which the river runs, is entirely inaccessible to a boat large enough to carry sufl5cient provisions to last them to their destination. Their lot will certainly be a deplorable one.

The wind blowing strongly in our favor, we tarried less than half an hour, then shot down the boisterous water with frightful rapidity.

At midnight it became foggy and dark; our boat collided with a huge log, which almost wrecked us, and we were compelled to go ashore and repair damages.

After passing Fort Rigley, where we made a very short stop, we soon reached Fort Norman. At this point the Bear river intersects the Mackenzie, and drains the Great Bear lake. The wind was blowing strongly from the southwest, which impeded our progress materially. All along the bluffs above the post, great ledges of coal crop out. Many of them had been set on fire, and no doubt have been burning for years.

Here we seized an opportunity to exchange our boat for a Peterborough canoe, which had been brought from that town in Canada by miners, and they disposed of it, little knowing its real value. It was only twenty feet long and four feet in width, made of bass (the lightest wood known), And weighed but one hundred and fifty-six pounds

when dry. It was a perfect Godsend to us, as it was exactly what we needed to ascend the rapids and cascades of Rat river, and to carry over the portage to the waters of the Pacific slope.

As the wind continued to blow fiercely from the southwest, we determined to set our sail to the northeast, up Bear river, and visit the ruins of Fort Franklin on the northwest shore of Great Bear lake. By rapidly sailing in our new canoe up the river, occasionally "tracking,"^ we made excellent time, reaching the lake the next evening. The wind subsided about midnight, when, after rounding a prominent point, we soon anchored under the shelter of the bluffs on which stood the old fort.

After anchoring our boat to a large rock, we ascended to the place so fraught with the impressions of a sad and historical past, that I could hardly realize where I stood. After a cup of tea we spread our blankets, but could not sleep, for the dashing of the mournful waves, the harsh chattering of the waterfowls, coupled with the memory of ■the horrible fate of the gallant Franklin and his brave followers, the story of which I had read in my childhood days, all combined to make this a solemn hour. As my thoughts recurred to that dreadful past, over half a century ago, the place seemed to be rehabilitated with the actors who once made it famous. The wild scream of loons could be heard in all directions; the coarse croak of the ravens, as they perched on the dead scraggy trees, scattered on that rock-bound coast, appeared to signify they had battened on the bones of the dead heroes and were waiting for more.

Everything appeared to intensify the halo of solemnity that surrounded that almost sacred spot, and I imagined

^ " Traisking." It Is very common for fur companies In the far North to transport goods a thousand miles up the rivers iu boats propelled by Indians, who walk on the shore, holding to one end of a long line, the other being attached to the boat, which is guided by a steersman, who stands in the bow with a long sweep. This method nf nayigation is called "tracking."

the lamentations of Lady Franklin could still be heard, saying:
"Canst thou not tell me, Polar Star,
Where in the frosty waste he kneels And on the icy plains afar
His love to God and me reveals? Wilt thou not send one brighter ray To my lone heart and aching eye? Wilt thou not turn my night to day, And wake my spirit ere I die?
"Tell me, O frozen North, for now
My heart is like thine ai-ctic zone; Beneath the darkened skies I bow.
Or ride the stormy seas alone. Tell me of my beloVed, for I know not
One ray my lord witliout; Oh, tell me, that I may not die
A sorrower on the'sea of doubt."
How it could be possible for Sir John Franklin and one hundred and thirty-seven heroes to perish in that northern region, is to me a mystery. I feel confident that if stranded on the Arctic shores, with a good Winchester rifle, plenty of ammunition and a pair of blankets, I would never tarry until reaching the most delightful clime in the world, which lies, in my best judgment, between the thirty-sixth and fortieth degrees of latitude.

There stood the identical cabin, erected so many decades ago, by the heroic explorer and his gallant crew, now in ruins, a monument of the daring spirits who had ventured so far to advance the interests of science. The logs of which the cabin was constructed were badly decayed, only its ghost remaining, figuratively. The door was gone, and the earth washed from the few remaining poles that formed the roof. A table still stood in one end of the r- lom, but it was slowly decaying under the influence of the continually warring elements. The stone chimney was as solid as when first built. There were evidently two apartments in the building, one larger than

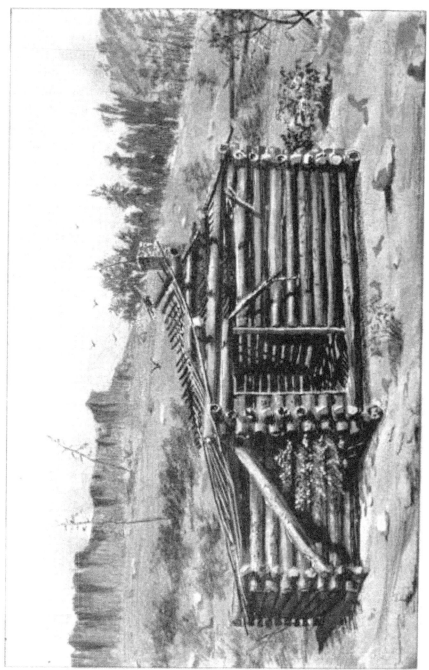

the other, with a connecting door. The smaller, doubtless, was used for storing goods, perhaps occupied for sleeping also.

Apparently there had originally been several buildings of less size than the one under discussion, constructed by Franklin's party or others, but they appeared to have been destroyed by fire,— probably the act of Indians.

Timber is very scarce on this bleak, rocky coast, and for what reason Sir John Franklin selected such a spot in which to pass the winter, I cannot imagine. By simply going down Bear river a day's journey, he would have found a country well wooded and much better sheltered from the terrible storms which prevail during that portion of the year. Perhaps his choice was made from the fact that immense herds of reindeer and musk-oxen, upon which he depended for food, made the contiguous region a favorite grazing-ground.

As tired and fatigued as we were, no sleep came to our ■eyes, and after resting a few hours at this enchanting spot, hallowed by so many cherished memories, we regretfully (yet apparently something irresistible impelled us on) tacked back to the mouth of the river, and were soon upon its broad bosom again. The tempestuous gale of the previous day having completely exhausted itself, we were hurriedly floated down to Fort Norman by the swift current. We stopped only long enough to procure a few fresh herring, the first place at which they could be obtained while going down the Mackenzie; and as we had never tasted them before, thought them delicious. The Mackenzie river is the widest stream I ever saw. Below its intersection with the Liard it averages fully two miles, while near its mouth no one knows how wide it is, as it has never been measured. It flows at the rate of two miles an hour, excepting when at a high stage, when it is increased to three miles an hour.

Before reaching the " ramparts," ^ so called, into which we were hurled with a force that was terrific in its impetuosity, the roar of the water over the loose bowlders could be heard for ten miles, before our arrival. Here the river is reduced to a half-mile in width, and its narrowness compared to its breadth above is conspicuous. Perpendicular walls of solid granite on each side, rising from three to five hundred feet high, constitute the gorge, of which I took a snap-shot with my kodak as our boat dashed through. The scenery is sublime.

RAMPARTS OF THE MACKENZIE RIVER

As we emerged from the ramparts, which are ten miles long, we caught our first glimpse of Fort Good Hope,

1 These ramparts are formed by a narrow gorge in the rocks, through which the whole volume of the river Is forced, as at the Dalles of the Columbia and those of St. Orolz.

FORT GOOD HOPE

449

which is at the edge of the Arctic Circle. We soon arrived at this prominent geographical locality, where I was surprised to find a garden planted with potatoes and other vegetables, remarkably prolific, and of excellent quality. Beautiful flowers covered the country. It was like a Garden of Eden, as compared to the Barren Lands.

CATHOLIC CHURCH AT FORT GOOD HOPE

Fort Good Hope is one of the oldest posts in the far North. It has been rebuilt several times, in different localities. There is a large Catholic church here, with a large cross in front, belonging to the mission, and it is the finest building of its character in the remote North. I took a picture of this building. There are no white people at this post, excepting one or two priests.

Leaving Fort Good Hope in a few hours, we sailed and — 29

floated down the river four days more, which brought us to the Arctic ocean, along the shores of which and through the deltas of the Mackenzie we coasted a day or two. We met' many Eskimos, dressed entirely in furs. Some seemed very old. They could not understand us, or we them.

Their boats were of framework, made of sticks lashed' together and covered with whale-skins. Their canoes were entirely covered, excepting a hole into which the occupant could crowd and wrap a lappel or aj)ron around his waist, thus shutting out all water, even if it rolled over the entire canoe. Thus they venture on the mighty billows of the Arctic ocean, which to ordinary boatmen would seem impossible. The men and boys over twelve years of age all wear ivory buttons in their under lips for ornaments. They resemble the Malayan race; are very ingenious, and are not at all hostile.

We sailed forty miles from the ocean back up the Mackenzie to the mouth of Peel's river, which we ascended until we arrived at the mouth of Rat river. Peel's river has an average width of about a thousand feet, while that of Rat river is but fifty.

We ascended Rat river twenty-five miles, to the point where we reached its first cascade. There all boats are knocked to pieces, out of which smaller ones are constructed, as boats of large size cannot be towed up the rapids. The loss of boats and other property at that place has been so great, it has very properly been named "Destruction City." Here the sun shines in summer for a period of forty days of twenty-four hours' duration each,— continual sunlight; therefore the night of intense darkness must be of corresponding length.

The majority of the travelers congregated there must spend the winter, and will be without fresh meat or fish and without vegetables. It is a safe prediction that the dreaded scurvy will break out among them. But, if they take proper precautions, gather plenty of the wild fruit I

A VENERABLE ESKIMO.

CANOE COVERED WITH WHALESKIN.

have mentioned, and descend to Peel's river, where they may procure fish, possibly they may get through safely. Some of them have already, in their despair, committed suicide, two of them on the Mackenzie river and three on the Yukon, within sixty days. For those who survive the terrible ordeal, I have prophesied that if they do not ascend the mountains to too great a height, they will keep warm, for there is an abundance of timber along that stream.

Most writers make the assertion that the Arctic Circle is near the limit of vegetation. They speak of the scrubby and barren character of the lower Mackenzie river region, while in fact, north of the Arctic Circle there is as fine a growth of spruce and birch timber as I have ever seen. Some of the young trees are so tall and symmetrical that they would be regarded as perfect for liberty-poles. Wild currants and a variety of small cranberries are to be found in greatest luxuriance, while grass and moss cover every spot.

At "Destruction City " we overtook many persons from all parts of the world; numbers of them had been traveling on their weary journey for over a year. In the whole assemblage there was but one woman. She had nobly braved the perils of the trip thus far; a Mrs. A. C. Craig, from Chicago. Her husband had been a contractor in that city, and with his wife had been on the road for more than twelve months. Here they abandoned their trip. To return ? No; there is no retreating. It would require three years to tow their boats up the rivers and cross the lakes in returning to Edmonton, the first place of civilization. All left for them to do was to return to Fort McPherson, eighty miles up Peel's river, there build sleds, and portage their goods over the divide to Belle river, during the ensuing winter and spring, so as to be ready to descend to the Yukon the following summer, to the gold-fields, their objective point,— consuming two whole years. I have met many of the friends of the people to

whom I have referred, since my return. They invariably ask," Why don't they return ? Why do they stay there ?" Their predicament recalls very forcibly the parable in the Bible, of the rich man Dives, who died and went to Hades. He could not reach the haven he desired, neither was he permitted to return and warn his kindred not to come to that place of torment.

While at Fort Resolution I received a letter from my sister, Mrs. Ed. Clayton, in Chicago, begging me, if I should meet the Craigs above referred to, to do all in my power to help them along, as they were friends of hers. Upon the acquaintance thus formed with Mr. Oraig, and with liberal inducements, I succeeded in persuading him and Mr. E. K. Turner, of Salt Lake City, to assist us in drawing our little boat up Rat river and over the portage. Mrs. Craig remained at the tent, keeping a vigil over the precious larder, which she and her husband cherished as they did their lives.

Poor woman ! her experience had been a remarkable one. She had been subjected to innumerable hardships, under summer suns and through winter snows; had descended rivers, and passed over their rapids; crossed Great Slave lake on the ice; steered their boat while her husband plied the oars, sometimes working theni herself when he was prostrated by his almost superhuman exertions. She had driven dog-sleds, and gathered wood in the thick underbrush to keep up fires while her husband was absent on long journeys, portaging their goods. She often pushed her way along the river's edge, towing the boat with a long cord. Her wearing apparel of necessity became tattered and torn, so much so that she was compelled to resort to men's clothing. Yet she was always brave, never uttering a murmur. If she successfully reaches the Pacific coast, she will be the first white woman who ever essayed the journey by this route, and will be entitled to be classed as a heroine.

I also met at this place the ubiquituous newspaper cor-

ESKIMOS ON THE ARCTIC OCEAN —SOCIETY BELLES.

respondent, in the person of Mr. Thiimser, of Chicago, who had been sent by the Associated Press as their agent to report upon the feasibility of the Edmonton route to Dawson City. He had not, however, been able to send back a word since leaving Edmonton in May. He had expected to forward his report by whaling-vessels, which he hoped to find in the Arctic ocean, but it is doubtful whether his messenger ever succeeded in reaching a ship. He would gladly have availed himself of the opportunity to send by Mr. Rea and myself, if he had had the slightest confidence in our reaching civilization before the next year.

We remained at this romantic city of tents but one night, leaving next morning, August 10th, but before starting discarded every conceivable article we could spare, so as to lighten our burden as much as possible. I even gave away my gun, field-glass, revolver, and many other articles which I had carried for years during my travels on the frontier. When all was ready, with the little amount of provisions left to last us until we could reach the Yukon river, loaded into the boat, we waded into the water, one man on each side of the canoe to keep it from dashing on the rocks, and two in front with the tow-line to keep it in the middle of the stream, the only place where there was sufficient water to float it, without injury. There was plenty of water on each side, of course,— often waist deep, in fact; but the bottom was so thickly strewn with rocks, whose jagged points neared the surface, that it would have been impossible for any craft to live there a moment. Some one may ask why we did not walk on the shore and tow our boat, as we have stated that the stream is narrow; but it must be remembered that often the rocky bed referred to widens out for twenty yards or more on either side of the narrow channel, and where narrow it is so crooked that we were obliged to pull with a short line, and directly ahead.

We left Destruction City full of courage, hoping to make rapid progress with such a light load; but we were

sorely disappointed, as in many places our combined efforts were not sufficient to drag the boat up the cascades. We were often obliged to carry our goods on our backs a half-mile at a time, then return and tow the empty boat to the top of the rapids. This required an immense amount of muscle and all the ingenuity we could command, as the current runs like a mill-race. We would have employed Indians for this hard work had it been possible, but the white men who had preceded us had scattered the microbes of la grippe from Edmonton all the way to Destruction City, and the Indians along the route were sick ; many dying daily. It was very fortunate that we secured the services of the two gentlemen mentioned, or we should have been compelled to pass another winter within the Arctic Circle.

During the first thirty miles we passed a great many parties, who, like ourselves, were struggling to the summit, frequently following one another so closely that the parties were not more than one hundred yards apart; but during the last quarter of our forty-mile journey through the rapids, very few outfits had succeeded in progressing thus far, probably less than a dozen that would be able to cross over before winter.

We consumed seven days in making forty miles, and when we landed our boat on the small lake which is the source of West Rat river it was the 17th of August. Here we bade farewell and Godspeed to Messrs. Craig and Turner, who had rendered us such excellent service.

On our long journey from Fort Resolution on Great Slave lake we had passed ninety-five boats and their crews, with the intense satisfaction of knowing that none had passed us.

We found a new route while crossing the portage between the two Rat rivers, by which we -were enabled to make a portage of only twenty-three hundred and fifty feet, while all the other parties had been compelled to carry their goods and boats twice that distance in ef-

fecting it. The cut-off was made by following a stream which entered the lake at the head of East Rat river, the stream flowing into the lake from the south and coming within that short distance of the other lake, which is the source of West Rat river.

Mr. McDougall, the civil engineer who mapped this Rat river pass, gives its elevation as eleven hundred and sixty feet, but his figures do not agree with my measurements. I find it to be eight hundred and forty feet higher. The only way in which I can account for this great discrepancy is that the Indians insist that Mr. Mc-Dougal never went there at all, but traveled overland from McPherson to the LaPere house on Belle river, while his guides hauled his empty boat up Rat river, thence over the portage to Belle river, where they joined him.

Many hundred gold-seekers will be compelled to spend another dreary winter on the Rat river, in that land of darkness, then haul what few effects they may have left in the spring on dog-sleds across to Belle river. Those who are far up Rat river doubtless will be able to portage their goods the short distance they have to travel, on their backs, to West Rat river, where they can descend in small boats, which they must construct of lumber sawed by hand. They too will learn that West Rat river is the place of all places to realize the sensation of "shooting the chutes." It is a continuous succession of cascades from source to mouth. As we rushed down it in our frail boat it furnished us some new sensations in boating in Arctic waters. Mr. Rea stood in the bow with a long pole, while I took a position in the stern with another. As we went flying down, Mr. Rea would thrust in his pole and guide the boat around the danger-point, which consisted of rocks protruding above the surface or very close to it. His action had a tendency to force the other end of the boat against the very one he was trying to avoid. Then came my turn for an exhibition of skill by keeping it off. A single slip or miss on my part would have

crushed our boat into kindling-wood, and all would have been lost in the turbulent current. It was clearly a game of life and death. It seemed to me that river was longer than the Mississippi. When we reached the last rapids, just before entering Belle river, the sharp points of a great many rocks made their appearance. Mr. Rea made a mighty effort with his pole to escape a particularly dangerous one, but in so doing only threw the boat on another just to our right. The boat fairly leaped into the air; turned clear around, going down the river stern first, and a stream of water burst through the bottom of the boat, about four inches in diameter. By the time we discovered it, and realized what had occurred, we were in the center of Belle river. We both quickly dropped our poles and pulled on the oars for the opposite shore. Before we reached it the water was half-way to the gunwales, and everything completely drenched, which compelled us to sleep in wet blankets that night.

Scientists claim that the Rat river pass was caused by the ice gorging at the mouth of the Mackenzie river during the glacial period, until it backed up the water so high it diverted the floods to the Pacific slope, and cut the mountains down about a thousand feet. But this theory is all guess-work, as the probability is no scientific man ever passed over that route. In my opinion the theory is not correct, for several reasons. One is sufficient to defeat such a possibility, viz.: If the water had been raised three thousand feet, by that time the snow falling on the mountains would have reached a tremendous height, as all agree that during the 12,000 years of the glacial period, snow fell to a depth of two and a half feet per year, which, when compressed, made over six inches of ice, after a year or two. This would have elevated the mountain 7,000 feet higher, or a total of 10,000 feet above sea-level, and would have sent the waters over the Barren Lands to the Arctic Ocean, or backed it over the divide into the Mississippi or Hudson Bay slopes.

The trouble is with some scientific men, they too often jump at conclusions without proving them.

Next morning we patched up the boat as best we could, and started on our long journey to the great Yukon river.

I must admit that with all its trials and hardships, the route we had traveled did not differ from what I had expected, as in the previous fall, before leaving Fort Resolution, I had met an Indian and talked with him as to the feasibility of returning that way. His description of the difficulties to be met with I found to be correct; so was not disapijointed, as were thousands of others who had foolishly taken the advice of people who knew no more about the topography of the country than they did of that of the moon.

Our success was clearly attributable to well-trained muscles and the hardships incident to the summer and winter of the year before, when we were sojourning in the Barren Lands. If any desire to make the trip to the Yukon by the "Edmonton route," they should first determine whether they have a constitution of iron, nerves of steel, and an indomitable will. That determined beyond a doubt, let them secure the lightest boat possible, take just enough provisions to last to the Yukon, and in a company of not less than three others, cast in the same mould as themselves. Then, if expert sailors, and the weather is not too boisterous, by securing a practical guide to take them through the rapids of Athabaska and Slave rivers and across the lake of the same name, with a guide from the Mackenzie up Peel's and Rat rivers to the source of West Rat river, they can feel assured of making the journey in one summer, provided they follow the ice when it breaks up early in the spring, keeping on their course both night and day.

Some half a dozen parties had preceded us over the Rat river route, and shot down the rapids through Belle and Porcupine rivers to the muddy Yukon; while others, a limited number, had portaged eighty-five miles from Fort

McPherson to the old LaPere house, on the Belle river, where they constructed rafts and floated down Belle and Porcupine rivers.

The most sensible course pursued by any of the many hundreds who had reached Peel's river was that of Messrs. E. A. Olds and J. H. Huntoon, of Los Angeles, Cal. They arrived at Fort McPherson early in June, where they met a number of Eskimos from Herschel's island in the Arctic ocean, with whom they exchanged a portion of their goods for twenty very strong dogs, on whose backs they packed the remainder of their supplies and made the trip across to Belle river. Their dogs carried from thirty to forty-five pounds each, and the acquisition of these animals proved a Godsend to them. At Belle river they built a large raft, and on it floated down to Fort Yukon, where they disposed of the dogs at fabulous lirices.

We overtook this party on Porcupine river, three days before they arrived at their destination. Fort Yukon. I wish I could present a photograph of their peculiar craft as it appeared when I first saw it, for it was the most comical thing I saw on my whole trip. They abandoned it at Fort Yukon, and with the amount of money received from the sale of the dogs, were able to take first-class passage to San Francisco, and had enough gold-dust left to establish their claim of having discovered wonderful mines, had they felt so disposed, as thousands of others had done,— creating a false excitement in relation to the mineral resources of that over-estimated region.

When three hundred and fifty miles up the Porcupine river I was surprised by meeting a large party of gold prospectors who had come in via Dawson City. They intended to winter at that point, and in the spring portage over about a hundred miles north, to the head of a river which they believed emptied into the Kotzebue sound. Among others was a Mr. Shank, of Omaha, Neb., whom I had met before. They were in the locality of Old

Crow river, the place of all j)laces for historical petrified relics, of the gigantic mastodon and other large animals.

About a hundred miles below where we met them, we were hurled into the ramparts of Porcupine river. This mighty gorge, through which the water shoots with tremendous force and rapidity, is about nijiety miles long. The walls on either side are so variegated in color in some places that they resemble the " Pictured Rocks" of Lake Superior. Midway of the gorge is Rampart House, until very recently a Protestant mission of the Fort Yukon district. This is where General Frederick Funston spent the winter of 1893-94. We stopped there over-night, where we met the Reverend T. H. Bawksley, who has been so diligent in educating Indians. He and a half-dozen jolly good fellows were up there for the purpose of moving the furniture and other goods of this mission on the Porcupine down to Fort Yukon. He was possessed of a'fine library, an organ and other musical instruments, and I really felt as though we had once more reached a land of civilization.

Early the next morning we were gliding down the rapids, and applied our oars as vigorously as if we were in mere eddies, making every exertion to reach Fort St. Michael's before the rivers were closed.

We saw a great many young geese and ducks on our route, and killed a few black bear, the tender meat of which we appreciated very much.

On the morning of the 27th of August we entered the great and muddy Yukon, and could j)lainly distinguish the outlines of Fort Yukon about two miles above. The wind being in our favor, we set sail, and soon anchored at the little Indian village. Many of the inhabitants stood on the banks watching us as we glided toward them up the swift current. On landing, an old Indian informed us it was the first boat he ever saw which could sail up the swift stream. Our boat was so light and its sail so large it was irresistible.

In Alaska we found some of the greatest rascals of the period, both in Canada and the United States,— especially among the custom-house and other officers. They often collect more duty from small crafts than their cargoes originally cost; while those boat-owners who were "up to snuff" merely slipped a ten-dollar bill or gold-piece into the official's hands, and passed without inspection. An official receipt is rarely given, to those they do inspect,— simply a slip of paper, on which is written something like the following: " This is to certify that I have examined Mr. 's outfit, and collected duty on same." They were very careful not to specify the amount or the names of the articles dutiable, and everybody knew the money received seldom, if ever, found its way into the treasury of their respective governments.

To show the extent to which this malfeasance obtains in that country, I was told by a gentleman at Minook, seven hundred miles below Dawson City, that he had written to the postmaster there several times during the summer to have his mail forwarded to him at Minook, but received no reply. He paid fifty dollars for passage to Dawson, and on arriving there fell into line, finally reaching the postoffice window, where he asked for his mail. The clerk said there was nothing for him. The gentleman insisted that he should look, for he knew there must be at least a basketful. The clerk still refused to look, declaring there was no mail. The surging crowd pushed the anxious inquirer along, and he was compelled to relinquish his search for that day. But the next day he returned to the postoffice. He had been told to "tip" the clerk, and this time he did so by handing him a twenty-dollar bill; and he again asked for his mail. The clerk turned away, and soon returned with forty-five letters and a package of papers.

This is only one instance of that character which I have space to recite, although I have the knowledge of many others. This nefarious method was practiced not only at

Dawson, in the British Possessions, but at many of the post-offices in the United States contiguous, where from five to ten cents was demanded before delivering a letter. The fact is, some of those officers, so remote from the seat of government, can make a small fortune before it is possible for a report to reach the Departments at Washington and Ottawa, their conduct investigated and successors appointed. Consequently, they are very extortionate and defiant.

We remained at Fort Yukon nearly a week, hoping to catch a steamer to St. Michael's; but before one arrived Mr. Rea went up the river to Dawson City. On his return he corroborated the extravagant methods of robbery reported. While at Dawson he gathered many interesting facts, some of which, if made known, would be astounding. I do not deem it expedient to insert his letter, as so much of a derogatory character has already been published about this much-talked-of place. fHPP|!Qf|^ IjlhTBriP

Very few boats touch at Fort Yukon, tni*<wice all-important "no place." I soon became tired of its terrible monotony, and concluded with three other gentlemen who had joined me, to take our canoe and drift down the river, hoping that a steamer would overtake us. The weather

was cold and stormy; rain and sleet fell almost continually. We had scarcely reached the lower end of the island, beyond which flows the main channel of the Yukon, when to our chagrin we saw two immense steamers passing down the stream. We were so far from them that we had little hoJ)e of their seeing or hearing us, yet we waved our hats, coats and blankets, and yelled ourselves hoarse — all to no purpose, for they proceeded on their way without noticing us.

The wind blew furiously from the northwest as we floated on the rolling waves, until night was upon us; then, cold and hungry, we sought shelter under the thick willows fringing the north bank.

The next day was Sunday; we neither went to church

nor Sunday-school, but had a little " Endeavor meeting " of our own,—endeavored to stem the terrific wind and waves, but made very little progress. We continued floating by day and camping at night, until Tuesday morning, just as we had finished our breakfast of slapjacks, bacon and coffee, a cloud of black smoke was borne on the breeze beyond a point of timber we had passed the night before. In a short time a monstrous steamer came in sight, and we all hurriedly paddled to the center of the river. As it approached us I jumped on our "grub-box" and gave the railroad signal for it to stop. At the same time all of us waved our hats and coats, but the steamer passed to the south of us and was swiftly gliding by, when the pilothouse window was opened and a man leaned out. I held up my arm and shouted, "Four passengers for St. Michael's!" He rang the reverse bell, the steamer stopped, and soon we were alongside of the Alaska Commercial Company's largest and finest boat, "Hannah." The purser was on the lower deck, and came to where we were. I asked him, "How much for four passages to St. Michael's ? " He replied, " One hundred and seventy-five dollars.". We were already half-way from Dawson to Bering Sea, and knew the fare at that time for first-class passage from Dawson to St. Michael's was fifty dollars. I intimated so, and offered one hundred and fifty. He answered with a most emphatic " No 1 " We quickly concluded to f)ay the exorbitant price, and climbed aboard. Then we cut the towline from our small boat and let it go adrift, with all our cooking utensils, etc. We arranged our proportion of the fare with Mr. Olds, and he paid the one hundred and seventy-five dollars to the purser.

I asked to be shown my stateroom, but the purser replied, "Just pay your fare and I will arrange the rooms." I replied, "Mr. Olds has paid for all." The purser answered, " He has only paid for one." We were all dumbfounded 1 One hundred and seventy-five dollars each was demanded, when our contract plainly implied it was

meant for all four, at least a dozen passengers and officers corroborating my statement.

What to do we did not know. Our boat was gone, but we did not propose to be robbed in that way. The purser handed the money back and gave us orders to get off as soon as the next wood-yard was reached. We protested, patted him on the back, and begged to be allowed to continue our journey and pay a reasonable fare, but without effect. Learning that the company's general manager, Mr. Wilson, was aboard, we appealed to him. We asked him to allow us to remain, even if we went as steerage passengers. He shook his head. I then proposed that we work our way down, and let them retain the money. The proposition was accepted, and we all went below, supposing, of course, that there would be some kind of a bed to sleep on, but discovered that only the wet, dirty deck or cord-wood was to be our couch. I made my bed the first night on the wood, but precious little sleep did I get. The next day I found a board four feet and a half long by eleven inches wide which served me a great deal better; and I was really thankful for the comfort it afforded. Our principal work was loading cordwood from the banks, and I always pitched it with such force and peculiar twist down the hills, as to make each stick turn four or five somersaults, which landed it nearly in its proper place near the boat. I soon found out I had made a great mistake, as I was always ordered afterward by the mate to the farthest pile from the boat. In fact, I worked just as hard as if I had not paid forty-two dollars and fifty cents for the privilege of being a deck-hand without wages.

After we reached the little hamlet of Andressy I was helping to pull the anchor-line on shore to make the boat fast, when, stepping on a block of wood, two rusty nails penetrated my moccasin and sank deeply into my foot. I hobbled back to the boat, too lame to perform any more work, and tried very hard to persuade the officers to assign me a room so as to doctor my wound, as well as a

severe cold I had contracted because of the miserable quarters I had been obliged to occupy. Although there were eight empty rooms above, they declined to grant my request. The Alaska Commercial Company is known by all that travel in Alaska as a "corporation without a soul"—one that has grown to the magnitude of a multimillionaire by being the pet of the United States in the peal fisheries and carrying government supplies. That company is now returning gratitude to the citizens of our great nation for favors received, by bleeding them. We did find men of kind hearts in the kitchen of the boat. They treated us with due courtesy and kindness, and to them we return everlasting gratitude.

There is also another corporation, the Alaska Transportation Company, which, too, is without a soul. These companies have laid claim to about two miles frontage of the best and almost the only available portion of the harbor at St. Michael's. The first thing I saw after landing on the pier was a notice posted in a conspicuous place by the commanding officer in charge of the United States military post there (which includes all the harbor), warning the public not to trespass upon the premises claimed by the corporations to which I have referred; consequently, no one is allowed to sell anything, no matter how small it may be. No boarding-house is allowed within these sacred precincts, excepting those of the great corporations, who have supply stores, hotels, etc., and charge their patrons most exorbitant rates.

I was told by a sergeant of the regular army stationed there, that the Alaska Transportation Company had agreed to have barracks ready for the troops on their arrival ; but they found only the foundations laid.

The commanding officer said the soldiers might assist the company in building the barracks, which would give them thirty cents an hour for spending-money. They quickly learned that wages were fifty cents an hour, and that there were many poor disappointed civilians there

who needed the work. They respectfully sent word to their commander they did not want to cut wages and beat needy workmen out of their jobs. In reply, a peremptory order was given for the soldiers to build the barracks and accept whatever the company saw fit to pay them; so there was nothing left for them but to obey. After they had finished, the company had the audacity to give them fifteen cents an hour. This heartless corporation is now receiving from the government thirty-six hundred dollars a year as rental for the barracks, built by its own troops. It probably cost the company less than its receipts for six months. These transportation companies, doubtless, are to a great extent responsible for the glowing reports about Alaska and the whole Northwestern country which have been sent out for the sole purpose of filling their coffers with the earnings of the many thousands they have allured there.

At St. Michael's, on the 17th of September, I boarded the ocean steamer Tillamook, bound for Seattle, Wash. We sailed about eighty miles northwest to discharge a cargo of freight at a point on Colovin Bay. This completed, the captain steered for the deep sea,— but soon landed us high and dry on a sandbar I There we remained for two days and nights. Finally, by extraordinary effort at high tide, and a favorable wind, we were freed from our dangerous mooring. It was fortunate that we got off when we did, otherwise we should have been left there the whole winter, for the wind soon shifted to the north and blew the water out of the bay.

About ten miles out after leaving the bar, a small steamboat in distress was discovered. The captain changed his course for it, and found it to be the Fortune Hunter. (The only fortune that ever came to it was when we reached it that day.) The engine of the boat had become disabled, and it was drifting to sea at the mercy of the wind and waves. Our vessel finally got near enough to heave a line, by which we towed the — 29

disabled steamer ashore. The result of our delay on the sandbar was the saving of the lives of fifteen helpless men.

After rescuing the Fortune Hunter we proceeded on our journey for Dutch harbor, on one of the Aleutian islands. That night the equinoctial storm commenced its pranks in that almost unknown sea. Our captain had only once before been over the route, but our only dependence was upon him. The billows rolled like mountains; the space between was like valleys, while the ship was tossed about in every direction. Nearly all the passengers were seasick, and the vessel was a desolate,* dreary-looking object.

The detention on the sandbar had caused us to run short of both water and provisions. During the storm the crew cursed, and threw up the little they had eaten. No wonder 1 for the food provided for both passengers and crew was unfit to set before human beings. The cooks were filthy in their habits, and the vessel was overrun with rats. The appearance of the food indicated that they had free access to everything edible on board.

Early in the morning of the fourth day out from Gulu-van Bay, we were surprised to find ourselves drifting among the Aleutian Islands, fully fifty miles out of our course. Every time the vessel plunged down into the great valleys of water, we expected to be dashed upon the numerous shoals, which we were surely rapidly approaching. Our captain was a courageous fellow, and was reported to be one of the best sailors of the Pacific ocean. He did not appear to be at all frightened, but was very solicitous regarding our possible peril. By heaving the lead and examining his charts, he soon found his bearings, and breathed easier, as did we all, when he turned the vessel about, and continued on the proper course.

Before noon we were safely landed in Dutch harbor, where we took coal and remained until the terrible gale had somewhat subsided. After we landed, both captain and crew declared it was the most terrific storm in all

their experience, and we congratulated ourselves upon having weathered it safely.

While at Dutch harbor the rats began to abandon the vessel, and upon the crew noticing it their superstitions were aroused, for among sailors this is considered one of the most ominous things that.can occur. Many of them talked among themselves of doing exactly what the rats were doing, and suggested that we should take another vessel. Finally they were ridiculed out of their notions, and we sailed away on the second day after our arrival. After passing through the group of islands the storm increased in violence, and was almost as terrific as before. On the evening of the second day, when the steward went below into the storeroom among the rats for supplies, he came rushing frantically back and reported to the^captain that the ship was in a sinking condition, with three feet of water in the hold. Immediately all hands were at the pumps, every bucket on board called into requisition, and both captain and crew and such of the passengers as were able worked till nearly morning, handling the pumps or passing up water from the hold, and at last the leak was gotten under control. It must have been a more serious affair than the passengers imagined, for both the captain and mate passed the greater portion of the night bailing out with the rest of the crew. No wonder the rats had been leaving, for the ship was really in a sinking condition when at Dutch harbor. The boat had been so fearfully thrashed about in the storm, that when she was rising on the crest of a wave anyone in the hold could see daylight through the wrenched sides. It was only by skillful seamanship and willing hands that we were kept afloat until reaching our destination.

Happy was everybody on board, the morning of the 6th day of October, 1898, when the " slow bell " rang, and we ran into the harbor of Seattle. Daylight had hardly made its appearance, but no sooner was the boat within jumping distance of the wharf than I was ashore. Imagine my feelings of delight at realizing that I was once more in my native country. But how strange everything appeared to me! I hardly knew how to keep on the sidewalk, and was often in the middle of the street or crossing a back yard. Finally I found a telegraph office, and sent messages to my friends that I was not dead, neither had I been sleeping. It was unspeakable delight to me to hear the whistles scream, the bells ring, the buzz of electric street cars, and all the other sounds of civilization to which I had so long been a stranger. One of the oddest and most ridiculous things to me was the crowing of roosters. I stopped and really laughed aloud, as their clarion notes and flapping of wings reached my ears. Then the cackling of hens and the "peeping" of little chickens all combined to make it a concert unfamiliar to my ears for a long time, but now recalling sweet remembrances of my childhood days on the old farm.

It was like flying through space, when I boarded the lightning express train for Troy, Kansas, the place that I had left many years previously. It was the home of my early manhood. I could hardly wait till the time when I should meet my family and the hosts of friends, the young men and women of long ago. Imagine my surprise, on arriving, at being invited into the opera-house, where a public reception was tendered me. When escorted to the stage and I looked into the faces of dear old friends, I was thrilled with emotions of thanksgiving that are indescribable. At that moment the pianist touched the keys, and the instrument seemed to say, " Mid pleasures and palaces though I may roam, be it ever so humble, there's no place like home." The great audience arose and sang that dear old song, which to the hearts of all

HOME, SWEET HOME

469

travelers in foreign lauds is most precious. A prayer of thanksgiving was offered, after which all joined in the Bong of songs, that fills the breasts of American patriots more than all others, " My country 'tis of thee, sweet land of liberty, of thee I sing." And no person ever appreciated songs and native land more than, at this time, did

THE END

Made in the USA
Monee, IL
29 December 2023

50767421R00149